The Corpse Bridge

Also by Stephen Booth

FICTION

The Corpse Bridge

A Cooper & Fry Mystery

STEPHEN BOOTH

WITNESS
IMPULSE
An Imprint of HarperCollins*Publishers*

This book was originally published in 2014 by Sphere, an Imprint of Little, Brown Book Group.

Excerpt from *Lost River* copyright © 2010 by Stephen Booth.

EPub Edition DECEMBER 2014 ISBN: 9780062382429

Print Edition ISBN: 9780062382405

10 9 8 7 6 5 4 3 2

For Lesley, as always

Blessed be the man that spares these stones,
And cursed be he that moves my bones

—EPITAPH ON THE GRAVE OF WILLIAM SHAKESPEARE

Chapter One

Dusk was falling on the Corpse Bridge by the time Jason Shaw reached the river. The broken stone setts felt slippery under his boots after a heavy shower, and the walls ran with moisture in the fading light. He shivered and shook the rain from his hair as he checked his watch one more time. He was going to be late.

Jason had come out unprepared for a downpour. He'd been in such a hurry, and the autumn weather was so unpredictable, that he'd been fooled into thinking a light jacket would be enough, and he'd left his waterproofs in the Land Rover. So when the shower started he'd stopped to shelter under a sycamore tree while the water drummed on the earth all around him and turned the river below into a seething foam. But it was the end of October and the leaves were almost gone from the trees. Within seconds his hair was plastered to his skull and water dripped inside his collar as rain cascaded through the branches. He decided he'd get less wet if he returned to the path and just hoped for the shower to ease off. By the time the sky cleared he was soaking.

And that was one of his problems. He always seemed to be in a hurry these days. There was too much going on in his life, so he was constantly rushing from one thing to the next. Sometimes he just wished everything would stop for a while and let him get his breath. If only he had time to think, at least. Perhaps he wouldn't make so many bad decisions. He might be more prepared for what the world threw at him.

But circumstances were conspiring against him all the time. The situation was out of control and he was being dragged along, as if by an irresistible current. The most important decisions in his life were being made by other people. He was aware of it, but couldn't do anything about it.

And Jason knew who was responsible for that. The one person he could never say 'no' to.

He was trembling with cold as he stepped round a patch of mud that had collected in a damaged section of the track. Every few yards the setts had been shattered or dislodged, exposing the earth beneath to serious erosion. Much of this destruction had been caused by off-roaders. The national park authority was trying to enforce a traffic regulation order on some of these narrow-walled byways and green lanes to keep four-by-fours and trail bikes from using them. There were places in Derbyshire where off-roaders swarmed in their hundreds on bank holiday weekends, with whole convoys of Land Rovers forcing their way down bridleways and gouging new tracks out of the hillsides. By the end of the summer you could see their wheel tracks for miles. Most were intruders from the cities, leaving their mark on the landscape.

It was as he was wiping the water from his eyes that Jason saw her. At first she seemed like an illusion – a pale shape glimpsed through a blur of water and the deceptive colours of twilight. He wasn't a superstitious person, but Jason felt a jolt of fear at the ghostly flicker and swirl as the figure dodged its way through the trees on the other side of the bridge.

But did the figure run? It hardly seemed the right word. To Jason, she appeared to float or hover, her feet hardly touching the ground. By the time she vanished from his sight on the opposite hill, he still wasn't sure whether he'd imagined the figure or not. He realised there had been no sound from her. But that could have been an atmospheric effect, a result of the damp air and the evening stillness.

And finally there was a noise. Something bigger and definitely physical was crashing through the undergrowth where the woman had disappeared. Jason saw nothing, but he felt the hairs on the back of his neck begin to stir, an icy chill surging through his limbs. He heard one shout, an incoherent yell with no words, a cry that might almost have come from an animal.

Then the crashing stopped, and there was silence.

Jason was left standing for a moment on the approach to the Corpse Bridge, listening carefully for a sound, but hearing only the rush of the river and the dripping of rain from the trees.

OF COURSE, GEOFF and Sally Naden shouldn't have been there at all. Not that evening. It was entirely the wrong night, a different time of the week from the one they'd planned. Yes, it was definitely a mistake. At least, that was what Geoff insisted.

Sally was in a bad mood even before they came out. She recognised her own moods, and knew that Geoff would say she was sulking. But she didn't really care tonight. She wasn't as young as she used to be, and she just wanted to get this over with.

'It was definitely you,' said Geoff. 'You got it wrong again. You're always getting things wrong.'

'Rubbish,' she said. 'It's tonight, I'm certain.'

Sally had been saying 'rubbish' all evening, since even before they left the house. She didn't have the energy or inclination to spell out her argument in coherent sentences. But she was starting to get bored with 'rubbish'. She might have to think of something else to say.

'You'll get things wrong once too often some day soon,' said Geoff, 'and that will be the end of you. I hope you've written your will.'

'Nonsense,' she said.

Of course, Geoff was talking through his elbow. But Sally had to admit he was right about one thing. Some mistakes could have disastrous consequences. You found yourself in the wrong place at the wrong time, met the sort of person you'd normally spend your whole life avoiding, and you could end up putting yourself in a dangerous situation. In those circumstances, one of you might have an accident. Out here, in a spot as quiet as this, an accident might be fatal.

Sally had been thinking about murder for a while now. Not all the time, just off and on when the mood took her. Sometimes it would be when she was in bed at night, trying to get to sleep but finding herself staring at the bedroom ceiling for hours, while the weight of her husband's comatose body dragged the duvet off her again. Or it might be while she was driving, frustrated by the traffic, hearing his parting words repeating in her mind over and over. Those were the times when she fantasised about finally putting an end to it all. It would be a kindness really.

She'd once heard someone claim that the best way to commit a murder and get away with it was to lure your victim up on to a high place, such as a cliff. As long as there were no eyewitnesses, it was almost impossible to prove from forensic evidence whether that person fell or was pushed. The fall had to be terminal, and unobserved. It needed to happen at a time when no one else was around.

But there was someone else here. Sally had been absorbed in such a world of her own that the sudden realisation came as a shock.

'Did you hear that?' she said.

Geoff had already stopped, his head tilted on one side. 'I'm not sure.'

'I thought there was something—'

He'd obviously heard the same thing, but Sally saw that he couldn't bring himself to agree with her, even now.

'Perhaps we should go back,' he said instead.

And that was typical. He wouldn't get into an argument, but would make it seem as though whatever they did next was entirely his own idea.

Geoff and Sally Naden turned back and began to walk up the track. They knew someone was nearby, and it made them nervous. Sally was still sure she was right. But this wasn't the way it was supposed to be.

JUST BEFORE SIX o'clock, Poppy Mellor was sitting in her car, parked against a stone wall on the Staffordshire side of the river.

Earlier that afternoon she'd been for a trip with some friends to Monkey Forest in Trentham. She'd always had an interest in apes and monkeys. And those forty acres of land south of Stoke were the only place in the country you could see them roaming free. A hundred and forty Barbary macaques in a Staffordshire woodland were the closest she could get, until she'd saved enough money for a trip to North Africa. Up in the Atlas Mountains of Morocco, that was where the macaques came from.

Poppy gazed down the slope at the dripping trees and bare fields. The Atlas Mountains were a bit different from the borders of Staffordshire and Derbyshire, she imagined.

She'd been sitting in her car for a few minutes thinking about the noise. She was in the middle of reading a text message from Imogen, one of her friends from the drama studies course at uni. Her dad would raise his eyebrows at the idea of her texting someone she'd seen only a few hours before. He would say it was a kind of compulsion. But she always felt this need to be in touch.

Those monkeys at Trentham lived in close family groups. She loved them for that. Whenever you saw them, they were either physically touching or talking to each other, sometimes both. Their hierarchy was complex too, though she supposed one always had to be the leader. Every macaque knew its role, and they could rely on each other totally for loyalty and support.

Poppy sighed. Humans had a lot to learn from other primates. She ought to tell her dad that. She could just picture his face now. Some people's reactions were so predictable. For months she'd longed for something to happen that would make her life more interesting.

She turned up her CD player and wondered if anyone had heard that scream. There were lots of strange noises out in the country at night. It could have been a fox, perhaps? It was mating season and vixens called like that sometimes.

But Poppy knew it hadn't been a fox. Even from a distance, it had unmistakably been a primate. Or more specifically, human.

FURTHER DOWN THE slope, on either side of the bridge, Jason Shaw and the Nadens were unaware of Poppy's presence. Jason peered cautiously into the trees as he climbed the slope, stopped, walked a few yards into the undergrowth, then changed his mind and came back again.

Three hundred yards away, Poppy had got out of her car. She glanced for a moment at the clouds scudding overhead, revealing brief glimpses of the moon, still pale against the twilight blue sky. Then she leaned on the stone wall and gazed down into the valley where the river ran through the darkening woods. Her eyesight was good, but she could see no movement, no sign of any human presence among the trees. Poppy thought of making a phone call, but knew it would be pointless. So she got back in her car, switched on the headlights and accelerated away down the road towards Hartington. The Nadens took longer to reach their home, after stopping to argue about the best route to take.

None of them would forget that night for a long time. Though, in the end, it was someone else who found the body.

Chapter Two

DETECTIVE SERGEANT BEN Cooper was still sleeping badly. He'd been relying on the help of tablets for months now, switching from herbal aids to chemicals and back again, fearing that he'd get too reliant on some particular substance and would never be able to sleep without it again.

But this particular night had been full of demons and ghosts. And many other creatures too. Vampires, witches, skeletons. And hordes of stumbling, bloodied zombies like the entire cast of extras from *The Walking Dead*.

Well, it was always like this on Halloween. By twilight the streets of Edendale had been full of groups of children in home-made costumes fashioned from plastic bin liners and toilet rolls. After them came the teenagers with their supermarket horror masks and pumpkin lanterns. Later the atmosphere changed as the pubs filled with flesh-eating monsters, their prosthetic fangs dripping with gore. All in the name of harmless fun.

So Cooper was awake at 2 a.m. From his ground-floor flat in Welbeck Street, he could hear the distant sounds of revelry from the pubs in Edendale town centre, just across the river. Though revelry was a kind word for it.

'Harmless fun,' he said with a sardonic laugh, breaking the silence of his flat.

There were police officers on duty out there, some of his E Division uniformed colleagues from West Street, assigned to the drunk shift. They would have been shivering in their vans for the past couple of hours, waiting for the bars to empty and the fights to start.

In the old days, before the formation of professional police forces, the duties of watchmen had included firefighting and sweeping the excrement from the street. Many officers would say they were still doing the same thing now.

Edendale wasn't much different on a Thursday, Friday or Saturday night from any other town up and down Britain. Halloween just meant the prisoner cages would be full of battered Draculas and legless Egyptian mummies. Fake blood would be mingling with the real stuff. And the pavements would be littered with the dead, staggering towards home.

'And do it quietly, please,' said Cooper. 'Like a good zombie.'

He was glad no one could hear him. He'd always thought people who talked to themselves were definitely a bit weird.

Cooper looked around for the cat, but found her asleep, curled up by a radiator. She was probably aware of his presence, but too wise to think it might be breakfast time so early. She'd grown used to his erratic hours over the last few months and refused to let his unpredictable behaviour affect her routine. Lucky animal. She seemed oblivious to the noise outside too, except for a twitch of an ear if someone passed too close in the street. Occasionally, there was a wandering ghoul, lost and drunk, clattering down the road and vomiting in the gutter.

What could you expect from a celebration based on fear? This was the time of year when graves opened and the spirits of the dead returned to the world. In traditional belief, these few hours of darkness saw the doors between life and death standing ajar.

But just these few hours. For some of his ancestors, the concept of the dead returning had been too much to bear. For them, Halloween was a time to shut themselves inside their homes and protect their families with prayers and charms.

For others, though, the time was all too short. There were so few hours until daylight came. Halloween just didn't last long enough. If it came to the crunch, Cooper knew he'd be counted among their number himself. It was the reality that he couldn't escape, the one fact that never left his mind all night. The dead never really got a chance to return to the world.

'No, never. Never.'

Cooper threw a tired glance round the familiar walls of his flat. The dead who would never return – they were here, too. Their photographs were lurking in the darkness. His father, Sergeant Joe Cooper, killed in the execution of his duty. His mother, Isabel Cooper, dead of natural causes. And civilian scenes of crime officer Elizabeth Petty, who died...

Well, she'd died anyway. And that was an end to it.

Just outside, in Welbeck Street, he heard banging and laughter, followed by the shriek of a car alarm.

'For heaven's sake, go away,' he said, more loudly.

Behind him, the cat made a small questioning noise. Cooper turned.

'Not you, obviously. I was talking to ... well, who *was* I talking to?'

The cat gave him a despairing look and went back to sleep.

'No, I don't know either,' said Cooper.

He thought of putting the lights on, but there didn't seem much point. At this time of the morning artificial light only made the flat look ghastly and unreal. He felt like a character in a film, hiding away in precarious isolation, fighting desperately for survival while the world outside disintegrated into chaos, as the dead walked and cities burned.

With a vague sense of surprise, Cooper looked down at the mug clutched in his hand. He'd forgotten that he'd been making himself a drink. Camomile tea, by the smell of it. His sister Claire had insisted he tried it to help him sleep. But it had gone almost cold in his hand as he stood here near the window, listening to the sounds of the night.

Life shouldn't feel so cold and wasted. Not at his age. He was only in his thirties, after all. It was too young for everyone he cared about most to be dead and in the ground. He shouldn't have to spend half his life visiting graveyards.

Cooper shuddered as a cold certainty ran through his limbs. There would be people out tonight who gravitated to cemeteries and graveyards. Halloween was their night. And cemeteries were their playground.

He sighed again. All Hallows' Eve. That was where it all started. It was supposed to be dedicated to remembering dead saints and the faithful departed. Souls wandered the earth, looking for one last chance to gain vengeance on the living. People would wear masks or costumes to disguise their identities and avoid being recognised by vengeful souls.

People often complained that Halloween was an imported American tradition. But surely it was only because Guy Fawkes and Bonfire Night had poached some of the customs of Halloween.

For centuries English people had preferred burning effigies of Catholics, rather than remembering dead saints. Halloween had become a focus of superstitions about witches and ghosts.

Just last week the *Eden Valley Times* had published a letter written by a local vicar complaining that the newspaper was encouraging Satanism and witchcraft by reporting Halloween events and publishing pictures of children dressed as ghosts and vampires. He'd done it every year, for as long as Cooper could remember. Like everyone else, the clergyman had probably forgotten the origins of the festivities.

'Not that anybody really believes in anything any more.'

He realised that he was mumbling a bit now. He wasn't even sure what words were coming out of his mouth. The last sentence had sounded like a meaningless jumble, even to his own ears.

With a weary stretch of his limbs, Cooper went to lie back down on his bed, though he knew he wouldn't sleep.

There must be so many people who'd lost loved ones during the past twelve months. Some of them must have been wishing that the dead really could return. How did they react to ghosts and corpses banging on their door all evening? What were you supposed to do, except offer a treat from a tub of miniature chocolate bars? A modern ritual to keep the spirits away.

But if he slept tonight at all, Cooper knew the dead would walk in his dreams.

FIFTEEN MILES FROM Edendale, Rob Beresford cursed to himself in the darkness. It wouldn't happen tonight. Something had gone wrong.

He pulled out his phone, tried to dial the number again, but could get no signal. Down here by the river, with dense trees around him and hills rising on either side, he was bound to be in a dead spot.

But they'd known this was likely to happen and they'd planned for it. That was why the timing had been so carefully worked out. So what had gone wrong? Why was he on his own out here?

Rob waited. He didn't have much patience, but what else could he do? Turn round and go home? He didn't want to be the one who did that. At least, when tomorrow came, he'd be able to blame the others for wrecking the plan. He wondered who had actually got cold feet. It could be any of them, of course. They were a bunch of wimps, mostly. And worse – they'd left him out here on his own, in the dark, with no idea what was going on.

He was beginning to get angry. Rob paced up and down, swinging his torch along the track, its bright LED beam flicking from stone wall to hanging branch, from a splash of water stirring a muddy pool to the flutter of a dead leaf in the breeze. He was oblivious now to their agreement not to make too much noise or show any more light than was necessary. It was obvious he was on his own. Abandoned, and made to look an idiot. And what a place to be in at this time of night. It was lucky he wasn't a nervous bloke or he could start imagining things.

But where was he exactly? There had been no map. He only followed the directions he'd been given. Nowhere looked the same in the dark anyway. People who lived in towns didn't realise how black it was out in the proper country at night. They never saw total darkness like this. So a map would have been useless.

A noise made Rob whirl round suddenly. It sounded like a voice – a garbled word spoken from the darkness, a liquid gabbling from a throat that surely wasn't human. But then the noise came again and he saw the river. He could see the surges of water bubbling over the rocks, sucking and gurgling through gaps and crevices in the riverbed. He saw the muddy bank and the skeletal outline of a stunted tree growing on the water's edge.

And something else.

Rob realised with a shock that he could see a pale face caught in the light. It was the mask of a ghoul, white and ghostly, with the unnatural gleam of cheap plastic. He had a glimpse of a profile pulled into a grotesque shape – a gaping mouth, a blank eye, a trickle of blood. It was surely a Halloween joke to scare the children. Just some bad taste prank.

The hairs on the back of Rob's neck stirred, and he swung his torch wildly across the trees until its beam lit the glittering water rushing between the banks and highlighted the arch of the bridge. His trembling hand swept the light backwards and forwards along the parapet looming above him and probed into the gap between the stones to pick out the ancient trackway. It was half in shadow and half illuminated by his wavering torchlight. It looked like an empty stage, garishly lit, awaiting the next scene of a drama.

Rob had lived in this area all his life and he knew what this place was. Everyone called it the Corpse Bridge.

Chapter Three

Friday 1 November

AND YET THERE was so little blood.

Ben Cooper crouched and leaned forward to look more closely. For a moment he felt light-headed from tiredness and almost slipped in the mud on the bank of the river as his head swam. But he recovered himself in time, a hand poised in mid-air almost touching the body. He hoped no one had noticed.

There was certainly a lack of blood. Sometimes a corpse could surprise you like that. At first glance it didn't seem possible that anyone could be dead, when they'd hardly bled at all. Here there were no more than a few drops on the corner of the stone, a narrow trickle that might just as easily have been a splash of muddy water or a leak from a damaged bottle. Not blood, but a spilled energy drink.

Cooper straightened up again, easing the discomfort in his back. Either way, the body had been drained of its vitality. The life force had departed hours ago.

An upper stretch of the River Dove was rushing under the bridge here. Though barely the width of a stream, the water was running fast as the earlier rain syphoned down off the hills on both sides. The body was trapped in the branches of a sycamore lying close to the surface. To Cooper's weary eyes, those dark, wet boulders all around it could have been a dozen bodies lying half-submerged. The roaring of the water might have been their cries of pain, that gurgle under a rock a victim's last, dying breath.

The north side of the bridge was green with mould and fungus. Uneven stone setts on the bridge were lined with dying brambles. Here the river had slippery edges, with no safe footing in the mud, and the body was only accessible on foot through the water. Divers had waded into the river and were now under the bridge attempting to recover the body. The victim had fallen into an awkward, tangled position, and the body was already partially rigid from the onset of rigor mortis.

The initial police response had accessed the bridge using four-wheel-drive vehicles from the Derbyshire side, right down to where a large lump of rock blocked the crossing. The water was shallow enough to have been a ford at one time, but the idea of driving across it had been effectively discouraged.

The bridge itself was much too narrow for vehicles. It was the type of structure generally described as a packhorse bridge, with low parapets and stone setts designed to provide a secure footing for horses. But this bridge had been known for a different function.

It was barely six in the morning when he'd arrived, and still dark by the river. Arc lights had been set up to illuminate the scene, but it might be a while before he got a proper look at the victim. Evidence would become more obvious in daylight. A story might start to emerge then. The story of how one more human being had encountered death.

One of his detective constables, Luke Irvine, had been here at the scene before him. That was the penalty of being on call-out. Irvine was a bit dishevelled and unshaven, which somehow made him seem even younger than he was.

Cooper tended to forget that the younger DCs had only a few years' experience. They were impressively competent and self-confident – much more than he himself had been at the same age, he felt sure. The other youngster on his team, Becky Hurst, was destined for great things in his estimation. She had that air about her, a quiet determination and absolute focus on what she wanted. Luke was okay, but a little bit rebellious and unpredictable. Somebody would knock those edges off him one day. Or something.

'Well, as you can see,' said Irvine, 'we've got a female, aged about thirty-five. Caucasian. She's not been in the water very long, by the looks of it. There's a clear head wound, but other than that—'

'Found by?'

'Finder's name is Rob Beresford. Actually, his full name is Robson – as in Robson Green the actor, you know?'

'Yes.'

'He's fairly local. Lives in Earl Sterndale. Mr Beresford says he was walking down here and saw the woman in the water. He had to go back up the trackway a hundred yards or so before he could dial 999 on his mobile.'

'He was on his own?' asked Cooper.

'It seems so. But—'

'What, Luke?'

Irvine shrugged. 'Well, you'll see for yourself when you talk to him, Ben. I know you like to form your own impressions.'

'Okay.'

'We've got him up the road there. Will you talk to him now?'

'In a second.'

The River Dove was the boundary not only between two counties, but between the East Midlands and West Midlands. It was the border between limestone country and sandstone too. In daylight the view across the valley made the contrast obvious, with the hills on the Staffordshire side looking so much more gentle and unimpressive compared to the rugged limestone at his back. As far as Cooper was concerned, there was no doubt about it, whatever some Staffordshire people said. Derbyshire had the best hills.

In between, on the flatter and more fertile land in a loop of the river, stood one of Derbyshire's historic houses, Knowle Abbey – a huge country mansion where the Earls of Manby had lived for generations, surrounded by acres of landscaped parkland. It had always seemed to Cooper like a sort of no man's land, sitting in its own little world halfway between the two counties, but having little connection with either of them.

There was a Staffordshire Police presence here too, Cooper saw. Their vehicles carried a badge with the Staffordshire knot instead of the Derbyshire coat of arms. It was a strange choice of logo, he'd always thought. The triple loop of the Staffordshire knot was supposed to represent the solution devised by a hangman to execute three felons simultaneously. It didn't really fit with the current public image the police tried to present. Looking round, Cooper identified a couple of uniformed constables, an officer from Staffordshire's Major Investigation Department, and a Forensics Investigation van from their station at Leek.

The body of the victim had been tangled in the roots of a tree close to the Derbyshire side. But the River Dove was very narrow here and the county boundary ran right down the middle. He supposed it was possible that part of the body had been lying or floating in Staffordshire's jurisdiction.

But this wasn't a case of territorial dispute. Not yet, anyway. The two forces were cooperating. It was obvious to everyone that the victim or her attacker were just as likely to have approached the scene from the Staffordshire side as from Derbyshire. Boundaries were irrelevant, especially while the scene was being examined for forensic evidence. Footwear marks, DNA or trace evidence were left with complete disregard to jurisdictions.

DAWN WAS BREAKING, and the sun would rise by seven. A bird was singing over some abandoned buildings on the eastern bank of the river.

The young man who'd found the body was sitting in the passenger seat of a police car with the door open and his long legs stretched out in front of him. His head was down and he seemed to be gazing at his feet as if they could explain everything. He was no older than twenty, and he was dressed in denim jeans and a grey hooded jacket. The feet he was staring at were encased in white trainers with thick soles. At least, they'd been white once. The mud covering them now left barely a glimpse of the original colour. Perhaps that was why the young man looked at them so morosely. They were probably the most expensive thing he was wearing.

'Mr Beresford?' said Cooper. 'Detective Sergeant Cooper, from Edendale Police.'

'I suppose you want me to go over it all again,' said the man sullenly. 'I've seen this bit on the telly. Over and over again with the self-same questions that the other lot have asked already.'

'Perhaps. But quite a few new questions too, I imagine,' said Cooper.

'Oh, great.'

Cooper settled himself against the stone wall and found a comfortable position, trying to bring himself closer to the young man's level. It was less intimidating than standing over him, and it allowed Cooper to get a closer look at Rob Beresford's face.

'I do need to ask you again whether you saw anyone else in this area tonight. Now that you've had a bit of time to think about it. You can appreciate it's very important.'

'I didn't see anyone,' said Beresford without hesitation.

The answer came so quickly that it heightened Cooper's attention to the man's choice of words. Did he detect slightly too much emphasis on the word 'see'?

'Perhaps you heard someone?' he said.

Beresford shook his head, still not meeting Cooper's eye. The answer was noticeably slower in coming this time. 'No. There was no one around.'

'That's a shame.'

He didn't bother to explain why it was a shame. He could let the young man interpret that for himself. If there really *was* no one else around, that left only one person known to have been at the crime scene, apart from the dead woman herself. Beresford must have realised that, surely. If he'd seen this sort of thing on the telly, he'd know who the first suspect would be. Yet he made no effort to point his questioners in another direction.

For a moment Cooper watched Rob Beresford's expression, which seemed to be set into a look of stubborn resignation. Then he glanced round at the bridge. 'You told my colleagues you were out for a walk, sir.'

'That's right.'

'An early morning walk. Very early. Do you own a dog, Mr Beresford?'

'We have a Jack Russell terrier.'

'So where is it?'

'At home,' said Beresford.

Cooper smiled at his tone. 'It's just that most early morning walks are accompanied by a dog in my experience. When someone is out before dawn for a walk, it suggests they have to start work early. That, or the dog has a bladder problem.'

Beresford didn't respond. But that was fair enough – Cooper hadn't asked him a question. The young man sat forward on the seat and stared down at his feet. His trainers were soaked.

'What do you do for a living, sir?' asked Cooper.

'I'm a student.'

'Really? Where?'

'University of Derby. I'm studying.'

'Buxton campus? The Dome?'

'That's right.'

'So you don't have far to go for lectures.'

'My dad usually takes me into Buxton on his way to work.'

'And what does he do?'

'He's a driver. He drives a van for a parcel delivery company.'

'That *can* involve an early start, I imagine. He'll have to get to the depot in plenty of time, so he can load up and get out on his route.'

'Yes.'

'Which company does your dad work for?'

'ABC Despatch. They have a distribution centre just outside Buxton.'

'I know it. On the industrial estate at Harpur Hill.'

'That's it.'

Cooper let a silence develop. Sometimes it was the best way to deal with someone like this. Beresford would be expecting the next question, the one he didn't want to answer. But if he was left waiting long enough, he wouldn't be able to stand the tension. Cooper was patient. Besides, he didn't really have the energy at this time of the morning to try too hard.

The young man began to fidget, and bit his lip.

'Well, the truth is, I needed to get away from the house for a bit,' he said.

'Ah.'

'The parents. You know what it's like.'

'Yes.'

Cooper didn't really. He'd never had the chance to reach that stage where you didn't want to be in the house with each other a moment longer. But he'd heard people say it often enough, so he'd come to believe it must be true.

'You had a row?'

'That's it. Nothing serious. But I had to get out, take in a bit of fresh air.'

'Why did you come down here?'

'I don't know. It was just handy.'

Cooper consulted the notes he'd been given. 'You live in Earl Sterndale, sir. You didn't walk all this way. It must be a couple of miles at least.'

'My bike is up the hill there.'

'A motorbike or…'

'Just an old pushbike. It's all I can afford. Student loans, you know.'

'I see.'

It was obvious that Rob Beresford wasn't an experienced walker. No one with any sense wore expensive trainers to go hiking in. You needed a pair of boots or good stout shoes on terrain like this, or you risked breaking an ankle, not to mention ruining your footwear. And everyone knew you didn't wear denims to walk in wet weather. They soon became sodden and heavy, and would take hours to dry out. The young man's jeans were a much darker blue below the knee, where they'd got soaking wet from the damp undergrowth.

Beresford looked up. 'There's one question your mates didn't ask. And you haven't asked me either.'

Cooper stopped. 'What's that, sir?'

'Whether I knew the dead woman.'

With a sinking heart, Cooper realised that he'd missed a vital point completely. He could only put it down to tiredness. But it was unacceptable that a witness should have to remind him of an important question he'd overlooked. He'd have to watch himself carefully, or someone else would be keeping an eye on him.

'And did you, Mr Beresford?' he asked.

Beresford nodded despondently.

'Of course I did,' he said. 'Her name is Sandra Blair.'

Chapter Four

DETECTIVE SERGEANT DIANE Fry didn't do early mornings any more. Not if she could avoid it. Since she'd transferred to the Major Crime Unit of the East Midlands Special Operations Unit, her life seemed to be getting back on track. The nights were more peaceful, the days more fulfilling. Apart from a brief setback, when she'd been obliged to return to Derbyshire's E Division to cover for sick leave, she was doing the job she'd always wanted to do. What's more, it meant she was able to move back to a city.

When Fry first came to the Peak District, the culture shock had been pretty traumatic. Compared to her old stamping grounds in Birmingham and the Black Country, this had seemed like, well ... not just the backwoods, but a barren wasteland. Those vast, bleak expanses of peat moor they called the Dark Peak were like the back of the moon to a city girl. The first day she drove past a road sign that said 'Sheep for 10 miles' she'd known she was no longer in civilisation.

Fry drank her coffee and bit into a piece of toast as she sat looking out of her window on to Grosvenor Avenue. She barely noticed the flat itself now. It already felt like a part of her past. She merely drifted in and out, boiled a kettle, ran a shower, lay down to sleep. It was no more her home than any hotel room in any dull town in some far-flung part of the country. She had no more roots in Edendale than the pot plant dying on her window ledge.

For a moment Fry stopped chewing and looked at the plant. She couldn't remember the last time she'd watered it, so there was no wonder it was dying. She peered a bit more closely and poked at a brown leaf, which crumbled at her touch. More dead than dying, then. Somebody had given her the plant, but she couldn't remember who. It hardly mattered now, did it?

She finally had a new place to move into, in a smart apartment building on the outskirts of Nottingham. Fry was looking forward to seeing traffic, theatres, a bit of nightlife. Proper street lights. And no sheep anywhere.

Proper crimes too. The Major Crime Unit investigated all the serious stuff in the region. There would be no dealing with vast amounts of low-level volume crime, the way they did on division.

Fry checked her phone. Reports were coming through this morning of a suspicious death in Derbyshire. Somewhere near Buxton, a few miles to the west of Edendale. If it was in Derbyshire, it was just within the remit of EMSOU.

She called her DCI, Alistair Mackenzie, to see what he wanted her to do.

'We do need you back here, Diane.'

'Of course.'

'You're not still hankering after the country life, are you?'

'You are joking. Sir.'

Mackenzie laughed. 'Perhaps.'

'Can we let Divisional CID run with it for now, then?'

'Yes, unless they encounter any problems. We'll keep a watching brief.'

Fry ended the call, finished her coffee and got ready to leave. She studied the people moving in Grosvenor Avenue. There weren't many – just a few students from the multi-occupancy Victorian houses like the one her flat was part of, and a Royal Mail van stopped a few doors up, the postman chatting to someone over a wall.

She turned away. That was enough watching for now. Perhaps for ever.

Yes, that would be the best thing. Very soon she would never have to think about Edendale again. Or any of the people in it.

BEN COOPER STOOD back and let the recovery team do their work. The victim had finally been removed from the water and placed on the Derbyshire bank of the river. Her hands had been bagged, in case evidence from her attacker was trapped under her fingernails. But the rest of her body was bundled up in heavy clothing, which was completely waterlogged, creating a limp, misshapen mound that hardly looked human. Dark hair spread in sodden strands around her face.

And the victim's injuries were obvious now too, with blood still leaking from a head wound. Though the bleeding had seemed so little while she was in the river, now the red stain quickly began to spread across the sheeting and on to the ground. The water had kept the head wound open, while washing away the blood downstream.

As he watched officers manoeuvre the body and crime-scene examiners record every detail with their digital cameras, Cooper began to wonder whether the victim's blood had reached both banks of the river or had drifted into Staffordshire on the current.

But it didn't matter. The body was here, on the Derbyshire side. It was his responsibility for now. The chief constable had said recently that there was no greater privilege than this – the job of investigating the death of another human being.

Sandra Blair was the victim's name, according to Rob Beresford. She lived nearby in the village of Crowdecote and worked in tea rooms in Hartington. As far as Beresford knew, she was unmarried. She was a friend of his mother's, he said. They were in some organisation together. The Women's Institute or the Mothers' Union, or a local historical society. Perhaps all of them. He was vague on the details beyond that point.

'Any confirmation of ID on the victim?' asked Cooper as the crime-scene manager, Wayne Abbott, broke away from the activity round the body.

'There are some house keys,' said Abbott. 'And a phone, but it's been immersed in water, so—'

'Forensics might be able to get something off it, do you think?'

'Possibly. Other than that, she had nothing much on her. There's no purse, just the odd bit of small change in the pockets. She was wearing a blue waterproof jacket, which must have weighed her down in the water. Walking boots too.'

'But the water is so shallow. It wouldn't have stopped her getting out, if she was still alive and conscious.'

Abbott shrugged. His scene suit was wet and streaked with mud. He looked cold too, and must have been very uncomfortable. But this was all part of the job. No one chose a crime scene with the comfort of the investigators in mind.

'That's not for me to comment on,' he said.

The divers in their wetsuits were still in the water, carefully exploring the riverbed, feeling under rocks, sifting through mud.

They were gradually making their way downstream from the location of the body, in case evidence had drifted away in the current and disappeared, following the streams of the victim's blood.

'No torch among her possessions?' asked Cooper.

Abbott shook his head. 'Not that we've found.'

'There must have been one. She wouldn't have come out in the pitch dark without a torch of some kind.'

'Well, someone else must have been here, I suppose. Maybe they had it.'

'Perhaps. But she seems to be dressed for the outing, at least.'

He was thinking about Rob Beresford, dressed in his unsuitable muddy trainers and sodden denims. The victim had come out here much better prepared, and presumably for quite a different purpose. What that purpose was, he had no idea. Not yet anyway. But Sandra Blair's life was about to become the focus of a lot of attention.

'And a hat,' said Cooper, thinking of the head wound and the dark strands of wet hair.

'Sorry?'

'She was probably wearing a hat. What happened to it?'

'No idea.'

Gradually, the entire team was gathering at the Corpse Bridge. The same old circus that any suspicious death attracted. Present at the scene now was Detective Inspector Dean Walker. Cooper knew him, but hadn't worked directly with him until now. His old DI, Paul Hitchens, had moved on – and probably wouldn't be back in E Division for any nostalgic reunions with his ex-colleagues, judging by his comments in the pub on his last day. Walker was only a temporary replacement, though. He was earmarked for better things, a job at headquarters in Ripley. There would still be a vacancy in E Division.

Walker was talking on the phone to a detective chief inspector, the only DCI they still had knocking around in this part of Derbyshire.

In the present circumstances everyone was expected to pick up the slack. The DCI and the DI were each doing two people's jobs. Further down the ladder many of the senior DCs were taking on a sergeant's role, while frontline uniformed PCs were acting as social workers, not to mention standing in for paramedics. Everyone had a story of taking an injured person to hospital in the back of a police car rather than wait for an ambulance that might never come because it was already waiting outside A&E with a previous patient.

Sometimes Cooper wondered who was actually doing the real police work. Community support officers, he supposed. The PCSOs – dressed up to look like police officers, but without any of the powers.

As a DS, he was right in the middle of this mess. He could probably use the freedom to show a bit of initiative, unless this became a major inquiry, in which case they would all lose control to EMSOU's Major Crime Unit.

'A quick resolution would be nice,' he said, though to no one in particular.

'Amen to that,' said DC Luke Irvine, who happened to be standing closest. 'You know I have all these other cases, Ben—'

'So have we all.'

'Fair enough, I suppose. What do you want me to do?'

Cooper looked at his watch. 'You can get up to Earl Sterndale and visit Rob Beresford's parents. Find out whatever they know about Sandra Blair. Obviously, we need an address for her, any family, the next of kin.'

'Got it.'

'Oh, and you can let them know their son is still with us, making a statement back at the station. He's phoned them already, but they're probably worried about him.'

'I'm on my way.'

Cooper looked round. DC Carol Villiers would be at West Street to take Rob Beresford's statement when he arrived. Becky Hurst had a rest day. That left just one member of his team.

DC Gavin Murfin was slouched against a stone wall, his body ballooning like the Michelin Man under several layers of clothing. Murfin looked detached, or at least semi-detached. But Cooper had known him to have the best insights at these moments, some nugget from more than thirty years of experience.

'What are you thinking, Gavin?' he asked.

Murfin shifted reluctantly from the wall. 'In the old days I'd be thinking, I wonder how much overtime I can make from this one.'

'No overtime now, Gavin.'

'Exactly.'

Cooper watched him slump back again. So did that mean Murfin wasn't thinking about anything at all? With Gavin, it was possible. Though there was also a likelihood that he was just contemplating food.

Another police Land Rover was working its way down the track, bumping over the ruts and splashing through a miniature lake of muddy water that had gathered on the bend before the final descent. Its white paintwork was already filthy and the wipers were struggling to keep an area of windscreen clear for the driver.

'You had a review with Personnel, didn't you?' said Cooper. 'What's going to happen?'

Murfin groaned. 'If I stay on any longer, it's bad news.'

'How do you mean?'

'I mean they might send me to Glossop,' said Murfin, with a note of despair.

'It's not the end of the world, Gavin.'

'No. But you can see it from there.'

'So, what? You're chucking in the towel? Collecting your pension and waving goodbye?'

'It seems so. Though I've got a different type of gesture in mind.'

The Land Rover had been forced to stop a hundred yards up the ancient, potholed trackway. There were already too many vehicles down here near the scene. No one was going to stand a chance of turning round when they came to leave. The back-up crew from the Land Rover had decided to take a shortcut across the field to reach the riverside.

Cooper watched them with interest, guessing they were from one of the bigger towns, Chesterfield or even Derby. One officer, climbing over a stock fence on to wet grass, took a couple of electric shocks. Perhaps, thought Cooper, he should have warned them to get the fencing turned off before they did that.

'So what are you going to do with yourself, Gavin?' he asked. 'I don't suppose Jean will want you getting under her feet all day long at home.'

'How right you are. I don't even have any hobbies that will get me out of the house. There's no shed for me to hide in. If I took up gardening, she'd think I'd gone mad and get me certified. Besides, I've just laid a new patio over the flowerbed.'

'A few cruises?'

Murfin sighed again. 'Have you ever been on one of those? You get all the same daft biddies and boring old farts on every boat. It's like *Death on the Nile*, but with fewer laughs. When we're not actually on shore trailing round tacky souvenir shops in ninety-degree heat, I spend my time propping up the bar. And I can do that just as well at home, not to mention that the beer's better round here.'

'You have a couple of young grandchildren now, don't you?' said Cooper. 'Surely you're looking forward to spending more time with them?'

'There is that,' said Murfin, without any great enthusiasm.

Cooper felt sure there was something Murfin wasn't telling him. What did he actually have planned for his years in retirement? Something he was embarrassed about, perhaps. Maybe Jean had it all mapped out for him and Gavin had no say in it at all. That would be possible. She might have decided her husband should go to adult education classes to learn Spanish or salsa dancing, or t'ai chi. Or even all three. That would keep him busy, all right.

But the leap of the imagination to picture Gavin Murfin as a Spanish-speaking salsa dancer and t'ai chi expert left Cooper feeling mentally exhausted. His brain wasn't ready for such a shock.

Above the trees Cooper could see the upper slopes of the hills now. On the Derbyshire side there had been a series of disturbing incidents recently – increasingly frequent reports of animals being found slaughtered on the moors. Sheep with their eyes gouged out and their genitals mutilated, a cow with its ears slit, a horse with its tail amputated. People were talking about Satanists and ritual sacrifice. But it didn't take much for Derbyshire people to start talking like that. In Peak District villages they didn't seem to believe in religion very much these days. But they believed in everything else.

Cooper realised they were going to have to extend the search area considerably. Who knew what had been going on in these woods? He would have to speak to the DI to get that organised.

'Still, you won't miss me when you've got these bright kids,' said Murfin. 'Look at young Luke there. He's the future. Happy as a pig in clover he is, with this sort of thing.'

'Do you think so?'

'He follows you about like a dog, Ben. He knows you'll find him a nice juicy murder case.'

'Could you actually get some work done, Gavin?' said Cooper.

'Like what?'

'Get across the border and see if you can assist our colleagues from Staffordshire.'

Chapter Five

DC LUKE IRVINE was breathless by the time he reached the top of the trackway where his car was parked on a grass verge. He was driving a Vauxhall hatchback, and it was his current pride and joy. He hated the idea of scraping its paintwork on a dry stone wall in one of these narrow lanes, or having some uniformed bobby snapping his wing mirror off with a Transit van.

As he climbed into his car, he wondered if there was a reason he'd been tasked with finding out about the victim's family. It might mean that he'd end up having to inform bereaved relatives of a death. It was the job everyone dreaded the most. Would Ben Cooper delegate that responsibility to him?

Irvine was conscious of certain subjects he mustn't mention to his DS. It was murmured around the office that Ben Cooper might still be vulnerable to an ill-judged comment. No one knew how he might react to the wrong word. Some said he was on a knife edge, though so far he seemed to be hiding it well. Irvine was even nervous of mentioning the Scenes of Crime department, or crime-scene examiners, or even some forensic detail. It was the department Ben's fiancée had worked in. Would it bring back intolerable memories?

But Irvine wondered whether he was being over-sensitive about this. Cooper was a professional. He could surely deal with these things; separate his job from whatever happened in his private life outside the office. Even the death of a fiancée.

With the car started, he checked his satnav for Earl Sterndale. Ben Cooper would have used a map, of course. He was an obsessive user of Ordnance Survey maps. No, scratch that. Ben would have known exactly which way to go without having to look at any map. Irvine had to accept that he wasn't as familiar with these remoter areas as his DS was. He wasn't a Derbyshire boy like Cooper. He'd grown up in West Yorkshire. Parts of that county were very similar to the Dark Peak, but it didn't help when it came to navigating these back roads.

As he inched his way to the road and turned towards a hamlet called Glutton, Irvine shook his head in frustration. It seemed so difficult these days to know what was the right thing to do or say. Perhaps it was working so closely with Becky Hurst that had done this to him. She'd made him paranoid about blurting out something that might upset or offend anyone listening.

But Becky was right a lot of the time, of course. You had to be careful; what you said, especially when you were a police officer. It didn't really matter what your personal opinions were, as long as you didn't act on them or express them out loud. Not even in an email or a tweet. Someone was bound to report you for inappropriate behaviour. It was almost the worst offence you could commit now. No one allowed police officers to be human, not in the way they once had. No office banter or canteen culture pranks, none of that black humour or contempt for criminals the old school coppers had expressed on a daily basis.

You'd think it was unhealthy to keep all this stuff bottled up, though. All those old guys around the station always seemed so much more relaxed. Take Gavin Murfin. He was so laid back he was practically lying dead on the floor. He said what he thought and didn't care about the consequences. He'd already put in his thirty years' service and could pack his belongings at any moment with the certainty of collecting his full pension.

Irvine couldn't imagine ending up like that. The job was so different now. You had to keep your lip buttoned if you wanted to survive long enough to call it a career. If he managed to make it to his thirty, Irvine suspected he'd be a screwed-up, paranoid mess. Probably a chief superintendent, in fact.

He drove the Vauxhall up out of the valley and through some of those curiously shaped hills that characterised this side of the county. Earl Sterndale was only a little way ahead. He was glad of the satnav's instructions when it came time to make the turn. The crossroads were almost anonymous and unrecognisable.

The Beresfords' house was a stone-built semi near the village church. He was able to park directly in front. But he waited for a few minutes, watching children leaving their homes and walking down to the bus stop to wait for the school bus. It made him feel like a lurking paedophile and he began to worry that a suspicious parent might take his registration number and report him.

Finally, he couldn't waste any more time. He climbed out of the car and checked his pockets to make sure he had his notebook, his warrant card and his phone. It was as he was looking down that he noticed his shoes were caked in mud. So were the bottoms of his trousers. There must be mud on the carpet in his car too, damn it. Just as bad was the fact that he now had to present himself at someone's front door in this state and expect to be taken seriously.

There was no point in trying to brush the mud off until it dried. Anything he did now would only make it worse.

Irvine cursed under his breath. He heard laughter and turned to see a couple of girls about thirteen years old walking past. They were giggling and nudging each other like idiots. He felt himself beginning to flush. He was glad his DS couldn't see him now.

He knew Ben Cooper had wanted children. Wanted them badly, in fact. Irvine had once run into Cooper on the street in town, when they were both off duty. It had been in Clappergate, near the entrance to the shopping precinct. He remembered the encounter well, because it had been one of the moments when details impressed themselves on his mind.

Cooper had been accompanied by his two nieces, the younger one holding his hand, the other a bit too old to do the same without embarrassment, but sticking close by his side. Irvine had tried to make polite small talk, the way you were supposed to. But he'd felt very awkward, and even a bit shocked, at this terribly domestic picture of his detective sergeant standing in the street like a proud dad.

Maybe it wouldn't happen for Cooper now. He might never have his own children to take shopping. Irvine was sure it must be what Cooper was thinking.

Irvine didn't like children much himself. He didn't possess that urge to be a parent. He couldn't help a horrified reaction to mothers sometimes. It was the way they seemed to regard motherhood as giving them not only special privileges, but some kind of superpower. Their sense of entitlement could be staggering and they instilled it in their children too. He'd never been brought up like that. Back home in Yorkshire he'd been taught a bit of humility and consideration for other people. It made him feel like some old fogey to be looking at these arrogant young kids and dreading what sort of society they'd create when they grew up.

At least he couldn't picture Becky Hurst as a mother. It would be far too disruptive to her future plans.

He turned his back on the girls, surreptitiously wiped his shoes on a patch of grass and went to knock on the Beresfords' door.

ONCE THE SEARCH area was extended, it didn't take long for the search teams to turn up their first find. When the shout went up from somewhere deep among the trees, Cooper felt all his senses prickle with anticipation. It was as if a shot of adrenalin had just gone through his veins. All the tiredness fell away like dead skin. There was an edge to the tone of the voices he could hear from the woods. It told him what he'd been waiting for. This was going to be something that would change the whole picture.

'What have you found?' he asked when he'd run up the slope to the point where the shout had come from.

'Look for yourself, Sergeant.'

Cooper pushed through members of the search team and looked. There was another trackway here, descending the hill diagonally from the north-east. There was very little trace of the stone setts, if there had ever been any. But the track was marked by a low wall on the side where it overlooked the valley.

Just at the point where this route dipped to approach the Corpse Bridge, a large slab of stone was embedded in the ground. Its top was flat and smooth, and it must have been almost six feet in length. On its own it looked anomalous. It was obvious that it had been sited here deliberately, but a long time ago. Over the centuries it had weathered and become scarred and worn by use. Its mossy sides blended in with its surroundings, but it had clearly been important. It was functional, not decorative. And Cooper knew what it was.

'A coffin stone,' he said. 'They would rest the coffin here before they crossed the bridge.'

The officers in the search team were looking at him expectantly now. That was the trouble with sounding as though you knew what you were talking about. Sometimes you didn't. Sometimes you were as baffled as everyone else.

'But as for *that*,' said Cooper. 'I have no idea.'

Lying on the coffin stone was a makeshift dummy. It was an effigy stuffed with straw or cotton wool, stitched into an outfit of clothes that looked to have been made for it specially – brown corduroy trousers, a tweed jacket, a floppy hat.

'It's a guy,' said someone. 'That's what it is.'

Cooper nodded. Yes, in some ways, it was a traditional Bonfire Night guy, the sort of thing that would be on bonfires all over the country in a few days' time. But most of them would be much less carefully crafted than this one. There was something chilling about the amount of effort that had gone into creating the features of the face. He felt sure it was intended to resemble some real person, though it was no one he recognised. What message was it intended to convey?

The effigy lay sprawled on its back on the coffin stone, its limbs bent into unnatural shapes, its torso wet and beginning to cover over in dead leaves. The unnerving face was grinning up at him from amid the first stages of decomposition.

And that was the message, surely. It was a body, waiting here. Waiting for its time to cross the Corpse Bridge.

'Staffordshire have made a find on their side too. Just a few yards up the track from the river.'

'What is it?'

'A piece of rope.'

'Rope?' said Cooper.

'Well, to be exact – it's a noose.'

Cooper gazed at the river crossing, with its two tracks coming down from the Derbyshire side and a third leading away into Staffordshire. Crossroads held a special place in folklore. In superstitious belief, places where tracks intersected were considered dangerous. They were protected by spirit guardians, because they were places where the world and the underworld met. Many people believed that the Devil could be made to manifest himself there.

Well, the Corpse Bridge wasn't quite a crossroads, but it was a focal point where three routes met. It would probably have filled the requirements for believers in the old crossroads lore.

Cooper looked at the body, still lying on the bank. He tried to imagine what connection the victim might have had to the carefully constructed effigy on the coffin stone or to a rope noose. But his imagination failed him for once. Perhaps the link was something beyond his comprehension.

People scoffed at the old beliefs now, of course. But the Devil had manifested himself here, after all.

Chapter Six

LUKE IRVINE CAME away from the Beresfords' house in Earl Sterndale wondering whether his visit had been as useful as he'd hoped.

Yes, he'd obtained an address for Sandra Blair in Crowdecote and learned that she was widowed, her husband having died five years ago. No children either. The nearest thing to a next of kin was probably a sister in Scotland, who the Beresfords didn't know. But that was about it.

Mrs Beresford didn't know anything about the husband, Gary. She'd never met him, having only come into contact with Sandra at the tea rooms in Hartington, and later at WI meetings. Sandra had talked about her husband quite a bit, but only spoke of the small things, the personal stuff – a holiday in Tenerife, Gary's favourite dog, their first house in Bowden, where they'd lived until her husband's death. She seemed to have avoided the less personal topics.

Sandra Blair was local, though, and not an incomer. That ought to help. More people would know her than if she'd only moved into the area in the last few years.

Irvine had already phoned these details to his DS. But would they be enough? Cooper had sounded distracted and distant on the phone. Of course, he liked his DCs to give him more than just the basic facts. He liked to get their impressions of the people involved, an opinion or instinctive reaction. Becky Hurst was great at that. And DC Carol Villiers too, of course. Ben always trusted her opinion.

Privately, Irvine felt he might be lacking in this department. He couldn't seem to form any subjective impressions of individuals while he was concentrating on asking the important questions and making notes. The temptation was to make something up, offer an opinion he didn't really feel.

Oh, well. He'd soon find out whether it was enough, by what task DS Cooper sent him on next.

BEN COOPER WAS waiting at the top of the trackway leading down to the Corpse Bridge. He was studying the landscape, trying to achieve an overall view of the topography in a way that he couldn't get from a map, or even from a satellite image on Google.

From here the bridge was invisible, standing way down among the trees at the foot of the slope. The only buildings within half a mile were those derelict field barns on the Derbyshire side. The ruins had been searched, but nothing else had turned up, no signs of recent activity or occupation. Not even a homeless person or lost hiker would have taken the trouble to fight their way into one of the roofless shells through the tangle of overgrown birch trees and dying brambles.

Each side of the valley, pathways snaked up the hillsides until they reached a narrow B-road and the occasional isolated farmstead. The nearest farms had been visited by uniformed officers, but no one could have seen or heard anything from there. Working farmers were in bed and fast asleep at the time Sandra Blair must have been killed. They'd awoken to the first signs of police activity.

With a frown, Cooper scanned the countryside around. To the south of the Corpse Bridge, the River Dove formed a loop and created that wide area of flat, fertile ground in the bottom of the valley. Lit by a shaft of sunlight in the distance was Knowle Abbey, sitting elegantly among its acres of parkland as if posing for photographers. Only the white scar of a disused limestone quarry immediately behind it created a slight flaw in the picture.

Cooper remembered a visit to this stately home when he was a teenager. His mother had loved these sorts of places. Chatsworth House, Haddon Hall – anywhere the aristocracy lived seemed to hold some strange kind of fascination for her. She enjoyed gawping at the antique furniture and endless family portraits, exclaiming at the size of the dining table and the four-poster beds, wandering round the immaculate gardens and choosing a souvenir from the gift shop. And she wasn't alone, judging by the crowds of visitors who flocked to these historic houses. Like Isabel Cooper, most of them had far more in common with the servants who'd worked away in the kitchens and pantries than with the aristocrats in the portraits.

Knowle wasn't quite in the Chatsworth House league, though. While Chatsworth's façade was a familiar sight on postcards and in guides to popular Peak District attractions, Knowle Abbey rarely made an appearance. The Duke and Duchess of Devonshire were much better known than the Earl and Countess Manby. The Manbys were a bit of a mystery. They never seemed to get their pictures in the papers supporting local charities or opening summer fêtes. Cooper knew the Devonshires by sight, but had no idea what Earl Manby looked like.

A little to the west, conveniently out of sight of the abbey, was the estate village of Bowden. Its quaint stone cottages were inhabited by workers on the earl's estate. The village had been built for that purpose, so that all the gamekeepers and gardeners and domestic staff could live near their work, while paying rent to the earl as their landlord.

Bowden had its own little church, where for centuries a clergyman appointed by the earl would have preached to his little flock about duty and morality, and about knowing their place. There was a village hall too, and at one time a small schoolhouse for the estate workers' children. The present children went to school in Hartington and the church saw only the occasional visit from an overworked vicar covering five parishes. But otherwise, Bowden hadn't changed much.

To the north of the bridge the River Dove came down from its source on Axe Edge Moor. On the Derbyshire side a long string of limestone quarries ran southwards from the town of Buxton along the A515. As a result this narrow strip of the county was left almost isolated between the quarries and the river. There were only a few small communities here – Earl Sterndale and Crowdecote, Glutton and Pilsbury. They were tiny places, with nothing of any size until you reached Hartington to the south.

The hills were strange too, even for a county like Derbyshire. Their shapes looked unnatural, like animals or artificial constructions from the ancient past. This was certainly an area where myths and legends would thrive. You only needed one look at those hills to make you believe in anything.

'What do you want me to do next, Ben?' asked Irvine after he'd reported to Cooper.

'You can come with me to Crowdecote. And then Hartington. The tea rooms should be open now.'

'Crowdecote? Well, I got the address...'

Cooper held up an evidence bag from among the items retrieved from the body.

'And we've got the key too,' he said.

THE ROADS IN this area were slippery with mud and wet leaves. Farm vehicles had been busy working well into the autumn, trimming hedgerows and verges, scattering more debris on the already difficult surfaces. Cooper drove carefully, conscious of his tiredness, the risk of a momentary lapse of concentration on a treacherous bend.

Sandra Blair had lived in a stone cottage in a small row of them close to the edge of a narrow road that dipped and twisted its way through the hamlet of Crowdecote like a ski slope, dropping down to the Dove. A few yards away, set back from the road, was the village pub, the Pack Horse Inn. And almost directly opposite, a lane swung off towards Earl Sterndale.

The cottage was separated from the road by a short stretch of iron railings. Behind them there was no room for anything that could be called a garden, just a climbing rose against the front wall and a bird feeder with an empty feed tray positioned right in front of the sash window. The cottage hadn't been decorated for a while, but a carriage lamp and a hand-painted ceramic name plate had been added by the front door in recent years. It had been given the name of Pilsbury Cottage.

'What car does Sandra Blair drive?' asked Cooper, hoping that Irvine had used a bit of initiative when he got her address.

'A red Ford Ka,' Irvine said promptly.

Cooper nodded. And there it was. A red Ford Ka, tucked into a tight parking area at the side of the cottage, where it was just clear of the road. Did Sandra get a lift from someone else last night to the place where she'd met her death? Or was she another bike owner, like Rob Beresford? Cooper's money was on the first possibility – it would certainly be much more helpful to the investigation. The second option seemed like too much of a coincidence, at the very least.

'When we've finished in the cottage, the neighbours will have to be spoken to,' said Cooper.

'We'll be looking for anyone who witnessed Mrs Blair leaving home last night,' said Irvine, looking over the Ka.

'Or, failing that, someone who can help us to narrow down the time. If a neighbour can confirm when she was still at home, that would help a bit. And of course—'

'Any sightings of a vehicle calling at Pilsbury Cottage,' added Irvine. 'Or the name of a boyfriend, anyone she might have been going out with last night?'

'Very good, Luke.'

Irvine peered through the driver's window of the Ford. 'Are the car keys on the ring with those for the house?'

Cooper jingled the keys. 'No. Let's see if they're inside.'

'Shouldn't we knock first?' asked Irvine.

'Why?'

'Well, just in case … there might be someone at home.'

'Go ahead, then.'

Irvine gave a loud rap on the front door, while Cooper waited, rattling the keys. He was conscious of faces appearing at windows nearby, wondering who they were and what they were up to. There might be a few calls to the local station shortly.

'Happy now?' said Cooper when there was no reply.

DIANE FRY TWISTED uncomfortably at her desk in the Major Crime Unit at St Ann's in Nottingham. She wasn't happy.

Fry had just come back from a meeting with her DCI, Alistair Mackenzie.

'We can't just leave them to get on with it,' he'd said.

'Why not?'

'It's our job.'

It was frustrating being the new girl all over again and not feeling able to argue too much. But Fry felt there were some things that weren't her job.

'We've got so much else on,' she said, though she was pointing out the obvious.

Mackenzie was unmoved. 'It makes no difference, Diane. Besides—'

'What?' She could see him getting round to breaking some kind of bad news. He wasn't sure how she was going to react. Fry knew herself well enough to realise it probably meant she was going to react badly. 'Sir? What is it?'

'We've had a request from Derbyshire. Specifically, E Division.'

'No, no, no,' said Fry. 'I spent enough time there. I filled in at Divisional CID in Edendale for months while Ben Cooper was on extended sick leave. It was too much. I couldn't stand going back and doing the same thing again.'

'That's not—' began Mackenzie.

'Besides, DS Cooper is back at work now. I know he is. I was there when he returned. There can't be someone else…?'

Mackenzie was shaking his head patiently. 'No, you're getting completely the wrong end of the stick, Diane.'

'Am I?'

Fry tried to restrain herself. But the sudden prospect that had risen in her mind was too scary. After Ben Cooper's tragedy in the pub fire, she'd been unable to decline the temporary assignment back to E Division, a secondment to take charge of her old team in Divisional CID. A refusal would have been impossible, especially in those circumstances.

And then there had been the unexpected final task, the more personal one for which she was totally unsuited. Breaking bad news, adding another psychological burden to someone who was already down. She had no personal skills for doing that. Ben Cooper must be used to hearing only bad news from her by now. The thought caused an unexpected stab of pain in her abdomen.

'Let me explain,' said Mackenzie.

So Fry reluctantly sat and listened to his explanation of the request from Derbyshire. She fidgeted at the thought of the task she was being presented with. It opened up all kinds of possibilities in her mind, some of which were completely unprofessional. She suppressed the flight of imagination immediately. Totally inappropriate.

'Why me?' she said when Mackenzie had finished.

The DCI raised his hands. 'You're the obvious person. You've got to admit that, Diane.'

'Perhaps.'

He looked at her more seriously. 'This is a compliment, you know. It's a sign of how highly you're regarded. Don't just throw that away.'

Fry bit her lip. She knew she was going to have to accept. In fact, her mind was already turning over the ways she might approach the task. Her relationship with Ben Cooper was complicated, but she had to put all that aside. Feelings couldn't come into it. Definitely not.

She gazed back at Mackenzie for a moment, and finally she nodded. There was only one thing to do. She would just have to take the bull by the horns.

Chapter Seven

THE INTERIOR OF Pilsbury Cottage was cramped and dark. The windows in these old cottages were always too small and the ceilings too low. It reminded Cooper that his ancestors must have been people of short stature who spent their time crouched in candlelight huddled against the cold.

'We need the lights on,' he said.

'Here.'

Irvine found the switches and the sitting room sprang into focus. It was still cramped, but the furniture and wallpaper were decorated in a series of bright chintzy patterns that made the light suddenly painful on his tired eyes.

'Check upstairs for any signs that anyone else has been here,' said Cooper. 'Then see if you can find a diary and an address book.'

'Anyone else? Oh, you mean like a boyfriend?' said Irvine. 'Shaver in the bathroom, slippers under the bed?'

'Possibly.'

While Irvine disappeared upstairs, Cooper stood in the middle of the sitting room and turned through three hundred and sixty degrees to perform a quick survey. The objects scattered around were a little out of the ordinary. They reminded him of the sort of thing his sister Claire collected. Abstract pottery, ethnic art, bowls full of crystals and stacks of scented candles. A Native American dreamcatcher hung from the ceiling and a pack of Tarot cards stood on a bookshelf. One wall was covered with a rug woven in vibrant colours with tribal African figures.

He noticed a large wicker basket next to one of the armchairs by the fireplace. When he lifted the lid, he found balls of wool, scraps of material, knitting needles, a case full of pins and cotton thread, another of buttons and small glass beads.

Cooper saw a phone on a table by the window. He pressed the answering machine button to play back the messages. But a recorded voice told him there weren't any. Even the old messages had been deleted. There was a calls list function too, but the only recent numbers it showed were listed as unavailable.

That was odd. It was almost like someone was trying to hide their contact history. It certainly wasn't a normal thing for the victim of a crime to do. People didn't expect to meet their death when they left the house.

Cooper walked through into the tiny kitchen and found a laptop computer sitting on the table. He looked out of the back door, where there was only a tiny square of garden tucked under the hillside. He could see over a stone wall into a few acres of sheep pasture.

'Can you see an address book or anything with phone numbers in?' he called, when he heard Irvine come back downstairs.

Irvine had begun opening and closing drawers in a pine dresser in the sitting room. 'Not yet. But come and have a look – I've found a diary.'

'Is it a big one?'

'No, tiny. A little pocket diary.'

'She didn't record every detail of her life, then.'

'No such luck.'

Irvine passed him the diary. The cover was plastic, but tex-tured to make it look like leather, and it had little brass corners to protect it from getting dog-eared from use by the end of the year. Cooper riffled through and saw the information it provided would be sparse. There were four days to a page and Sandra Blair had used the space mostly to record dates when she was working, the times of WI meetings, dental appointments, an eye test.

He turned to Thursday 31 October. But the section was blank. To Cooper's eye, it looked suspiciously blank. After the absence of messages on the answering machine, it looked as though Sandra had deliberately failed to mention where she was going last night. Not even to her own diary.

But what about tonight? Well, here was an entry at last. So Sandra hadn't planned to die last night. For Friday 1 November, she'd written: 'Meet Grandfather, 1am.'

'What does it say?' asked Irvine.

'"Meet Grandfather, 1am." What do you think that means?'

'Well, someone was meeting their grandfather, I guess.'

'Grandfather?' said Cooper. 'How old was Sandra Blair, Luke?'

'We think she was around thirty-five. But that's an estimate from Mrs Beresford.'

Cooper did a quick mental calculation. 'It's possible, I suppose. But her grandfather would be approaching eighty, at least.'

'My grandfather wouldn't be out meeting anyone at one o'clock in the morning,' said Irvine. 'He's in bed with his hot chocolate by ten at the latest.'

'There are grandfathers and grandfathers, though.'

Cooper was remembering his Granddad Frank, his mother's father. He'd been a tough old bird, who'd spent most of his life working on the roads as a foreman in the county council's highways department. That was in the days before health and safety, when Frank and his colleagues worked on all kinds of jobs and in all conditions wearing their overalls and flat caps. As foreman, Granddad Frank had insisted on wearing a tie too. He could have walked twenty miles when he was aged nearly eighty, and he never seemed to get more than three or four hours' sleep.

'Whose grandfather, then?' asked Irvine.

'I have no idea.'

Irvine frowned. 'That's a shame, Ben. She was supposed to be meeting him tonight, whoever he is.'

'Tonight?' said Cooper. 'Or last night?'

'It's an entry for today, isn't it?'

'Yes, but at one in the morning.'

'Oh, I see what you mean.'

'If you were going somewhere at one o'clock in the morning, would you enter it in your diary for that day or the day before?'

'Where would I be going at 1 a.m.?'

'I don't know. I'm not familiar with your social life. An all-night party? A rave?'

'Chance would be a fine thing.' Irvine thought about it for a moment. 'Probably the day before. Because that's when I'd need to remember it. The next day would be no good. If I was the sort of person who might forget something like that.'

'Speaking of which,' said Cooper. 'I haven't seen any car keys yet. You?'

'No. There's a handbag here with the usual sort of stuff in. A purse, but no keys.'

Cooper looked round. They'd left the front door open when they entered the house, just in case someone passing by got worried about them being burglars.

'Close the door for a minute, Luke,' he said.

Irvine looked surprised, but he pushed the door shut. On the back of it was a row of coat hooks, which held two or three jackets, a waterproof and a scarf.

'Try the pockets of the top jacket,' said Cooper.

Irvine patted the pockets, dived in with a hand and pulled out a set of car keys on a fob with a logo.

'Eureka,' he said with a happy grin.

'Let's take a look in the car, then.'

It was while they were searching the car that a member of the public stopped to ask what they were doing. Irvine showed his warrant card and assured him there was nothing to worry about. Cooper watched the man as he left reluctantly. It would be all round the village in half an hour that something was going on at Pilsbury Cottage. But it couldn't be helped.

'Nothing in the boot,' said Irvine, except some bags of old clothes. 'It looks as though she was planning to take them to the charity shop.'

Cooper smiled. He opened the glove compartment, pushed aside some old car parking tickets and till receipts, and put his hand on an address book.

'Excellent.'

They went back inside the house, away from prying eyes again.

'Luke, did you find a sketch pad in any of the drawers?' asked Cooper.

'A what?'

'A sketch pad. Blank pages that you can draw on.'

'No, nothing like that.'

'Let me know if you see one.'

'By the way, we'll need a formal identification, won't we?' said Irvine, peering into a broom cupboard.

'Of course. But it's more important to use these first few hours trying to pick up as much evidence as we can before the lines of inquiry start to go cold.'

'Yes.'

'Besides,' said Cooper, 'I think we can be fairly sure of who our victim is.'

He picked up a framed photograph from the dresser. Sandra Blair was pictured with a dark-haired man leaning against a stone wall. They were smiling broadly and had their arms round each other. 'This must be her husband that she's with. How long ago did he die?'

'Around five years. His name was Gary.'

There were other photos on the dresser. One was apparently from the Blairs' wedding day, with Sandra in an elaborate white dress and Gary looking embarrassed in his suit and tie, with a white buttonhole. Another was of an earlier family group, taken perhaps twenty years ago – mother and father, with two teenage girls. Sandra and her sister, he assumed, though Mrs Blair was un-recognisable as a fifteen-year-old.

'Do we know the sister's name?' asked Cooper.

'No, the Beresfords couldn't remember. They think she might live in the Dundee area, and she's married with three or four children. But that's all we have at the moment.'

'We must get on to that. Neighbours—'

'I know. I'll go now.'

'Thanks, Luke. Then we'll try her colleagues at the place Mrs Blair worked in Hartington. And the Women's Institute too, if necessary.'

When Irvine had left to call at the houses on either side of Pilsbury Cottage, Cooper looked through the address book. Well, it said 'Addresses' on the cover, but it turned out to have very few addresses in it. Names and phone numbers, yes. But many were just first names. Only a few numbers such as the dentist's and the doctor's surgery were immediately identifiable. Someone would have to go through the book entry by entry and call all these people. First of all, it would help to identify a Dundee dialling code.

Cooper pulled out his iPhone. The easiest way was to do a quick Google search, provided there was a good signal here. It took a few seconds for him to find the code was 01382. He flicked through the pages of the address book, but found no matches.

It was frustrating that there were no addresses given. Of course, there must be an address list somewhere, even if it was only for sending out Christmas cards. Unless Sandra Blair was the kind of person who sent digital cards by email. He went to the kitchen table and switched on the laptop. As soon as it booted up, he saw that it was password protected, as he suspected. That would be a task for a computer forensics analyst who would be able to crack the password and extract files and emails.

Then Cooper went upstairs. Luke had already been up here, so he didn't spend much time looking for evidence of a second person being present. The neighbours would know about that, if anyone did. It was impossible to miss much of what was going on in an area like this.

At the bottom of the bedside cabinet, he found what he was looking for. It was folded inside a copy of *Woman's Weekly Craft Special*, among several other magazines. At first glance it looked like a pattern book. Sandra had covered it with a swatch of velvety material. Cooper ran his hand over its smoothness. She'd made a nice effort of it too. But it was the right size and feel.

When he opened the book, it fell directly to the last page. The page where Sandra Blair had made her sketch of the Corpse Bridge effigy.

Chapter Eight

COOPER PARKED THE Toyota in Hartington Market Place, close to the duck pond. Legend said that it was actually a 'ducking pond', originally used for subjecting suspected witches to water torture to make them confess. But today half a dozen white ducks were on the pond anyway, doing their bit to wipe out the memory of its true purpose. They couldn't have done a better job if they'd been paid by the tourist authority.

In fact, Hartington was an odd mixture of tourist and traditional, with tea rooms and an antiques shop rubbing shoulders with the village stores and a post office with its Victorian postbox still standing outside the door. Self-catering cottages stood opposite the Royal British Legion club, where a notice advertised grocery bingo on the third Sunday of every month.

'So that's all the neighbours knew,' Luke Irvine was saying. 'Sandra kept herself to herself pretty much. She was interested in crafts, joined the WI.'

'We know that,' said Cooper.

'And she'd been going out quite a lot in the evenings recently. They didn't know where.'

'Or with who?'

'No. In fact, they were surprised to see that she didn't go out in her own car last night. There isn't much in the way of public transport.'

'Somebody must have picked her up,' said Cooper. 'Perhaps just not from in front of her house.'

'Why would she go to the trouble of sneaking away like that?'

Cooper shook his head. 'I don't know. Not yet.'

He locked the car and glanced around the village.

'Do you know Hartington at all, Luke?' asked Cooper.

'Not really. I think there's a DI from Derby who lives here somewhere, isn't there?'

'Yes. He has a house up Hall Bank, near the youth hostel. But we won't bother him. He'll be busy.'

Irvine smiled, and Cooper wondered if he'd made a joke. It seemed a long while since that had happened.

'So what's the village's claim to fame?' asked Irvine, looking round.

'Cheese,' said Cooper.

'Cheese?'

'Yes, cheese.'

A passer-by turned to stare at them. Cooper laughed now. He suddenly had a picture of himself and Irvine as a couple of tourists having their souvenir photo taken. '*Say cheese, and let's have a big grin for the camera.*'

But it was true. Until recently Hartington had been a centre for Stilton cheese-making. The cheese factory was built at the Duke of Devonshire's creamery, where cheese was made from the milk produced by his tenant farmers. There had been other cheese factories in this area – one at Glutton Bridge and one across the river near Sheen. But Hartington had supplied a quarter of the world's Stilton at one time. The factory closed when it was bought out by a rival company in Leicestershire six years ago. It had been looking increasingly derelict since plans for a residential development on the site were turned down by the planning authority.

Cooper could see the old cheese factory down a side lane off the marketplace. The paint was peeling on the doors and window frames, rubbish was scattered outside, and the sheds and loading bays were gradually losing any sense of function or purpose as they lay abandoned.

In a way the history of the Hartington cheese factory reflected the role of large landowners like Earl Manby. Nearly two hundred people were employed here at the height of its production, many of them living in the village of Hartington itself. They depended on the factory, and its closure took away their livelihoods. Some of them were probably forced to move away to find alternative work.

'Which tea rooms did Sandra Blair work in?' asked Cooper.

'Hartdale. It should be close to the square somewhere. Mill Lane.'

'Over that way,' said Cooper.

Some enterprising individuals had reopened the Old Cheese Shop in the village and were making their own cheese from a farm nearby. If he got chance, he ought to call in for a chunk of Peakland Blue. His cat was a bit of a cheese connoisseur and blue cheeses were her favourite.

The pub across the road was called the Devonshire Arms. Of course, Hartington was the Duke of Devonshire's territory. In this part of Derbyshire every second pub was called either the Devon-shire Arms or the Cavendish Arms, after the family name of the owners of Chatsworth House. Even some of the larger houses in the villages had stones featuring the stags' heads from the family's coat of arms. The Devonshires were much larger landowners than the Manbys, and always had been. So the owners of Knowle Abbey had bigger neighbours – and grander, too. A duke outranked an earl in the order of precedence, the aristocrats' league table.

Hartdale Tea Rooms were located in a converted farm build-ing, near the corner of Mill Lane. It had no parking of its own, but it was handily placed between the village centre and the overspill car park further up the lane. The proprietor was alone, except for a teenage girl wiping tables and tidying chairs.

The windows were small – probably because they hadn't been able to change the original exterior of the barn in view of Har-tington's conservation area status. But it created a cosy feeling inside, even at the beginning of November. Cooper could imagine it would be pleasant in here later in the year with snow falling outside, and the smell of coffee and hot crumpets inside.

Florence Grindey was a woman in her sixties. In his mind Cooper felt as though he ought to be thinking of her as a lady, rather than a woman. She had that air about her. A certain con-fidence and style natural to people who'd grown up that way. She was tall and slim, with greying hair tied back from well-defined cheekbones. In fact, she resembled an ageing actress. If he'd encountered her in different circumstances, he might have won-dered if he'd seen her as a leading lady in films from the 1970s. He would have been sifting through his memories trying to place her name, but failing. Even now he couldn't say who exactly it was she reminded him of.

'Miss Grindey? I'm Detective Sergeant Cooper from Edendale CID,' he said, showing his warrant card. 'This is my colleague, Detective Constable Irvine.'

Miss Grindey looked flustered for a moment. It was often the way, even with the most law-abiding of citizens. People tended to search their memories, or their consciences, for something they'd done wrong. Almost everyone had broken a law at some time. But Miss Grindey's search didn't seem to last long. Her expression changed to concern. It must be bad news.

'Poor Sandra. It's so dreadful,' she said, when Cooper broke the news of her employee's death to her. 'Do we know what happened?'

'Not yet, I'm afraid. But obviously, that's what we're trying to find out.'

'Of course.'

It was odd, that use of 'we'. It was the tone of a nurse addressing an elderly patient or a mother talking to a child. Not so much a paternal manner, as maternal.

'So what can I tell you, Detective Sergeant?'

'First of all we need to trace her movements yesterday. Was she working here?'

'Yes, but only until lunchtime was over. We're very quiet on a weekday at this time of the year. Some days we don't open at all in the winter. We rely on the weekend for most of our business.'

'So what time did Mrs Blair leave?'

'Oh, about two-thirty.'

'Do you have any idea what she was planning to do for the rest of the day? Or in the evening?'

'None at all.'

'It was Halloween. You're sure she didn't mention any plans?'

Miss Grindey shook her head. 'I'm sure she didn't.'

'Did she seem worried about anything? Was there anything unusual about her manner?'

'No.'

Cooper turned to look at the teenage girl, who had stopped working to listen to the conversation.

'Kimberley wasn't here yesterday,' said Miss Grindey. 'She only helps us out part-time, mostly at weekends. Though what I'm going to do now without Sandra...'

'Even so,' said Cooper. 'Might my colleague DC Irvine chat to Kimberley for a few minutes?'

'I suppose so.'

He nodded at Irvine, who managed to lead the girl into the kitchen area without any reluctance on her part. Irvine might not get anything from her, but at least now she was out of earshot.

Cooper found Miss Grindey watching him expectantly. A knowing expression had come into her eyes.

'I suppose you're going to ask me about Sandra Blair's private life now,' she said.

'Well—'

'It's always what the police are interested in, isn't it? The prurient details. The victim's sex life. How did she get on with her husband? Was there a boyfriend involved?'

'Well, we know her husband has been dead for several years,' said Cooper calmly.

'Indeed.'

'So was there...?'

He waited patiently. Finally, Miss Grindey sighed. 'Not that I'm aware of.'

Cooper had the feeling she wouldn't have told him even if she'd known that Sandra Blair had a string of lovers. It was something about the way she'd said the word 'sex' in a hushed tone, as if it were a subject never mentioned in a Hartington tea room. He knew that wasn't the case, of course. When some people got together over a pot of tea, they talked of little else. He was sure that Miss Grindey must be the sort of person who noticed little things about her customers.

'She never mentioned any friends at all?' he asked.

'Not by name,' said Miss Grindey. 'She was in a few local organisations, I understand.'

'Yes. What sort of interests did Mrs Blair have? Did she talk about any of her activities?'

'Oh, she was interested in all kinds of crafts,' said Miss Grindey. 'She brought little things in to show us sometimes. I think it was something she took up after her husband died. Poor dear. You do need something to occupy your time in those circumstances.'

'Is that why she took the job here too? I mean … no offence, Miss Grindey, but it was hardly launching herself into a new career, was it?'

'No, you're right.' Miss Grindey lowered her voice. 'Actually, I believe she needed the money.'

'Oh?'

'Her husband's death didn't leave her very well off, from what I gather. She was able to buy her little cottage at Crowdecote. But even that wasn't cheap. I'm sure you know what property prices are like in this area.'

'Yes, I do,' said Cooper.

The unexpected jolt of memory made him gulp. He'd spent many months looking at properties with Liz, when they were planning their future. He could probably have put an accurate asking price on anything on the market below two hundred thousand pounds. And he knew there were many houses to be found at that price.

'I think it was thanks to a life insurance policy that she was able to do that,' said Miss Grindey. 'Otherwise she would have been stuck in rented accommodation.'

'Didn't she have a house to sell when her husband died?'

Miss Grindey shook her head. 'Oh, no. Until he died they lived at Bowden.'

'Of course.'

Cooper mentally kicked himself for his naive question. Bowden was one of the estate villages for Knowle Abbey and its residents were all tenants. Their landlord was the owner of the Knowle estate, Lord Manby himself. He owned Bowden.

'We urgently need to track down Sandra Blair's family,' said Cooper.

'She has a sister in Scotland.'

'So I understand. Do you have any idea of the sister's name or where she lives?'

'No, I'm sorry.'

He looked across at Irvine, who seemed to have finished with young Kimberley.

'You could try Mr Naden,' said Miss Grindey, finally volunteering information now that she sensed the police were about leave her tea rooms.

Cooper turned back to her. 'Who?'

'Mr Naden. He and his wife come in here for afternoon tea sometimes. I always had the impression that they knew Sandra quite well. Not that they chatted or anything. But just the way they spoke to each other, you know.'

'I know,' said Cooper, glad that his instinct about her had been correct. 'Thank you for your time, Miss Grindey.'

'I don't know their address, but Geoff Naden looks after the churchyard,' she said. 'You might find him there.'

Chapter Nine

OUTSIDE, THE CENTRE of Hartington village was gradually getting busier. Some of the people he could see were probably local, calling at the post office or filling up their cars at the little petrol station in Mill Lane. But there were visitors too. There were always folk looking for somewhere to spend their time at the weekend, as long as the weather wasn't too bad. And even then some hardy individuals would venture out in the snow.

Near the village stores they passed a row of eighteenth-century cottages. The door of one stood partly open, with a sign offering free range eggs and pure Hartington honey straight from the hive.

'The part-time girl, Kimberley, hardly ever saw Sandra Blair,' said Irvine. 'She knew a lot more about the old dear she works for.'

'Miss Grindey? Anything interesting?'

'Not really.'

They turned into Hyde Lane, where the village hall stood. This end of the building still showed traces of its original sign, which had been painted on the wall. Hartington Amusement Hall.

Cooper wondered if the amusements in those days had been the same as those enjoyed by Hartington residents now.

He opened a small gate and they climbed a set of steps into the graveyard of St Giles' Church. According to a plaque, the bench at the top of the steps was a gift from His Grace the Duke of Devonshire in 1978. That must have been the old duke, father of the present incumbent at Chatsworth. From somewhere in his memory, Cooper dredged the fact that the eldest son of the duke held the title of Marquis of Hartington, at least until he succeeded to the dukedom.

As in many English villages the signs of the ancient landowners were everywhere, even if they no longer owned any of the properties. That part of English history would take a long time to disappear. It would still be evident while the pubs existed and while some of these houses remained standing.

Cooper turned at the bench and looked back at the village. The organisers of events held at the amusement hall would probably have been obliged to get approval from the duke for their entertainments. He must have had the final say in pretty much everything else.

In the graveyard they found a thickset, middle-aged man vigorously raking leaves off the paths into a big heap. He was wearing a baseball cap and he had receding grey hair sticking out in untidy clumps. He didn't see them coming at first and Cooper was struck by his grimly determined expression as he lashed out with the rake. He was digging out the last of the dead leaves from cracks between the stones, but his mind appeared to be dwelling on something entirely different that made him angry.

'Mr Naden?' called Cooper when they got closer.

The man looked up, startled. Almost frightened. For a moment Cooper wondered if he was deaf, or listening to an iPod while he worked. But it appeared he'd just been so deeply engrossed in his thoughts that he was noticing nothing around him. That took quite a bit of concentration.

'Yes? Can I help you?' he said, with the rake poised in mid-air. 'I can't show you the church. I don't have the keys.'

'We're not visitors, sir.'

Cooper produced his warrant card and introduced himself and Irvine.

Naden looked around him and hefted the rake in his hand. For a second Cooper thought he was going to do a runner or lash out at the two police officers. He almost took a step backwards to put himself out of reach of a weapon, but stopped himself. He was surely just imagining things. Everybody was starting to look suspicious.

'What can I do for you, Sergeant?' asked Naden finally.

'We're making enquiries about a lady called Sandra Blair,' said Cooper.

'She works at the tea rooms.'

'That's the lady.'

Naden began to poke at some more leaves, but in a desultory fashion. There was no longer the passion he'd been showing with the rake when Cooper first set eyes on him.

'We're trying to contact her family. Would you know—'

'There's a sister in Scotland, I think.'

'We're aware of that.'

'But that's all I know.'

Cooper sighed. He was beginning to wonder if this sibling north of the border actually existed. Could she be a figment of Sandra Blair's imagination, casually mentioned to everyone she met in order to give the impression that she had a family like everyone else? If the sister in Scotland couldn't be tracked down, he might have to turn his attention to finding the family of the deceased husband. For some reason he couldn't explain to himself, he had no faith in the existence of a grandfather who'd arranged a meeting at one o'clock in the morning.

'Are you the churchwarden or something?' asked Cooper.

'No, I just help out,' said Naden. 'We all have to do our bit.'

'And how did you first meet Mrs Blair?'

Naden shrugged. 'I'm not sure, really. I suppose she's always been working at the tea rooms.'

'I don't think so.'

'Well, that's where we always saw her. She doesn't live in Hartington.'

'No, you're right there.'

Out of the corner of his eye, Cooper noticed Irvine had walked a few yards away and was kicking at a pile of leaves. He was getting bored.

But Cooper waited a little longer. Naden raised his head, sensing from the silence that he was supposed to say something else.

'What's happened to Sandra Blair, then?' he said. 'Has she had an accident?'

I thought you'd never ask, thought Cooper.

'Something like that, sir,' he said.

'WELL, HE WAS a washout,' said Irvine as they returned to the car. 'Mr Grumpy with the rake. What was his name?'

'Mr Naden,' said Cooper.

'He didn't tell us anything.'

'He might do, though. Given time.'

Irvine laughed. 'I don't know how you can have so much patience with people like that, Ben.'

'Sometimes it's the only way,' said Cooper.

'Are we going back to West Street now?' asked Irvine.

'Yes.'

'What next, then?'

'That address book has to be gone through,' said Cooper. 'Sandra Blair's remaining relatives must be in there somewhere. The sister in Scotland…'

'And her grandfather,' said Irvine.

'Yes. Well, possibly. And perhaps someone who knew her a bit better than her employer and her neighbours. Gavin should be in the office. You can do the job between you. But let me know if you think you've traced the sister. We'll need her to come down for a formal identification and start going through all the formalities.'

'Couldn't someone else do the identification? Someone who knew Mrs Blair well?'

'Yes, of course, if we really needed it,' said Cooper. 'We could get Miss Grindey to do it. But it's a sensitive issue for the family of a murder victim. They feel it's their job, to make that official confirmation of the death of their family member. They don't understand when it's been left to some person they didn't even know, and they can get very upset about it. It just doesn't feel right to them. They should be the first to know about the death, too. But in this case…'

'Understood.'

Cooper took a last look around the centre of the village. His route back to Edendale would be up through Hartington Dale and north on the A515 to the turning for Tideswell.

Despite the visitors, Hartington was actually quieter than he remembered it. That was due to the closure of the cheese factory, he supposed. There were no delivery vehicles coming and going to the empty factory in Stonewell Lane. There was no major employer in the village now. And he didn't have time to buy that piece of cheese either.

'After that you can call it a day, Luke,' he said. 'It's not as if there are any house-to-house enquiries to do near the crime scene.'

'There are no houses there,' said Irvine.

'Exactly. I'm going to get the press office to start putting out some public appeals as soon as possible. Tomorrow we'll see what forensics have come up with. Then we ought to have some leads to follow up.'

'Suits me,' said Irvine. 'I've got a date tonight anyway.'

Cooper looked at him as he started the Toyota. He couldn't help a twinge of envy. He'd been Luke Irvine's age once and it wasn't all that long ago either. But he couldn't remember the last time he'd been able to say those words to a colleague: 'I've got a date tonight.' It sounded so innocent. The sentence seemed to hang in the air inside the car, oozing with freedom and hope for the future.

With a jerk, Cooper put the car into gear and drove away from Hartington.

'Good luck with that then, Luke,' he said.

Chapter Ten

THE FIRST APPEALS for witnesses were broadcast on the local TV news early that evening. They appeared on Twitter feeds for the police and BBC Radio Derby, and were soon all over the internet. Detectives wanted to hear from anyone who'd been in an area of the Upper Dove Valley last night near a location known as Hollins Bridge.

When Cooper heard the appeal, he realised the press office had decided against using the familiar colloquial name for the bridge. Instead they had chosen the official name, which featured on Ordnance Survey maps of the White Peak but was never used by ordinary people. At least, it wasn't used by local people – only by visitors who relied entirely on maps.

That was a pity. The individuals they were hoping to hear from would surely be local. Too often people didn't have enough knowledge about their own locality. Not accurate, factual knowledge. They just knew the stories and legends, and the vernacular names.

So he just had to hope that someone with useful information would make the proper connection. But wasn't that the whole principle behind solving crime?

Cooper tidied the paperwork on his desk, pulled on his jacket and left the office. He drove out through the barrier from the police compound and headed down West Street towards the town.

Dusk was long past and it was dark over Edendale. Below him street lights sparkled in the cold air and windows of houses glowed in their pale colours. It would only need the first heavy frost to arrive and the town would start to look quite Christmassy.

The thought reminded him that he had some shopping to do. Instead of continuing all the way to Fargate, he turned off into Hollowgate and found a parking place in the market square near the war memorial.

When he got out of the car, Cooper listened for a few moments, enjoying the sound of the River Eden running below him in the darkness. At night its sound had a mysterious quality, as if thousands of tiny, invisible creatures were out there, whispering and murmuring until daylight came again. He could picture the mallard ducks that lived on this stretch of the river through the centre of town. They would be bobbing gently on the surface as they slept with their heads towards the weir. The flow of water didn't seem to bother them. He'd always admired the ability of the mallards to float calmly in whatever torrent of water came their way.

He turned towards the town. The high street was only a few yards away and some of the shops were still open. Even at the beginning of November, there were groups of young people sitting out in the beer gardens of the pubs. The smoking ban had made some of them quite hardy.

Cooper thought he might even walk down to the Hanging Gate for a drink before he went home to Welbeck Street. It was certainly a tempting thought.

SALLY NADEN WAS having a bad day with the pain. Sometimes the tablets weren't enough to keep its excruciating surges suppressed all day long. By the middle of the afternoon the pain could break through its anaesthetic restraints like a deranged killer ripping out of a straitjacket. Once loose, the agony swept through her body in uncontrolled waves and left her exhausted and helpless.

So her mind was distracted and she wasn't quite thinking straight by the time the phone rang and Geoff began to tell her this garbled story about people being killed and the police looking for someone. She thought he was describing the plot of some TV programme he'd been watching. He was a great one for sitting in front of episodes of *Lewis* and *Midsomer Murders* and trying to guess who did it. In fact, he would get really tetchy if you interrupted him at the wrong moment and he missed a vital clue.

As she listened to him gabbling down the line, she thought he must finally have lost touch with reality. That was the risk of watching detective drama stories all the time. You ended up confusing them with the real world. Life wasn't actually like that. People didn't get killed every day, the way they did in Inspector Barnaby's world.

Finally, Sally began to realise what he was telling her.

'Seriously? You mean—'

'We were there,' said Geoff.

'It's not possible.'

'Well, I think it is. What are we going to do?'

Geoff had calmed down a bit and she could hear him trying to formulate a plan. What was in his own best interests? That would be the concern foremost in his mind.

'The chances are, they'll find out we were in the area, one way or another,' he said. 'Someone will have seen us or our car, or ...

Well, you know – it will come out sooner or later. And it will look bad if we haven't mentioned it.'

Sally laughed, but winced with the pain it caused her. 'You mean they might suspect you of murder? That's a joke.'

'Both of us,' said Geoff firmly. 'We were both there.'

Sally felt another surge of pain as she thought about what they'd have to do. But, for the first time in many years, she knew that her husband was right.

It was a difficult decision for Jason Shaw too. That evening, after he'd listened to the news, he sat in his little cottage in Bowden and stared at the log fire for quite a while, gulping from a can of lager. When that one was finished, he went to the fridge to fetch another. He needed something to help him think.

He remembered very clearly the figure he'd seen running through the woods near the Corpse Bridge. That pale shape in the twilight dodging through the trees. Its unnatural appearance had made him wonder whether his eyesight had been blurred by the rain.

More worrying had been the noises. The sound of something crashing through the undergrowth and that wordless yell. Who had been shouting and who were they calling to?

Jason had heard many noises in the woods at night. Often they were nocturnal animals. Foxes or badgers, or even owls. Their screeching could be unnerving if you weren't used to it. But at least their presence was natural in the darkness. Sometimes there were gamekeepers or poachers. But they didn't shout to each other like that. Or at least, the poachers didn't. They wanted to remain unnoticed, so they moved as quietly and unobtrusively as possible. Jason knew that as well as anyone.

But now and then, he knew there were other people out in the woods at night. Sometimes there were kids playing games.

Popping the tab on another can, Jason took a swig. Yes, perhaps that was who it had been near the bridge. It was Halloween, after all. They might have had to go off and mess around on their own. But the bridge was a long way from anywhere. And it had been raining. Kids weren't so tough these days, were they? The first drop of rain and they were back in the house with their PlayStations.

So that just left the final group. The ones who were doing things he didn't understand, and didn't want to. He'd glimpsed them from time to time, whole groups of them, sometimes silent, but other times talking or singing. He'd found dead animals too – animals that hadn't been caught by a poacher or trapped by a keeper. Neither would do those things to a sheep that he'd seen, or leave such a bloodied mess. The reasons for that were beyond his imagination.

Jason heaved himself up from the armchair and stepped to the back window of his cottage. He heard his dog grumble outside in the kennel where it slept. Lights were on in most of the cottages in Bowden. Behind their curtains people were watching TV, maybe just hearing about the body found at the Corpse Bridge, wondering if anyone would come forward.

The bridge was too close to Bowden for anyone's comfort. People would soon find themselves asking each other if the killer might be nearby. They would be afraid. They would wonder whether they and their families were safe. Jason was wondering the same thing. Because he was frightened too.

Suddenly, the lager tasted sour in his mouth. It made Jason feel sick with fear to think that someone might have been watching him from the trees near the Corpse Bridge last night, especially if it was one of *those* people – the ones who did evil, inexplicable things in the woods.

Well, he'd seen someone and the chances were high that they'd seen him. Jason put the lager can down and picked up the phone.

BEN COOPER WAS walking back through the streets of Edendale when his phone rang. A mobile number he didn't recognise. Should he answer it? It might be a wrong number or a sales call, even at this time in the evening. He should let it go to voicemail.

But something made him answer the call instead.

'Yes?' he said cautiously.

'Ben? That *is* you, isn't it? You don't answer your phone very professionally these days. You sounded very surly.'

Cooper stopped walking. He'd suddenly found that he couldn't walk and talk at the same time.

'Diane?' he said.

'Who else did you think it was?'

'You've got a new phone. I didn't recognise the number.'

'It's me, nevertheless. How are you doing?'

'I'm okay. Hold on, though … what do you mean by "surly"?'

It sounded trivial, but he was so surprised that he couldn't think what else to say. The last thing he'd anticipated was a call from Diane Fry. So he fell back on the first thing that came into his mind.

'Rude, ill-tempered, unfriendly. You sounded as though you didn't want to speak to anyone.'

'Not the old Ben Cooper you know and love, then,' he said.

But as he said it, the sharpness in his tone was obvious, even to himself. Blast her, she was right again – he *was* getting surly.

Fry sighed down the line. 'Well, that's the pleasantries over with,' she said.

Cooper thought he detected actual disappointment in her voice. Surely she couldn't have expected a delirious greeting, given their history?

He bit his lip. Well, not all of it had been bad. Fry had shown some loyalty over the years, even been the one who understood him and came to his aid when he needed it. But somehow she'd always managed to ruin things and sour their relationship again. He'd always assumed she wanted it that way.

'So what are you doing at the moment?' asked Fry.

'Nothing much.'

'Are you in town?'

'Yes,' he said. 'Why?'

'I'm packing.'

'What? Oh, yes, I heard. You're moving, aren't you? Leaving Edendale.'

'Yes, I'm going to live in Nottingham. It makes sense. It's far too much of a trek getting to St Ann's every morning from here.'

'I understand. So?'

'Well…'

She hesitated. Cooper hadn't heard her hesitate very often. She'd always seemed very confident in her views and always knew what she wanted to say.

'Well, the new flat is part-furnished,' she said, 'but I've got a couple of pieces of my own furniture here. Only small stuff, but awkward. I can't get them into my car. So I thought…'

'Go on.'

'I remembered you had that big four-wheel drive. You do still have it, don't you?'

'The Toyota, yes. It's getting a bit old now. I was thinking of replacing it.'

'But it has plenty of space in the back, if I remember.'

'I suppose so,' said Cooper.

'Enough to get my bits and pieces in, I think. If I asked nicely.'

'Nicely? Diane, are you asking me for a favour? You want me to help you move your stuff to Nottingham?'

'Only if you're not doing anything else.'

'Ah.'

So that was it. She thought he could be taken advantage of because he had nothing better to do with his time any more. Or perhaps she felt sorry for him. Cooper wasn't sure which was worse.

'You know perfectly well I'm not likely to be doing much,' he said. 'I don't have a personal life left, of course.'

Cooper knew he was sounding ill-tempered again. Rude and unfriendly, even. He felt certain now that this was actually the reason she'd called him. She'd known he had nothing better to do, that he was just as sad a case as she was herself, ever since that fire at the Light House pub had snatched his entire future away.

No doubt it wasn't really his load capacity she wanted, but a glimpse of Ben Cooper at his lowest ebb, just as he was moving on.

He almost ended the call then and there, with his rudest comment yet hovering on his lips. But a small voice at the back of his mind made him change his intention. He *wasn't* at his lowest ebb, was he? Yes, months ago he'd been in a bad way. That couldn't be denied. But he'd submitted himself to the counselling sessions, he'd worked all his feelings through and dealt with them. He was okay now. He was fine. He could let Diane Fry see that he was back to his normal self. More than that, he could show her that he was full of energy, raring to go. And *he* was ready to move on too. She would see that he wasn't going to miss her at all. His life was totally back on track.

'All right,' he said. 'I'll be there in a few minutes.'

He could hear the surprise in her voice. She'd thought he wasn't going to agree.

'Thanks, Ben,' she said. 'I appreciate it.'

And that was probably a first too. Cooper couldn't remember hearing Fry thank him before. He might actually enjoy this task.

When he ended the call, Cooper realised he was staring into the window of a children's bookshop in Hollowgate. He didn't remember it being here before. The shop must have opened some time during the last few months, when he wasn't really noticing things like this.

As he focused his gaze into the shop, Cooper found himself looking at a display of books with bright, cheerful covers – *The Snappy Playset Garage*, *The Things I Love about Bedtime* and *The Things I Love about School*. Next to them were *My Home* and *My Family*. Each title seemed to taunt him from behind the glass, until the accumulated effect was unbearable.

He felt the urge to find a brick and toss it through the bookshop window, as if that would destroy the image. The physical action and the sound of glass smashing might make him feel better for one fleeting moment.

But it was worse than that. Cooper knew the really disturbing images were inside his head, and there was nothing he could ever do to smash them.

Chapter Eleven

DIANE FRY'S FLAT was in one of the large detached Victorian villas in Grosvenor Avenue, just off Castleton Road. Although the tree-lined street had once been prosperous, almost all the properties were in multiple occupancy now – one-bedroom flats, smaller bed-sits and some houses where the tenants shared communal facilities.

Cooper knew this as a student area, mostly for young people studying at the High Peak College campus. He had no idea why Fry had chosen to live here when she came to Derbyshire. And he had even less understanding of her reasons for staying in Gros-venor Avenue when she could so easily have afforded somewhere better on her detective sergeant's salary.

But that might have been because he'd never asked her about her reasons. Or he'd never asked her properly. There was a lot about Diane Fry he didn't understand, but she only shared infor-mation about herself on a need-to-know basis. At least that meant he wasn't the only person who didn't understand her. Nobody at West Street did. The only person he'd ever met who might have a bit more insight was Diane's sister, Angie. Cooper reassured himself with that fact.

A couple of the other tenants were just leaving the house as he parked outside the gate. They didn't look like students, though. They were a bit too old and bundled up in old clothes as if off to a night shift at a job where they didn't expect to stay clean. When he said hello to them, they answered readily enough, in accents that sounded East European. Of course, Grosvenor Avenue wasn't just student territory any more. The High Peak College students were competing for cheap accommodation with migrant workers from countries in the European Union.

He remembered something Fry had said to him years ago, when he moved out of Bridge End Farm into his own little flat on Welbeck Street. 'A cheap rent just means something really grotty that nobody else wants,' she'd said. But number 8 Welbeck Street was a lot better than this.

Cooper rang the bell set among half a dozen others by the front door and it was opened almost immediately.

'Hello, Diane.'

'Hi. Come in.'

She left him to close the door and set off up the stairs. She was dressed in unfaded denim jeans and a sparkling white shirt, like someone who'd decided to dress casually but found she didn't have any casual clothes. He'd rarely seen her when she wasn't wearing black suit trousers, aiming for the smart professional look. Yet this look suited her. It somehow managed to soften her edges. Her fair hair had grown a little longer too, and it masked the hard lines of her face, which in the past she'd always seemed keen to emphasise. Whatever had caused the change in her appearance, he was glad of it. Though he knew better than to comment on it. Fry never took compliments well.

'Aren't you supposed to say "thank you for coming" or something like that?' said Cooper, though he was speaking to Fry's retreating back.

'Oh, yes. Thanks, Ben.'

'You're welcome,' he muttered as he followed her up the stairs. 'Always a pleasure.'

Fry's flat was on the first floor of the house. It consisted of a bedroom, a sitting room, a bathroom with a shower cubicle, and a tiny kitchen area. As soon as he entered, Cooper noticed that it had been redecorated since the last time he was here. He recalled striped wallpaper in a faded shade of brown and a carpet in washed-out blues, pinks and yellows, a pattern that looked as though it had been designed to hide substances spilled on it. The redecoration had done wonders. Fresh paintwork in cleaner, bright colours and a new carpet on the floor. Was Fry responsible for this? Or had the landlords insisted? That seemed much more likely. They would be looking to attract replacement tenants now.

Fry's own possessions seemed to be scanty, judging by the cardboard boxes around the flat. They would barely fill the back of a small van. Surely there must be some books, music, a few prized objects she'd collected over the years. Okay, perhaps not souvenirs of the Peak District. But, well … something. He suspected these boxes contained clothes, bedding and not much else.

'Have you moved some stuff already?' he asked.

'A bit,' she said.

'Do you want these boxes moving?'

'No, I'm taking those myself. I can get three or four in the boot of my Peugeot each trip. It's just this table and the bookshelves. Oh, and the TV is mine.'

Cooper nodded. 'No problem.'

So there were bookshelves, but that didn't mean there had been books. In fact, he couldn't imagine what sort of books Diane Fry might read in her leisure time. *Blackstone's Police Manuals Volumes 1–4.* That would be about the shape of it.

'The shelves will have to be dismantled,' he said.

'Oh.'

'It's easy enough. Just a few screws to take out.'

Fry frowned and looked around her. 'I don't think I have a—'

'I've got a set of screwdrivers in the Toyota,' said Cooper.

'Brilliant.'

He watched her for a moment as she folded towels into a plastic carrier, her slim hands working quickly and precisely, the sleeves of her shirt rolled up above wrists that looked too fragile to have any strength. A strand of hair had fallen over her face and she had a faint sheen of sweat on her temple. She gave the job of packing as much concentration as she did any other task and she didn't seem to notice his observation. He'd ceased to exist again just in that moment.

It was so typical of this woman. For Fry, a person was either useful to her or just a nuisance. And she could switch them from one to another in the blink of an eye. Cooper wished he had the ability to tune people out the way she did. But he just couldn't do it. Right now he was aware of almost nothing else but Diane's presence so close to him in the cramped sitting room. Yet she seemed to have forgotten his existence for a moment. It was strange that he didn't resent this more. Instead, it made him feel sorry for her.

'I'll put the TV in the car, then I'll bring the tools back up with me, shall I?'

She looked up. 'That'll be great, Ben.'

So he unplugged the TV set and carried it downstairs. Luckily, Fry wasn't the type to go for a massive sixty-five-inch widescreen. This one would fit in the back of the Toyota without difficulty. And he could carry it on his own too. Not that he had much choice.

He found the little toolbox, covered the TV set with a coat and locked the car carefully. When he returned to the flat, Fry was sitting down looking unnaturally relaxed. And she'd made him a coffee.

'I thought we'd take a break,' she said. 'Have a seat.'

Cooper did as he was told, but with trepidation. Looking at Fry's jeans and shirt, it struck him for the first time that she'd dressed specially for the occasion – and that wasn't just for the packing. There was something else she'd planned.

Fry leaned forward. 'So...' she said.

'So?' Cooper repeated.

He had a sudden dread that Fry was going to start asking him personal questions. And not just any old questions, but the full cross-examination – all the same questions that people had asked him over and over again in the months after Liz was killed.

And he was right. But it was such an odd thing. Within a few minutes of Fry broaching the subject, he found himself telling her exactly what it had been like. He spilled it all out – the plans he and Liz had been making, what the wedding was going to be like, their dreams for the future, the possibility of having children very soon.

And then that afternoon at the Light House pub, when he and Carol Villiers had been examining the cellar while Liz searched for forensic evidence in one of the bedrooms upstairs. And there was the fire.

That was the most difficult part to talk about. He'd been through it many times for the subsequent inquiry, the inquest, the trial hearings. But it didn't make the telling any easier, no matter how many times he ran over the events as if they'd happened to someone else. The stink of smoke, the roar of flames, the crash of shattering windows, the terror of being trapped in the burning building. The knowledge that his fiancée was two floors above him, alone, and unaware of the blazing stairs. And finally the moment when he realised that she was no longer behind him as he fought his way to safety. The moment he lost her to the flames.

Cooper felt himself drifting into his memories as he talked. His immediate surroundings faded away, the dismal first-floor flat receding into the distance. He saw only Diane Fry's face in front of him, her eyes curiously compelling, as if this had been the opportunity he'd been awaiting for so long.

It was only when it came to talking about the aftermath of the fire that he faltered. The period when he was away from work on extended sick leave was the most difficult to explain. Liz's death had been tragic and meaningless. But the things he did in the following few months were inexplicable. When he looked back now, they had no logic. He'd lost his senses and he couldn't explain that to anyone.

'After it happened,' he said, 'I mean, after the fire, there were months and months when I kept telling myself it was all a mistake and Liz wasn't really dead at all. Some of the time I think I actually believed that.'

Fry nodded.

'I understand,' she said.

But Diane Fry wasn't that good an actress. He didn't believe she understood at all. She just knew it was something people said in the circumstances. And yet she'd taken in every word he'd told her. He had no doubt about that.

Cooper felt suspicion welling up again. Was all this concern genuine? Surely not. Fry had some ulterior motive. What it was, he had no idea. He supposed it would become evident one day. And whatever it was, it wouldn't be to his benefit.

After a moment he managed to change the subject. 'I suppose you're looking forward to living in Nottingham,' he said.

'Well, what do *you* think?'

'You can't wait, I suppose.'

'You got that right. Look at this place. Well, I know it's where you're from and all that, but really...'

'Is there anybody here you'll miss?' asked Cooper tentatively.

'Oh, yes,' said Fry.

'Really?'

'Mr and Mrs Khan at the corner shop. They've always been very nice to me.'

The silence was broken when Cooper's phone buzzed. At first he tried to ignore it. But Fry looked at him expectantly.

'Perhaps you'd better answer that,' she said. 'It might be important. Some urgent development in your murder inquiry.'

She was right, of course. It might have been that. But the call was from the East Midlands Ambulance Service. They'd been given his name by a patient who'd just been admitted to the Accident and Emergency department at Edendale General Hospital.

He listened for a few moments while Fry watched him curiously, no doubt alerted by the sudden change in his manner.

'What's up?' she said when he finished the call.

'It's my landlady, Dorothy Shelley. She's been taken to hospital. It sounds as though she's had a stroke.'

'That's a shame. You've grown quite close to her, haven't you? I heard you look after her quite a bit.'

'Yes.'

But Cooper felt a wave of guilt. He hadn't been paying much attention to Mrs Shelley recently. The old girl had been very good to him, ever since he first turned up to look at the flat in Welbeck Street. She'd treated him pretty much as a grandson and he was sure his rent ought to have gone up substantially in the past few years, but for her indulgence. He should have returned the consideration by keeping a closer eye on her as she got increasingly frail and confused.

He certainly ought to have been there tonight when she needed him. She could have just banged on the wall and he would have gone straight round. He wondered if she'd been able to call the ambulance for herself or if someone else had come to her aid. He wondered how long she'd been obliged to wait for help.

'She gave them my name,' said Cooper, in a tone that expressed far more than the mere words conveyed. 'I'm sorry. But I have to go.'

DIANE FRY WENT to the window and watched for a few minutes as Cooper left the house and got into his car. He didn't look back. He had someone else to worry about now.

Fry closed the curtains and turned back to the half-empty cardboard boxes littering the floor of her flat. She seemed to have spent a large part of her life watching Ben Cooper walking away.

Chapter Twelve

Saturday 2 November

IT WAS so hard to get used to the change from British Summer Time. The clocks had gone back the previous weekend and suddenly the sun was setting before he managed to get away from work. Cooper looked out of the window and saw the sun had gone from the sky. It was dark by the time he got home, which was always too depressing.

Of course, it happened every year, but that didn't seem to make any difference. It caught him out every time. No matter how many times he was reminded about changing his watch, the reality of its effect on his daily routine didn't sink in. Not until it happened. And then, somehow, he felt deceived.

It made Cooper feel the way he had when he was a child, expecting the summer to go on for ever and feeling that sense of loss and disappointment when the light faded and he knew that winter was on its way. He could recall the feeling now, remembered how let down he'd always felt, as if even the calendar were prepared to betray him.

Yes, he certainly learned that lesson as a boy. The whole world was the same. People too. He'd discovered that you couldn't rely on anything or anyone. If you let yourself be fooled into trusting someone, the same betrayal was inevitable. The day would eventually come when the weather changed and winter arrived.

Mrs Shelley's stroke last night had been a serious one. His landlady's nephew had turned up at the hospital. Cooper had never liked him – he suspected the man had no interest in his aunt, except for the prospect of inheriting her two properties in Welbeck Street. There was no doubt that Cooper's rent would go up when that happened – but only until the houses were sold off to the first property developer who came along.

Dorothy Shelley looked more than just frail as she lay in her hospital bed in the intensive care unit. She looked deathly pale and so thin that her fragile bones protruded from the sunken skin on her shoulders. Her eyes were deep set and the shape of her skull stood out as clearly as if it were a specimen in an anatomy class.

It hardly needed saying, but the medical staff had to say it anyway. One stroke was often followed by another, and then another. And if Mrs Shelley suffered just one more stroke as serious as the first, it might well be fatal.

Well, it was the weekend and he wasn't supposed to be on duty, but the hospital could get in touch with him at any time if they needed to. Though he supposed they would contact the nephew now. Family members always took precedence in hospital procedures. Next of kin and all that. But at least if he heard nothing, he could call later, perhaps on Sunday. Waiting was always the worst thing.

The fact that tomorrow was Sunday put an idea into his mind. There was a retired clergyman he'd known for many years. The

Reverend William Latham had been their local vicar for decades. He'd conducted the wedding of Joe Cooper and Isabel Howard, and baptised all of their children, including Ben. He'd guided the young Ben towards confirmation and given him communion a few times. And he'd expressed his disappointment when Ben stopped going to church.

The Reverend Latham was rarely called on now. Retired clergymen were often relied on to stand in and conduct services when there were vacancies. But the old man generally declined invitations, preferring to let the younger clergy do the work. The last time Cooper saw him was at his mother's funeral.

But he knew Latham was still around. He sent a Christmas card every year – one of the few cards Cooper still received with an overtly religious theme, usually a nativity scene with angels and shepherds. He wasn't sure the old vicar really believed in the Nativity story, or anything that appeared in the Old Testament. An air of irony always seemed to seep from his cards when they were opened. Sometimes there was a subtle joke included in the message inside. The Reverend Latham definitely had a subversive sense of humour.

Like a lot of Victorian clergymen, Bill Latham had an obsessive interest in history, particularly stories from the past of his own parishioners. Unlike the Victorians, he'd never had time to indulge his interest while he was serving as a Church of England minister. The old joke about only working one day a week hadn't been true for a long time. A vicar was more likely to be rushing from one parish to another, attending meetings and training courses, and involving himself in the community. But since he'd retired the Reverend Latham had made up for lost time.

'Ah, young Ben,' he said in surprise, when Cooper called him. There was a short pause, during which Cooper could almost hear the old clergyman mentally checking through his recollection of the stories he'd heard and making sure he'd got it right. 'I was so, so sorry to hear about your loss…'

'Thank you. It's in the past now.'

'Of course.'

In fact, Latham had taken the trouble to write to Cooper at the time of Liz's death – a long handwritten letter that arrived at Bridge End Farm addressed to him, along with the more usual sympathy card. Cooper still had the letter, stored away in its envelope. He'd taken it out and read it a few times during those months on sick leave and alone at home in Welbeck Street. It was strange how much comfort you could glean from a few heartfelt paragraphs written by someone you respected, a man who'd played an important part in your life. They didn't need to share a religious belief for that to matter.

'So you're keeping well, Ben?'

'Yes, I'm fine.'

'I'm very glad to hear it.'

Latham enquired about the rest of his family. Once he'd dug into his memories, they seemed to start flowing unstoppably, like a rusty tap being turned on. He not only remembered Matt and Claire, but he knew the name of Matt's wife Kate and recalled that they had two children.

'Two girls, am I right? They must be, oh … I suppose they're almost grown up now. It's been such a long time.'

'They're teenagers anyway,' said Cooper.

'Ah. Well, perhaps not such a long time, then. It's difficult to keep track. And your Uncle John and the rest of the family?'

'All fine.'

'Good, good.'

Latham paused, possibly feeling that he'd achieved a success. He must be approaching eighty now. Cooper remembered him as being very active and fit, so he was pleased the old man's mental faculties seemed to be intact too. It encouraged him to ask the favour he wanted. The reaction was enthusiastic.

'Oh, I'd be delighted,' said Latham.

'Are you free today?'

'Any time you like.'

'I'll pick you up later,' said Cooper.

GEOFF AND SALLY Naden were sitting together in an interview room at West Street. Mr Naden had managed to tame the wild tufts of grey hair that had sprung from the sides of his head when Cooper saw him in the churchyard at Hartington. But his expression hadn't improved. He still looked just as angry.

His wife sat primly next to him, her arms folded and her knees pressed tightly together, as if she were afraid of touching anything. Perhaps she was frightened of being contaminated by the taint of crime that might be staining the table and seeping out of the walls. Cooper couldn't really blame her for that. He sometimes thought he could smell it himself.

'Mr and Mrs Naden, thank you very much for coming in,' said Cooper, sitting down across the table from them. 'We really appreciate your help. This is my colleague, Detective Constable Villiers.'

Carol nodded and smiled. Her smile always looked genuine and trustworthy. She could play the 'good cop' role very well, if required.

'We saw the appeal on the news,' said Mrs Naden. 'It was asking for people to come forward. If they were in the area where ... you know.'

'Yes, that's correct.'

Her husband looked surprised and irritated that she seemed to have appointed herself spokesperson. There was a definite edginess between them. It dawned on Cooper that it might have been his wife that Mr Naden was thinking about yesterday, when he was wielding that rake so passionately.

'We heard there had been an incident,' said Naden. 'A body.'

'You did the right thing,' said Cooper. 'It could be very useful to us. But we'll try not to keep you too long. If you could just tell us in your own words what you saw or heard that night.'

'Well, it was dark of course,' said Naden.

'Ah yes,' asked Cooper. 'Is it your usual practice to go for walks at night?'

'It wasn't that late actually,' said Mrs Naden. 'It was barely dark at all. Dusk, really.'

'It's the quietest time,' put in her husband.

'Anyway,' said Sally hurriedly, as if she thought he'd said the wrong thing, 'we saw something, so we thought we'd better come in and tell you about it. Didn't we, Geoff?'

'No, we *heard* something,' said Naden. 'To be accurate.'

His wife pursed her lips. 'I,' she said firmly, 'I thought I *saw* something.'

Her husband sighed. 'I'm afraid my wife has a bit of an overactive imagination, Detective Sergeant Cooper. She starts putting two and two together in her mind and gets five, then she convinces herself it's a scientifically proven fact. I'm sure you must know what women are like.'

'Er...'

Cooper could sense Carol Villiers shift uncomfortably next to him, as if about to argue. But Villiers was no Diane Fry. She wouldn't let any animosity show. She knew when to hold her tongue and let people talk.

Mrs Naden's face was set into rigid lines, her mouth turned down at the corners. She looked sour and obstinate. It was probably her normal expression.

'Perhaps we could just let you tell your stories one at a time,' suggested Cooper.

'Certainly,' said Naden. 'I'll go first, shall I?'

'Well, that was the trouble, right from the start,' said his wife. 'He insisted on going first, as always. He thinks he knows better than everyone else. But he's usually wrong.'

'Rubbish,' said Naden, turning slightly pink. 'If you'd just shut up for a few minutes—'

Cooper held up a hand. 'We're not here to offer marriage guidance counselling,' he said. 'So if you don't mind, could we stick to the subject?'

Now they both looked offended. But there was a limit to anyone's patience.

'Well, we were just there, that's all,' said Naden sullenly.

Mrs Naden tapped her fingers on the table, then seemed to remember the risk of contamination and tucked her hands hastily into her lap.

'And what did you hear, sir?'

'A noise. You'll ask me to describe what kind of noise, of course.'

Cooper nodded expectantly.

'Screaming, I suppose you might call it. But not, you know…'

'What?'

'Well, it didn't sound like someone being attacked, if you know what I mean.'

'Mmm. Not exactly.'

'Shrieking,' said Mrs Naden, 'is what I would have called it. If I'd been asked.'

Cooper looked from one to the other. 'Would you agree with that, Mr Naden?'

'It might just have been high spirits,' he replied.

Sally Naden snorted derisively and her husband began to look angry again.

'Anyway,' he said, 'someone was definitely there. That's what you wanted to know, isn't it?'

Cooper turned to Mrs Naden. 'And you say you might have seen something.'

'I believe so. Just ... something white, there in the trees.'

'Something white? A person? Or a light, perhaps?'

'I don't know. It could have been either.'

'You're not certain, Mrs Naden?'

'No,' she admitted reluctantly.

Geoff Naden tilted his head on one side and regarded Cooper seriously, as if about to pass judgement.

'You see, we're all much better off when we just stick to the facts, aren't we?'

Mrs Naden coughed and glanced at Villiers' notebook.

'Detective Sergeant,' she said tentatively, 'you spoke to my husband yesterday in the churchyard at Hartington.'

'Yes, Mrs Naden.'

'Do we take it that the person who was killed ... well, was it Sandra Blair?'

'Actually, we're still waiting for a formal identification,' said Cooper.

She nodded. 'I understand. We did wonder. We know her a bit, you see.'

'From the tea rooms,' said Naden.

'Yes, from the tea rooms,' agreed his wife.

Cooper smiled at them. It was quite satisfying to see the Nadens in agreement for the first time since they'd arrived at West Street.

Chapter Thirteen

COOPER HAD BARELY managed to get back to his desk in the CID room after the Nadens left, when Carol Villiers took a phone call.

'Ben, someone else is coming in,' she said. 'Name of Jason Shaw.'

'Another one in response to the appeals?'

'It seems so.'

'Amazing.'

Cooper had to admit he'd been wrong about the use of the official name by the press office for the location of the crime scene. At least three local people had recognised the name of Hollins Bridge, after all. And their response had been very prompt.

But it felt too good to be true. The Nadens' account seemed unreliable at best. Their story wasn't very convincing. He wondered if Mr Shaw would be the sort of person who put two and two together and got five.

BUT, IN FACT, Jason Shaw was very matter of fact about it. There was no messing around with imaginative leaps or hesitation about what he might or might not have seen near the Corpse Bridge that Thursday night.

'There was somebody running through the trees in white. Somebody else chasing her. One of them, I don't know which, shouted something, but I couldn't make out any words. And that was it.'

Shaw looked at Villiers as she wrote it down. When she'd finished the last word, he seemed to be about to get up and leave the interview room.

'Her?' said Cooper.

'You what?'

'You said "her". This figure in white was a woman, then?'

Shaw licked his lips as he considered how to answer. He was a different type to the Nadens certainly. He was one of those members of the public who thought they just had to make a statement, say what they wanted to say, and they would never be asked any questions.

'Er ... it could have been.'

'You're not sure?'

'I'm not totally sure,' he said. 'It was just...'

'An impression?'

'Yes.'

Jason Shaw was about thirty years old, with a complexion darkened not by sunbathing but by a lot of time spent outdoors. He had a few days' growth of dark stubble and a silver stud in his left ear. His eyes were a bright blue, which was always a striking combination in someone so dark-haired. Shaw was dressed in blue jeans and a well-worn Harrington jacket, which smelled of something earthy that Cooper couldn't quite identify. Smells like that were always amplified in an interview room at West Street. It resulted from the fact that there was no air conditioning or ventilation, and no windows to open.

Over the years Cooper had experienced some interesting aromas from suspects during interviews. Often the individual himself didn't seem to be aware of the odour, until it was bounced back at him from these claustrophobic walls. It could work as a perfectly good interview technique. It made a suspect feel uncomfortable about himself, without resorting to tactics that might breach the procedures of the Police and Criminal Evidence Act.

'But you're quite confident there were people in the trees,' said Cooper.

'Right. That's it.'

'What vehicle do you drive, sir?'

'Why does that matter?'

'In case someone saw it near the scene, then we can identify it as yours.'

Shaw nodded. 'It's a Land Rover Defender. Blue.'

'Thank you. And you say that at the time you were walking your dog on the trackway.'

'It's a Border Collie,' said Shaw. 'His name is Patch.'

Cooper exchanged glances with Villiers. Unlike Diane Fry, Carol knew what he was thinking. She was always on the same wavelength.

'Mr Shaw, did you see anyone else on the track? Any other walkers?' asked Villiers.

'Not a living soul.'

Cooper gazed into Shaw's blue eyes while he answered Villiers, but he saw not a flicker of amusement or deceit.

'Do you know some people called Naden?' asked Villiers.

Cooper held his breath. That was a good question. He watched Shaw pause for a moment.

'Naden? Naden … no, I don't think so. Should I?'

'Perhaps not.'

There had been a slight hesitation there, though it might mean nothing. A lot of people had trouble remembering names. If they saw each other, it might be different. Maybe Cooper should have arranged an accidental face-to-face encounter before the Nadens left the station, and observed the reactions. But it was too late now.

'Well, thank you for coming forward, Mr Shaw,' he said.

Shaw nodded. 'I hope it was a help.'

Cooper saw him pause, as if he wanted to say more.

'Is there any other detail you'd like to add, sir?'

'No, but … I was wondering, has anyone else come in? After the appeals, I mean.'

'We've had some other response,' said Cooper.

'Good.'

Shaw stood and Villiers got up to show him out.

'By the way, sir,' said Cooper before he reached the door. 'Where do you work?'

'Me?' said Shaw. 'I work at Knowle Abbey.'

THE SCENE AT the Corpse Bridge was much quieter today. There was a marked police car blocking the entrance to the trackway and a scene guard further down, with a crime-scene examiner still working in a tent erected over the stretch of riverbank where Sandra Blair had been found.

But Cooper didn't want to go all the way down to the scene and nor did the Reverend Latham. The elderly clergyman was content to stop and rest on a bench halfway down the track, where they could see the river and the arch of the stone bridge below them, as well as the hills on the Staffordshire side of the Dove, and even a corner of Knowle Abbey behind a plantation of trees.

'I think something was going on here,' said Cooper. 'More than just a simple murder, if there is such a thing.'

Latham murmured to himself, but said nothing. The old man was thinner than Cooper remembered him, his hands bony and shaking slightly. He supported himself on a stick, but his posture was still upright and his eyes were bright and inquisitive. His voice had lost some of its power – he would struggle to make himself heard in the pews at the back without the help of a microphone. And before he left his house near Edendale, he'd taken the time to wrap himself up warmly in an overcoat and a long scarf, with an incongruous red woollen hat that he said had been knitted by a parishioner.

'This was what they call the coffin road,' said Cooper. 'It leads to the Corpse Bridge.'

'Indeed,' said Latham.

'But am I right in thinking there was more than one coffin way?'

'Yes, you're right. There were several old coffin roads from these small settlements along the eastern banks of the Dove. They all converged on this bridge.'

'Why, though?'

Latham shook his head sadly. 'For many years coffin roads were the only practical means of transporting corpses from these communities to the graveyards that had burial rights. You see, when populations increased, more churches were built to serve new communities. But that encroached on the territory of existing parish churches and their clergy. It threatened their authority – and, of course, their revenue. They insisted that only a mother church could hold burials.'

'Just burials?'

'They were the most lucrative of the triple rites of birth, marriage and death,' said Latham.

'So it was all about money?'

'Money and power,' said the old clergyman sadly. 'I'm afraid the established church was to blame for a lot of injustices in those days.'

'Only in those days?' said Cooper.

Latham looked at him sharply, but couldn't resist a twinkle coming into his eyes.

'No comment, officer.'

'So where were they taking their dead?' asked Cooper.

Latham pointed with his stick. 'Over yonder.'

Cooper followed his gesture. 'To Knowle Abbey?'

'Almost. To the burial ground at Bowden. It's within the abbey estate now, of course. In fact, it always belonged to the Manbys – or to the Vaudreys before them. It housed their workers, just as it does today. The church belonged to them as well. The earl appointed the minister and insisted that everyone attended church on a Sunday, on penalty of dismissal. In those days if they lost their jobs, they lost their homes as well. So people had to do what they were told. And that sort of control spread to other villages.'

'People even had to bring him their dead.'

'Indeed. For people living in these villages, bodies had to be transported long distances to reach the burial ground at Bowden, often over difficult terrain like this. And the corpse had to be carried, of course, unless the departed was a particularly wealthy individual. There weren't many of those in this area.'

They were both silent for a while. Carol Villiers, who had walked down to the crime scene, looked up and began to climb slowly back towards them.

'Where were the other coffin roads?' asked Cooper after a few moments.

Latham waved his stick vaguely across the hillside on the Derbyshire side. 'Oh, I believe there was one from the north, near Harpur Hill. Another came from a village that has long since disappeared under the quarrying operations. And the third was a little to the south, from the direction of Pilsbury. You'll find only small sections of them now.'

'Of course.'

'You mentioned the coffin stone?' said Latham, raising his head from a contemplation of his bony hands.

'Yes, someone left an effigy on it. Laid out like a body.'

Latham nodded. 'Coffin stones weren't just there to let the bearers take a rest. They were designed to prevent the ground from becoming tainted by death or allowing the spirit of the deceased an opportunity to escape and haunt its place of death.'

Cooper turned and looked at him. 'You know the stories too, then?'

'Why wouldn't I? People still told them in my day.'

'And even now,' said Cooper.

'Really? Perhaps they're a bit more circumspect when they're talking to me, then.' Latham laughed quietly. 'But with coffin ways – well, what would you expect? I suppose it was inevitable that each one gathered a mass of folklore about phantoms and spirits. Wherever there are corpses, there must be ghosts.'

Cooper spread out his Ordnance Survey map. Many of the coffin roads must have long since disappeared, while the original purposes of those that had survived as footpaths were largely forgotten too.

But here there were two reminders. At the bottom of the hill on the eastern side of the river was the coffin stone, a flat lump of limestone on which the coffin had been placed while the bearers rested. And then there was the name of the bridge itself, still known locally as the Corpse Bridge, though it was clearly marked on the Ordnance Survey map with another name. When they heard it mentioned, many visitors to the area probably thought it was a quaint local corruption of some entirely different word. Glutton Bridge wasn't named for its gluttons, or Chrome Hill because it was made of chrome.

On the brow of the hill, he could see that the path crossed Church Way Field. He supposed it might have been possible once to plot the course of a lost coffin road by the sequence of old field names, and perhaps from local legends and vanished features of the landscape marked on antiquated maps.

But all of those things were gradually disappearing themselves. Even farmers forgot the names of their own fields as traditions were lost from generation to generation. Now they were more likely to refer to a field by its size in acres or its position in relation to the farm. In time Church Way Field would become the Upper Forty. Its associated legends would vanish under the plough and a layer of chemical fertiliser.

'That's the way it always was,' the Reverend Latham was saying. 'The bearers and the funeral party making their way down the hill, resting the coffin, dividing and coming together again across the water.'

'Yes, Bill,' said Cooper.

But he wasn't really listening to the old man now. The map had engaged his imagination. The coffin road to the graveyard at

Bowden must have covered a distance of more than four miles and crossed two streams as well as the River Dove. It was so difficult to conceive of the hardship willingly undertaken by those mourners, struggling over the hills with their burden. And resting the coffin for a few minutes on the stone down there, in constant fear of the taint of death or a fugitive spirit.

Cooper was thinking of mentioning to the Reverend Latham his thought about the Devil manifesting himself at crossroads. Just to see what the clergyman said. Did the old man believe in the Devil? Or was that too Old Testament a concept for him?

But before he could speak Latham turned his head and looked up the trackway. He must have sharper hearing than he let on, because he'd noticed someone approaching before Cooper had himself.

'Is this a colleague of yours?' he said.

Cooper opened his mouth in astonishment. 'In a way,' he said.

Chapter Fourteen

DIANE FRY SMILED her ambiguous little smile when Cooper introduced her to the Reverend Latham. He had no idea what she was thinking, but he knew it wouldn't be anything complimentary about either of them.

'I thought I'd find you here, Ben,' she said. 'Despite the fact that you're supposed to be off duty, according to your office.'

'An informal visit. The Reverend Latham is just giving me some insight into the history.'

'I can imagine,' she said.

Fry looked round. 'That's your crime scene? The bridge.'

'Yes,' said Cooper.

He looked for Carol Villiers.

'Carol, would you give the Reverend Latham a lift back to Edendale?'

'Certainly,' said Villiers. 'I can see you've got your hands full.'

'Don't, Carol,' said Cooper quietly, unable to suppress a pleading note from his voice.

Villiers said nothing, but gave him a quizzical look. She knew all about Diane Fry. Possibly more than he could guess.

'Under the bridge,' said Latham, as he rose and supported himself on his stick to go with Villiers.

'What, Bill?' said Cooper.

'The body. It was under the bridge.'

'Yes, it was.'

But even as he answered, Cooper realised that Bill Latham hadn't been asking him a question. His words had formed a statement. *It was under the bridge.* Latham already knew that. But how?

Latham nodded. 'It fits,' he said. 'Under the bridge. Yes, it would have to be.'

Cooper was distracted by the sound of Fry's voice.

'I won't be a minute,' she called. 'I'm just going to take a look at what's on the other side of the bridge.'

'Be careful,' said Cooper automatically, as Villiers and Latham left.

'Of course.'

There was a smaller stream on the Staffordshire side, with a footpath running alongside it. A few yards along, the stream was crossed by a very slippery wooden footbridge, consisting of nothing more than a single plank wedged into the mud on either side.

Cooper watched Diane Fry walk up the footpath to examine the spot where Staffordshire officers had found the coil of rope. Then with her eyes fixed on the water, she decided to cross the stream. He saw her step casually towards the makeshift footbridge with a horrified fascination.

Despite all her time in the Peak District, Fry had never learned how to choose appropriate footwear. She always seemed to wear the minimum she thought would be required. The flat shoes she was wearing now might have been fine for driving out here from Edendale, and they'd just about coped with the uneven setts on the trackway, as long as she went slowly and took care. But when she left a solid surface, she would be in difficulties. Her soles had no grip on them. The moment she set foot on that greasy plank, the outcome was inevitable.

Instinctively, Cooper stepped forward. He quickly came up behind Fry and was able to grasp her arm to support her just as she began to lose her balance. She hardly seemed to notice his assistance.

'Where do we come to if we go this way?' she asked.

'We're in Staffordshire now,' said Cooper. 'This track leads up towards a village called Hollinsclough.'

'Staffordshire? Really?'

'Of course.'

Cooper kept his eye on her. Even Fry didn't have any jurisdiction in Staffordshire. It wasn't in the East Midlands, so it was out of the EMSOU's patch. They had to rely on mutual cooperation with a neighbouring force.

'It's strange really, to think that you've crossed a border,' said Cooper, turning to look back at the Corpse Bridge. 'It's such a narrow stretch of water and such a small bridge. Yet it's always meant so much to people because of its position and significance.'

'A crossing from life to death?' suggested Fry.

Cooper swung round sharply. 'What made you say that?'

Fry smiled again. 'I just thought it was something you would be thinking, Ben.'

'I see.'

'Well, wasn't it?'

'Something like that.'

Fry nodded, apparently pleased with herself. Just because she'd guessed at a notion flitting through his imagination. Was that what she regarded as insight?

'And what about this way?' she said, pointing to the main route of the trackway where it climbed through the trees.

'That's the coffin road,' said Cooper. 'It goes to Bowden.'

'Derbyshire?'

'Just about.'

Cooper explained the nature of the estate village and its relationship to Knowle Abbey.

'And that's where the coffin way leads to?' she asked.

'Yes, to Bowden. It's where they had to take their bodies, for burial in the graveyard there.'

He could see the concept was difficult for Diane Fry to understand. And why wouldn't it be, for someone who had grown up in a city like Birmingham? To Fry, the idea of trekking across the Peak District countryside carrying a coffin probably sounded like just another inexplicable rural tradition.

Cooper showed her the route of the coffin road on his map and carefully explained why people from the hamlets to the east had been forced to carry their dead all this way. It hadn't been their choice, or a random whim. They were completely at the mercy of those who had all the money and power.

'But this track crosses the bridge, then recrosses the river a few hundred yards further down,' pointed out Fry. 'Why would they do that? It doesn't make sense. You just end up back on the same side of the river that you started from.'

He could see Fry frowning at the map in bafflement. What she said was accurate, of course. That was exactly what the coffin road did. And she was right, too, that there seemed no sense in it. No rhyme or reason, or apparent purpose.

Or at least, no reason in the purely logical, modern world that Diane Fry lived in.

'Spirits,' said Cooper.

'What?'

'Spirits,' he repeated, with that sinking feeling of resignation. He knew what her response would be when he tried to explain this. Derision and disbelief. But he was quite used to that now.

'Do you really mean—' she began.

'Yes, spirits,' he said. 'Spirits can't cross water.'

'Oh, for heaven's sake.'

'Perhaps.'

Fry turned away and began to walk up the track and Cooper followed her. As they climbed away from the banks of the river, the trees soon began to close in again.

Cooper couldn't escape the feeling that Diane Fry was observing him constantly. He supposed she was waiting for him to slip up and make a mistake. She'd be watching him for any sign of weakness or hesitation, an indication that his mind wasn't fully focused on his work, that his powers of concentration still hadn't fully returned. She'd be hoping that he wasn't up to the job.

'Shrieking in the woods, white figures moving through the trees,' she said. 'What would the folklore say, Ben?'

If he'd been talking to anyone else, Cooper might have mentioned corpse candles. It was the name given to a flame or ball of light seen travelling above the ground on the route from a cemetery to a dying person's house and back again. For some reason the light was usually blue. A similar light appearing in a graveyard was believed to be an omen of approaching tragedy. Cooper seemed to recall that they appeared on the night before a death. The stories told about corpse lights were like those of the will-o'-the-wisps, mischievous spirits who attempted to lead travellers astray.

As Diane Fry would certainly have pointed out, there were always logical explanations for these things. Anyone observing a will-o'-the-wisp might be seeing nothing more than a luminescent barn owl. A wildlife officer had once told him that some barn owls possessed a form of bioluminescence caused by honey fungus. The white plumage of the birds could look eerie enough at night, if you glimpsed one in your torchlight. A luminescent barn owl flitting through the darkness would be enough to spook anyone. And corpse candles? Witnesses might just have been noticing the effect of methane gas, the product of decomposing organic material in marshes and peat bogs.

But even in the twenty-first century, the prosaic scientific explanations weren't always what people wanted. Everyone liked a bit of mystery. Generation after generation, the more superstitious inhabitants of Derbyshire had preferred to believe in spirits.

'Who told you that anyway?' asked Cooper.

'DC Villiers. I heard about the statements from your members of the public this morning.'

'Oh.'

'Have you got a problem with that? We're colleagues, aren't we? We should be working together.'

'If you say so.'

Cooper stopped. He'd caught a glimpse of something blue glittering among the trees, a flash of light, as if from a piece of glass reflecting the sun. The sight was irresistible, a signal tempting him from the path. He had no option but to turn aside and investigate.

When he got closer he could see that what he'd seen was a ball of smoky blue glass, the kind of thing sold in craft centres and gift shops for use as a table ornament or a flower vase. His sister would have taken it home and placed a scented candle inside it.

But inside this one was a tangle of threads. There were lengths of cotton of every colour – not only white and black threads, but bright strands twisted among them in no discernible pattern. It was just a random hotch-potch of colour, all given an eerie glow by the blue of the glass. The neck of the ball was attached to a branch of a rowan tree by a pair of ribbons and it moved slightly in the breeze, spinning one way and then the other. It had been placed at a height just above Cooper's head, but he could reach up to stop its movement. Then he saw the scraps of paper entangled among the threads, rolled into little tubes and thrust into the multicoloured mass.

'What is it?'

Cooper turned at the sound of Fry's voice. As happened so often, her words intruded like a cold dose of reality from the outside world at a moment when he was contemplating the mysteries of the rural imagination, feeling the centuries of belief in magic running disturbingly through his veins. There was something about these old superstitions that made him shiver, not only with apprehension, but with understanding too.

'You don't want to know, Diane,' he said.

'I suppose that means it's something absurd and rustic.'

'Well, it's a witch bottle,' said Cooper.

Fry snorted. 'Exactly.'

Cooper looked at her, not at all surprised this time that she'd noticed him leaving the path and decided to follow him. It was like being under twenty-four-hour surveillance. He wondered what she would have done if he'd simply sneaked off to relieve himself behind a tree. Would she have stood there making notes?

'It should probably be called a "watch ball" actually,' he said. 'It's used to guard against evil spirits. Its purpose is to draw in and trap negative energy that might have been directed at its owner. It can counteract spells cast by witches or prevent spirits moving about at night. That's why it's placed here, by the coffin road, because it's the route spirits would take. It's a sort of diversion sign, to deflect evil and keep it away from something, or someone.'

Despite her initial reaction, Fry was peering more closely into the blue glass as Cooper held it still. 'So the pieces of paper inside?'

'Charms,' said Cooper. 'If we can get them out and interpret them, they might give us an idea what evil the witch bottle is designed to counteract and who the charms might be aimed at. And perhaps who put them here.'

'Well, that sounds like a job for a superstitious country boy,' said Fry. 'I wonder where we'd find one of those.'

Carefully, Cooper began to untie the ribbons from the branch and reached out to grasp the ball.

'Fingerprints,' said Fry automatically.

'You're right, of course.'

Cooper found a fresh pair of latex gloves in his pocket and pulled them on before handling the ball. It was surprisingly light. The glass must be very thin, he supposed.

'What's in the ball?' asked Fry. 'What are all those bits of paper?'

Cooper couldn't make out the language written on them or interpret the symbols. But he had a good idea what they would be.

'Spells,' he said. 'Probably curses.'

'Oh, right.'

And there was something else shoved right into the middle. A piece of clay, formed into a distinctive shape. Not human, though. A bird.

'Now that I recognise,' said Fry. 'It's an eagle's head.'

'Yes.'

'Does it have some significance?' she asked.

'Around here it does.'

Cooper placed everything into evidence bags for the forensic examiner. As he turned the ball in his hand, he wondered how the colour was introduced into the glass when it was made. The swirls of blue looked so in- substantial and translucent. They could almost have been tiny evil spirits themselves, trapped in the surface of the bottle.

Chapter Fifteen

BEN COOPER PARKED his Toyota outside Earl Sterndale's best-known landmark – its pub, the Quiet Woman. The swinging wooden sign outside was much photographed by tourists in the summer, because it showed an image of a headless woman. According to the story behind the pub's name, that was a previous landlord's solution to the problem of keeping his garrulous wife quiet.

There was a campsite next to the pub, though it was empty. Marston's Burton Ales. Outside the door stood an old sink and a brush for boot washing, and plastic bags were kept in the porch for walkers to put over their dirty boots before entering the pub. It was the same principle as the one used at crime scenes, where forensic examiners and police officers wore plastic overshoes to avoid contaminating the scene with trace evidence and footwear marks.

The pub had milk delivered from a dairy in Hazel Grove. The bottles were still sitting in the porch, even though it was past midday. Of course, the Quiet Woman was closed. Many landlords in the more outlying villages found there was no point in opening their pubs during the day, especially in the winter months. There just wasn't enough lunchtime trade to pay for the overheads.

Cooper looked across the road to locate the Beresfords' house. Luke Irvine would be unhappy that his DS seemed to be covering the same ground, as if Irvine hadn't done a good enough job the first time round. But that couldn't be helped. Not today. It was bad enough having Diane Fry tagging along like a spare part. Didn't she have anything better to do with her time? He supposed he could ask her, but he would only get a sarcastic answer.

'Are you coming?' he said.

'No, I'll wait here,' said Fry. 'I've got a few phone calls to make.'

'Fair enough.'

Across the road he found Mrs Beresford was at home on her own, which was fine by Cooper.

'One of your colleagues came the other day, you know,' she said straight away when she answered the door.

'I know. Just a couple more questions.'

She was a small woman with a chilled look, her ears and nose pink with cold as if she'd just come back from a brisk walk on the moors. Even as Cooper introduced himself, she was removing a quilted body warmer. Perhaps he was lucky to have caught her.

'I don't know what else I can tell you,' she said.

'It's about Sandra Blair's husband,' said Cooper.

'Gary? He died. I did tell—'

'Yes. About five years ago?'

'That would be about right.'

'Do you happen to know where Mr Blair's family are?'

'His family? Well, I don't think his parents are still around. They used to live at Bowden, of course.'

'The estate village for Knowle Abbey.'

'Yes. Sandra and Gary lived with his parents for a while after they got married. But there was no way they could ever have had children there, in one of those little houses. And they were planning a family. At least … Sandra said they were.'

'And no other relatives in the area?'

'Not that I know of. Some of the people at Bowden would have a better idea, perhaps.'

'Thank you.'

Cooper went back to his car and drove through Earl Sterndale. Ahead he saw a distinctive hill called High Wheeldon. He glanced at Fry, but she was still busy with her phone, talking to someone at her office in St Ann's.

'Everything okay, Diane?' he said, hoping she was being called back to Nottingham.

She nodded. 'Absolutely fine.'

Cooper sighed and drove on. Fry hadn't even asked where they were going next.

Viewed from the road out of the village, High Wheeldon looked like a Derbyshire pyramid, a transplant from Egypt, or something casually dropped by a passing alien. Artificial, certainly. Nature wasn't capable of constructing such a regular, conical shape. Yet when you got closer and the road skirted its eastern side, you could see that it had been an optical illusion. High Wheeldon wasn't shaped like a pyramid at all from here, but was just another irregular hump in the landscape, mysterious enough in its own enigmatic way, lending itself to leaps of the imagination, the way so much of the Peak District landscape did.

ONCE YOU TURNED off the main road to Longnor, it became obvious that Bowden was no ordinary village. To enter it you had to pass through a gateway and over a cattle grid, past the signs warning you that it was private property and part of the Knowle Abbey estate.

The houses were all well constructed from local stone, but in a surprisingly wide variety of architectural styles. It was as if the architect, or the earl who'd commissioned him, couldn't quite make his mind up which design he preferred. There were Norman arches, Tudor-style chimneys, medieval turrets, Swiss roofs and Italianate windows. The paintwork on all the cottages was a collective Knowle Park green. But the houses with arched windows and balconies were larger and more ornate in style, distinguishing them from the plainer cottages. There had always been a social hierarchy, even among workers on the same estate.

It looked as though there had been a farmhouse here. But the house and its outbuildings had been converted. A barn had become a series of small apartments for staff. A lodge with castellations and imitation arrow slits guarded the entrance to Knowle Park itself. Cooper recalled seeing a matching lodge at the north entrance.

Sheep were grazing in an adjacent field and across the park he could see a small herd of cattle. Limousin cross, if he wasn't mistaken. During the landscaping of the park, the course of the River Dove had been altered slightly and a new bridge had been built. Big landowners could do that in those days, if it improved the view. Planning permission was never a concern. Nor was consideration for your neighbours, probably.

Bowden had a small church with a disproportionately tall spire. But the doors were locked and weeds were growing in the porch. On two sides of it was the burial ground, with several untidy rows of headstones, many old enough to be worn and corroded by the weather, their inscriptions almost illegible.

This was where the mourners from those small hamlets to the east would have arrived after their arduous trek across the hills and over the Corpse Bridge. Many of the coffins mouldering under these headstones would have been carried for miles and allowed to rest for a while on the same coffin stone where they'd found the effigy on Friday. Cooper found it hard to grasp the fact that all those people had been brought here at the end of their lives and laid to rest on the earl's property, as if they were a final tribute.

Though he could hear a few children playing somewhere, there seemed to be very few residents of Bowden actually at home. On a small field next to the graveyard he could see piles of wood heaped up in a large stack, ready for Bonfire Night on Tuesday. A short distance away from it a yellow bulldozer was parked behind the church. It must be handy to have that sort of equipment available.

They began to knock on doors and it was Diane Fry who found someone first. Cooper got a call from her on his phone and he walked back across the central green to meet her.

'This is Mrs Mellor,' said Fry. 'Mrs Mellor, my colleague Detective Sergeant Cooper.'

She was a woman in her mid to late sixties, with a welcoming smile and a faint smell of pine disinfectant and toasted cheese. In the background Cooper could hear what sounded like daytime TV, perhaps an old episode of *Lewis* or *Midsomer Murders*.

'Hello. Come in,' she said. 'Would you like a cup of tea? I don't see many people during the day, even on a Saturday.'

Fry followed him into the house. Cooper wished he was alone in circumstances like this. He would find it easier to get on with people and encourage them to talk. But he seemed to be stuck with her for now.

They sat down in a cosy sitting room and the kettle was soon boiled for tea. Mrs Mellor produced a plate of biscuits and it occurred to Cooper that it must be around lunchtime. He felt hungry.

'I gather you knew the Blairs,' said Cooper. 'They used to live in Bowden.'

'Yes,' said Mrs Mellor. 'They were just across the way there. They lived here for many years.'

'All these properties at Bowden still belong to Knowle Abbey, don't they? The cottages were built for estate workers.'

Mrs Mellor poured the tea for them both. 'Oh, yes,' she said. 'The earl himself is the landlord. Though I don't think anybody sees much of him these days. Not this present one, anyway. We deal mostly with the estate manager or one of the office staff.'

'So the people who live here are all workers at the abbey or on the estate?'

'Knowle Abbey staff and pensioners.'

'Pensioners?' he asked.

'You know, retired staff or estate workers. You don't get kicked out of your house as soon as you retire. At least, that's been the arrangement in the past.'

'So Gary Blair's father must have worked for the estate? Or he used to?'

'He was a forester. Alan Blair was part of a team maintaining the woodlands around the estate. Mostly to keep the paths clear and remove any damaged trees. But they produce a bit of commercial timber too. He started working at that job a long time ago, under the old earl.'

'The old earl,' said Cooper. 'He was popular, wasn't he?'

Mrs Mellor sat down opposite him and sighed.

'All the estate workers loved the old man,' she said. 'He was lovely. The old earl liked to ride round his land and see what was going on. Somehow he managed to know all the men personally and asked after their families by name. And he always gave them a big dinner at Christmas too as a "thank you". The children of the estate were given two parties a year, one in the summer and one in December. Of course, Father Christmas always managed to make a surprise appearance. The earl used to love doing that job himself, until he got too old for it. I believe there was quite a lot of beer drunk in honour of the old man. But it doesn't happen now.'

'I see.'

Cooper felt torn over whether that was a good thing or not. Paternalistic employers had certainly disappeared. There might not be so many toasts in the present earl's name, and he probably didn't know all his staff personally, but the old-style landlords had exercised a kind of autocratic control over their workers. He bet that the previous earl would have had no hesitation in sacking a man on the spot if he misbehaved or was disrespectful. With workers living in these tied cottages in the estate villages, that meant a man would lose his home too, and his family would be evicted. At least the current earl would be expected to obey current employment legislation.

'At one time there was even a school here for children of the estate workers,' said Mrs Mellor. 'It was set up by one of the Manbys who had a particular interest in his tenants. They say that school had as many as sixty pupils in its heyday. But it was demolished long ago. Children are picked up by bus to go to the local primary school now.'

'So what happened to the Blairs?' asked Cooper.

'Oh, Alan dropped dead from a heart attack one day. It was quite a shock and Pat became very ill. She was in hospital for a long, long time. In fact, she never really recovered, poor woman. She died of pneumonia in the end.'

'Gary and his wife Sandra lived with them for a while, I believe.'

'Yes, they couldn't get a house of their own. It's difficult for young couples.'

'I heard they wanted to start a family of their own. So they stayed here while trying to save up to buy their first house.'

'Perhaps,' said Mrs Mellor. 'But I think they were hoping for a tenancy of their own here on the estate.'

'Oh?' Cooper hesitated, not sure he'd understood correctly what she meant. 'Mrs Mellor, do you mean Gary Blair worked for Knowle Abbey too?'

'Yes, of course. Didn't you know that?'

'No.'

For a moment Mrs Mellor looked as though she might regret having told him something he didn't know. But it was just a fleeting confusion. Cooper must have given the impression he knew more than he actually did.

Diane Fry took up the opportunity presented by his silence.

'What job did Gary do?' she asked. 'Was he a forester too?'

Mrs Mellor turned to her. 'That's right. He learned the work from his father and went into the job himself when he left school. He was very good at it, so I've heard. He knew how to manage a chainsaw.'

Cooper ate another digestive as he watched the two women in conversation. Fry hadn't even touched her tea, let alone the biscuits. She was probably unaware of how rude it looked to people when she did this. Since Mrs Mellor had taken the trouble to make the tea, she ought at least take a sip or two out of politeness.

But Mrs Mellor didn't seem to have noticed.

'It was sad, but Gary got very depressed after his father died and his mother was so ill. I think they all went through a difficult time. And then there was the accident, of course…'

Fry's ears almost visibly pricked up. 'Accident?'

Mrs Mellor took a deep breath and shuddered. She leaned towards Fry and lowered her voice. 'With the chainsaw. Horrible.'

'They're very dangerous things.'

'I know. But Gary Blair, of all people. They all get the training and the safety equipment. But this particular day … well, no one knows what really happened. He was on his own at the time, working out of sight of the other men. I suppose he must have slipped.' She shuddered again. 'It's too awful to think about.'

'Was he badly hurt?'

'Oh, yes. They had to remove his arm. Then he couldn't work as a forester any more. He wasn't qualified for anything else. They offered him a job in the car park, just a few hours a week. But he went downhill rapidly from then on. Well, you can imagine.'

'Did Gary and Sandra have to leave Bowden after that?'

'Oh, they knew they were going to have to leave,' said Mrs Mellor. 'They were told they wouldn't be able to take over the tenancy of the cottage after Gary's mother died. That was the biggest blow. I think that was what finished Gary off.'

Cooper brushed some crumbs from the table on to the now empty plate.

'Mrs Mellor,' he said, 'how did Gary Blair die?'

'You don't know?' she said, turning to Cooper. She looked at him as if he were the only one here who was ignorant.

'I'm afraid you're going to say that he took his own life,' he said.

Mrs Mellor nodded. 'Yes, he killed himself. He just couldn't take it. It's such a shame about that family.'

OUTSIDE MRS MELLOR's cottage Fry stopped to ask a question.

'Why do they need so many houses here,' she said, 'if they're for workers at Knowle Abbey?'

'Believe it or not, there are about three hundred people employed on the estate in various ways,' said Cooper.

'You're joking. Doing what?'

'They're either in the abbey, working on maintenance and looking after the visitors, or they're in the gardens, the restaurant, the shop. They're on the farms, in the woodland, looking after the fisheries and game, or working in the offices. And probably lots of jobs I haven't thought of.'

Cooper stood on the central green and looked around at the houses of Bowden. The Manby emblem was set into the gable end of the cottages and the larger properties featured stone carvings of the crest above their front doors.

Like the Devonshires, the Manbys had owned many of the local villages in their time. Their name wasn't as ubiquitous, but it was certainly here at Bowden. It was on the church, the community hall and some of their workers' properties. And so was their emblem. It was a profile turned to the right, with a hooked beak like a scimitar. An eagle's head.

'Where to next?' asked Fry.

'I think it's time to go visiting the aristocracy,' said Cooper.

Chapter Sixteen

LOCAL PEOPLE WOULD tell you that Knowle Abbey had never actually been an abbey. Well, so far as anyone was aware – not in the sense that it had housed monks or nuns, ruled over by an abbot. It had always been the home of the Manby family and that was the end of the story.

But Cooper knew from that visit with his mother that the history books said differently. Knowle had originally been the site of a Cistercian abbey. But when the Dissolution of the Monasteries came along, the abbot and his monks had been pensioned off and their abbey confiscated by the state.

In fact, when it first became a country residence, this had been as a home for the Vaudrey family, a declining branch of an old Norman line who'd lost most of their lands by picking the wrong side in a rebellion. A dilapidated Knowle Abbey had later passed to the Manbys by marriage. Unlike the Vaudreys, the first Earl Manby was a new aristocrat on the rise and his descendants had become powerful and wealthy. They'd built the present house some time in the eighteenth century, adding to it in various ways over the years according to the whims of successive earls.

Cooper had called into his office at West Street and found DC Carol Villiers on duty. She wasn't very surprised to hear from him. Carol was quite used to his ways by now. They'd known each other since they were children, after all. Since she'd left the RAF Police and been recruited into Derbyshire Constabulary. It had made a refreshing change for Cooper to have someone on his team in CID who actually understood him.

'Carol, can you check if there have been any incidents reported recently at Knowle Abbey, or anywhere on the estate. Anything involving the Manby family or their staff. I've a feeling there was something a while ago.'

'You mean *the* Manby family?' said Villiers. 'The earl himself?'

'That's the one.'

'Of course, Ben. No problem.'

Then Cooper phoned ahead to the estate office at Knowle, and was assured that someone would meet him at the abbey.

'You don't need to come along,' he said to Fry.

She shrugged. 'What else would I do?'

Cooper thought of mentioning that she was supposed to be moving to a new flat this weekend, but it might not be the right subject to raise when he'd abandoned her so suddenly last night.

They drove down into the landscaped parkland that occupied the fertile valley of the River Dove and extended well up into the lower slopes of the hills on either side. For several minutes they seemed to be passing along a perimeter wall around the estate. Dense plantations of trees covered much of the landscape.

'Are there wild animals in these woods?' asked Fry.

'Bound to be.'

'There'll be badgers, I suppose?'

'What?'

'Badgers. They spread TB.'

Cooper shook his head. 'Only to cattle, Diane. You're perfectly safe.'

Badgers were a difficult subject at Bridge End Farm. Matt was likely to explode if anyone mentioned them as being cute, cuddly animals. Unlike the situation in other parts of the country, Derbyshire County Council had banned a badger cull in the county, despite incidents of TB being reported among local cattle. So it was quite likely that somewhere on the Knowle Abbey estate, the badgers would be below ground, waiting for the night.

Further on the abbey itself came into view. From this angle it seemed to be an almost random collection of porticos, balconies, windows and castellated extensions. Its size was impressive, but its architectural design would never have won any awards.

Villiers called Cooper back just as he was driving through the ornate front gates of the abbey.

'Hi, Carol.'

'Yes, Ben, you were right. Nothing too serious, but there have been some reports of threats and vandalism. An intruder reported one day in the grounds, that sort of thing.'

'Threats? Against who?'

'General abuse, most of it. Though the earl's name was mentioned, of course. They had some obscene graffiti. There was even an anonymous letter, which is a rather old-fashioned way of doing it. Most people like to write their threats and abuse on Twitter or Facebook these days.'

'Most *young* people,' said Cooper.

'That's a point. But wouldn't you think—'

'What?'

'Well, the average middle-aged Derbyshire resident doesn't resort to writing threats and abuse to people they don't know.'

'I suppose it depends whether they have a reason,' said Cooper.

He followed direction signs to the estate office. Just inside the park they passed a walled topiary garden, with hedges clipped into the shape of an eagle's head. The Manby family emblem.

THE ESTATE OFFICES at Knowle Abbey were housed in part of the old coach house block, next door to the restaurant and craft centre. They were met by a young woman with short red hair and a brisk manner. She was wearing a navy-blue body warmer with her name on a badge. Meredith Burns described herself as an assistant estate manager.

'Thank you for coming along. You must know about our unfortunate incidents,' she said.

'I'm sure your neighbourhood policing team has been to speak to you,' said Cooper.

'Yes, they have. But we didn't expect too much to come from it, to be honest. Not a visit from a detective sergeant anyway.' She looked at Diane Fry. 'Or two, in fact?'

'Yes,' said Fry.

'How unusual.'

Cooper could sense an instant animosity developing between Fry and Meredith Burns. It was something that seemed to happen when Diane Fry was involved. She must give off some specific pheromone that he couldn't detect.

'I believe you received an anonymous letter,' said Cooper.

'Yes, about three weeks ago. We didn't really think anything of it, until the vandalism.'

'Oh, yes. Can you show us?'

'This way.'

Meredith Burns led the way along a gravel path that headed away from the stable block along the east wing of the abbey itself.

'Apart from a few medieval stone carvings, the only remnant of the abbey's early history is the former Chapter House, which is now the Manby family's private chapel,' she said.

When they turned a corner of the abbey, it was immediately obvious that the arched front of the chapel was suffering from the ravages of time, along with the effects of weather and pollution. Meredith Burns explained that it had been placed on the Buildings at Risk Register ten years previously. Specialist conservation work had been started, but the money ran out. Now lots more cash was needed to save it from complete destruction.

'We estimate that the necessary work will take around eight years to complete, at a cost of over a million pounds,' she said. 'Our immediate priorities are to prevent water penetrating the core of the building and damaging the delicate carvings and statues. Obviously, we also need to conserve and repair the eroded masonry. We'd like to examine the façade for any traces of medieval paintings, before they disappear completely. And the entrance steps to the west front will need repairs too.'

They were approaching the rear of the chapel, where a small mausoleum became visible in its shadow. Burns turned to Cooper.

'We don't have many years left to do these things, before some parts of the chapel get beyond repair,' she said. 'That's why we're seeking donations and sponsorship to help us rescue it. This is a national treasure.'

'Sponsorship?'

'We're trying to get grant aid from the English Heritage Lottery Fund. But there's a lot of demand for grants and it wouldn't cover the total cost of conservation anyway. We're asking visitors to make cash donations for the appeal via donation boxes inside the house and café. We've approached several local and national companies to become sponsors of the campaign. But times are hard for everyone.'

A sheet of blue plastic had been secured over the back wall of the chapel, as if repair work was under way. But when Burns lifted a corner of the sheet, they could see that it was concealing the graffiti that had been sprayed on the stone wall in red paint. It was clearly something you wouldn't want your paying visitors to see.

'Why is it that people who spray graffiti never know how to spell "Fascists"?' commented Fry.

Burns dropped the plastic back into place. 'They always know how to spell that other word, though,' she said.

'And the letter?'

'Come through into the office for a few minutes,' said Burns.

Inside the abbey every room had huge Georgian sash windows with wooden shutters. Here in the east wing, all the window frames were rotten. Cooper reckoned it wouldn't take more than a few seconds with a jemmy to remove the panes of glass or wrench out the catch. What on earth did the insurance companies have to say about an arrangement like this?

In places there were bare floorboards and cracked plaster on the ceiling. The heads of various species of antelope and impala mounted on wooden plaques stared at each other from the walls.

One room they passed through was enormous, two storeys high, with furniture including a grand piano and a full-sized billiards table. A large fireplace was dominated by an almost life-sized family portrait and a couple of red sofas had been roped off to keep the public away. Cooper shook his head at the sight. Did the earl and his family sit here of an evening, gathered in this huge, draughty room that must be impossible to heat properly, perched uncomfortably on those ancient sofas, looked down on by mounted antelope heads, staring at the glass cases with their collections of stuffed animals?

'There are bullet holes in the wall here,' said Cooper when they reached the offices.

'Friendly fire,' said Burns.

'What?'

'There was a detachment of American soldiers billeted in this part of the abbey during the Second World War. I gather some of them were a bit trigger happy.'

'It looks as though they used the impala for target practice.'

'I think that's right.'

Cooper recalled visiting Newstead Abbey in Nottinghamshire once and being told by the guide about Lord Byron's habit of enjoying indoor pistol practice, resulting in bullet holes in the walls and doors. That must have been in the early nineteenth century. Nothing much changed, really.

'If you leave via the main entrance of the abbey, you should take a look in the old nursery on your way out,' said Burns. 'Just follow the signs.'

'Did you keep the anonymous letter?' asked Cooper.

Burns reached into a drawer and produced a tattered envelope. 'Yes. I thought you might want it.'

Cooper winced, thinking of all the fingerprints and extraneous trace substances now contaminating the evidence. Fry produced a pair of gloves and a plastic bag. She extracted the letter and they both read it. Like the address on the envelope, the message was produced on a laser printer, and it was very short.

Our dead are never dead to us, until we've forgotten them.
Remember: Death will have his day!

'A QUOTATION, I suppose,' said Fry. 'What is it from?'

'We never really troubled to find out,' said Burns. 'It didn't seem important at the time.'

'Come on, Ben, you're the literary one.'

But Cooper was frowning over the message. 'It sounds like a quotation,' he said. 'But I think it's a bit of a hotch- potch.'

'"Death will have his day" sounds familiar,' said Fry. 'It's got to be either Shakespeare or the Bible.'

'Possibly.'

'Or am I thinking of "Every dog will have his day"?'

Cooper handed her the letter and she slid it back into its envelope. He wondered what she was really doing here, if she was trying to help. She certainly wasn't helping very much so far.

'It doesn't necessarily seem like a threat anyway,' said Fry. 'It's just a quotation. It could mean anything. What do you think, Ben?'

'Well, it wouldn't stand up in court,' he said. 'Not on its own.'

'It's addressed to "Earl Manby and family, Knowle Abbey". They've even used the postcode. First-class stamp, but the postmark is unreadable of course. I can't remember the last time I was able to read a postmark.'

'Do you have any idea what it means, Miss Burns?' asked Cooper.

She shook her head. 'It's too vague. We didn't take the letter seriously – we almost threw it away in the office, but for some reason I left it in a tray and it stayed there.'

'And that was about three weeks ago?'

'Yes. The vandalism is more recent. One of the staff found it on Friday morning, fortunately before the first visitors arrived.'

'I think there was a report of an intruder in the grounds.'

'Yes, we've had a few incidents in the past. They're usually harmless, of course. Just the curious or drunk. Usually, they get too close to the buildings and trigger a security light, then they disappear as fast as they can. We do get poachers now and then. There's a herd of roe deer in the park. But this one seemed different. A bit more disturbing. One of the security team spotted him and said he was dressed in dark clothing and just seemed to be watching from a safe distance in the trees, where he was out of range of the sensors. He'd gone when they went to look for him.'

'Do you know of any reason why the earl or any of the members of his family should be targeted in this way?' asked Cooper.

Burns shrugged. 'It's just general envy, isn't it? Some people get very bitter.'

Cooper glanced at Fry. 'I suppose so.'

'But I'm aware that we have to take a few precautions. In case there's anybody who decides to take their grievance further.'

'Absolutely.'

'You said the graffiti was found on Friday morning,' said Fry. 'Yes?'

'What was going on here at Knowle Abbey on Halloween night?'

'Ah, take a look for yourself.'

Burns took a leaflet from a pile on her desk. 'We have to find any opportunity to put on special events and get people in. We're starting to prepare for our Christmas events now.'

Fry took the leaflet, scanned it quickly and passed it to Cooper. On a spooky background of ghosts and bats flying across the moon, it read:

Knowle at Halloween. Thursday 31 October. Explore Knowle Abbey's dark and spooky interior. Definitely not for the faint-hearted! Gather in the restaurant for a spooky themed meal or a glass of Dutch courage before departing up to the abbey by timed ticket. The restaurant will be open from 6pm for pre- and post-performance suppers and refreshments. Please note that due to low light levels and time constraints, this event is not suitable for visitors with limited mobility. Tickets £20 per person. Must be booked in advance.

'TWENTY POUNDS?' SAID Fry flatly. 'How many people did you get coming along for that price?'

'Oh, a few dozen.'

'So you had strangers wandering around the abbey in the dark all evening from 7 p.m.?' said Cooper.

'Not wandering around exactly, Sergeant. All the groups were accompanied by a guide.'

'Even so...'

'I'm afraid it's not exactly difficult to get into the abbey grounds at night, if you're determined to do so,' said Burns. 'Of course, we have security. And alarms.'

'But if all you want to do is creep up to the chapel and daub some graffiti on the wall, while the public are trooping in and out of the abbey for some Halloween event...'

'Yes. Anybody could have managed it.'

'"Explore Knowle Abbey's dark and spooky interior",' quoted Fry. 'I take it that means...'

'Of course. We had all the lights turned off. For atmosphere, you know.'

'Is the earl himself at home at the moment?' asked Cooper.

'Yes, he and the countess are in residence, along with their younger son and their daughter, Lady Imogen.'

'And do you happen to have a photograph of Lord Manby that we could use?' asked Cooper.

Burns looked surprised. 'Why on earth would I have one of those? He's hardly some kind of rock star handing out signed photographs to his fans.'

'No, I just thought—'

'In fact, Walter is a very private man,' said Burns stiffly. 'He prefers not to be recognised, even when he's here around the abbey. And he doesn't do much in public, if he can avoid it. To be honest, I think he would rather find some other way of paying for the upkeep of the abbey, instead of letting all these visitors in. It's his home, after all.'

'I understand.'

When they left the estate office, Cooper and Fry followed the arrows pointing towards the main entrance. But Cooper paused in a passage lined with peeling doors. While Fry fidgeted impatiently, he opened a door marked 'Nursery'. Even if he hadn't been told by Meredith Burns, it would have been obvious that the army had been billeted in this part of the house. There were maps and flags scattered among the toys. The wallpaper was filthy, and the doors and skirting boards looked as though they had been kicked repeatedly by heavy boots.

In the Great Hall the walls were lined with enormous Manby family portraits. The present earl was there – Walter, 9th Earl Manby of Knowle Abbey. In previous generations his ancestors seemed to have been christened with wonderful aristocratic names like Algernon, Peregrine and Clotworthy.

The collection of earls and their relatives gazed down with apparent astonishment at the crowds of strangers who must come through this hall every weekend to gawp at the abbey. Walter's Victorian grandfather, the seventh Lord Manby, looked particularly outraged at the prospect.

WHEN THEY GOT back to the car Fry sat and stared at the façade of Knowle Abbey for a while. From her expression she didn't seem to be impressed by the quality of the architecture. Maybe the pillars and porticos weren't quite symmetrical enough for her taste.

Or perhaps something else was causing the sour look on her face.

'What are you thinking, Diane?' asked Cooper curiously.

'Have a guess.'

'You're wondering whether they used this as a location for filming *Downton Abbey*?'

'Idiot.'

'Thanks. So, what, then?'

Fry was silent for a moment, so Cooper waited. Finally, she started the car and let the engine turn over slowly before putting it into gear.

'I'll tell you what I'm thinking,' she said. 'I'm asking myself why ordinary people should be expected to cough up millions of pounds to maintain a privately owned pile like this, when there's no money available for proper policing.'

Cooper nodded. 'Fair point. But she did say it's a national treasure. And the earl can't afford to maintain it himself.'

'Personally,' said Fry, 'I don't care if his chapel leaks and his statues erode.'

Chapter Seventeen

IN THE CID room at West Street, Cooper found a message waiting for him that Detective Superintendent Branagh wanted to see him ASAP. And that meant before the morning briefing took place on the Sandra Blair inquiry.

All of his team had come in for the briefing, except Luke Irvine. Cooper had a couple of jobs he needed doing. First of all he asked Becky Hurst to hunt out a photograph of Walter, 9th Earl Manby.

'There should be something on the internet,' he said.

'Everything is on the internet, Ben.'

'So I hear.'

'The ninth Earl,' said Hurst.

'Yes, the living one. Walter. If you find something and I'm not back before the briefing, pass it to DI Walker.'

'Okay.'

Cooper turned to Carol Villiers and asked her to produce a list of residents in Bowden.

'All of them?' she said.

'If possible. The adults anyway.'

'Okay, Ben.'

Cooper straightened his tie. 'I won't be long. I hope.'

Down the corridor the door of the superintendent's office was standing partly open, but Cooper knocked anyway. Detective Superintendent Hazel Branagh got up from her desk and waved him to a chair.

'Come in, DS Cooper,' she said. 'It's nothing to worry about. I just want to catch up. Tell me how things are going generally.'

Cooper sat down, not entirely reassured. Rumours around the station said that Branagh had been on a diet recently, though she would never have admitted it. She seemed to have lost weight around her face, though, and the combination of broad shoulders and lean cheekbones made her even more intimidating. Cooper was actually glad when she sat down again.

'Fine, ma'am,' he said. 'I'm very happy with my team in CID. They're doing nicely.'

'Ah, yes.' Branagh consulted a note on her desk. 'You have DC Villiers – I've heard very good reports of her since she joined us.'

'She's a valuable asset,' said Cooper, conscious that he was immediately falling into management speak, but unable to prevent himself.

'And DCs Hurst and Irvine. Very promising, would you say?'

'Absolutely, ma'am.'

She paused, placing a finger on the list in front of her. 'And I see you still have DC Gavin Murfin at the moment.'

'Yes.'

'Well, we'll be giving him a good send-off soon,' said Branagh. 'There's no point in going over his faults now, is there?'

'I've found Gavin's experience useful,' said Cooper.

Branagh glanced up at him. 'Very loyal, DS Cooper. Of course, we'll look at the possibility of finding you a replacement for Murfin when he goes. But I'm sure you understand, in the present circumstances ... The budget cuts...'

'With respect, ma'am, there should be five detective constables in my team, according to the official establishment. I'm already one down.'

'I know. But I'm afraid we have to get used to these reductions across the board. It's the same for all of us.'

Cooper said nothing. He'd heard a lot of officers express the opinion that Derbyshire Constabulary was a victim of its own success. The crime rate in the county had been reduced by about 15 per cent in the past year. And this was despite the fact that all the neighbouring forces had higher rates of crime and larger urban centres of population, with the result that Derbyshire was often a target for travelling criminals from Greater Manchester, Nottinghamshire or South Yorkshire. If your crime rate was falling, even in those circumstances, then clearly you didn't need so many police officers. It seemed counter-intuitive and very short-term thinking.

But Superintendent Branagh had probably heard that view plenty of times. There was no point in Cooper repeating it now.

Branagh pushed her list to one side. 'But what about *you*, DS Cooper? How are you doing yourself?'

That was a question he couldn't hesitate in answering. Not for even a second.

'I'm absolutely fine, ma'am,' said Cooper firmly.

'Good. Excellent. That's what I like to hear. But could I suggest, perhaps...'

'Yes?'

'That you need to push yourself forward a bit more. You're in danger of getting overlooked.'

'Overlooked?'

'For promotion.'

'Oh.'

Cooper hadn't really thought about further promotion yet. There didn't seem much point. There was already a log-jam in human resources since promotions were frozen by budget cuts.

'You've talked up all the DCs in your team,' said Branagh. 'Even DC Murfin, who we all know about. But you don't talk yourself up at all.'

'I suppose that's true,' admitted Cooper.

Since he'd been promoted to Detective Sergeant, Cooper had concentrated on taking the trouble to bring his DCs on. He wanted to let them take responsibility and get some credit for their work. Not everybody did that. But it was true what Branagh said. The police service had become a competitive business. Like lots of people working in private sector businesses, you had to be able to justify your job these days.

'You can be too self-effacing, you know,' emphasised Branagh. 'In this profession you have to get yourself noticed if you want to get on. Otherwise they'll just bring somebody in over your head. People who lie down get walked over.'

'Yes, I do know that,' said Cooper.

Branagh watched him carefully, then nodded. Her shoulders relaxed slightly.

'Well, if it does happen, Ben,' she said, 'let's hope it's a police officer at least, and not someone brought in from managing a supermarket.'

'Yes, ma'am,' said Cooper.

He realised the interview was over and got up to leave. Branagh was exaggerating, of course. But only a bit. The government's new scheme would soon bring in twenty direct-entry police superintendents from other businesses and professions, along with eighty fast-tracked inspectors, graduates on a three-year scheme taking them straight from constable rank to the first rung of the management ladder. Many were already on training courses at the College of Policing.

There were very few police officers who didn't believe that experience working on the frontline was essential for anyone holding a senior management position on the operational side. How could you expect someone to make high-pressure decisions in an emergency situation when they'd never had to respond to an emergency themselves? Surely they needed first-hand knowledge.

But it was too late to fight the changes. The new scheme would allow outsiders to leap over thousands of officers who'd spent years building experience, working in a variety of roles across the force. One day a chief constable would be appointed who had never made an arrest.

Those new inspectors had to be graduates with good degrees, but would at least have spent a short time as constables and sergeants. But neither of those was a requirement for a direct-entry superintendent, though that was two ranks above inspector. The new batch of supers might be from the armed forces or the intelligence services. They could be prison governors or existing members of civilian staff. But the guidelines said they could equally be 'people with experience of running private sector operations'.

So Branagh's half-joking reference wasn't quite accurate. A newly appointed inspector couldn't come straight from being a supermarket manager. But a new superintendent could.

It's time to get out.

Cooper had heard those words said more and more often over the past few months. And it wasn't just from Gavin Murfin either.

'By the way,' said Branagh as Cooper left her office.

'Yes, ma'am?'

'Detective Sergeant Fry is with us for the briefing. Representing the Major Crime Unit, of course.'

'Yes.'

Cooper waited, sensing that Branagh had something else to say. If it was in connection with Diane Fry, it might be something he didn't want to hear.

'It would be good,' said Branagh, 'if we could manage without the assistance of the MCU on this occasion.'

He nodded, not sure what she expected him to say in response to that.

'I feel it would be good for the division,' she said. 'And especially ... Ben, it would be especially good for you. It would be wonderful if we could fill a vacancy at inspector level before those direct entrants start to arrive.'

Cooper swallowed at the enormity of the challenge he was being presented with. Was he ready for this? But Branagh was waiting for an acknowledgement of some kind.

'Ben, remember what I said, won't you?'

'Yes, ma'am,' he said.

Chapter Eighteen

THE BRIEFING ROOM wasn't as full as it ought to have been. Cooper remembered it being packed out in the past, with standing room only for those at the back. Superintendent Branagh led the briefing herself, with Detective Inspector Dean Walker alongside her. Walker was relatively inexperienced, but Branagh had many years as a senior investigating officer.

Currently, the Sandra Blair inquiry was treated as a suspicious death. Results of the post-mortem examination were expected later today and would surely raise the classification to a murder case when the cause of death was established.

The details known about the victim were already familiar to Cooper. He and Luke Irvine had obtained most of them over the weekend. But forensic examination of the scene at the bridge had been continuing for the past forty-eight hours. So had the search of the woods on either side of the river, the search area gradually expanding to cover most of the hillside and the tracks leading down to the bridge. Witness statements had been taken from the young man who discovered the body, Rob Beresford, as well as from Geoff and Sally Naden, and Jason Shaw.

Now there would be an assessment of what lines of inquiry could be followed up and which would be most urgent.

'According to the forensic medical examiner, the victim died somewhere between 6 p.m. and midnight on Friday,' said Branagh. 'That's an estimate based on body temperature and the extent of rigor mortis and lividity. As usual we can't get a more specific timeframe. No witnesses have come forward who had contact with the victim between those times. The body was found at around 1 a.m. by a young man called Robson Beresford, whose statement we have. The other witness statements are vague, but I think we can take them as indicating the presence of at least two people in the woods near the scene earlier that night. One of them may have been our victim. But we can't be sure of that.'

Becky Hurst raised a hand to get attention.

'Yes, DC Hurst?'

'These statements suggest that someone was being chased,' said Hurst. 'Were there any signs on the victim that she'd been running?'

'Such as?'

'Scratches on her hands and face from the undergrowth, mud splashes on her clothing. She might have been sweating from the exertion.'

'There was certainly mud on her shoes and some of her clothes. But that could simply have resulted from being on the riverbank. We'll get an analysis of the spread of the mud splashes if we can. But bear in mind that the victim was lying in the river. Much of the mud will have dispersed.'

Cooper nodded across at Hurst. 'It's an important point, ma'am,' he said. 'If the victim had been running, that sort of physical exertion makes a difference to the rate of onset of rigor mortis.'

'Yes, it would speed up the onset of rigor, particularly in the legs,' agreed Branagh. 'On the other hand, the weather was cold and she was partially submerged in water, both of which would slow the process down. So it's a case of swings and roundabouts, I suppose. Rigor was certainly fairly well advanced by the time we attended the scene.'

She was right, of course. Cooper recalled the rigidity of the victim's limbs as she was removed from the river. When her muscles relaxed at the moment of death, she'd fallen into an awkward, tangled position, then rigor mortis had begun to set in, first in the small muscles of the face and neck before spreading to the rest of the body. Even Rob Beresford had remarked on the flat, staring eyes that had so frightened him. The eyes were among the first parts of the body to be affected by rigor.

Branagh consulted her briefing notes. 'As far as the victim's movements are concerned, all we know is that she left her place of work between one and one-thirty on Thursday afternoon. That's the Hartdale tea rooms in Hartington. She seems to have returned to her home in Crowdecote at some time during the afternoon, but went out again later on. Since her car was still parked outside her house when it was visited by DS Cooper and DC Irvine on Friday, we have to conclude that she either went with someone else or took a taxi, or possibly set out on foot.'

The superintendent paused and looked round the room, but no one commented. Perhaps she expected someone to cast doubt on the idea that Sandra Blair would have walked from Crowdecote to the bridge. It was the best part of two miles, even using the footpaths that skirted the hillsides in the Dove valley, and a good bit further by road. Diane Fry might have been the person to scoff at that possibility, but even she said nothing. Cooper glanced across at her and saw that she was holding herself tense and restrained, her lips pursed shut, as if making a determined effort not to interrupt.

Cooper waited for Branagh to continue. Personally, he had no doubt that the victim might have set off to walk from her home. He thought the idea of her calling for a taxi was by far the least likely.

'So over the next few days,' said Branagh, 'we'll be deploying all of our additional manpower...'

She paused again, but only very briefly to ride the automatic laughter from the officers present.

'... in both Hartington and Crowdecote to conduct house-to-house enquiries. Here are the priorities for the house-to-house teams. We need to know if anyone saw the victim after she left the tea rooms and before she left home again that evening. Did she call at one of the shops in Hartington? Did anyone see Sandra Blair in her car between there and her home? And obviously, we'd very much like to hear from anyone who saw her, and a possible second person, between her home and Hollins Bridge that afternoon or evening. Somebody will have to check local taxi firms.'

Cooper restrained himself from shaking his head. Taxis were a waste of someone's time, but the options had to be covered. As for her drive home, Sandra Blair was a local. He bet she wouldn't even have thought of going via the main A515 up to Sparklow, but would have taken the back road from Hartington, which wound its way across the hill above the hamlet of Pilsbury. It was a much quieter route. He could think of only three or four farms set back from the road until you reached the junction at High Needham. Not much chance of anyone noticing a small red Ford Ka passing. Their best hope would be that someone saw Sandra later, after she'd left her house. Yes, that would definitely constitute an early break.

Branagh handed over to DI Walker, who had been at the scene. He was a young detective inspector, who'd risen quickly through the ranks, but who might yet be overtaken in his career by those fast-tracked graduates just starting their three-year programmes. Slim and blond-haired, Walker looked more like an actor auditioning for the role of a fictional aristocratic detective than a real police officer. It was said that he had public school and university education too – though surely that didn't make any difference in today's police service?

'Our search of the scene is still ongoing,' said Walker. 'Given the statements from witnesses, we've extended the search area quite considerably.'

He indicated a large-scale map on the wall of the briefing room. Around the area of Hollins Bridge, the map was shaded in sectors to show the designated areas. As Walker said, the search teams were working their way steadily further from the bridge itself.

'We've almost completed the area on our side of the river,' the DI was saying. 'We're waiting for our colleagues in Staffordshire to do the same. They have some difficult terrain on their side, where it's a bit steeper, so it's taking longer. I'll be liaising with them later today on that. Meanwhile, these are the items we've found so far.'

Photos were pinned up on a board next to the map, with indicators to show where each item had been found. The noose was there and so was the witch ball with its screwed-up bits of paper and the clay eagle's head. Most distinctive of them was the effigy discovered lying on the coffin stone, which caused a lot of murmuring through the room.

'It's just a guy, isn't it?' said someone.

'Yep, someone had it ready for Bonfire Night and lost it,' added a second officer.

But a third shook his head. 'I've never seen one like that. It's too well made. Why would you go to all that trouble, just to burn it?'

DI Walker agreed. 'That's what we think, too. It may have been designed deliberately to look like someone. I think it would be fair to say that it isn't our victim, anyway.'

There was a ripple of laughter again and Walker looked pleased. In that moment he seemed even more like a performer, gratified to get a reaction from his audience.

'However, we have one suggestion put forward for the identity of the effigy,' said Walker cheerfully. 'DS Cooper has a theory.'

All eyes turned to Cooper and he stood up. Briefly, he explained his reasoning, from the eagle's head to the emblem of the Manbys, then the situation at Knowle Abbey, with the anonymous letter, the mysterious intruder and the vandalism of the chapel.

'So it's possible this is part of a campaign by someone with a grudge against the Manby family,' concluded Cooper.

'And who's the effigy of?' asked a voice from behind him in the room. 'Is it the earl? I have no idea what he looks like.'

Walker pinned a photograph on to the board next to the picture of the effigy. It was a blown-up detail from a formal occasion that had been featured in *Derbyshire Life*. The Right Honourable Walter, Earl Manby, was pictured in white tie and tails, beaming at the camera with his best air of bonhomie. He was clean shaven, with iron-grey hair neatly clipped and slicked down. His cheeks were full and his skin shone with a slightly florid glow, which might just have been a sign that he'd been enjoying a convivial evening. Apart from that, Cooper had to admit the photograph bore no similarity to the effigy at all.

'The photo is a year or two old,' said Becky Hurst, against a deafeningly dubious silence. 'But it was all we could lay our hands on.'

'Well, be that as it may,' said DI Walker, 'it's something to bear in mind that there may be a connection with Knowle Abbey. The presence of the rope noose within a few yards of the effigy is worrying. It starts to look like a serious threat.'

Another murmur ran round the room. Walker waited for it to subside.

'Although it also seems a possibility from the evidence at Sandra Blair's house that the victim may have made the effigy herself,' he said. 'We're waiting for confirmation of that.'

'Why would she do that?' asked someone.

'We don't know. In fact, a better question might be "Who did she make it for?"'

It was a good point, of course. Cooper had to admit that. He decided to sit back and listen to the rest of the briefing in dignified silence.

'We're still working our way through the diary and address book belonging to the victim, but the good news is that we've located Mrs Blair's sister. Her name is Maureen Mackinnon and she'll be arriving from Scotland in the morning.'

Cooper frowned. Why hadn't he been able to locate a Dundee phone number in Sandra's address book?

DI Walker might have seen his expression. He hesitated, looked down at his notes and said, 'Mrs Mackinnon lives in Dunfermline, I believe.'

Oh, well. Dundee, Dunfermline. It was probably too easy to confuse them. It must have taken Luke Irvine a while to sort that one out.

'There was the note in the diary about meeting "Grandfather",' said Cooper, forgetting his resolution to keep quiet.

'According to Mrs Mackinnon, the victim doesn't have a grandfather,' said Walker with an air of finality. 'Not a living one she could have been meeting.'

And Cooper wasn't surprised to hear that.

'Okay, thank you,' said Superintendent Branagh. 'Let me say at this point that we won't be releasing any details to the public of what we found at the scene. Specifically, there will be no mention of the effigy or the noose. Understood? All right. What about forensics?'

The crime-scene manager, Wayne Abbott, took over the floor. He was a marked contrast to the DI, heavily built and shaven-headed like a football hooligan but totally on the ball when it came to the details of a crime scene.

'Our scene is pretty messy,' said Abbott. 'Muddy, badly churned up, rained on and trampled. It couldn't have been worse really. There's no viable DNA to work with, for a start, and trace evidence is fragmentary. We've recovered some shoe marks close to where the body was found. They'll be difficult to identify with any certainty, but we're working on it.'

'Fingerprints?'

'We've retrieved a few partials from the victim's clothing and from the effigy,' said Abbott. 'Many of them are the victim's own, of course. The others we haven't been able to identify. There's no match from the database.'

'That's privatisation for you,' said someone.

Cooper turned round to look, but couldn't see who had spoken. It could have been Gavin Murfin, but he looked too innocent and his mouth was full anyway.

Creeping privatisation was a standing grievance among some officers. And fingerprint records had already been privatised during the past twelve months. There was no storage room left at the Regional Identification Bureau in Nottingham. So, like other East Midlands forces, Derbyshire had decided to digitise their records and move to an entirely electronic process. Half a million paper records were being destroyed after they were scanned and stored on a secure server.

'That's nothing to do with it,' said Superintendent Branagh sharply. And no one seemed ready to argue with her.

Abbott looked across at where Cooper sat and met his eye.

'The one thing we have established,' he said, 'is that the material used in making the effigy matches samples of fabric found in the victim's home. There's also a sketch that resembles the final design. So it seems we can confirm that the victim created the effigy herself.'

Cooper breathed a sigh of relief. At least he'd been right about something. He looked across the room and gasped in surprise. If he wasn't mistaken, he'd almost caught Diane Fry smiling.

Chapter Nineteen

In Edendale that evening the streets were wet with more rain. The Christmas lights hadn't gone up in the town yet. But it wouldn't be long, now that it was November. Most of the shops just couldn't wait to get the Halloween costumes and Guy Fawkes masks off their shelves and fill the space with Christmas gift wrap and tinsel.

Ben Cooper had almost forgotten that he was expected somewhere that evening. He was supposed to be helping his sister Claire get her new shop ready for opening.

Well, his family expected him to forget things, or to be too busy to turn up, or to get called away. And sometimes, lately, they'd expected him just not to be up to it. But that had changed now, hadn't it?

Claire had closed the old shop months ago. To be fair, it had been a bit of a niche venture, even when times were good. He could have told her that at the time, but he knew she wouldn't be willing to hear it. If you wanted to do something badly enough, you needed encouragement and support from your family and friends, not discouraging words and predictions of disaster.

Still, it was certainly true that the market for healing crystals and scented candles had fallen through the floor when the economic downturn came along. Edendale people didn't really go for that sort of thing. The older residents were happy with their goose fat and paraffin lamps. The younger ones thought you could get it all on the internet.

And visitors to the area were spending less money than ever in the town. Even those with a bit of spare cash preferred to spend it in the farm shops or the outdoor clothing stores, or perhaps to visit one of those historic attractions like Knowle Abbey. Small local businesses were struggling against the competition, whatever area of retail they were in.

Cooper thought of the dreamcatcher and the Tarot cards in Sandra Blair's cottage at Crowdecote. It was ironic to think that Sandra might have been a customer of Claire's at one time, in the old shop. But Sandra Blair was dead and Claire Cooper had moved on.

The new shop was just off the market square in Edendale. It stood in the steep, cobbled alley called Nick i'th Tor. There had been a half-hearted campaign recently to change the name of the street on the argument that visitors couldn't pronounce it so were too embarrassed to ask for directions to it. But the idea never stood a chance. Edendale was too proud of its history and too fond of its traditions – even if no one knew what they meant.

He could see through the front window that his brother Matt was in the shop, putting up some shelves for one of the displays. Claire wouldn't lash out money on professional shopfitters when she could persuade members of her family to do the job for her. But then all the Coopers were like that. It seemed to be an inherited trait.

'Hi, Matt,' he said as he entered.

As soon as he opened the door, he was hit by the powerful smells of fresh paint and plaster, and newly sawn timber.

Matt turned. His broad shoulders and increasing girth had been crammed into an old set of blue overalls that hadn't really fitted him for a couple of years now. Only the lower buttons were fastened on the front, exposing an ancient woolly sweater full of holes. He looked like a grizzly bear struggling to get out of a duvet cover. His face was red and there was a smudge of grease on his cheek. In fact, he looked pretty much as he always did back at the farm.

'Oh, you made it,' he said. 'I thought I was going to be on my own again tonight.'

'Where's the boss?'

'Who?'

'The owner of the shop. Shouldn't she be here supervising?'

'Oh, Claire's not going to be here tonight. She's been down in Birmingham for some trade exhibition or something. Networking and looking at new product lines.'

'Looking at new product lines?'

'That's what she said.'

'Oh, I can just hear her saying it.'

'Well, her train from Birmingham doesn't get in until later. She has to change in Sheffield, you know.'

'Of course. So what needs doing?'

'You can finish off the paintwork behind the counter.'

'No problem.'

Ben found a brush and opened a half-used tin of gloss white. A dust sheet was already spread on the floor to catch drips, and the panels on the wall behind the counter were primed and ready for painting.

The place was already completely unrecognisable. This used to be a second-hand bookshop, which had been empty for a while since the death of its owner. Ben could remember all too clearly the dusty upstairs rooms above the shop, where only certain clients were invited to browse. But Claire was only converting the ground floor, so far at least.

It was a smart choice of location, he had to admit. He'd always liked these narrow lanes in the oldest part of Edendale, between Eyre Street and the market square. Claire's new shop was only a couple of doors down from Larkin's, a traditional bakery whose window was always full of pastries and cheeses – apricot white stilton, homity pies and enormous high-baked pork pies. And a few yards away in the market square itself was a celebrated butcher's and game dealers called Ferris's. Between them these two establishments were among Edendale's most popular businesses, with locals and visitors alike. They were such a draw that this corner of the market square could qualify as a retail destination, as far as Edendale had one.

So Claire had wisely gone for a complementary business, an outlet for local farmers' produce. Most of it was organic, of course. Rare breed meats, gluten-free products, dry cured bacon and home-made cakes. A sign already in the window advertised her venture into a more upmarket range. Uncle Roy's Comestible Concoctions – fudge sauces and wholegrain mustards, seaweed salt and country bramble jelly.

Ben noticed a large sign propped against the wall near where Matt was working. It was probably ready to go in the window display when the stock began to arrive.

'What does that sign say?' he asked.

'Totally Locally,' said Matt.

'And that is?'

'It's the Totally Locally campaign. You must have heard of it.'

'No, Matt.'

'Look, it says here. If every adult in the area spends five pounds a week in their local independent shops instead of online or in the big supermarkets, it would mean an extra one million pounds a year going into the local economy. More jobs, better facilities, a nicer place to live.'

Matt nodded vigorously at the sign. Claire had certainly found an enthusiastic supporter for that one.

'Well, it makes sense, doesn't it?' said Matt.

'Yes, it does. Will it work?'

'Have faith.'

They both worked in silence for a while, apart from the occasional curse from Matt. After a few minutes he seemed to remember his brother was there.

'Are you okay with that, Ben?'

'Of course. I've got the easy job.'

'Yes, you have.'

'It makes a change, though.'

'Oh, yeah. Right.'

There was another pause. Ben finished one panel and shifted position to start the next.

'So how's it going, then?' said Matt. 'Have you been assigned your own police tractor yet?'

Matt laughed uproariously at his own joke. It wasn't one of his most appealing characteristics. It had been a regular jest of Matt's ever since June, when a tractor liveried in police colours had been used to encourage members of the public to sign up for the Farm Watch scheme. Matt had come across the tractor on display at the cattle market in Bakewell, where it had been loaned by the manufacturer, New Holland. Of course, the tractor had then continued to turn up at markets and shows right through the summer, prompting another burst of hilarity from Matt every time he saw it.

It was a bit frustrating. Thieves had been targeting farms across the county and making off with a huge range of items, from livestock to fuel. They'd taken numerous quad bikes, muck spreaders and generators, and six incidents of sheep rustling had been recorded. Many farmers had signed up for Farm Watch, including Matt. But it didn't stop him making jokes about the police tractor. Well, at least it kept the scheme in his mind.

Ben didn't bother to answer. It hardly seemed worth it. But Matt tried again.

'So where have you been today? Anywhere interesting?'

'I've been over at Knowle Abbey and Bowden village.'

'Oh,' said Matt, immediately losing interest. 'Staffordshire people.'

'No, actually.'

It was odd how Matt's interest in the affairs of his neighbours ended at the border. No one who lived west of the River Dove was of any concern to him.

'Not Staffordshire?' he said.

'Don't you know where your own county ends?'

'Not really. Why would it matter to me? As long as my ewes don't wander that far.'

'Talk about parochialism,' said Ben. 'You're the living, breathing embodiment of it.'

'Cheers.'

'Well, it's true. If it doesn't happen on your patch, it doesn't exist.'

Matt was right, though. Why should it matter to him? He hardly needed a passport to get in and out of Derbyshire, so he would never notice where the border was. The dry stone walls around his farm were the only boundaries he cared about.

Ben watched his brother line up the shelves on one of the walls. He was frowning in concentration, with a couple of screws sticking out of his mouth. He would do a good job of it. His unrelenting practicality made Ben feel almost useless.

Sensing his brother watching him, Matt looked round.

'I suppose it's this woman who was killed at the bridge,' he said, speaking indistinctly round his mouthful of screws.

'That's right.'

'They call it the Corpse Bridge, don't they?'

'You've heard of it, then? And the coffin roads?'

'Yes, I remember all that stuff vaguely. Old stories.'

'I had the Reverend Latham out there this morning,' said Ben.

'Old Bill Latham? Is he still alive?'

'Definitely.'

'Good for him. He must be as old as I feel.'

Matt used a spirit level to check that his shelf was exactly at the right angle. Nothing would be falling off this display.

'And there's a connection to Knowle Abbey, is there?' he said.

'There may be.'

'That's another old story.'

'What is?'

'You don't remember the tale?'

'Which one, Matt?'

'The Revenge of the Poacher's Widow.'

Ben laughed. 'Oh, *that* story. Yes, Granddad Cooper told it to us when we were children. In fact, I think he probably told it several times over the years.'

'Yes, he did.'

'And he got all his folk tales from some book he was given by *his* parents. Though he embellished the details a bit more every time he told them, of course.'

'We loved them as kids,' said Matt. 'The more gruesome the better, too.'

'Right.' Ben shook his head. 'I don't quite remember, though.'

'You don't?' Matt stopped working for a moment and crinkled his forehead in an effort of memory. 'There was some old duke at Knowle Abbey...'

'An earl,' said Ben.

'Whatever. Well, he caught a poacher on his land, nicking his deer or something. And instead of just handing him over to the cops, he turned the poacher loose in the woods and let his aristocratic mates hunt him down like an animal. He reckoned he could get away with doing things like that, because he was so rich and important.'

'When was this exactly?'

'Oh, a couple of months ago.'

'Right.'

Matt laughed again. Ben found it a bit unsettling to hear his brother being so jolly.

'Anyway,' said Matt, 'the poacher got shot and killed. And nobody did anything about it, of course. So the poacher's widow vowed revenge and put a curse on the duke.'

'The earl.'

This time Matt ignored his interruption. He finished driving a screw in with his electric screwdriver and brushed some wood shavings off the finished shelf. Then he stood back to admire his handiwork with a smile of satisfaction. Ben found himself beginning to get impatient.

'So what happened to the duke?' he said. 'I mean, the earl.'

'Oh, he died,' said Matt airily.

'Everyone dies eventually.'

'Ah, but he died a *horrible* death. I can't remember exactly how. But I know it was horrible.'

Ben sighed. 'You're not a born storyteller, are you?'

'Not like Granddad Cooper,' admitted Matt.

Outside, the centre of town was getting noisy again as the pubs filled up.

'It's time to knock off here, I think,' said Matt, 'before they let the animals loose from the zoo.'

They put out the lights and Matt set the alarm and locked the door. He turned to Ben.

'Do you want to come back to the farm for a bit?' he said. 'Have you had something to eat? I dare say Kate can—'

Ben shook his head. 'No, I'm okay. Thanks anyway.'

'Suit yourself.'

Matt couldn't resist casting another sideways glance at him from the corner of his eye as they turned towards the market square.

'I'm fine, Matt, really.'

'Good. But if ever...'

'I know.'

'Well. Think on, then.'

When Matt had gone, Ben felt oddly reassured by the conversation they'd just had, standing here on the corner of Edendale market square. There had hardly been any words involved, but what had been said meant a lot. That was exactly the way he and his brother had always communicated with one another when they were boys at Bridge End Farm. Their mother would have said they just grunted at each other. But they'd been so close that they had an understanding beyond words.

Ben smiled. It had felt so good to have that back again, just for a few minutes. At least some things stayed re- assuringly the same in this world. And his brother was one of them.

Chapter Twenty

With a heave, Diane Fry dragged her overnight bag off the back seat of her car and slammed the door. The Audi was streaked with mud and its windscreen was filthy. Its black paintwork always showed the dirt at the best of times. But right now the wheel arches seemed to have accumulated half the topsoil of the Peak District. If she had that mud analysed, no doubt she would find a high percentage of sheep muck too.

She sighed and turned towards the lit-up entrance. The A38 Aston Expressway was only a hundred yards away and the buzz of evening traffic was loud and continuous. It was a noise she had grown up with, but which she rarely heard in Derbyshire. Its presence was like the return of the cuckoo in spring. Tuneless, but reassuring.

Fry checked in and found her room. It was like any other budget hotel, anonymous and without character. There were few staff to be seen and her fellow guests took no notice of her as she passed, some of them even turning their heads away as if they didn't want to be recognised. It suited her down to the ground.

In her room the first thing she did was turn off the TV. She hung her clothes in the tiny wardrobe, though she was only staying overnight. She checked her phone, saw the text she'd been expecting. Just enough time to shower and get changed.

They'd arranged to meet in a pub near Aston University. Fry set off to walk along the canal towpath from the back of the hotel, passing under Dartmouth Middleway, with its set of lock gates beneath a grim concrete bridge. From the edge of the Corporation Street dual carriageway, she turned down Holt Street towards the campus.

It was an old pub with leaded windows and wooden floors, and pictures on the walls depicting the history of Birmingham. Naturally, it was full of students, but they seemed to be drinking rather than eating. Fry crossed the bar to a far corner and found her sister already there.

'Hi, sis,' she said.

Angie stood up to give her an uncomfortable hug. 'Di. How are you doing?'

'I'm fine.'

Diane sat down and looked at her older sister. Every time she saw her it was like meeting a new person. Angie had run away from their foster home in the Black Country when they were both teenagers. They didn't see each other until one memorable day in the Peak District, when the two of them had been brought together by Ben Cooper, of all people.

That day Angie had seemed like a complete stranger. But Diane had been setting eyes on her for the first time since she was fourteen. Her teenage illusions were easily shattered.

They'd spent a lot of time together since then and Angie had even stayed with her for a while in her flat in Edendale. Yet it was odd to look at her now and notice that she was starting to look middle-aged. Her eyes were tired and the lines around her temples, formed by years of pain, seemed more deeply etched.

And surely Angie had put on weight too? It was something Diane herself had never been able to do. Food just didn't hold the same attraction for her that it did for other people. It was necessary fuel, but not a subject for lengthy conversation, let alone something to write stacks of books or produce endless TV shows about. So she eyed Angie's outline with interest and examined her arms, no longer so thin that they looked as though they would snap. Her sister had always been slim. Since Diane had tried to emulate her in every way when they were teenagers, it seemed wrong that Angie could now so easily abandon her function as a role model.

They ordered straight away, because Angie was keen to eat. Diane chose a pasta pomodoro, a penne pasta with tomato sauce, sun-dried tomatoes and basil.

'I suppose that's the lowest calorie dish on the menu,' said Angie.

'It might be,' said Diane, though she knew perfectly well it was.

Angie laughed. She seemed much more relaxed than her sister had ever seen her before. It was odd and she didn't quite know what to make of it.

Their food came quickly. Diane watched her sister eating skewered chicken breast pieces with peppers and barbecue sauce.

'Things are going well, then?' she said.

'Great.' Angie looked up from her chicken skewers. 'I told you I've got a new bloke, didn't I?'

'I believe you mentioned it in your texts. Several times.'

'We've been an item for a few months now.'

'I'm happy for you.'

Angie smiled. It was a curiously smug expression, more like a smirk. Diane immediately became suspicious.

'What's going on?' she said.

'What do you mean?'

'Come off it. I know you too well.'

But Angie shrugged. 'Stop being a copper.'

'Mmm.'

They ate silently for a moment, allowing the background noise of the students to wash over them.

'Speaking of which,' said Angie, 'how's the lovely Ben?'

'What?'

'Don't pretend you don't know who I mean.'

'Ben Cooper?'

'Of course.'

'He's all right, I suppose.'

Angie nodded. 'He's got over all that business with the fire and his fiancée being killed? I mean, it's a while ago now, isn't it? People do get over these things and move on with their lives.'

'Obviously.'

Diane didn't like the way the conversation was going. Angie had always shown an inexplicable interest in Ben Cooper. But she had her own bloke now. They'd been an item for months and it sounded serious. Why was she still talking about Cooper?

'So,' said Angie, 'he's, you know ... available again.'

'Well, I guess so. But I thought you were happy with your new bloke.'

Angie gaped at her and dropped her fork on to her plate with a clatter. She threw her head back and laughed. She had a peculiar, hiccuping laugh that always made heads turn in astonishment.

Diane cringed with embarrassment and tried to turn away from the gawping faces in the bar.

'Diane, you idiot,' said Angie, when she'd taken a drink to stop herself choking.

'What on earth is the matter with you?' said Diane.

'Never mind. How's the pasta?'

'Fine.'

When they'd finished their meal, they sat for a long time over their drinks. Finally, Angie put down her glass with a decisive air.

'So,' she said.

'What?'

'I have something to tell you.'

Diane's heart sank. She'd only ever heard bad news from her sister. Or so it seemed when she looked back over the years.

'What is it, sis?'

'You know I was saying about this bloke? His name's Craig, by the way.'

'I think I remember.'

'No, you don't.'

'Well…'

'It doesn't matter. Anyway, what I'm trying to tell you is this. We've been together for a while and we decided that … well, the fact is, Di – I'm pregnant.'

BEN COOPER HAD decided not to go straight back to his car after he left the shop, but headed away from the market square. Though it was right in the centre of Edendale, this stretch of the River Eden was a peaceful spot, particularly at night. It was only a few yards from the shopping centre, but it always felt to Cooper as though he'd stepped out of the town into a different world once he turned the corner and stepped down on to the riverbank.

In the darkness he could see only a few flickers of light off the water as it foamed over the weir. But he could hear the sounds. The soothing whisper and murmur of the river was enough to calm him down and let him think quietly to himself.

He was aware of the mallard ducks who lived on the river here. They were floating out there somewhere on the water near the weir, apparently asleep, with their beaks tucked under their wings. But he knew their feet must still be paddling like mad below the surface to keep them in position, or they would be swept downstream by the current.

Cooper sat on a bench for a while, enjoying the quiet and the chance to think. It wasn't the Sandra Blair inquiry that was bothering him. The solution to that would surely turn out to be something perfectly ordinary and sordid. Almost predictable, in fact.

It wasn't even Dorothy Shelley he was worried about. He'd phoned the hospital earlier in the evening to check on her condition and had been told she was 'comfortable'. He knew from experience that it was what they said when there was no hope of recovery. But her family were at her side and it wasn't his place to intrude. There was nothing more he could do.

No, it was Diane Fry's behaviour that baffled him. He'd tried to make friends with her when she'd first come to Derbyshire, but he'd failed. He'd tried to understand her, hoping she would relax a little and open up. But in the past she'd hardly noticed his attempts at empathy. She'd simply passed him by, as if he were no more than a piece of furniture. But then, she behaved the same way with everyone else, didn't she?

Yes, Fry's lack of empathy was legendary. He'd been reminded of it by one moment during Liz's funeral. In fact, he'd seen it at almost every funeral he'd ever been to. If you looked behind the church or crematorium, you'd sometimes see the drivers of the hearse and the funeral cars laughing and smoking among themselves during the service.

Well, the undertakers didn't really care that your fiancée had died. They attended two or three funerals every day and they couldn't be prostrated by grief every time, especially for people they didn't know. But for a while Cooper found it hard to understand how people could do the job at all. How did you spend time with a crowd of people who *were* grief stricken and not share their emotions? How could you go to funeral after funeral, every day of the week, all the year round, and not be affected by it? It needed a particular type of person to spend their life dealing with death, thinking about death, and meeting those who'd just been bereaved, and yet be able to chat and joke with their friends as if they didn't have a care in the world.

After Liz's funeral he'd come away with the conviction that people who did the job must be sociopaths. Only a serious personality disorder would enable you to look so solemn while you carried a coffin, then take off your tie, go home and eat dinner, watch the TV, and tell the wife you'd had a good day at work.

In fact, he'd envied those people. For a long time, he wished he could be like them. But he knew he would fail.

That idea, though, had made him look at Diane Fry differently. If it was true about funeral directors, then what about a police officer? Someone who dealt with nothing but murder cases and rapes, and serious violent crimes? Were they also sociopaths who just happened to have found themselves a profession where their personality disorder was an advantage? No one wanted a cop who empathised too much. It made them less professional, not so good at their jobs.

Cooper shivered with cold and knew it was time to go home. He stood up suddenly, startling the ducks and making them rattle their wings in the darkness.

No, he had never been able to achieve that level of detachment himself. No amount of trying got him to a position where he could create that protective façade. He'd become convinced this was what might prevent him from moving up the promotion ladder in the police service. It was the Diane Frys they wanted these days.

But then he recalled the new version of Diane he'd encountered in her flat on Friday night. The softer, more relaxed Fry. The one who actually asked him for a favour. Was this the same person? Could it be the woman he'd always suspected might exist behind the brittle exterior?

If so, this new Diane Fry was like a glimpse of some illusory oasis, glittering in the distance but defying the most determined traveller to reach it. The nearer he got, the further away she would seem. It felt inevitable, the story of his life. It was certainly the story of his relationship with Fry.

The ducks quacked quietly in agreement as he walked away from the peace of the river and headed back towards the town.

WHILE BEN COOPER sat by the riverside in Edendale, Luke Irvine was in the pub. His date hadn't gone too well the night before. No matter how often he checked his phone, there were no text messages. So he couldn't imagine she was expecting to hear from him again tonight. But that seemed to be the story of his life at the moment. Opportunities came along, but were allowed to escape.

As he watched the other customers in the bar of the Angler's Rest, Irvine knew that Ben Cooper would still be out asking questions about the woman whose body had been found at Hollins Bridge. Overtime meant nothing to his DS. Though he admired Cooper in lots of ways, Irvine hoped he never ended up like that himself. Dedication to the job was great, but it was so much better to have a life away from the office.

Irvine lived in the village of Bamford, between the Hope Valley and the Upper Derwent. It was a short drive over the hill to Edendale, but quiet enough to give him the village life he'd grown up with in West Yorkshire.

A man he knew vaguely from a few houses down the road came and sat down on a vacant seat nearby. He nodded and said, 'Hi'. Irvine acknowledged him cautiously. Conversations in the pub could be difficult, he'd discovered.

'Good to see the place so busy,' said the man.

'Yeah, great.'

'It just goes to show.'

'You're right, it does.'

Irvine took a swig of his beer, holding the bottle to his mouth a bit longer than was strictly necessary. He knew what the man was talking about, without any telling.

People in his community had spent months raising the money to buy their village pub. They formed a cooperative society to take ownership of the building, with hundreds of residents buying shares. They successfully applied to get the pub registered as an 'asset of community value' under the government's new Localism Act. They drew up a business plan, outlining a scheme for a community hub with a café and shop, and accommodation for visitors. Their village post office was due to close too and they negotiated to move counter services into the pub. They appeared in the local media, manned stalls at shows and fêtes, and enough money came in to make the dream possible.

For a while it had all seemed to be going well. With the financial targets hit, solicitors were instructed to begin the conveyancing process. But on the same day the company that owned the pub announced it was exchanging contracts with a third party – a developer who would make the deal pay by building houses on the car park.

Irvine remembered calling into the pub one night for a drink when the news had just broken. The mood was disturbing. Everyone he spoke to was frustrated and angry, convinced they had been betrayed by big business and exploited for a quick profit.

One of his neighbours, who'd had a couple of drinks too many, buttonholed him at the bar while he was ordering a bottle of Thornbridge Sour Brown. Like a doctor, Irvine found he could never escape the fact that he was a police officer, even when he was off duty. In fact, it had been worse since he joined CID and became a detective. Everyone wanted to hear gory details of cases, tell him their theories, or ask him for clandestine forms of assistance that would undoubtedly lose him his job.

That night, though, there was only one topic of conversation. The last-minute betrayal over the sale of the pub had turned people's minds to committing crime rather than solving it.

'This could definitely be a motive for murder,' this same neighbour had said, leaning close to him at the bar. 'With a hundred and eighty-five potential suspects at the last count. They might all commit the crime together, like the plot of an Agatha Christie story.'

'By far the least believable Christie plot,' said Irvine, who had watched *Poirot* on TV.

The man tapped the side of his nose and almost winked. 'Where there's a motive, people will find a means.'

But a week or two later the public outcry against the decision had changed the minds of both the pub's owners and the potential buyer. The project went ahead and Bamford owned its community hub. When he went into the Angler's Rest now for a Sour Brown, people again asked for gory details or the kind of assistance that would lose him his job.

'I suppose you're involved in that case over near Buxton,' said the man now, with an inquisitive lift of the eyebrows.

'Maybe so.'

But as Irvine looked at his neighbour, he recalled that earlier conversation. An Agatha Christie plot? He wondered if he should phone Ben Cooper right now with the interesting idea that had just come into his head.

But of course not. Unlike Cooper, he had a life after all.

'Do you fancy another drink, mate?' he said.

Chapter Twenty-one

Sunday 3 November

CAROL VILLIERS HAD produced a list of names and it was waiting for Cooper on his desk when he arrived in the CID room on Sunday morning. He wasn't supposed to be on duty, but there was nothing for him to do at home. It was a choice between being here and painting shelves in the shop. No contest. He loved his brother, but the thought of spending all day working with Matt filled him with dread.

The list Villiers had drawn up contained the names of all the residents of Bowden, plus Sandra Blair and her husband Gary, who were former residents, and those of Jason Shaw and the Nadens.

After a moment's thought, Cooper added Rob Beresford and his parents to the list. Was there anyone else he should consider? No, that seemed to be about it.

Cooper glanced through the list again. There were quite a few familiar surnames on it. That was inevitable, after all his years in E Division making arrests, interviewing suspects, reading intelligence files on known criminal associates. Certain family names cropped up time and time again. Others he remembered particularly after just one meeting – an individual could make such a deep impression on him he would never forget them for as long as he lived. There were even one or two who'd been helpful to him in the past and who might not run a mile when they saw him coming.

One of those individuals was suggested by a name on this list. The Kilners were a widespread family in this part of Derbyshire. But one particular member of the family, Brendan, was well known to Cooper.

Brendan Kilner had been the owner of a garage that was targeted during a proactive operation tackling an increase in the number of expensive, top-of-the-range cars being stolen in North Derbyshire, most of which were never recovered. The suspicion was that they were being processed locally and shipped abroad through a third party. There was always a market for stolen BMWs and Mercedes in parts of the world where fewer questions were asked.

But Kilner himself had never been convicted of anything. Two of his mechanics had gone down for a few years after the police operation located a couple of lock-ups in Edendale where the two employees had been working on stolen vehicles in their spare time. The inquiry had focused on tracking down the dealers who organised the shipping – they were the really serious players, part of an organised crime gang. Once their stage of the enterprise was disrupted, the market disappeared. They also made most of the profit, of course, so they were a much juicier target for an action under the Proceeds of Crime Act, which extracted large amounts of money from convicted criminals. Some of the proceeds even went towards maintaining levels of policing in the county.

It had never been entirely clear whether Kilner was squeaky clean in relation to the stolen car scam, but he'd been remarkably helpful at the time. He opened up his records to the police investigation and shared everything he knew about the activities of his two mechanics, who were by then safely in custody.

During the interviews Cooper was unable to escape a niggling doubt about the garage owner and whether there might be some hidden paperwork somewhere, a possibility the leading officer in the case decided not to pursue. Since then Brendan Kilner had nothing recorded against him, either in Criminal Records or in the intelligence databases. Going straight, then. The garage was still there, BK Motors – now in a double unit on an industrial estate on the outskirts of Edendale.

Cooper looked up a number and grabbed the phone. Kilner was surprised to hear from him, that much was obvious. A bit suspicious too. Maybe there was still a trace of guilty conscience in his reaction to an unexpected contact with the police. But that was a good thing, in the circumstances.

After a bit of cautious small talk, some polite enquiries about the family and how well business was doing, Cooper got round to telling Kilner that he wanted to talk to him.

'Where can I meet you?'

'What, today?' said Kilner, still reluctant.

'Yes, this afternoon.'

'Well, I'll be at Axe Edge. There's a race meeting.'

'Buxton Raceway? I know it.'

Kilner didn't hang up straight away. Cooper could hear him breathing, a slight wheeze as if he were about to start coughing. A nervous cough, or was Kilner a smoker? He couldn't remember that detail.

'Can you tell me what it's about?' asked Kilner.

'I'll tell you when I see you.'

'Okay, then. I'll get you a hot dog, shall I?'

BUXTON RACEWAY. THOUGH Cooper had often passed it, he'd never actually visited the races. It wasn't the sort of place Liz would ever have wanted to go with him for a Sunday afternoon outing.

The site stood in a bleak spot off the Buxton to Leek road, at a point where it crossed Axe Edge Moor. This was the highest stretch of moorland close to the border between Derbyshire and Staffordshire. Many of the Peak District's major rivers rose on Axe Edge Moor and the source of the River Dove itself was only a few hundred yards away in a patch of marshy ground near Dovehead Farm, just on the Staffordshire side of the border.

After he'd parked the car Cooper found Brendan Kilner at the end of a small stand for spectators. He was clutching a hot dog in a paper napkin from the stall behind him. The scent of fried onions mingled with a powerful smell of exhaust fumes, despite a strong breeze blowing across the moor.

Kilner gestured with the hot dog.

'Do you want one?' he asked by way of greeting.

'Not at the moment, thanks.'

'Suit yourself.'

He hardly looked at Cooper, but kept his eyes fixed on the circuit, where nothing much seemed to be happening. He'd put on weight since Cooper saw him last. Too many hot dogs and burgers, perhaps. But then, he'd always been a man whose idea of exercise was leaning into an engine compartment with a spanner.

'Sorry to drag you here,' said Kilner. 'This is almost the last meeting of the season. I couldn't miss it.'

'There's no racing in the winter?'

'No. It gets a bit wild up here, like.'

'I can imagine.'

Now he was standing still, that wind blowing across the landscape from Axe Edge Moor certainly felt a bit icy. Cooper looked around at the groups of people standing nearby.

'Can we walk round the other side of the track for a while?'

Kilner wiped his fingers as he swallowed the last piece of hot dog.

'If you like.'

The circuit consisted of a tarmac oval around a central refuge where a few official vehicles were parked, including a tractor and a paramedic's car. There were already some disabled racing cars lined up awaiting retrieval after the meeting was over. The circuit ran in front of the stand and past spectators who were parked at the trackside, protected by a black-and-white barrier and a high mesh safety fence. The landscape behind the raceway looked even more bare and rugged. In the background Cooper could see the distinctive jut of a rock face. He recognised it as a feature standing between the site of the Health and Safety Executive's laboratories at Harpur Hill and a flooded quarry once known by local people as the Blue Lagoon.

As they strolled away from the stand Cooper began to see cars and their drivers. The drivers wore racing overalls, crash helmets and fire-retardant gloves, just like the stars of Formula One. But their vehicles were a bunch of beaten-up hatchbacks. Datsun Sunnys, Ford Fiestas, Vauxhall Novas. Although really all that was left of each car was the chassis. They had been stripped down and armoured. In addition to heavy front and rear bumpers, iron cages had been welded along the sides. They were all painted in bright colour schemes.

'These are 1300cc saloon stocks,' said Kilner as a series of cars began to move out on to the track.

A man wearing goggles and ear protectors stood on a white breeze-block podium with a set of flags. About fifteen cars began to move round the circuit, slowly at first as if they were merely in a procession. Then there must have been a signal that Cooper didn't see, because engines roared simultaneously as drivers accelerated towards the starting flag, jostling for position in the first straight.

'I heard you were in the fire up at the old Light House,' said Kilner. 'It was in all the papers and everything. That was a bad business.'

'Yes.'

Cooper would have been amazed if Kilner didn't know all about it. Everyone else in the area did.

Kilner was watching the cars thoughtfully. 'I suppose you don't want to talk about it.'

'Not to you, Brendan, anyway.'

'Fair comment. I can't blame you for that. Put things behind you, get on with life. That's the motto, like.'

On the track a car spun three hundred and sixty degrees, but the driver recovered and kept going, trying to regain ground. Ahead of him another collided with the barrier, bounced and came to a halt. A blue-and-yellow car seemed to be in the lead all the way, so far as Cooper could tell.

'There's not the sort of excitement you get in some types of racing,' said Kilner. 'Super bangers or hot rods. You can pretty much predict who's going to come in first. But it's the spectacle, you know. The noise, the smell, the whole thing. It's like a drug, I suppose.'

Cooper had never been much of a petrol head himself. But his brother Matt would probably have enjoyed himself here. He was forever tinkering with one of his tractors back at Bridge End Farm. For years Matt's pride and joy had been a vintage Massey Ferguson that never did any work around the farm, but turned out a couple of times a year for a tractor rally and trundled around the roads with scores of others. The Massey had soaked up too much cash, though, which the farm couldn't afford, and it had been sold off.

With a glance around to make sure no one was near them, Cooper showed Kilner an edited version of the list that Villiers had produced for him.

'Recognise some of these names, Brendan?' he said.

Kilner fiddled in his pockets until he found a pair of reading glasses. Old age was creeping up on him too.

'Of course,' he said. 'All of them, I think. You probably guessed that or you wouldn't be here.'

'Apart from Bowden, can you suggest anything they all have in common?'

As the stock cars came past their position again, the noise of the engines was deafening. Cooper missed something that Brendan Kilner was saying.

'What?'

'I said, "They've all got an axe to grind." But then, haven't we all these days? Even the cops, I bet.'

Kilner laughed and Cooper got the whiff of fried onions again, but at second hand.

'So what axes do the Nadens and Jason Shaw have to grind?' he asked.

Kilner shrugged. 'It's all about family. Ancient history if you ask me. But that stuff means a lot to some people, doesn't it? Me, I can never bring myself to visit the place where my mum and dad were buried. Come to think of it, we didn't actually bury my dad – we burned him, then scattered him.'

'What are you talking about, Brendan?' asked Cooper.

'The graveyard, of course.'

'Graveyard?'

Kilner turned to look at him. 'What, you don't know about the graveyard? Where have you been these past few months?'

A stock car was nudged and went into a spin, stopping against the fence. It was unable to get back on the circuit, and the others came round and passed it again before track officials stopped them with a series of orange flags. The drivers waited patiently on the circuit while a tractor dragged the damaged car clear. It seemed a surprisingly civilised process – not really what he'd expected from the battered condition of most of the vehicles. They were like battle-scarred chariots under their heavy armour.

'Can you be more specific?' asked Cooper.

Kilner put a hand on his arm without taking his eyes off the circuit. 'I shouldn't say any more. You just go and look at the graveyard. You'll see for yourself easily enough.'

The flag man was counting down the remaining laps now as cars approached his podium. Then suddenly they were into the last lap and the blue-and-yellow car was still out in front. A car kicked up a cloud of dirt as it hit the edge of the central refuge and stalled.

Then the chequered flag came down and there was just time for the winner to do a victory lap in the back of an official car before preparations got under way for the next race. Brendan Kilner cheered and clapped with the rest of the crowd.

'Who won?' asked Cooper.

Kilner laughed. 'The same guy who always wins,' he said.

SCOTT HEYWOOD SWUNG his bike off a bend in the road above Pilsbury and coasted along the path towards the site of the castle.

It was a fine morning now – cold, but not raining for once. November was so unpredictable for weather. But then, every month was unpredictable in the Peak District.

He went through the gate and wheeled his bike as far as the information board, where he removed his helmet, pulled his Boardman water bottle from its cage and took a drink. In front of him was a sharp limestone outcrop with a tree growing from its furthest slope. Scott knew this wasn't part of the castle. It had probably been incorporated into the site as a natural defensive feature.

When he'd finished his drink, he shooed a couple of grazing sheep out of the way and walked up the grassy slope until he reached the edge of the outcrop. From here he had a fantastic view over the strange mounds where the castle had been and across the valley of the Dove. He could see as far as the even stranger shapes of the hills to the north. The air was bracing and he could feel himself cooling off quickly as the sweat dried on his skin.

Then Scott looked down.

'What the heck is that?' he said.

One of the sheep answered him and it made him jump. A plaintive croak, like the sound of a broken gate. It echoed mournfully around the crag.

'I think … No, it can't be,' said Scott.

After a moment's hesitation he began to slither his way down the far side of the slope, clinging to a branch of the tree to prevent himself sliding all the way down on his backside. By the time he got to the bottom he could see that he wasn't imagining things.

'Hello!' he called. 'Are you okay?'

He felt embarrassed by the sound of his own voice. He knew it was futile. The person was lying much too still at the foot of the slope, folded over into an unnatural shape. He could see that it was a man. He could distinguish a broad back and a large backside, with one arm twisted on the grass and ending with a pudgy hand turned palm upwards. A sheen of moisture gleamed on the clothes and on a patch of bald scalp in a fringe of dark hair.

Scott had never seen a dead body before. But he was surprised to find that there was no mistaking one when he saw it.

Chapter Twenty-two

THE REVEREND WILLIAM Latham lived in a small bungalow on one of the newer estates on the edge of Edendale. This wasn't quite sheltered housing for the elderly, but most of the people Cooper saw were past retirement age. They'd reached the time in their lives when they couldn't manage a big garden and didn't want to be coping with stairs.

He supposed it was a pleasant enough location. You could see the hills from here, and there was a bus route into town at the corner of the road. But it felt like the last stop on a journey, the sort of place you would never leave.

The Reverend Latham was cautious about visitors. When Cooper rang the bell he shuffled down the hall and called through the door to ask who it was.

'Bill? I'm sorry to disturb you. It's Ben Cooper again.'

Latham opened the door and peered out before lifting the security chain.

'Can't be too careful,' he said.

'Quite right.'

'So what can I do for you? More questions about coffin roads?'

'No,' said Cooper. 'A burial ground.'

'Ah. Interesting.'

Latham invited him in, though he left Cooper to close and lock the front door, which rather undermined his caution about visitors. The old man led him down the hall into an untidy sitting room. As Cooper looked around he realised that untidy would be a kind word for this room. It looked like benevolent chaos.

Cooper was used to seeing homes occupied by drug addicts and low-end criminals. They were invariably chaotic, a mess of used needles, empty alcohol bottles, rotting food and dirty clothes. That wasn't the case here. The disorder consisted of books and newspapers, pens and paper clips, cardboard boxes and piles of typed A4 sheets. There was a table under there somewhere and several chairs. An ancient leather sofa was occupied by two grey long-haired cats, sitting happily among the scattered papers and the remains of chewed cardboard.

'This is Peter and Paul,' said Latham, gesturing at the cats. 'Say hello.'

Cooper wasn't sure whether the old man was speaking to him or to the cats. But he said hello anyway. The cats glared at him and showed no signs of moving from the sofa to let him sit down.

'There's a chair here,' said Latham, picking up a pile of multicoloured folders which slipped out of his grasp and cascaded on to the carpet. Cooper bent to pick them up, but the old man stopped him. 'No, no, it's all right. They're as well filed on the floor as anywhere else, I suppose.'

Cooper removed a pair of glasses from the chair and placed them on the table. 'Are you writing a book or something?' he said.

'How did you guess?'

'Oh, I don't know. It just looks like a writer's room. What is the book about?'

'It's just a little memoir,' said Latham, waving a hand in a self-deprecating gesture. 'The difficulty I have is that my memory isn't as good as it used to be. It's requiring rather a lot of research to get the facts right. Dates and names and so on. I suppose it's my age.'

Latham perched himself on another chair and gazed vaguely at Cooper.

'Are you hoping to get it published?' asked Cooper, failing to keep a faint note of incredulity from his voice.

'I'm told it's very easy to publish a book yourself these days,' said Latham. 'Modern technology has opened up all kinds of doors. There are things called ebooks now.'

'Yes.' Cooper eyed the piles of paper. 'Where's your computer?'

'My what?'

'You have a laptop, at least?'

Latham shook his head. 'I do have a typewriter somewhere. I haven't used it for a while. There was a problem getting new ribbons.'

Cooper didn't know what else to say. If he went any further into the subject, he might end up volunteering to do the work himself. And that was beyond the call of duty.

'I was at Bowden yesterday,' said Cooper. 'You know, the estate village for Knowle Abbey?'

'Oh, the Bowden burial ground?' said Latham. 'Surely you know all about that?'

'No, I don't,' said Cooper.

Latham raised an eyebrow at him and Cooper realised his tone had been a bit too sharp.

'I'm sorry,' he said. 'I don't know anything about the burial ground.'

One of the cats stirred uneasily and dragged itself off the sofa. As it strolled out of the room, Cooper could see that it was beautifully groomed, but obese.

'I'm afraid there's nothing anyone can do about it,' Latham was saying. 'It's all perfectly within the rules and regulations.'

'What is?'

But now he'd set Latham off on a train of thought, the old man wasn't going to be steered by someone else's questions. 'When a church or burial ground has been consecrated, it comes under the jurisdiction of the bishop,' he said. 'In the case of a churchyard, the legal effects of consecration can only be removed by an Act of Parliament or the General Synod. But if the land or building isn't vested in an ecclesiastical body, then the bishop has the power of deconsecration.'

'So?'

Latham nodded at him. 'That's the case at Bowden, you see. The church was built by a previous Earl Manby and it belongs to the estate. So the bishop of this diocese has agreed to deconsecrate. There was no reason for him to refuse. The church itself isn't used any more, you know. It's the burial ground that has been most at issue.'

'Are you telling me the present Earl Manby is planning to sell off the church and burial ground at Bowden?'

'Well, of course.'

'For what purpose?'

'That I can't tell you.'

'He must have some scheme in mind for the land. But can he really do that to a graveyard?'

'By law, any graves more than seventy-five years old can be removed, though the removal and destruction of gravestones is subject to controls under the Cemeteries Act.' Latham looked at his chaotic table. 'I could quote you the specific section, if I can find the reference.'

'It doesn't matter.'

'Then there would be the Disused Burial Grounds Act,' said Latham. 'That dates from the 1880s, but I'm sure it still applies. The prohibition against building on a churchyard can be overridden if the church is declared redundant. Then the land can be deconsecrated and disposed of for any type of development, I think. Remains can be relocated but, if not, you're obliged to allow access to relatives.'

'There must have been objections from families with relatives buried there,' said Cooper.

'Indeed. But there are no plans to build on the actual burial ground, as I understand it. You'd have to consult the plans for more information, I suppose.'

Cooper watched the cat return, casually stalking past his legs as if he were just another pile of discarded paper.

'I wonder what the earl has in mind,' he said. 'It's bound to be something he can make money from. A residential development, perhaps.'

The Reverend Latham gazed at the returning cat and his expression became dreamy. He reached for a pen and an exercise book from the table and began to scribble in it.

'That reminds me,' he said. 'Thank you, Ben. It will make an interesting chapter for my ebook.'

'What?'

'Well, we had another example in this diocese,' said Latham. 'St Martin's Church. It was deconsecrated back in the 1980s. But it stood derelict for almost twenty years before a young couple bought it. I heard that they invested nearly three times the purchase price and it was very interesting what they did. They kept the stained glass and many of the fixtures intact, added skylights in the roof, installed under-floor heating and constructed a rather dramatic staircase up to a galleried library. They even used the wood from the pews to build kitchen counters and a dining room table. The project took them six years to complete, as I recall.'

'I remember that too,' said Cooper. 'When they finished the conversion, they listed the property for sale for about six hundred thousand pounds.'

'Ah, yes.' Latham wrote down the figure. 'Six hundred thousand pounds. It sounded like an awful lot of money to me. But it was a very unusual property. They let me see inside it once. It had an enormous living area. It incorporated the chancel and nave, and the ceiling must have been about thirty-five feet high. Just imagine what you could do with that.'

Cooper was imagining a vast cathedral-like space filled with stacks of paper and cardboard boxes, but Latham hadn't finished.

'Well, the really interesting thing,' he said, 'is that St Martin's had a small graveyard. Over the years graves had been dug deep and coffins stacked on top of each other to make maximum use of the available space. When the church was deconsecrated, the coffins were exhumed and moved to other graveyards. Rumour has it that some of them were never located and might still be buried under the grounds today.'

'Really?'

Latham laughed gently. 'Well, if it's true, there's a jacuzzi and a barbecue patio over the top of them now. Fortunately, those deepest graves would be very old burials. The forgotten ones.'

Cooper thought of Bowden village and Knowle Abbey, and some of the people he'd spoken to during the last few days.

'I don't think there are any forgotten ones in this case,' he said.

HALF AN HOUR later Cooper was walking along the ragged lines of headstones in the burial ground at Bowden and looking at the names inscribed on them. Several familiar surnames appeared. Shaw, Beresford, Kilner, Mellor, Blair.

The church was still locked, even though it was Sunday. But then, it wasn't just closed. It had been declared redundant. It would never be opened again, not as a place of worship at least. The bulldozer waiting behind the church took on a new meaning now. He could see it had nothing to do with the bonfire.

Mrs Mellor must have seen him from the window of the cottage and recognised him. She came across the green and walked through the graveyard to see what he was looking at.

'Yes, some of my family are here too,' she said, touching one of the gravestones.

'So I see.'

'I take it you know what's going to happen to this? To the church and the graveyard?'

'Yes, I know. But there have been objections from the families, haven't there?'

'Of course,' she said. 'But there are no plans to build over the burial ground itself. The church will be converted, probably for residential use. Then the burials that can be found will be removed and the graveyard will be landscaped. That's what the plans say.'

'Residential use, you think?'

'Well, we've heard there's a local artist who wants to turn the church into an art gallery. But it will probably be a holiday home for someone with plenty of money. Like the cottages.'

Cooper looked up. 'Cottages?'

Mrs Mellor pointed. 'There are a couple of cottages a bit further into the park. They used to be workers' homes, but the tenants were given notice. They're going to be converted into holiday rentals for tourists. Another money-spinner, no doubt.'

'Was one of those the Blairs' home?'

'That's right.'

She looked quite pleased with him, now that he had figured something out for himself, without being told.

'It's terrible about Sandra,' she said. 'I heard they confirmed that the body found at the bridge was hers.'

'Yes.'

'That family seem to have been fated.'

Mrs Mellor began to drift slowly away as Cooper stood for a few moments by the graves. For generations workers from the estate had been buried in this graveyard. They'd lived in tied cottages on the estate, paid their rent at the estate office, and owed their livelihoods to the earl. When they died, they were buried on the earl's land. Where else would they go?

The Manbys themselves had their memorials at the Lady Chapel attached to the hall, instead of down here with the workers on the edge of the park. Now some of the workers' cottages had to be vacated. They were going to be converted into holiday rentals for tourists. The burial ground would be deconsecrated by the bishop, the burials probably transferred to the cemetery at Buxton. The church would be advertised as a potential residential conversion. It would suit a couple looking for rural seclusion and wonderful views, as long as they had enough money to spend.

'Mrs Mellor,' called Cooper before the woman had left the graveyard. 'Do you know Jason Shaw? Does he still have family here in Bowden?'

'Jason? He has no family and no friends. Nobody has much to do with him. Why?'

'We know he was in the area near the bridge when Sandra died.'

'I can't tell you much about him. He works at night. In fact, he's a bit strange like that. He hardly ever goes out in the daylight.'

'Well, it's true it was dark at the time,' said Cooper. 'Mr Shaw said he was walking his dog that night.'

Mrs Mellor scowled. 'He never walks that dog. It lives in a run in his yard. I call it cruel myself.'

Chapter Twenty-three

DIANE FRY HAD just finished a phone call with her DCI, Alistair Mackenzie. A team would be arriving from St Ann's soon. This was no longer a case that could be left to Divisional CID.

The second body had been found at a place called Pilsbury Castle. Fry knew enough about the Peak District by now to guess that her mental image of a medieval fortress with high towers and a drawbridge leading over a moat to a portcullised gate would be completely wrong. Maps of England were still marked with the names of castles all over the countryside, but most of the buildings themselves seemed to be long gone.

And she turned out to be right, of course. Like so many other sites, there was nothing left at Pilsbury but a series of mounds and hollows, and a fragment of crumbling stone wall that only an archaeologist could have identified as a castle. Well, if it wasn't for the interpretation boards anyway. You could read about the history, even if you couldn't see it.

Apart from the forensic examiners and some uniformed officers, the only CID presence when she arrived was DC Luke Irvine.

She'd been Irvine's sergeant when she was serving in Edendale. She knew he was loyal to Ben Cooper. But that hardly mattered now.

At the inner cordon Fry found the crime-scene manager, Wayne Abbott, stripping off his mask and pulling back the hood of his scene suit. He grinned when he saw her. His face was slightly flushed, either from the warmth of the suit or the physical exertion of his task, or perhaps for some other reason entirely. He seemed unusually cheerful this morning, she thought. In fact, he was almost giggly. In other circumstances she might have said he was a bit tipsy. But surely not even Abbott would come on duty like that.

'So what have you found?' she asked when she reached the CSM.

'Oh, eight million fingerprints,' said Abbott breezily.

He laughed and Luke Irvine joined in. If Abbott had made a joke, Fry didn't find it very funny. Not for the first time, she felt as though she were missing out on some aspect of everyday conversation. She hated the use of obscure allusions whose meaning seemed to be shared by relative strangers, but not by her.

'*Exactly* eight million?' she said, with a frown.

Abbott sighed and shook his head. 'Never mind.'

Fry looked at Irvine for an explanation, as she often did when she was baffled by something like this.

'It's a popular culture reference, Diane,' he said patiently.

'Oh. Don't tell me – a TV show?'

'Yes. *Homeland*. I suppose you've never heard of it?'

'Some kind of property programme?'

'No, Diane.'

Irvine seemed reluctant to explain it any further, so she left it at that. It didn't matter anyway. Whatever *Homeland* was, it couldn't be of any importance.

'It looks as though your victim took a header off the crag up there,' said Abbott. 'There's a bit of scuffling and more than one set of shoe marks. And we found a rip in the sleeve of the victim's jacket, which doesn't look as though it was caused by his collision with the tree.'

'Anything else?'

'The victim probably came in through the gate there,' said Abbott. 'His prints are on it, but then so are, well...'

'Eight million others?'

'Something like that. It may have been an exaggeration the first time.'

'What about the information board?' asked Fry.

'Lots of prints on there too. It's amazing how many people seem to read with their fingers.'

'But not the victim's prints?'

Abbott shook his head. 'Not that we can confirm. But there are so many partials, it's asking the impossible to get a definite negative.'

'Understood.'

Fry cast her eye over the body. The man was aged around fifty or fifty-five, his hair still dark but showing signs of hereditary baldness from the gleam of scalp on top of his head. He was also a couple of stone overweight, she guessed, though it was difficult to tell given the extent of post-mortem bloating on the torso and limbs. The visible skin was badly discoloured, a series of ugly shades from red to green. The victim was wearing dark trousers, like the bottom half of a business suit, but sensible stout shoes and an expensive-looking padded jacket.

'A tourist?' she said.

'No,' replied Irvine promptly.

Fry looked up. 'Do we have an ID already, then?'

'Yes, the victim's name is George Redfearn,' said Irvine. 'A company director. He's listed as being on the board of Eden Valley Mineral Products.'

'And what do they do?'

'Oh, small-scale limestone quarrying. Mr Redfearn has an address over at Taddington.'

Fry waited. Irvine shouldn't need asking. He'd worked with her before, so he ought to know that she didn't carry a map of the Peak District in her head, the way some officers did.

'That's about seven miles away, if you know where you're going and take the Flagg road,' said Irvine.

'And how many miles is it the way I'd go?' asked Fry.

'Ten.'

'What about a car?'

'There's a black BMW parked by the road just down there at Pilsbury. I did a check on the number plate and confirmed it's registered to Mr Redfearn.'

'Yes, I saw it on the way here,' said Fry.

'It even has a personalised number plate,' said Irvine. 'The last three figures are GR8. That's his initials, you see. George Redfearn. But you can say it as "great".'

'Yes, thanks, I got it,' said Fry. 'But Pilsbury I don't get. I saw two or three houses...'

'That was it,' said Irvine.

Fry noticed Irvine's attention slip past her and over her shoulder, along with an expression of relief. She turned and saw Ben Cooper and Gavin Murfin arriving, just passing through the outer cordon and giving their names to a uniformed officer guarding the scene.

'Oh, by the way, any ghosts or spirits seen in the area?' asked Fry with a smile.

'Spirits?' said Abbott.

'Yes, didn't you know?'

'Who's talking about spirits?' asked Murfin as he lumbered up. 'I wouldn't mind a nice drop of Scotch myself right at this moment. A ten-year-old malt, for preference. Is there a pub in the neighbourhood?' He looked around him, as if noticing the landscape for the first time. Then he sighed. 'No, I didn't think there would be.'

'Actually,' said Cooper, 'we're only a stone's throw from Crowdecote. The Pack Horse Inn.'

Murfin screwed up his face. 'Crowdecote? Isn't that near a bridge?'

'Yes, the nearest road crossing over the Dove is at Crowdecote. In fact, it's the only one on this stretch of the river between Hartington and Glutton.'

'Speaking of gluttons,' said Fry. 'Some around here could do with taking up a more healthy diet.'

'I get my five a day,' said Murfin defensively.

'When they say that, they don't mean five meals a day, Gavin. They mean five portions of fruit and vegetables.'

'That's ridiculous.'

BEN COOPER WASN'T surprised to see Fry at Pilsbury Castle before him. It was inevitable now.

'The Major Crime Unit will be taking over after this, I suppose,' he said.

Fry just nodded. Well, it was only what he'd anticipated. He'd been expecting it ever since Fry first appeared at the Corpse Bridge.

In fact, it was almost as if he'd had a premonition when he thought about the Devil manifesting at a crossroads. Diane Fry might not quite be Satan, but she made a good stand-in when required.

'So what do you think now about blaming all this on someone with a grudge against Earl Manby and his family?' she said.

'It's still … possible,' said Cooper, feeling immediately defensive.

'It's just a theory, Ben. A theory is no good on its own. When you think that's all you've got, you want to hang on to it at all costs. It can affect your judgement. You lose objectivity.'

Cooper watched her leave. He reflected that Diane Fry had honed into a positive talent this ability to walk away from a conversation with the last word hanging in the air as it left her lips. Often her final shaft of wisdom was spot on, an accurate barb that struck his heart.

But she wasn't right this time. Yes, there were some things he'd wanted to hang on to in his life. Things he'd wanted desperately to cling to, but had lost anyway.

Cooper looked at the body of the latest victim lying at the foot of a tree. His theory about the grudge wasn't something he felt so desperate to hold on to that it would affect his judgement. Well, was it?

Instinctively, Cooper took a step closer to the body, until Abbott put a hand up to stop him. He wasn't wearing a scene suit.

Then Cooper sniffed. 'What would you say that smell is, Wayne?' he asked.

Abbott began sniffing too. 'It's petrol, I think.'

'Have there been any vehicles down here?'

'Not recently. The tyre marks would be clear enough in the mud. We can only make out a few mountain bikes, that's all.'

'Strange. It's a pretty strong odour.'

Abbott nodded. 'We'll see if we can identify any traces from the soil and vegetation close to the body, shall we?'

'That would be great.'

Pilsbury Castle had occupied an area of high ground overlooking the River Dove. The Normans had built it to re-establish control of the area after William the Conqueror's campaign to devastate and subdue the north of England. In medieval times the site would have overlooked a key crossing point of the river.

Cooper looked out over the valley of the Dove towards the peculiar shapes of Parkhouse Hill and Chrome Hill in the distance to the north. He would be able to see the Corpse Bridge from here, if it wasn't for the trees around it. He could certainly make out Knowle Abbey quite clearly. And across a stretch of parkland, located at a suitable distance from the abbey, he could see the village of Bowden.

Chapter Twenty-four

ONCE THE PHOTOGRAPHS had been taken and the scene thoroughly examined, the safe retrieval of the body from its position at the foot of the outcrop was going to be difficult. The slope was close to being perpendicular.

Ben Cooper walked round the outer circumference of the castle site. Of course, the steep slope and the limestone knoll had been part of the natural defences for the site. The castle itself was either destroyed after its owners took the wrong side in a twelfth-century rebellion or it may simply have become redundant as the village of Pilsbury became increasingly depopulated. Its timber defences were long gone, anyway. Now there was little to see except for the mounds, and the remains of ditches and earthworks.

From the Pilsbury side of the river, he had a good view of a steep descent on the opposite side of the valley. The green lane that snaked down towards the Dove was called Marty Lane, but was still known locally as 'the old salt way'. From here it headed up on to the limestone plateau, then over the Derbyshire hills towards the towns of Monyash and Bakewell, and onwards to Chesterfield.

When he'd done a complete circuit, he found Luke Irvine waiting for him.

'Ben, uniforms have been calling on the houses in Pilsbury,' said Irvine. 'It didn't take them long.'

'And?'

'Well, we've got some witnesses.'

Cooper turned to Irvine with automatic interest, then stopped himself.

'Shouldn't you be telling DS Fry this?' he said.

'She's not here,' pointed out Irvine.

'Fair enough.'

'They're just down in Pilsbury.'

'Okay, we'll go and talk to them.'

'By the way, I was thinking about the Sandra Blair case,' said Irvine. 'Last night in the pub.'

'Is that what you spend your time doing when you're in the pub?' asked Cooper.

'Not usually.'

'I'm glad to hear it.'

Irvine explained to Cooper his idea based on the Agatha Christie plot.

'A conspiracy?' said Cooper. 'More than one perpetrator involved?'

'I know it sounds crazy,' began Irvine.

'No, it's interesting that you thought of it too,' said Cooper.

'Really?'

'A conspiracy? Maybe. Let's hope so, anyway.'

'Why, Ben?'

'Well, every conspiracy needs a network,' said Cooper. 'And every network has a weak link.'

IT SEEMED THAT a party of late-season tourists had been renting a six-bedroom property on the Derbyshire bank of the Dove, an imposing three-storey Georgian house that used to be part of the Knowle estate. When Cooper saw it, he knew it must originally have been the home of someone significant – the estate manager at least, or perhaps an elderly relative of the earl, who had to be given a place to live on the estate but wasn't wanted too close to hand. Premium rental properties came at a high price in the Peak District, even in November. This house probably cost around two thousand pounds a week to rent.

'So what's their story?' asked Cooper as he and Irvine headed down the few yards of track to the hamlet of Pilsbury.

'Some people called Everett rented the property for a birthday celebration and invited three other couples to join them,' said Irvine. 'They're all friends from the Manchester area. Young professionals, you know the type. Too much money to spend on indulging themselves.'

'I've heard of the type,' said Cooper.

'Well, according to local residents, they've been behaving oddly ever since they arrived. They've been wandering around at night in the dark. People have reported hearing raised voices, right through into the early hours of the morning. This is a quiet area, as you can see.'

'That's an understatement.'

Raised voices in the early hours of the morning was normal for the centre of a town like Edendale. But not out here, with only three or four houses and a couple of farms, and a road that nobody ever used on the way to somewhere else.

'Let's go and speak to them,' said Cooper.

Pilsbury was what they called a shrunken village. Though it claimed to date back to Anglo-Saxon times and appeared in the Domesday Book, the few present-day houses were late-seventeenth or early-eighteenth century. It might have been a busy little spot in past centuries, he supposed. The castle was built to defend a river crossing that had been an important trade route through Pilsbury. But the centuries had passed it by and history had abandoned it. There were other settlements like this scattered around the landscape, some marked only by the bases for houses and garden plots enclosed by half-defined bankings, buried among hawthorn bushes and limestone outcrops.

There was no answer to the door at the elegant three-storey house in Pilsbury. Cooper peered through the front windows, while Irvine walked round the back and checked the garage.

'It doesn't look occupied,' said Cooper.

'And there are no vehicles. According to what we were told, there should be three cars.'

A farmer passing in a Ford Ranger stopped when he saw them.

'They're gone,' he called. 'Buggered off. Done a bunk.'

'When?'

'Just now. I saw the last bloke going down the road here in his Merc thirty seconds ago.'

'A Mercedes?' asked Cooper.

'Yes, a green Merc.'

'Do you mean they've taken the Hartington road, sir?'

'Yes, but if you hurry—'

Cooper laughed.

'Oh, don't worry,' he said. 'He won't get far.'

The farmer laughed too. 'Aye, daft sod. He left the first gate open. He couldn't stop long enough to close it behind him, I suppose.'

Cooper knew this stretch of road. Wallpit Lane was a gated single-track road between Pilsbury and Hartington, skirting the eastern bank of the Dove. He recalled there were perhaps five or six iron gates across it between here and Hartington, the first of them right here by Pilsbury Farm, which had now been left standing open.

'Why did they run, do you think?' asked Irvine as they passed through the first gate.

'Presumably they saw all the police activity,' said Cooper.

'Guilty consciences?'

'Yep.'

'Shall I call it in? We can get units to intercept him in Hartington?'

'No need. Ten to one we catch up with him before that.'

'If you say so, Ben.'

'Well, look – it's a gated road. I don't suppose they're used to them in Manchester.'

Like so many arrangements in the Peak District, the method of closing these gates was a bit random. Some used short lengths of rusted metal bent into a hook to catch the upper bars of the gate. Others relied on a loop of rope to go over the top of the post. One or two were hung so that their own weight kept them open. The rest had to be wedged just right against a strategically placed lump of limestone. You didn't get to make a quick getaway on this road.

When Cooper came round the next bend, he saw the green Mercedes stopped fifty yards ahead. The driver was out of the car and wrestling with a gate that had been closed across the road.

He'd stopped at the gate, only to discover that it swung towards him and his car was in the way, preventing it from opening. The outer bar of the gate was now wedged against his bumper. Cooper could see his mouth moving as he cursed and gesticulated.

The driver turned round and was about get back in to his car to reverse when he saw Cooper's Toyota approaching. His shoulders sagged and he clung to the door of his car with a disgusted look at the bonnet, as if it had let him down somehow.

'The first gate opened away from me,' he said. 'How was I to know this one would be any different? If they're going to put gates across roads like this, there should be a proper system.'

'It isn't fair. Is it, sir?'

'No.'

'Would you be Mr Everett?'

'I suppose so. Who's asking?'

Cooper showed Everett his ID. 'Shall we go back to the house for a while, sir?'

ONCE INSIDE THE house he could see that the group had definitely tried to leave in a hurry. The main lounge was in a state of disarray, with cushions knocked off the sofa and drawers left open. It looked as though the house had been searched by a fairly incompetent burglar.

As they were passing down the hall Cooper stopped and looked into the kitchen, where he could see washing-up left piled in the sink. A silver tray stood out from the rest of the dirty pans and used plates. He turned it over and saw faint traces of a white residue on the smooth base.

'Are you coming, Ben?' said Irvine.

'In a second.'

Cooper pressed the pedal on a bin next to the kitchen units. Among the waste he saw some tiny clear bags, a set of discarded drinking straws and a small plastic rectangle carrying the name of a nightclub in Manchester.

Marcus Everett was leaning against a marble fireplace, trying to look casual and relaxed. He was lean and well groomed, and as Cooper entered he ran a hand over his blond hair to smooth it back.

'Is this your first visit to the area, sir?' asked Cooper.

'No, we were here in September and we really loved it. That's why we came back with a few friends.'

'What did you do in September?'

'We went out with our guns and shot some pheasant.'

'Did you? What day was this?'

'It was the second week in September.' Everett smiled at his expression. 'Oh, don't worry. The Glorious Twelfth was well past.'

'Yes, it might have been,' said Cooper. 'But the twelfth of August is the start of grouse shooting season. It isn't open season for pheasant until October first. So your shooting expedition was still illegal.'

Everett opened his mouth to laugh and seemed to be about to make a smart reply. Then he remembered who he was speaking to.

'Well ... you know,' he said, 'it was just a few brace of pheasant. They won't make any difference. Everyone takes a bird for the pot here or there.'

Cooper didn't smile, though he'd shot a few brace of pheasant himself. Once October first had passed, those birds lived in jeopardy every minute of their lives.

'I thought perhaps you didn't like the Peak District,' he said.

'No, it's great. You have a beautiful area here, Detective Sergeant Cooper. We all love it. We tell our friends how great it is.'

'So why were you leaving so early, sir? I understand you had the property booked for a few more days yet.'

'Oh, the weather hasn't been too good, you know. A bit disappointing. And business to do back in Manchester...'

'And perhaps the stash ran out?' said Cooper.

'I beg your pardon?'

'You and your friends were in such a hurry that you didn't spend enough time cleaning up,' said Cooper. 'You've left some paraphernalia in the kitchen. It's funny. I would have expected you to use a credit card and rolled-up fifty-pound notes for snorting the coke. That would have been more in keeping with the image. But the silver tray for cutting the lines is a nice touch.'

'I don't know what you mean.'

Cooper shrugged. 'Shall I make a call? Then we can just sit here and chat while we wait for the sniffer dog to arrive. They're very good at locating traces of drugs.'

Everett went pale and smoothed his hair again. 'Is all this really necessary, Detective Sergeant? I have a good job, a nice house, a family. I'm a law-abiding citizen.'

'Then perhaps you'd like to cooperate a bit more.'

Everett sighed. 'Look, I'm sorry we decided to leave in a hurry. I realise it might have looked a bit suspicious. But my friends were freaked out by the sight of all the police cars. We had a quick conference and decided to call it a day. I suppose some of the locals have been talking about us. We just came here to have a bit of fun, though. We weren't doing any harm.'

'I'm interested in what you were doing late at night,' said Cooper. 'I hear you were outside into the early hours of the morning. Is that right? Even in November?'

'We're a hardy bunch in Manchester.' Everett laughed. 'You ought to see the kids out clubbing in Deansgate, dressed as if they're going to the beach with six inches of snow on the ground.'

'Were you out every night?'

Everett reached for a cigarette case in his pocket, looked at Cooper and pushed it back.

'Pretty much,' he said.

'Did you and your friends happen to go up as far as the castle?'

'Castle? Oh, up there on the mounds? No, it was too much of a climb for us when … I mean, in the dark. We liked it down by the river, just sitting in the dark watching the stars. You don't see the stars much in the city.'

'Do you know anybody in this area?'

'No. Why would we?'

Everett was starting to look a bit more confident now. He'd decided that Cooper wasn't going to do anything about the drugs paraphernalia or call in the sniffer dog.

'Anyway,' he said, 'there are other people out at night around here. You might want to wonder what they're up to, rather than persecuting people who are just having a good time.'

'What people?'

'We saw them going up there one night,' said Everett. 'To the castle.'

'How many of them?'

'At least two. There were two cars, so it must have been at least a couple of people. Now, you can bet they were up to no good.'

'What night was this?' asked Cooper.

'Er, I couldn't say exactly. It was a few days ago.'

'Could it have been last Thursday?'

'Yes, I suppose it could have been.'

'You saw at least two people going up? But how many coming down?'

Everett looked blank. 'It was probably too late for us by then.'

'Oh, I see,' said Cooper. 'Too late for you to remember anything.'

Chapter Twenty-five

DIANE FRY HAD found herself in Taddington, without really knowing where she was. She'd followed Luke Irvine's advice and taken the Flagg road. It was the sort of back road she would normally avoid, but it seemed to have worked.

Several officers were already in Taddington at the Redfearns' house and knocking on doors. A family liaison officer was in the house with George Redfearn's daughter, waiting for the wife to arrive. DC Becky Hurst and DC Gavin Murfin were both here too. They looked unsure what do when they saw Fry arrive.

'Anything useful so far?' she said.

Murfin shrugged and grunted. But Hurst seemed to make a different decision.

'The daughter has no idea what her father might have been doing or who he was meeting,' she said. 'But there's a lady across the road worth speaking to. The house with the blue door. She has an interesting bit of information. Gavin has spoken to her already.'

'Thank you, Becky.'

Fry walked across the road. The neighbour was agog with curiosity at all the activity. Some people got impatient when they were asked to repeat a story they'd already told, but this lady was only too eager.

'Yes, we had a man round here asking questions,' she said. 'He was a property enquiry agent.'

'What's one of those?' asked Fry.

'He said he was making enquiries on behalf of a prospective house purchaser. He wanted to know what the neighbourhood was like, whether it was quiet, how many children there were living in the area. That sort of thing.'

'Did he ask questions about your neighbours?'

She looked a bit embarrassed. 'Well, I'm not sure he asked questions about them exactly, but I suppose I might have ended up telling him a few things. There's always a bit of gossip in a village like this.'

'About the Redfearns, for example.'

'I didn't give away any secrets,' she protested. 'I only told him things that everyone around here knows.'

'Of course. Did you happen to get a name for this man?'

'I'm not daft. I asked him for his identity.' She put a hand to her mouth. 'Oh, he left me a business card. I forgot to tell the other police officer that.'

'Can I see it, please?'

'Give me a minute and I'll find it for you. It's around here somewhere.'

'Thank you.'

But she didn't go straight away to look for the card.

'Did I do something wrong?' she asked.

'Not so far,' said Fry. 'But you might be more careful about who you talk to in future.'

When she'd seen the card, Fry called Ben Cooper. She guessed he would still be at Pilsbury trying to sniff out a lead of his own.

'There's a job I'd like you to do,' she said. 'I think you'd be the best person for it.'

IT WAS ONE of the most remote farmsteads in the area. Even the narrow back road over the eastern slope of the moor seemed like the back of beyond. Cooper had reached a point on the road where he could see nothing in any direction except vast expanses of exposed moorland and lots more hills in the distance to the north.

And this was the spot where he had to turn off. He found a cattle grid and a muddy entrance to a track, which wandered away over the brow of the moor, apparently leading nowhere. He wouldn't have known it was the right place, except for a small sign on the fence. Bagshaw Farm.

'What was this man's name?' Cooper had asked Fry.

'Daniel Grady. Do you know him?'

'Why on earth should I?'

'Well, you always seem to know everyone.'

'Not this one.'

Cooper followed the potholed track between swathes of rough grazing land, where clumps of coarse grass battled with heather and whinberry for survival in a harsh environment. One patch of ground seemed to have been levelled and seeded for some purpose – possibly for use by hang-gliders, given the air currents funnelling in from Axe Edge.

As he crested the rise the track took a wide swing to the left and a view opened out into the valley and across to the Staffordshire hills. Suddenly, right in front of him, he saw the Dragon's Back, appearing much closer than he'd expected. But still he seemed to be heading nowhere. A scatter of stones on a prominent mound could have been the remains of a wall, an old farm building, or something much more ancient and mysterious.

And there, below him on the western slope, was Bagshaw Farm itself. Two houses surrounded by a sprawling cluster of barns, sheds and outbuildings. The track took another couple of swings before it skirted along a wall past more fertile looking in-bye land and reached the farm entrance.

As Cooper turned in he was surprised by the number of vehicles parked in the yard and in front of one of the biggest sheds. They were mostly pick-up trucks and Land Rovers, but there were a few muddy saloon cars too, parked up between trailers and farm equipment.

He'd seen this sort of thing before – an unnatural amount of activity at an isolated farm like this was sometimes a warning sign. Who knew what kind of activities went on here, where no one would see them? It could be something perfectly innocent, of course. But it would be worthwhile keeping his eyes and ears open while he was at Bagshaw Farm.

He found Daniel Grady in an office in the newer of the two houses. He pretty much matched the description that Fry had obtained from the Redfearns' neighbour in Taddington. There was nothing outstanding about him. He was average height, with medium brown hair cut short, but not too short. Aged in his mid-thirties, perhaps forty or so – it was difficult to tell. Dressed in an unremarkable suit, he was clean shaven, with a hint of a stoop and a very courteous manner. He could have been purpose-designed for the job of asking questions without attracting suspicion.

Cooper glanced around the office. It was lined with shelves full of colour-coded box files. Two filing cabinets stood behind the door, and Grady had squeezed in a desk with a laptop and printer. More equipment was in the corner. Cooper spotted a desktop scanner and a digital camera with a long lens.

'You're a property enquiry agent, sir?' he said. 'I've never heard of that profession.'

'It's a new idea,' said Grady with a smug smile. 'An entrepreneurial opportunity. We all know that one of the most important factors in living a peaceful and contented life in a new home is what sort of neighbours you have. Yet there's no established way of finding anything out about your neighbours before you actually commit yourself to buying a house. That's where I come in.'

He produced one of his cards and handed it to Cooper. It was headed by a logo showing a rose-covered cottage and the slogan 'Who will you be living next door to?'

'When you're considering a new property, the estate agent won't tell you anything about the neighbours in the sales details,' said Grady. 'They'll list the local schools, the transport links, the nearest golf course. But they don't mention what the people next door are like. Among all those checks and searches your solicitors do into planning permissions and rights of way and mining subsidence, there's no background check on the local residents.'

'But there's a questionnaire,' said Cooper.

Grady switched on a smile. 'Oh, are you thinking of buying a house?'

'Not at the moment. Well, not any more.'

For a moment Grady's smile almost slipped. 'Ah. Well, yes, you do have a questionnaire filled in by the vendor. "Have you had any disputes with neighbours during the past five years?" But what seller in their right mind would answer "yes" to that and jeopardise their own sale? By the time you've completed the purchase, exchanged contracts and moved in, it's much too late. When you find out the horrible truth, you're stuck with those neighbours that you knew nothing about.'

'I see.'

Grady nodded eagerly as he got into the swing of his sales pitch. 'We're filling that gap in the market, providing an essential service for prospective house buyers. Come to us and we'll tell you what your future neighbours are like. We're totally independent and objective, too.'

Cooper waited until he'd wound down.

'You're just a snooper, aren't you?' he said.

Now Grady looked disappointed. 'That's rather harsh, Detective Sergeant Cooper. Background checks are perfectly common these days in other fields. You can't get a job in teaching or childcare, or work as a volunteer for some charities, without having to go through a Criminal Records Bureau check.'

'That's true.'

'The Church of England won't let you do the flower arrangements in your local church without a pass from the CRB. Nobody objects to that. So why shouldn't we gather some basic information about the people we're going to be living next door to?'

'But what sort of information are you collecting? You're just an ordinary member of the public. You don't have access to criminal records.'

'Absolutely. That would be illegal.'

'So?'

'I'm sure you don't expect me to reveal my methods, Detective Sergeant.'

'Of course, if we should find during our enquiries that anything you're doing *is* unlawful...'

Grady held up his hands. 'My conscience is clear. Look, my hands are clear. Do your worst, Detective Sergeant.'

'So who were you working for when you were asking questions in Taddington recently?'

Grady smiled again and Cooper knew what the answer would be before he spoke. He'd heard it almost as often as 'no comment' in an interview room.

'Client confidentiality,' said Grady. 'I'm sure you understand. We could hardly be giving out that sort of information.'

'You were specifically asking questions about Mr and Mrs Redfearn of Manor House, Taddington. Mr Redfearn is now the subject of a murder inquiry.'

'No, I gathered intelligence about a number of residents in that area. If you check, you'll soon be able to confirm that.'

Cooper had no doubt Grady had covered himself in that respect. Whatever else he was, he seemed to be a professional who knew his job. The team in Taddington would find that he'd visited several properties and made a point of asking about neighbours other than the Redfearns. Once he'd collected a snippet of information from one person, he could give the impression he was enquiring about someone else entirely.

Grady must have a special knack that enabled him to get people to talk freely. Cooper wished he knew what that knack was. It definitely wasn't working for him. Perhaps being a police officer didn't help. He ought to suggest to Superintendent Branagh that they might employ Daniel Grady to conduct a training course for detectives in E Division.

'Will you tell us who your client is?' he asked. It was a futile attempt, but he had to try. There was no way of forcing the information out of Grady.

'I have lots of clients,' said Grady. 'Fortunately, business is doing very well, though it's early days. Actually, I hadn't considered working for the police as a consultant, but we could discuss terms if you're interested. You do have my card.'

Cooper looked more closely at the small print at the bottom of the business card.

'EVE,' he said. 'You're working for Eden Valley Enquiries.'

'I'm an associate,' said Grady. 'I'm establishing a separate division under the EVE corporate umbrella.'

Cooper looked out of the window at the activity in the yards around the farm.

'Would property enquiries be your only business, sir?' he asked.

'It's my most recent enterprise,' said Grady cautiously. 'I do have other interests.'

'So is this a working farm?'

'Of course.'

'You seem to have a lot of employees.'

Grady followed his glance. 'Not mine. I rent this house from the owner of the farm. I think there's an engineer here to do some repairs on the machinery or something. And I've heard they have a rat problem in some of the fields. The farm manager has organised a few men for a vermin control exercise today. I believe that would explain the dogs and the shotguns.'

'Yes.'

Cooper was used to seeing dogs and shotguns. He was wondering more about what was in the back of the vans. They had no names written on the sides and their rear windows had been painted over. But he had no justification for checking the vehicles and he couldn't think of a pretext right now. Grady's explanation was perfectly logical.

Outside, Cooper didn't head straight back to the car. He was watching a man with a dark, bushy moustache which drooped in the traditional Mexican style. Cooper felt sure he recognised the moustache, if not the face of the owner. But it took him a few minutes before he was able to make the connection. And no wonder, when the context was so different. The last time he'd seen this man, he was a Confederate soldier.

Cooper had been to a country and western night one Saturday in the social club at Sterndale Moor, just a few miles from here. There had been a shoot-out with .22 air rifles, rebel flags round the dance floor and people dressed as cowboys and US marshals. On stage had been Hank T or Monty Montana, or someone like that. Members of the club performed the American Trilogy, folding the flag and singing 'I Wish I Was in Dixie' for the South and 'Glory, Glory' for the North.

Sterndale Moor was an odd place, nothing like Earl Sterndale or any of the other villages in the area. He wouldn't be able to remember the name of the man with the Mexican moustache, but he might be able to find him in Sterndale Moor.

Cooper filed the idea away for future reference as he drove back up the track from Bagshaw Farm and on to Axe Edge Moor.

Chapter Twenty-six

LATER THAT DAY the Home Office forensic pathologist Doctor Juliana van Doon reported the results of her post-mortem examination on Sandra Blair. And the conclusion wasn't what anyone had expected.

Ben Cooper drove across town to the mortuary as soon as he heard. Yet when he pulled into the car park he saw that Diane Fry's black Audi was already there. She'd arrived before him.

'Damn,' he said to himself as he parked. 'Is there no escaping her?'

He hurried into the mortuary. Fortunately, Fry had only just walked through the doors. He caught her up as she walked down the corridor. She turned without surprise at the sound of his footsteps.

'Ben,' she said.

'We must stop meeting like this.'

She didn't smile. 'We might as well hear the results together.'

'Well, since we're both here…'

Cooper hadn't seen the pathologist for a while. It struck him that she, too, might be getting close to retirement age. For years she'd

hardly seemed to change in appearance, but suddenly she was looking older and more tired. The creases had deepened around her eyes
and she'd allowed her hair to turn a natural grey. And of course
Mrs van Doon barely took the trouble to hide her impatience with
irritating police officers who infested her post-mortem room.

The room itself was all polished stainless steel and gleaming tiles,
the smell of disinfectant hardly masking the odour of dead flesh
and internal organs. The walls echoed strangely whenever someone
spoke, as if the faint voices of the dead were answering them.

The pathologist tapped a scalpel thoughtfully against a
stainless-steel dish, a familiar habit that seemed to help her focus
her thoughts, or perhaps restrain her irritation. The metallic tone
reverberated in the room, stilling the ghostly voices for a moment.

'This individual died of natural causes,' said Mrs van Doon.
'She suffered a myocardial infarction, causing cardiac arrest. In
other words she had a heart attack.'

'She's not a murder victim, then?' said Fry.

Cooper couldn't tell from her face whether she was disappointed or relieved. He would have given a lot to know which of
the two reactions lay behind that controlled expression of hers.

'It's not for me to say. Well, it's theoretically possible for someone to deliberately cause a heart attack in their victim. But personally I've never heard of such a case. And there's certainly no
evidence of it from my examination of this female. Perhaps at the
crime scene?'

'Unfortunately not,' said Cooper.

'Ah.'

'The head injury?'

'Well, it could have been due to an assault. But on the other
hand it's also consistent with a fall on to rocks, say.'

'She was found lying on stones in the river, beneath the bridge.'

The pathologist nodded. 'Yes, the level of impact would be about the same. There would have been quite a lot of blood. The scalp bleeds heavily, even from a minor laceration. But if she was in the river, I expect the water washed the blood away.'

'And there was no blood on the bridge itself.'

'We thought she might have been killed on the bank and pushed into the river,' said Fry. 'But this would explain why we never found a blood trail.'

'There are some small lacerations on the hands,' said the pathologist, 'and one on the left temple. But they wouldn't have bled very much.'

'On her hands? Defensive injuries, possibly?'

'Only if someone was attempting to beat her with a bunch of twigs.'

Cooper nodded reluctantly. 'Scratches from the undergrowth, I suppose.'

'That's more likely.'

Mrs van Doon pushed back a stray hair from her face. She was still wearing a green apron and a medical mask, but she'd peeled off her gloves. The skin of her hands looked dry, with the faint suggestion of incipient liver spots.

'So,' she said, 'otherwise we have a well-nourished Caucasian female. From her physical condition, I would estimate her age to be in the late thirties.'

'She was thirty-five,' said Fry.

The pathologist raised an eyebrow. 'Some people do lie about that sort of thing, I believe. Though perhaps she just had a difficult life.'

'Perhaps.'

'I've recorded a height of one hundred and sixty-eight centimetres and a weight of seventy-eight kilos. Rather overweight, according to the standard body mass index. But then, aren't we all?'

Cooper thought Mrs van Doon wasn't an ounce overweight – quite the opposite, in fact. And Diane Fry had never been a woman who looked as though she had a good appetite. But he knew better than to comment, or even move a muscle in his face.

'This individual has never given birth to a child,' said the pathologist. 'Apart from the signs of coronary heart disease, which she ought really to have been aware of, she was in reasonable physical condition. She probably had a poor diet and an unhealthy lifestyle. It's an old story. And that's all I can tell you really, apart from…'

'What?'

She looked from Cooper to Fry and back again, perhaps trying to work out which of them she ought to be reporting the information to. She compromised by looking away, her eyes resting instead on the still, sheeted form of Sandra Blair.

'Well, when we did the toxicology tests,' said the pathologist, 'it transpired that this female had substantial amounts of cannabis and alcohol in her blood. It's impossible to say for certain, of course – but in my opinion they might have contributed to her death.'

LUKE IRVINE AND Becky Hurst looked as though they might have been having one of their disagreements. They knew better than to argue when their DS was in the office, but they got on each other's nerves too much to hide it sometimes. Gavin Murfin was lurking in the background, pretending to hear nothing, wrapped up in his world, probably thinking about the next meal break.

'That's a shock. You don't think of women in their thirties having heart attacks, do you?' said Irvine, when Cooper delivered the post-mortem results on Sandra Blair.

'It depends on what she had to put up with during her life,' said Hurst with a sharp look.

Irvine shrugged. 'Well, she didn't have any children or anything.'

'It wasn't children I was thinking of.'

Cooper intervened. 'If she had heart disease, it was probably hereditary,' he said. 'It seems academic now anyway.'

He looked round for Murfin, who seemed to have been spending a lot of time on the phone in the last couple of days. Cooper wasn't even sure it was anything to do with his job. And it wasn't like Gavin to be so shy and reticent.

'Anything from you, Gavin?' said Cooper.

Murfin reluctantly heaved himself out of his chair and came forward with his notebook.

'Yes, house to house enquiries have picked up some sightings of Sandra Blair on the day she died,' he said.

'Really? Share them with us, then.'

Murfin flipped back a page or two. 'After she left work at the Hartdale tea rooms, she was seen near the cheese factory in Hartington, though we can't confirm whether she called in any of the shops in the village. Later that afternoon she was seen again, this time a few miles away in Longnor General Stores buying a copy of the *Leek Post and Times*.' He looked up, with a ghost of a smile. 'That snippet is thanks to our friends across the border in Staffordshire.'

'Cross-border cooperation working then, Gavin?'

'Up to a point.'

'Longnor?' said Irvine. 'How would she get there?'

'It isn't far from her home in Crowdecote,' said Cooper. 'Less than a mile, I should think. She could easily have walked there and been picked up in Longnor.'

'But by who?'

'That's something I'd like to know.'

MAUREEN MACKINNON HAD arrived from Dunfermline and confirmed the identity of her sister. Though she'd been interviewed, Mrs Mackinnon had been unable to offer any particularly useful information. She could only describe Sandra's interest in a wide range of activities since the death of her husband Gary five years ago.

'We all thought it was a good thing for her to have so many interests,' she said. 'Especially when she was on her own. It stops you brooding, doesn't it? Sandra was into handicrafts and nature. She took a lot of walks. And, well … there were more esoteric things that personally I didn't understand. She was a very spiritual girl.'

According to her sister, Sandra had occasionally complained of pains, but was under the impression she suffered from heartburn. She sometimes mentioned sweating excessively and feeling dizzy. But Sandra simply treated herself with a variety of herbal remedies. She never worried that they might be signs of heart problems, said Maureen. And then, a little guiltily, she remembered that their grandfather had died of a heart attack, and perhaps a cousin too. So there was a family history, after all.

When pressed, Mrs Mackinnon admitted that her sister might have used cannabis occasionally. So she knew about that. But she had no idea of the existence of a boyfriend, if there was one. And sisters normally told each other these things, didn't they?

DIANE FRY WALKED into the CID room. She seemed to have appropriated a spare desk as her own for a while. But it hardly mattered. There were always spare desks in every department at West Street these days. Cooper wondered where she'd been since they left the mortuary together.

'So what about our second victim, Mr Redfearn?' said Fry, when she'd brought herself up to date with the latest developments. 'Mrs van Doon says we won't have her post-mortem report until tomorrow. But there must be something to go on. Time of death, for a start.'

She looked expectantly around the room.

'The FME says three days,' said Becky Hurst at last.

'What? Since he died?'

'Yes.'

'That makes it Thursday night,' said Cooper. 'It's only an estimate, of course…'

'I know.'

'There hasn't been a missing person report,' added Irvine. 'We've contacted Mr Redfearn's company here in Edendale and they say they weren't expecting him in the office today, so they weren't concerned about his absence.'

'What about his family?'

'He has a wife, Molly, but she's been away on a shopping trip with some friends in Paris. According to Mr Redfearn's secretary, it was a regular pre-Christmas trip that Mrs Redfearn took every year. It seems the husband regarded it as a bit of a break for himself too.'

'How long has she been away?' asked Fry.

'Since last Thursday. She's due back in the country tomorrow.'

'She must have tried to call him during that time, surely?'

'Well...'

Fry stared at Irvine. 'Don't you think so, Luke?'

Irvine glanced at Cooper. 'Well, perhaps not. It depends what sort of marriage they had, doesn't it? If they've been together for a long time, I mean...'

'What are you saying, Luke?' put in Hurst in a challenging tone.

Immediately, Irvine became defensive. 'You know – absence not only makes the heart grow fonder, it can be essential to keep a relationship going.'

'So they were happier when they were apart?'

'I'm just suggesting that some people are. A break from each other for a few days. She goes shopping with the girlfriends. He can go off and play golf, or whatever. It suits both parties. You must have heard about that sort of arrangement.'

Hurst frowned. 'Well, I suppose so.'

Cooper didn't want to believe it either, but he knew it was true. No one really understood what went on in other people's relationships.

'Besides, everyone knows the spouse is top of the suspect list in a murder inquiry,' said Irvine, as if playing a trump card.

'Not in this case – you've just told us she wasn't even in the country at the time.'

'Never heard of a contract killing? The Redfearns are well-off. She could afford someone good, instead of just some low-life off the street.'

Cooper nodded. It was a possibility they would have to cover, even if it seemed unlikely at this stage.

'We'll need to get Mrs Redfearn in as soon as she arrives,' he said.

'To confirm ID on the body?' said Hurst. 'It won't be very pleasant for her. Couldn't we do it from photographs?'

'That might be better,' agreed Cooper.

So the body of George Redfearn had lain at Pilsbury Castle for three days. Even in the best of circumstances a human body rapidly became difficult to identify. There was little point in expecting family members to make a visual identification of their loved one's remains after they'd been lying out in the open for an extended period of time. Fire, explosion or long-term immersion in water worked even more quickly to destroy any recognisable features. Identification then came down to more scientific measures – DNA comparisons or forensic odontology to confirm identity from the teeth.

Cooper recalled that Mr Redfearn's body had already started to look badly bloated when it was found. Even after twenty-four hours, when the remains had cooled to the temperature of the environment, the skin of the head and neck turned greenish-red and discolouration began to spread across the rest of the torso. The facial features could become quite unrecognisable.

Fortunately, the weather had been cold and this body was exposed to the air. But once bacteria started to dissolve the tissues, gases formed blisters on the skin, and the body swelled grossly and began to leak. In another day or two it would no longer have looked human.

Fry turned towards Cooper. 'So what connection are we making between these individuals, if there is one?' she said.

'I don't know, Diane. We haven't found one yet.'

'I presume you're looking?'

'Of course we're looking. What do you think we're doing – sitting around on our backsides with our thumbs in our mouths waiting for someone to come all the way from Nottingham and tell us how to do our jobs?'

She raised an eyebrow and Cooper's anger subsided.

'But you haven't found anything,' said Fry calmly.

He sighed deeply. 'Not yet, no. It's difficult to point to any significant similarities. Whether deliberately or accidentally, both victims seem to have fallen far enough for the impact to be fatal.'

'It hardly constitutes a pattern.'

'Not on its own, no,' agreed Cooper. 'Apart from that … well, the victims aren't even the same age or gender. True, they're both white and ethnically British, but—'

'But the ethnic minority population in this area is – what? Two per cent?' said Fry.

'About that.'

'It's hardly a multicultural melting pot, is it? So your killer would have to try really, really hard if he wanted to find a black or Asian victim. As far as the evidence goes, these individuals could just have been chosen at random.'

'Random,' said Cooper. 'I hate random.'

'I know. Me too.'

Those were always the burning questions. Not how the murderer committed the crime, but what motivated him or her to take those specific, drastic measures.

'But you still think the two incidents are linked?' said Fry.

'Yes, I do.'

When Cooper told her the story of the Bowden burial ground, Fry couldn't help herself. Her reaction was accompanied by a cynical laugh.

'Your friend Meredith Burns didn't mention the graveyard, did she? *Just general envy*, she said.'

'That was wrong of her,' agreed Cooper.

'Trying to avoid bad publicity for the earl, I imagine.'

'But they reported the incidents – including the graffiti. They must have known questions would be asked.'

'Wait a minute, though. Burns said the graffiti was discovered by one of the staff before the first visitors arrived on Friday.'

'Yes, she did.'

'Well, what if that wasn't the case? What if members of the public saw that graffiti before it was covered up? It would be too late to keep it quiet then. They would have been talking about it all over the area by the end of the day. Some of the visitors would have been taking photographs of it on their phones.'

Cooper nodded. Fry was probably right. He could hear the discussion that might have gone on in the estate office.

'So they decided to make a pre-emptive call,' he said. 'Damage limitation.'

'And I bet they thought it had worked. A visit from the Neighbourhood Policing Team, probably a PCSO making a few notes for her report and tutting sympathetically. Burns said they didn't expect anything to come of the visit. She meant they were *hoping* nothing would come of it. She really didn't want to see us turning up at the abbey. Though she put a good show on, I'll give her credit for that. Ms Burns had you more interested in looking at the nursery than enquiring into any reason for the incidents.'

'That's not true,' protested Cooper, aware that he was starting to flush, feeling the familiar discomfort that Diane Fry was so easily able to provoke in him.

'And now the murder of Mr Redfearn,' she said. 'If there's no evident connection between the two individuals, why do you insist on believing these two incidents are linked?'

'Oh, that's easy,' said Cooper. 'Because of the Corpse Bridge.'

ON HIS DESK Cooper found the leaflets that Meredith Burns had given him on Saturday. He put aside the one advertising the Halloween Night and opened the leaflet about the attractions of Knowle Abbey.

For a few minutes he read about its claim to historic associations and the generations of Manbys who'd lived there. He skipped through the stuff about antique furniture and fascinating collections of curiosities, turned the page on details of the restaurant and the craft centre, and the walled nursery. Then he reached a few paragraphs about the extensive parkland on the Knowle estate.

Finally, he dropped the leaflet back on his desk with an exasperated groan.

'How could I have been so stupid?' he said.

'What is it, Ben?' asked Irvine in surprise.

'Grandfather,' said Cooper.

'What?'

'*Meet Grandfather, 1am.* It's not a person. It's a place.'

Chapter Twenty-seven

'THE FAMILY TEND to refer to him as the Old Man of Knowle,' said Meredith Burns as she led the way from the estate office at the abbey. 'It's a traditional Manby joke, I think. A reference to the previous earl. The "old man", you know?'

Cooper nodded. 'Yes, I see,' he said.

As he and Diane Fry followed Burns along the signposted trail into the parkland, Cooper reflected that the old Derbyshire lead miners had often talked about 't'owd man' too. But they'd meant something quite different. They'd usually been referring to the Devil.

But who knew what went on in a family like the Manbys? In any family, in fact. Perhaps there was more than a coincidence in the similarity between the miners' superstition and the way the Manbys referred to the old earl. That portrait of the seventh Lord Manby in the Great Hall made him look a real tyrant. And when had Knowle Abbey begun to deteriorate so much? Had a previous owner neglected its maintenance, while spending his fortune on something else entirely? That would be enough to cause some degree of resentment among his descendants when they inherited a crumbling estate up to its chimneys in debt.

They'd entered the edge of the trees, and as the trail took a sharp bend they lost sight of the buildings they'd just come from.

'I don't like forests,' said Fry. 'You ought to know that by now.'

'This is hardly a forest,' said Cooper. 'It's landscaped parkland. Some previous earl obviously planted a few trees to create a view from the east wing.'

'But you said there are wild animals.'

'Roe deer. They're far more frightened of you than you are of them, Diane.'

Fry didn't look convinced. But he knew no animals would come near her, if they could help it. She was hardly Snow White, attracting wild creatures to feed trustingly from her hand. She was more the kind of person who would introduce a badger cull, then willingly extend it to include anything that moved in the dark.

'One of the great things about these big trees is that they make such wonderful landmarks,' Burns was saying. 'You might not be able to find your way through a wood where all the trees are the same age and look identical. But anyone can find this grand old chap.'

'And lots of people do, I suppose?' said Cooper.

'Oh, he's a tourist attraction in his own right. We have signs on all the trails to point the way to him. Visitors love to come and stand underneath his branches and have their photos taken, or see how many of them it takes to reach all the way round his trunk. British people have a very affectionate relationship with this particular species.'

'Do they?' said Fry.

Cooper laughed. Her horrified expression suggested she was imagining a much more intimate relationship than anything Burns had meant.

'There he is,' said Burns. 'The Grandfather Oak.'

The Old Man of Knowle, or the Grandfather Oak, was a thousand-year-old oak tree. Its status as a unique tourist attraction was the reason it was mentioned in the leaflets about Knowle Abbey.

Cooper paced round the tree. He didn't really know what he was looking for, but he could find none of the things that he might have expected from examining the scene at the Corpse Bridge. No effigy, no noose, no witch ball filled with curses. Not even any graffiti or obscene messages carved into the ancient bark. There were no signs that anyone had been here with malicious intent. And it would be useless to do a forensic search of the woods. Far too many people came through here, leaving signs of their presence.

He looked up into the branches. It would make a great vantage point, he supposed. But these branches were old and brittle. A couple of the larger boughs were propped up by lengths of timber to prevent them from snapping under their own weight. He wouldn't want to try climbing this tree without proper safety equipment.

Cooper turned to look at the abbey. It was barely visible from here. Just a small tower on the south corner in the distance could be glimpsed through the trees.

As they made their way back along the trail, the abbey came into sight again. Cooper spotted a small, slightly overweight figure moving towards the back of the house. He was dressed in wellingtons, mud-spattered jeans, a tweed jacket and a felt hat.

He pointed at the figure.

'Is that...' he began.

'Yes, that was the earl,' said Burns. 'I think Her Ladyship has sent him to do some mucking out in the stables.'

'Who's "Her Ladyship"?' asked Fry.

'The Countess. Lord Manby's wife.'

'Countess? I thought her husband was an earl, not a count?'

'Well, we don't have counts in England any more. They replaced the title with a more Anglo-Saxon version centuries ago.'

'And they never bothered introducing a female form of the new title,' added Cooper.

'Typical.'

Fry dropped back and leaned closer to Cooper when Burns was out of earshot. She waited to be sure that Burns wasn't listening.

'With all the staff he employs,' said Fry, 'don't you think Lord Manby would have someone to do the mucking out for him?'

'I think Meredith was joking,' said Cooper.

'Really?'

'Yes, really. You missed that?'

'I must have done.'

'It was a reference to the way the earl was dressed. Actually, I think she felt a bit embarrassed about us seeing him.'

'Ah. Perhaps he was presenting the wrong image.'

'I believe that was exactly it,' said Cooper.

But as they returned to the estate office, Cooper was wondering why Fry hadn't noticed the significance of the earl's very different appearance, once he was at home and relaxing among his own rolling acres instead of in white tie and tails at a formal occasion. Now Lord Manby looked exactly like the effigy on the Coffin Stone.

In her office Meredith Burns became defensive when Cooper asked about the earl's plans for the church and graveyard at Bowden.

'As I told you, we have to do everything we can to bring in revenue for the maintenance and repair of the abbey,' she said. 'I explained that to you last time you came. The monthly wage bill alone is staggering. The staff is enormous – you'd be surprised how many people there are working here.'

'About three hundred?' said Fry.

Burns was clearly taken aback. 'Yes, around that figure.'

'But you didn't mention the graveyard at Bowden,' said Cooper.

'It's just one of a range of projects,' protested Burns. 'Some of the old staff properties will become holiday lets. We're also hoping to get planning permission to build some new chalet-style units on the western side of the burial ground, within the walls of the park itself. Those units will have a very desirable setting.'

'And there's the church, of course.'

'Yes, and the church will be sold. We've had several expressions of interest, but unfortunately we don't have a confirmed buyer yet.'

'Does it surprise you that many of the people whose family members are buried at Bowden have strong objections to these plans?'

Burns shrugged. 'It was bound to happen. Some of these decisions are painful, but they have to be made. Otherwise what would happen to Knowle?'

She sat down at her desk and stared at a large plan of the Knowle Abbey estate on the wall in front of her.

'You know, at one time, this estate consisted of more than fifty properties and about three thousand acres of parkland and farms,' she said. 'Inheritance tax and divorce settlements have taken their toll over the centuries. But it has to be admitted that much of the decline was due to bad management by successive earls who were more interested in hunting and shooting, or in hosting lavish dinner parties for the local gentry.'

Cooper was satisfied to hear his speculation confirmed. But it was Fry who voiced what he was thinking. She had always been more prone to blurting out her opinions – probably more than was good for her.

'I don't think anyone would be surprised by that,' said Fry.

'I realise it's an image still common among the more ill-informed members of the public,' said Burns.

Fry opened her mouth to object and Cooper thought for a moment he was going to have to intervene in a peacekeeping role. But Burns didn't seem to notice Fry's reaction. She pointed at the map of the estate in front of her.

'When the present earl took over the estate, he launched himself into a whole series of projects,' she said. 'As Walter himself would tell you, he inherited a great many wasted assets and he wanted to make them work for their living. His first idea was the conversion of the old coach house into a restaurant. Then the kitchen gardens were turned into a plant nursery, and a craft shop was created in the joinery workshop. We've recently applied to the county council for a licence to use part of the abbey as a wedding venue. But none of these activities brings in enough money – and as revenue streams they're unpredictable, because they rely on the general public. An extended spell of bad weather could ruin us.'

'Or negative publicity?' asked Cooper.

'Well … quite.'

Cooper recalled the picture postcard view of Knowle Abbey he'd admired from across the river, above the Corpse Bridge.

'What about using the abbey as a location for filming?' he said. 'I've heard that's a thriving business.'

'We've tried, but we're competing with Chatsworth House and Haddon Hall, and a dozen other places in the county. Yes, we benefited a little from the *Downton Abbey* phenomenon. But the last TV crew to visit Knowle were from *Bargain Hunt*. Do you know it?'

'No, I'm sorry.'

'Daytime television, I believe.' She looked at Fry. 'Someone called Tim Wonnacott?'

Fry shook her head too. 'No.'

Burns sighed and gazed at Cooper seriously.

'There's a grand plan to save the Knowle estate,' she said. 'But it needs a massive long-term injection of cash. Somehow we have to find millions and millions of pounds of revenue – and from a consistent source.'

'*DOWNTON ABBEY*,' SAID Fry as they drove out through the parkland in the gathering dusk. 'I've actually seen that one. Is *Homeland* like that?'

'Not exactly like that,' said Cooper. 'Why?'

Fry turned to him. 'Well, just a thought. I was wondering if you remembered that you still have my TV in the boot of your car?'

When Cooper's phone rang a moment later he answered it automatically. But it was bad news.

'Has it just happened?' he said. 'Last night? Why didn't you call me? Well, okay. Yes, I suppose so. Thank you. And, well … I'm really sorry to hear of your loss.'

Cooper ended the call with a curse. 'Damn.'

'What is it?'

'Mrs Shelley,' he said.

'Oh … she's your landlady.'

'She was,' said Cooper. 'But she's dead.'

WHEN HE GOT back to Welbeck Street that evening and let himself into his flat, Cooper was immediately struck by how different it felt.

It made no sense, of course – especially as Dorothy Shelley had been in hospital since Friday. And even when she was living next door, he'd hardly been aware of her presence most of the time. But now that he knew she was dead, it made all the difference. Logic didn't come into it.

As he walked through the rooms he found it quite unnerving how much number eight no longer seemed the same. Deep down he knew the reason for the feeling. Death had crept a little bit too close to his walls, reminding him once again that there was no escape. As if he could forget.

Cooper checked his messages and fed the cat. He dug a chicken and sweetcorn pasta bake from the freezer compartment of his fridge, pierced the foil and slid it into the microwave. Six minutes at full power before it needed stirring. Then he switched on the TV for the news.

As he watched stories about bad weather and a firemen's strike, his mind began to drift. He thought it was odd that Diane Fry should remind him he had her television in the boot of his Toyota, then not ask for it back. She hadn't even arranged a time for him to deliver it to her new apartment in Nottingham, though surely she must be living there now – the old flat in Grosvenor Avenue would be empty and not fit to live in, even for someone with Fry's spartan needs. It was almost as if she'd wanted her TV to stay where it was. Well, he couldn't blame her. There wasn't much worth watching. It wasn't as if she were missing any episodes of *Homeland*. Or even *Bargain Hunt*.

A few minutes later Cooper sat down at the kitchen table with his pasta bake, watched by the cat and trying very hard not to stare at the empty chair opposite him. Liz had planned a big kitchen in their new home, with oak units and marble worktops. Even then her dream had seemed a million miles away from number eight Welbeck Street. And now it was just a half-forgotten fantasy. The reality was this cramped space at the back of a terraced house in an Edendale side street, with a microwave oven and a place set for one.

And this wouldn't last either, not once the new owner of the properties arrived. Cooper considered his options. Perhaps he should start house-hunting again. But the prospect filled him with dread. Every estate agent's window would have too many painful associations. Every set of property details would feel pointless.

When he first moved into this flat from Bridge End Farm, Cooper had never known a silent house in his life. He remembered a foreboding of how depressing, how desperate, and even how frightening it might be to come home every night to a dark and empty house. The post would still be lying on the mat where it had fallen in the morning, a single unwashed coffee mug would be in the sink where he'd left it after breakfast. And the house would have that feel of having got along all day without him, that his existence was unnecessary, maybe even unwelcome.

He recalled that first taste of loneliness now – sour and unexpected, a burst of metallic bitterness at the back of his mouth, like a spurt of blood on his tongue.

As he ate his pasta Cooper gradually tried to nudge his thoughts on to a different track, the way he'd been taught months ago by the grief counsellor. He ran his mind back over the events of the day, seeking some useful insight.

Each of the visits he'd made to Knowle Abbey reminded him that the Manbys' historic mansion was as much out of his comfort zone as it was for Diane Fry, a woman who never seemed truly at home anywhere. There were so many things he didn't understand about the way that place was run. The Right Honourable Walter, Lord Manby of Knowle, was an enigma to him and would probably stay that way. Even if he got a chance to interview the earl, which seemed unlikely, he wouldn't expect to learn anything helpful. Someone like his lordship would undoubtedly be as well practised at putting up a façade as any career criminal protesting his innocence in a court-room. It was all about public perception, letting people see whatever they wanted to see.

Cooper couldn't get the ideas of the coffin roads out of his head. Sandra Blair and the Corpse Bridge were at the centre of everything, he was sure. The discovery of George Redfearn's body had distracted most of the attention today, including his. The post-mortem result on Mrs Blair hadn't helped.

As a consequence his time had been taken up interviewing a middle-class cocaine user and a dodgy enquiry agent, not to mention a giant oak tree. Instead, he should have been trying to find a way of breaking open the group of people Sandra Blair had been involved with. He should have been seeking the weak link he'd mentioned to Luke Irvine.

Cooper could feel his position weakening hour by hour, though. Without more evidence, his justification for concentrating on Sandra Blair and Knowle Abbey was being eroded away and soon his stance would become untenable. And there would be no shortage of people willing to point it out.

As COOPER FINISHED his pasta, Diane Fry was driving through the gates of a modern executive development on the outskirts of Nottingham and drawing up outside her new home. She'd rented a double-bedroom, top-floor apartment with an open-plan lounge and kitchen area, a master bedroom with fitted wardrobes and juliet balcony, and a secure door entry system. The rent was about six hundred pounds a month, but it did have its own parking space. And it was only a stone's throw from the A52 for her commute into the city.

She sat in the car for a few moments and looked at the other properties, with their neat grass verges and the little access roads between them. There was barely a sign of human occupation, but for lights behind curtained windows and a car parked in front of a garage door.

It was amazingly quiet here – much more peaceful than the house in Edendale, with its constant comings and goings, the endless flow of noisy students and migrant workers, the neighbours who wanted to stop and chat in the street, the friendly family in the corner shop who always smiled and asked after her health.

It didn't seem right, really. The city ought to be noisier and livelier than a small country town. But she was in the suburbs here, twenty minutes from the city centre with its pubs and shops and theatres. Suburban life had its own rhythm.

Fry let herself into the apartment, remembering to clear the burglar alarm. It was something she'd never had to do in Edendale. But then, she didn't have anything worth stealing. She'd never felt the urge to surround herself with material possessions. But she lived here now. Perhaps she would feel obliged to go shopping.

She walked to the windows and looked outside. She found herself worrying about where she should put her wheelie bins without making the development look untidy. And she realised with a shock that she must have become middle class.

Fry took off her jacket and dropped her keys on the table. She had to admit that the rooms sounded empty and strange. She turned and looked at the corner of the lounge, where a table stood waiting for her TV set to arrive.

Well, that was one thing that kept her connected to Edendale. There was one small part of her that still hadn't left.

Chapter Twenty-eight

Monday 4 November

IT WAS A typical early morning in November. A frost lay on the ground and a thick mist blanketed the valley. Above the mist the humped backs of Chrome Hill and Parkhouse Hill were lit by the sun, like whales breaking the surface.

Ben Cooper couldn't believe he was out so early. He'd been sleeping better for the past few nights, but this morning he woke so promptly that he was out of the house at dawn. Barely half an hour later he was here on the edge of the county, watching the sun rise.

The very top of Parkhouse Hill felt almost razor sharp. With that vertical drop on one side, you wouldn't want to lose your footing on a day like this. He imagined two people up here together. It would be so easy, wouldn't it? He could see the picture now in his mind and hear the conversation.

'Watch where you're walking. It's slippery.'

'I'm okay.'

'Here, let me hold on to you…'

It wouldn't take much. A quick push, a momentary loss of balance. And the result would be serious injury or even death.

He continued to walk until he'd passed through the mist and emerged into sunlight. With a deep breath, Cooper turned and looked northwards. From here the view was stunning. It fired his imagination like no other vista in the Peak District.

Seen from Parkhouse, Chrome Hill was clearly the body of an ancient dinosaur, a dragon sleeping in the Derbyshire landscape. It was half buried in the ground, its sides covered with grass over the centuries. The dragon was quite clear, and obvious. He could see its ridged back and scaly tail. If he leaned a few yards to the left, he'd be able to make out its massive head. Its belly lay beneath those scrubby trees on the southern flank. The rise and fall of its breathing was almost visible to him.

Cooper saw it all so clearly that he even doubted for a moment if the dragon was sleeping at all. Perhaps it was about to rise to its feet with a roar, angered by his unwelcome presence in its lair.

Because that was what this place must be – a dragon's lair. Parkhouse and Chrome were prehistoric anomalies. One glance told him they belonged to a distant past. They shouldn't exist here, in the twenty-first century. These strange hills were a fragment of some parallel universe, dropped into Derbyshire by a momentary connection between their two worlds. He was standing in reality, but looking at legend.

Cooper found a flat rock and spread out his map. He marked Bowden, with its chapel and graveyard. Then he located the villages to the east. With a bit of guesswork, he could trace the probable routes of the coffin ways from each of those villages, the twists and turns the mourners would have taken to reach the crossing at the Corpse Bridge. One track came over the Pilsbury Hills and skirted the site of the castle as it descended to the river.

Another of the routes had passed through an area now swallowed up by an enormous limestone quarry. It was one of a whole series of quarries still operating south of Buxton – vast holes blasted out of the rock, their cliff faces carved into ledges like Roman amphitheatres, with diggers and dumper trucks that looked like Dinky toys as they trundled backwards and forwards on the roadways below. They were much larger than the disused quarry, the remains of which he could see now behind Knowle Abbey. They had become massive white limestone basins gleaming in the sun, but bowls of choking dust when the machinery was loading crushed stone. That route from Deeplow had once been a public right of way, now diverted at the request of the quarry owners, in an attempt to keep walkers away from the quarry.

And of course there had been a third coffin road, at least. He could see it on the map as it approached the bridge from the north. But where did it originate? It was hard to tell, but it looked as though mourners taking their dead to their final resting place at Knowle must have followed a very tortuous route. Their way had led across an area of ground now marked with a scatter of isolated structures arranged in a pattern unlike any community or industrial site he knew of in the Peak District.

Cooper could recall the Reverend Latham's voice describing the funeral. *The bearers and the funeral party making their way down the hill, resting the coffin, dividing and coming together again across the water.*

But wait a minute. Dividing? Was that what Latham had said? He was quite sure of it. He could hear the words clearly in his head. *Dividing and coming together again across the water.* Did he mean the funeral party? Surely he must have done. But why would they have divided? They stopped and rested the coffin at the bridge, on the stone put there for the purpose. That was to allow the bearers to change over, the men who'd been carrying the coffin down the hill getting a rest and fresh shoulders taking up the load. So what else happened there?

Cooper looked down at the river. As he watched the waters of the Dove splashing and dancing over the stones, he realised what had happened to him. Somehow he must have been infected by Diane Fry's cynicism, inhaled some of her incessant disbelief like carbon monoxide gas leaking from a faulty stove. Her sneering had affected him, despite his instincts. She'd made him feel reluctant to acknowledge those ancient, deep-down beliefs that his ancestors lived with. And not only lived with, but acted on in their daily lives. His forebears believed in spirits – not just as some quaint, archaic superstition, but as a real and present danger in the landscape. If they were told they needed to cross water to block a spirit's path from the grave, that's exactly what they would have done. Not simply on some occasions if it was convenient, but every time, as a necessity.

Cooper turned and looked down towards the Corpse Bridge, hidden in its belt of trees. A body at the bridge, one at Pilsbury Castle. Did it mean there would be more deaths, one on each of the coffin roads?

WHEN COOPER REACHED West Street later that morning his team were already hard at work in the CID room, making him feel a twinge of guilt. He was supposed to be showing qualities of leadership.

'How are things, Gavin?' he asked.

Murfin looked up from his desk. 'Like a bad day at the mortuary,' he said.

'It's going that well?'

'There's good news, though,' said Murfin. 'There's a lass here who's come in to see you. She asked for you specifically too.'

'Who is it?'

'Her name is Poppy Mellor.'

'Mellor,' said Cooper. 'That's interesting. When you say a lass, Gavin?'

Murfin shrugged. 'Twenty-one, maybe.'

'Good.'

POPPY MELLOR SAT nervously in Interview Room One. She looked intimidated by her surroundings, as people often did who had never expected to find themselves in a police station. Looking at her, Cooper thought it had probably taken a lot of courage for her to come here.

She sat with a plastic cup of coffee in front of her on the table. She was staring at it as if she didn't quite know what it was. Cooper could sympathise with that. He'd tasted the liquid that came out of the machine and he couldn't tell what it was either.

'Miss Mellor?' he said. 'I'm Detective Sergeant Cooper. You were asking for me.'

She stood up when he came in, then sat down again suddenly, her legs wobbling and unable to support her properly. She looked relieved when she heard his name.

'Poppy,' she said. 'No one calls me Miss Mellor.'

She was a tall, athletic-looking girl with dark hair, quite pretty in a way, with long hands moving restlessly against each other on the table, her fingers twisting a set of rings. She'd draped a cream jacket casually over the chair and was wearing a white T-shirt with an esoteric design Cooper couldn't place without staring too closely.

'Poppy,' said Cooper, sitting down opposite her. 'I met a lady at the weekend—'

She nodded. 'My great-aunt Caroline. She lives at Bowden.'

'Did she mention me to you?'

'Yes. It's amazing that she remembered your name really. She can be quite vague. You must have made an impression on her.'

Cooper looked at the plastic cup. The coffee had gone cold and a grey skin was forming on the top. It looked disgusting.

'Would you like me to get you another one of those?' he said.

'No. Thank you.'

'I don't blame you.'

He put the cup aside and sat back. She seemed to be relaxing a bit more, but it would be a mistake to push her too hard.

'Take your time, Poppy,' he said. 'Just get it clear in your mind what you want to tell me. There's no rush.'

'Oh, I've thought about it already,' she said. 'I know what I want to say. It's about Rob.'

'Rob Beresford?'

'Yes.'

'He's a friend of yours?'

'Yes.'

'He was part of the scheme, wasn't he? I mean, the whole performance at the Corpse Bridge with the effigy and the noose.'

Poppy looked crestfallen. 'He didn't do much, you know. In fact, he didn't do anything in the end.'

'So what was his role?'

'He was supposed to be the person who found the effigy,' she said. 'He deliberately didn't play any other part. He had no contact with the others beforehand, so that he would just be an innocent person stumbling across the dummy.'

'Why didn't they just leave it for some genuinely innocent person to find?'

Poppy shook her head. 'It might not have been found for weeks, especially if the weather turned bad. And they were worried who might find it. It could have been somebody who didn't bother to report it. It could have been a child. They didn't want to leave that to chance.'

'So the next step was going to be making sure it got as much publicity as possible, I suppose?'

'Yes.'

'They were going to take photos, I imagine?' said Cooper.

'Of course. Carrying a digital camera would have been a bit too suspicious, but Rob was going to take photos and a short video on his iPhone, then pass them on everywhere he could.'

'Local papers?'

'Yes, but Facebook and Twitter too. The video would have gone on YouTube. They were hoping to go viral, he said.'

'It would certainly have drawn attention to the cause.'

Poppy nodded. 'That's what they figured. There was no harm to it really.'

'But it went wrong. What happened?'

'I don't know,' she said. 'And Rob doesn't know either. He wasn't there. Like I said, he had no contact with the others beforehand. They weren't even supposed to have each other's numbers on their phones, just in case. They know you look for things like that.'

'Yes, we do,' admitted Cooper.

'But Rob recognised Sandra, obviously. He didn't see how he could claim otherwise. You would have found out. There was no point in him pretending.'

'We'll need to talk to Rob directly,' said Cooper. 'He'll have to give us a statement.'

'I know. But I didn't want you to go along thinking he's a suspect. He isn't.'

Cooper noted that Poppy Mellor seemed to be under the impression that Sandra Blair was murdered. Did she actually suspect Rob Beresford of being responsible? Was that why she'd felt compelled to come in and tell this story on his behalf? Not so much protecting the innocent, as standing by the guilty?

Well, nothing could be taken at face value – even someone who seemed so genuinely well-intentioned.

'And what was your part in his scheme, Poppy?' asked Cooper.

'Me? I didn't do anything. Rob wanted me to. I thought it was a good cause, protesting against the earl's plans for the holiday cottages and selling off the church. And the car park, of course.'

'Car park?'

'On the burial ground at Bowden. He wants to concrete it over and turn it into a parking area for the holiday lets.'

'I don't think he can do that,' said Cooper.

'Well, it's what they say.'

'Perhaps they do.'

Cooper thought it sounded like a touch of exaggeration, a bit of added propaganda to make the plans sound even worse and cause that extra edge of outrage. Concreting over a graveyard? Who wouldn't object to that?

'When the group first got together they just talked about things,' said Poppy. 'Letting off steam, I suppose. But then they decided to walk all the old coffin roads, as a symbolic gesture. It was on one of the walks they had the idea of a bigger protest. Something more dramatic.'

'Who actually suggested it?'

'Rob says he can't remember.'

'We'll ask him again, of course.'

'He doesn't trust the cops. But he might talk to you.'

Cooper smiled. Well, that was a compliment, he supposed, to be considered not truly a cop.

'Anyway,' said Poppy. 'I couldn't do it. I was supposed to be there that night, according to the plan. But I got scared. I sat in my car for a few minutes and then I drove away and went home.'

'It's nothing to be ashamed of, Poppy.'

'I bottled out. That's what Rob would say.'

'But you've talked to Rob since?'

'Oh, yes. He texted me after it all happened and we met up the next day to talk about it.'

'On Friday.'

'Yes. I tried to persuade him to come in and talk to you, but he wouldn't do it.'

'He won't be happy about you telling me this, then,' said Cooper.

'No, he won't. But it's for the best. I've thought and thought about this, and I'm concerned for him. He didn't do anything wrong, you see. But I'm frightened there are other people in that group who are much worse. From what Rob says, they might be violent.'

'Do you know who the other group members are? Do you have any names?'

She shook her head. 'No, I wasn't that closely involved. I just knew Rob.'

'I see.'

'He's a good guy,' insisted Poppy. 'Really he is. Rob isn't guilty of anything, except trying to protect other people.'

Chapter Twenty-nine

When Poppy Mellor had gone, Cooper thought back to his conversation with Rob Beresford that early morning near the Corpse Bridge. After Halloween night he'd been dog-tired or he might not have missed so much.

While he sat waiting in the police car at the Corpse Bridge, Rob Beresford must have had plenty of time to think things through and consider his position. It would have been obvious to him the victim would soon be identified. The fact that she was known to him would emerge during the investigation. If he hadn't mentioned straight away that he recognised her, it would have looked bad for him when the facts came out. It would certainly have put him under suspicion. Only the guilty made a secret of something like that.

So Beresford had definitely made the sensible decision, coming straight out with it. He must have been worried when Cooper failed to ask him the right question. It was easy in those circumstances to start thinking the police knew more than they actually did. Perhaps Rob Beresford had given Cooper more credit than he deserved. When Beresford blurted out that he knew the victim, it had been one of those moments when you grasped your courage in both hands and took an irrevocable step, when you made a decision there was no going back from. It had almost worked for him, too.

Cooper wondered if it was a sign of another weakness in his own attitude that he'd accepted the likelihood of Rob Beresford and Sandra Blair knowing each other. It was the way things were around here. If you'd lived in one of these villages for a while, you did know everyone. Cooper grew up that way, thinking nothing odd at all in the fact that if you saw a face you didn't know, it would certainly belong to a tourist, someone who would be gone back to their own part of the country next week. Those who belonged to the area were all people he knew, or at least recognised.

So perhaps it should have struck him as too much of a coincidence that Rob Beresford knew Sandra Blair, but it didn't at the time. That was a situation where another officer might have taken a different attitude and made a better decision. Diane Fry, for example. Her city girl scepticism would have been a great advantage.

Cooper shook his head. It wasn't often he found himself thinking that. Or perhaps he'd let the thought cross his mind a few times, but dismissed it too easily.

He went slowly back into the CID room, where he stopped by Luke Irvine's desk.

'Well, Luke,' he said, 'now I know who the weak link is.'

'Sorry?'

Cooper called Gavin Murfin over and explained Poppy Mellor's story to them.

'We're going to need background checks on everyone involved,' said Cooper when he'd finished. 'You can share the tasks out between you.'

'Who was in this group, then?' asked Irvine.

'All of them, I think,' said Cooper. 'Rob Beresford, Jason Shaw, the Nadens – and Sandra Blair herself. But there might be more we don't know about. The Nadens and Shaw only came forward after the appeals because they thought someone else had been there at the bridge that night who might have seen them and been able to describe them to us.'

'Someone who wasn't a member of the group, you mean.'

'Exactly. Either innocent members of the public or individuals who were involved in some activity of their own. Whichever it was, they knew it would look bad if they didn't admit straight away to their presence. Just as Rob Beresford figured he should admit that he knew Sandra Blair. They would have looked guilty if we found out from another source.'

'They weren't just opportunists, were they?' said Irvine.

'Not at all. They'd thought about this and planned it. When it went wrong they did the sensible thing. It might have worked out too, but for Poppy Mellor. She thinks she's defending the innocent. But perhaps not.'

'And the target of their bizarre scheme is the Manby family.'

'It seems so. They're protesting against development plans for the graveyard at Bowden.'

'Everyone keeps saying "the Manby family". But who is there living at the abbey, apart from the earl himself?'

'I can tell you that,' said Murfin, flicking through the pages of his notebook. 'I've got it here. There's the earl's wife, Countess Caroline. And three grown-up children. The eldest is Lord Peter Manby. Then there's the Honourable Richard, and Lady Imogen. Peter is the heir. He'll be the next earl in due course. That's why he gets to be called Lord, when his younger brother is just Honourable.'

'You've done a bit of research, then, Gavin.'

'I thought if we were going to be mingling with the aristocracy...'

'Well, we're not.'

Murfin sighed. 'It's probably for the best. You'd only embarrass us with your uncouth ways.'

'I'm not sure the younger Manbys spend much time at the abbey,' said Cooper. 'No more than they have to, anyway.'

'Well, would you? It must be like living in a fish tank, with people gawping at you all day long.'

'Doesn't Peter Manby have some other claim to fame?' said Irvine. 'His name rings a bell vaguely.'

'He worked in the media for a while, then ran his own production company making strange little indie films. It was never a success. Then he stood as a parliamentary candidate for the High Peak a couple of general elections ago.'

'He wanted to be an MP?'

'I don't know whether he seriously hoped to get elected. He stood as an Independent candidate. They never get in, do they? Not around here.'

'He must be in his mid-to-late thirties now.'

'The last I could see, he was working for an advertising agency in London.'

'Well,' said Irvine, 'it sounds as though he's doing anything he can to get away from Knowle Abbey.'

'I imagine he's just trying out a few things while he has the freedom to,' said Cooper. 'Once he succeeds his father, he'll be tied to Knowle. All the responsibilities will be his then. Personally, I don't really envy him.'

BEN COOPER HAD a lot of notes to write out before the morning briefing. When he reported his interview with Poppy Mellor, he found himself stumbling a bit over his own scrawl, trying to cast light on the motives and identity of the group of which both Sandra Blair and Rob Beresford had been members.

'What's your next move, DS Cooper?' asked Superintendent Branagh.

Cooper thought he detected a dwindling of her interest in the tone of the question.

'I'll despatch a team to pick up Rob Beresford. And we'll need to talk to the Nadens and Jason Shaw again. We should try to get some more names from them.'

'Are we considering charges?'

'If we can establish which of the group was responsible for the threatening letter, the graffiti...'

'Yes, of course.'

Then Branagh turned away.

'And what about George Redfearn?' she said.

'We're still awaiting the post-mortem results,' said DI Walker. 'But we've had reports that at least two people went up to Pilsbury Castle that night in separate cars, and they didn't all come back down. His wife is due to arrive from France today. We've managed to contact her to inform her of her husband's death, so at least she'll be prepared when she arrives.'

Cooper was unable to concentrate fully on what was being said next, until he heard his own name mentioned.

'Oh, and DS Cooper asked us to establish whether there were any traces of petrol at the scene,' Wayne Abbott was saying.

Branagh switched her attention back to him suddenly and he sat up straight.

'Why would you do that, DS Cooper?' she asked.

'A smell, ma'am.'

'Got a nose for these things, have you?'

Cooper grimaced. 'Yes, ma'am. Well, I just thought it was quite noticeable.'

'And was there any petrol?'

'No,' said Abbott, leaving a dramatic pause. 'In fact, it was diesel fuel. We found evidence of diesel, as well as traces of ammonium nitrate.'

'Near the body?'

'It was on the victim's clothing.'

SUPERINTENDENT BRANAGH CALLED Cooper into her office after the briefing.

'DS Cooper, you seemed to be distracted. What's on your mind?'

But Cooper didn't answer directly.

'There will be another victim, you know,' he said. 'Possibly two.'

She looked annoyed. 'Ben, people in that part of Derbyshire are getting very jumpy,' she said. 'They're already frightened in those small villages. We must not let the idea get out that we expect more killings.'

'No, ma'am.'

'If your idea about a corpse on each of the coffin roads starts to be spread around—'

'No one outside this building will hear it from me,' said Cooper. 'But ma'am…'

'What?'

'I think some of those people will be putting two and two together themselves before very long.'

THEY'D BROUGHT GEOFF and Sally Naden in for a second interview. When Poppy Mellor's version of events was put to them, they confirmed it almost willingly. Their admission seemed to come as quite a relief.

'It was a group thing,' said Geoff. 'We were all going to be there together, in unity. A joint effort.'

Cooper blinked. That was quite a verbal achievement. Naden had made five attempts to spread responsibility within a few sentences.

'But you say you didn't get as far as the bridge in the end?'

'Well, we thought we had the wrong night,' said Geoff.

'*He* thought we had the wrong night,' said his wife. 'But planning was never one of his strong points. I had a different opinion.'

'You were right on this occasion, Mrs Naden,' said Cooper.

'Of course I was.'

'But it was lucky that you listened to your husband. It might have kept you out of danger.'

Naden grimaced at the thought. 'We never intended any harm,' he said.

'I'm sure you didn't.'

'It was just a protest. A statement. People do a lot worse things when they feel strongly about a cause.'

'I was never convinced,' said Sally. 'I still didn't think it was the wrong night. I told him as much when we got home.'

'Several times,' said Geoff.

'And the other people in the group?'

'Beresford,' said Naden.

'Yes.'

'And Jason Shaw,' he added.

'Right.'

'And Sandra, of course,' said his wife. 'And there was some girl, though I don't think we ever saw her.'

'Beresford's girlfriend,' said Naden.

'Anyone else?'

They both shook their heads.

'There were some others, in the beginning,' said Sally. 'But they just talked and grumbled, and never actually did anything. You know the sort.'

'That's right,' said Geoff. 'I suppose you might say we were the stalwarts.'

'But some of us were worse than others,' said Sally suddenly.

Then she put her hand to her mouth, as if she'd spoken too much. But for once her husband seemed to agree.

'Sandra was crazy, you know,' he said. 'All that weird stuff about magic. It made no sense. And she was always dosing herself with herbal medicines. At least, that's what she called them.'

Sally's mouth had drawn into a tight, disapproving line. When Cooper looked at her closely now, he could see the shadows in her face, the tension round her eyes. He wondered what was wrong with her. She looked like a woman who knew about pain.

'Goodness knows what she was doing to herself,' said Sally. 'You know what I mean.'

'Were you aware that Mrs Blair was taking drugs?' asked Cooper.

They glanced at each other.

'We guessed,' said Sally. 'And she was drinking too, of course. But then, we all know people who drink a bit too much, don't we?'

Geoff Naden cleared his throat loudly.

'Anyway,' he said, 'it might interest you to know that Sandra was by far the most extreme member of the group.'

'Was she, sir? Extreme in what way?'

Chapter Thirty

COOPER RETURNED TO his desk and pulled out his map again, with the routes of the coffin roads marked on it.

But as soon as he sat down Becky Hurst looked up from a call.

'Ben? Ben?' she said, an unmistakable note of urgency in her voice.

'Don't tell me,' said Cooper, still gazing at the map. 'We've got another dead body.'

The conclusion seemed inevitable, a logical fit to the network of coffin ways converging on the bridge. Where there were two bodies, there must be a third.

'No,' said Hurst. 'No dead body. Well, not yet. But the officers we sent to Earl Sterndale. They can't locate Rob Beresford and his parents are reporting him missing.'

'Put out an alert for him. He won't have gone far.'

'Okay.'

'What about Jason Shaw?'

'Carol and Luke are tracing him now.'

Cooper ran a hand through his hair, envisaging disaster. His initial witness, the person who found Sandra Blair's body, had

Naden could see that he had Cooper's interest. He leaned forward across the table and lowered his voice to a conspiratorial tone.

'She was most in favour of what they call direct action. She wanted to go further. You understand?' Naden paused. 'We were afraid that she might go too far in the end. We thought she might be driven to violence.'

'Really?' Cooper couldn't keep the tone of scepticism from his voice. 'Was Mrs Blair particularly close to any of the other members of the group?'

'Ah now,' said Naden, 'you'll have to ask someone else about that.'

slipped through his fingers. Worse, Rob Beresford might end up as the next of those bodies.

He heard a cough and found Wayne Abbott standing at his shoulder.

'I thought you'd like to know straight away,' said Abbott. 'Digital forensics have managed to retrieve some interesting images off Sandra Blair's computer. It looks as though she took them on her smartphone, then emailed them to herself.'

'Great. Let's have a look.'

Abbott placed a laptop on his desk and flipped open the screen. A familiar image appeared, caught in a glare of sun.

'As you can see, first we have some shots of the bridge,' said Abbott. 'Taken in daylight, of course.'

'The Corpse Bridge, taken from west and east banks of the river. It must have been a planning visit. They were well organised.'

'Right. And here are some of the dummy, but taken indoors.'

'That's Mrs Blair's sitting room,' said Cooper.

He was looking at a badly lit picture of the effigy of Earl Manby. It was sitting in one of the chintzy armchairs at Pilsbury Cottage with the African rug on the wall behind it.

'Why would she take a photograph of it, do you think?'

'She was very proud of her handiwork,' said Cooper.

Abbott nodded. 'This will interest you most. Digital forensics managed to retrieve an image from a few months earlier. The quality isn't very good, but they've done their best to enhance this one. It might be important. It was taken in London, I think. Some kind of railway depot. Perhaps a repair yard or a sidings for old rolling stock.'

Cooper leaned forward eagerly. There they were in the photograph, all of them. Geoff Naden stood slightly in front, as if leading a guided walk, with Sally at his elbow. They were flanked by Rob Beresford, Jason Shaw and, lurking to one side, Sandra Blair herself.

The group were standing on a path with trees behind them. The background was fairly unremarkable and undistinguished, except for one thing. The most striking detail in the picture was a London Underground train on a track in a dip between the group and the belt of trees. The last carriage of another train could just be made out past Sandra Blair's head. It looked as if the train were drawn up in a sidings.

There was one more photo. It was of Sandra herself, standing on her own. The shot was taken by flash at night, so her skin was washed out and pale, her eyes flared red, her figure stood out in unnatural detail from her surroundings as if she were an illusion or phantom. In that instant of the flash going off, Sandra Blair already looked like a ghost.

'What's the date stamp on this?' asked Cooper.

'October thirty-first.'

'The night she died.'

Cooper peered more closely. Though the colours weren't accurate, he could see Sandra was wearing the same clothes that her body had been found in, including the blue waterproof jacket and the walking boots. And he'd been right about the hat. It was woollen, with ear flaps and decorated in some kind of Scandinavian design. Sandra's dark hair peeped out of it over her forehead. She was holding something in her hand, close to her body. Cooper couldn't see what it was, but his bet was on a torch. That was missing from the scene too.

'Can we zoom in a bit?' he said.

'Sure.'

In the background he could make out the distinctive arched outline, only just visible but recognisable, even in the darkness. Its wet, moss-covered stones glittered eerily in the light of the flash. Sandra Blair was standing right in front of the Corpse Bridge, no more than a few feet from where she died.

Cooper asked Abbott to go back to the group shot again.

'Yes, strange, isn't it?' said Abbott. 'A couple of Tube trains. It must be in the London area somewhere. There are no Tube trains in Derbyshire.'

'Where do you live, Wayne?' asked Cooper.

'Me? In Sheffield.'

'That explains it.'

Abbott stared at him in puzzlement. But Cooper was remembering what Poppy Mellor had said. *They walked all the old coffin roads.* Of course they did. And this was one of them.

'No Tube trains in Derbyshire?' he said. 'Actually, I think you'll find there are. Or at least, there were when this photograph was taken.'

DC LUKE IRVINE had been sent to Bowden with Carol Villiers. They parked near the church and walked across to Jason Shaw's address.

Villiers had seen Shaw before, but it was the first time Irvine had set eyes on him. He was recorded as being in his early thirties. Irvine noted the dark stubble. He envied the silver ear stud – he would have one himself, if he could.

They'd found Shaw in a small backyard behind his cottage. It was paved and only large enough to contain a couple of wheelie bins and a dog run. A blue Land Rover Discovery was drawn up by the side wall.

The dog began barking before they went round the corner of the house, so Shaw knew someone was coming. He'd put down a bowl of dog food and some water in the run and was just closing the door. The dog was a collie cross of some kind. Irvine couldn't have been more accurate, though he was sure Ben Cooper would have known.

Shaw knew who they were straight away. He didn't seem at all surprised.

'I thought you lot would be here before long,' he said.

They showed him their IDs anyway. The dog began barking again, but Shaw yelled at it and it cowered away from the fence.

'You know why we've come, then,' said Villiers. 'You didn't tell us the truth when you came in to make a statement in Edendale on Saturday morning.'

'I didn't lie,' said Shaw. 'I told you some of the truth. The part that mattered.'

'Well, we don't agree with that attitude, sir. It all matters to us.'

Shaw wiped his hands on his jeans. 'I don't see that it's relevant. I came forward like a good citizen when I heard the appeals. That's the end of it.'

'Obviously we have to ask you about the protest group you're a member of. We need to know what was going on last Thursday night at the bridge.'

'I honestly don't know what I can tell you about the group,' said Shaw.

'You didn't tell us anything before.'

'Okay, but – you've talked to some of the others already, haven't you? So you'll know all about it by now. More than I could tell you, anyway. I'm just a humble foot soldier. The others are the ones with the brains. They did all the talking and I just trailed along behind, if you get my meaning.'

'So who sent the threatening letter to the Manbys and wrote graffiti on the wall of the chapel at Knowle Abbey?'

Shaw shrugged. 'No idea,' he said. 'I don't think that was ever part of the plan. Somebody taking a bit of individual action, by the sound of it. Graffiti? Ask Rob Beresford, that would be my suggestion. It sounds like his sort of trick.'

'And what about Sandra Blair?'

He stalled for the first time and looked genuinely upset for a few moments. But the expression passed. 'That was a real shame. She was okay, Sandra. I bet the others told you she was a nutcase. Well, she was a bit wacky in some ways, I suppose. But she meant well.'

'You were with her that night at the bridge, weren't you?'

'Only up to a point,' said Shaw.

'What do you mean?'

'Well, I had her stuff in my Land Rover – you know, the effigy thing and the other bits and pieces.'

'A noose? A witch ball?'

'I think that was it. I'd collected the stuff from her earlier in the week. Then that afternoon, when she finished work, she walked across from Crowdecote and I met her in Longnor, in front of the general stores. She wouldn't have got her own car anywhere near the bridge, you see. But with the Land Rover, I got right down to the last few yards, until the track was too broken up. I mean, she wouldn't have wanted to walk down to the bridge with those things. If anybody had seen her, that would definitely have looked weird.'

'Then what did you do?'

'I left her to it,' said Shaw.

'You left her there on her own?'

'Yes. Well, she was on her own when I drove back up the track. I had to get the Land Rover clear. If anybody saw it going down, they would just think I was another off-roader. But if it was parked by the bridge for a couple of hours, well – that looks suspicious.'

'Who worked all this out?' asked Irvine.

Shaw laughed. 'Not me, anyway. I just did what I was told.'

'So why were you there on the track again later?'

'Once I shifted the Land Rover, I was supposed to go back. That was the plan. We were going to get photos when it was all set up. The group standing round the noose. We'd have our faces covered by hoods and scarves. It was going to be like a terrorist video – you know, when they kidnap some tourist and put pictures on the internet standing round him with their Kalashnikovs. You know what I mean?'

'Yes. But it didn't happen, did it?'

'No,' said Shaw. 'Well, I told you the rest, when I came in the first time. I don't know any more than that.'

'You're saying you have no idea what happened to Sandra Blair at the bridge?'

'Not a clue. Did … did someone do that to her? They killed her?'

'Who do you think might have done that, Mr Shaw?'

'I don't know.'

'One of the group?'

'Like who?'

'You tell me.'

He shook his head slowly. 'I honestly can't imagine. I mean, they didn't always see eye to eye. They argued sometimes. Particularly…'

'Yes?'

'Well, Sally Naden. She didn't think much of Sandra. I heard her say once that Sandra was a liability. But it wasn't serious. She would never kill her. Why would she do that? It doesn't make sense.'

'It was your suggestion.'

'I'm just trying to help.'

'As it happens,' said Villiers, 'the post-mortem examination suggests that Mrs Blair wasn't deliberately killed. She may just have had an accident.'

Shaw looked faintly relieved. 'Well, even so – it's still a real shame.'

Irvine cast around for any questions that Villiers hadn't asked. As usual he found himself wondering what Ben Cooper would do or say. Something a bit unexpected, which might catch their interviewee.

'You work here at Knowle Abbey, don't you, sir?' he said.

Shaw looked at him. 'I'm on the estate staff. Gamekeeping mostly.'

'Have you always worked on the estate?'

'No. I used to have a job in Hartington. It was good work too. But that went belly up.'

Villiers frowned. But Irvine had picked up a thing or two while he was with Cooper.

'Did you have a job at the cheese factory?' he said.

Shaw's entire attention was on him now and it made Irvine smile.

'Yes, I was in the warehouse,' said Shaw. 'I did a bit of forklift work too. You know what happened to the factory, then?'

'Yes, of course,' said Irvine, feeling smug. 'It was sold and you were all made redundant.'

Shaw scowled. 'That's the truth. And it's the same story everywhere you go.'

Chapter Thirty-one

THE LAST TIME Cooper had been to Harpur Hill was for a match at Buxton Rugby Club's ground, which claimed to have the highest posts in the country. They often played in appalling weather conditions up here. But then, Buxton was notorious for its weather, ever since a cricket match was interrupted by snow in the middle of June.

The village itself lay between the outskirts of Buxton and the quarries off the A515. A large proportion of Harpur Hill had been occupied for years by the sprawling, derelict buildings of an old University of Derby campus, which had once been High Peak College. After a new campus was created from Buxton's former Devonshire Royal Hospital, the empty Harpur Hill buildings lay damaged and rotting, like a set of broken teeth, an incongruous lump of urban decay that split an ordinary village housing estate in half.

As Cooper passed through, he recalled that the site had attracted intruders, despite the security fencing. Thieves removed lead from the roofs and stripped out wiring. Once, a large pentagram had been found scratched into the floor of the refectory. Empty buildings were like a magnet for the curious and the opportunist.

DCs Becky Hurst and Gavin Murfin were in the car with him, the only officers available and willing to follow his instinct. He was lucky they hadn't already been appropriated for other assignments.

At least he seemed to have got Diane Fry out of his hair for the time being. Her attention was on the George Redfearn inquiry, like everyone else – though Cooper had a strong suspicion the results might lead her straight back to him before long.

'So what's in Harpur Hill?' asked Hurst doubtfully as they slowed almost to a halt behind a tractor towing a trailer of manure.

'Elf 'n' safety,' said Murfin. 'The temple of our new God.'

'Is it?' said Hurst. She twisted round to look at Murfin, who was slumped in the back seat. 'I thought your God worked at the local pie shop.'

Cooper glanced in the rearview mirror. Murfin might well have a pie hidden somewhere in his pockets. He could smell the warm juice now, drifting through the car.

'You're just a heathen,' said Murfin. 'You wait until Judgment Day. Then we'll see who gets chosen.'

'You're too heavy to float up to heaven,' said Hurst. 'You'll sink the other way.'

Murfin sniffed and maintained a dignified silence for a few moments.

'And the Blue Lagoon,' he said suddenly. 'Am I right?'

'The what?' asked Hurst.

'Yes, you're right,' said Cooper.

Directly opposite the old university campus, the flooded Far Hill Quarry had also hit the headlines for a while. For years it had been known as the Blue Lagoon, because of its azure colour, which made it a popular place for swimming. It was also one of the most polluted stretches of water to be found anywhere in Derbyshire.

The attractive colouring had been caused by the surrounding limestone rocks, which leached calcite crystals into the water, turning it turquoise. Its alkalinity came from calcium oxide, a by-product of the quarrying process. The lagoon was known to contain car wrecks, dead animals, excrement and other kinds of toxic rubbish. Despite the signs warning that high pH levels could cause rashes, eye irritations, stomach problems and fungal infections, parents could be seen pulling their babies around in rubber rings on the water. Whole families regularly made the trek to the lagoon, gazing at the blue water as if to convince themselves they were in the Bahamas. It had been beautiful to look at, but horrendously dangerous.

But it wasn't pretty any more. On the principle that the lagoon's attraction was all about surface appearance, the council dyed the water black. When they visited Far Hill Quarry now, people didn't think they were in the Bahamas any more. They knew perfectly well they were in Derbyshire.

'One of the coffin roads started from somewhere near here,' said Cooper.

'Oh.' Murfin gazed out of the car window. 'You wouldn't think you'd died and gone to heaven, would you?'

Hurst laughed. 'I'm with you there, Gavin.'

Past Hoffman's Bar, Cooper turned off by the Parks Inn and followed a twisting road that led up to the industrial estate. He found an engineering factory, a pet crematorium, then the gleaming, modern laboratory complex operated by the Health and Safety Executive.

From 1938 the RAF had turned a vast area of hillside above Harpur Hill into a series of underground munitions stores. Tunnels were dug out to house large amounts of ammunition and ordnance, including howitzer shells loaded with mustard gas and phosphorus. When the RAF left, the tunnels were used as a mushroom farm, then as a cold store for cheese, and finally as a warehouse for wines and spirits. Many of the bunkers could still be seen in the surrounding landscape, which was now used as testing grounds for the Health and Safety Laboratory.

Cooper wondered how many health and safety regulations had existed at the time when cheese was stored in the same tunnels that once contained chemical weapons. Local people had all kinds of stories about this place. The number of underground bunkers and mysterious explosions accounted for many of the rumours.

A sign pointed to a half-overgrown path that led down through the trees to a steep hillside and an area of limestone pasture. When Cooper got closer he saw that the sign was for the Buxton Climate Change Impacts Laboratory.

'It's an enormous site,' said Hurst. 'And there are just the three of us. How are we going to do this, Ben?'

'Don't you understand yet?' said Cooper. 'We only need to find the route of the old coffin road.'

He was aware of Hurst and Murfin looking at each other when he said that. Murfin gave a subtle shrug. His DCs were loyal, but even they didn't believe in his theories.

The HSE's own security teams had been asked to check the parts of the site nearest to the laboratories. But two or three public footpaths ran through the old RAF camp and these were the readily accessible areas. The route of the old coffin road must have followed one of these public rights of way. Sandra Blair's group must have worked out the route for themselves. Not only did they walk it as a group, but they had their photograph taken around here. Was this the moment when someone suggested taking their protest further?

There were signs everywhere bearing the same message: 'You are about to enter an area where hazardous activities take place.' He was warned to watch for red flags flying to indicate danger.

A dark strip of woodland separated the Health and Safety testing grounds from some University of Sheffield laboratories on the western side. The Department of Civil and Structural Engineers, the Communications Research Group and CEDUS. What was that? Cooper couldn't remember what the initials stood for, but he had a feeling it was to do with research into the blast effects of high-velocity explosives.

Hurst began to cast about like a terrier sniffing the ground for a fox. Murfin made a desultory show of peering through the windows of an abandoned building.

'I hear you've been talking to Brendan Kilner,' said Murfin, without turning round.

Cooper stared at him. He hadn't mentioned his conversation with Kilner or his visit to Buxton Raceway. But he tended to forget how long Gavin Murfin had been in this job and how many people he knew. Gavin's network of informants must be pretty extensive by now. No doubt someone in the crowd at Axe Edge saw him talking to Kilner and mentioned it to Murfin in the pub last night. He ought to have known that was a possibility.

'He can be useful,' he said.

'Kilner is a lifelong criminal,' said Murfin. 'A born scrote. He probably mugged the midwife before he was five minutes old. These days they say he's into the drugs trade because it's more profitable.'

'It doesn't mean he can't be useful for providing a bit of information, Gavin. You know that. Don't be so cynical.'

Murfin grunted and kicked at a lump of broken concrete. 'So you think it's okay to spend your time with the bad guys?'

'If it's necessary. Now can we get on with it, Gavin?'

'Just so we're clear.'

The whole site was scattered with concrete bunkers, chimneys, ventilation shafts and scaffolding structures emerging from the ground, a CCTV camera on a gantry watching for walkers getting too close. A drop tower and old bomb stores. He passed Bunker 90. Further on the red flags were fluttering at half-mast. So no danger at the moment.

Ahead were the large main buildings, looking like any other modern office complex. They made the rest of the site seem like a vast playground filled with tunnels and towers, railway tracks and climbing frames, and places where you could just make things go *bang*. The high explosive testing tunnel ran for about a quarter of a mile across the site and was said to contain the scorched remains of a headless test dummy, still perched in a blackened chair in the path of an explosive blast.

Cooper produced a print of the photograph of the group taken on Sandra Blair's phone.

'About here, perhaps?' he said.

Hurst squinted at the picture and the landscape in front of them. 'Could be.'

Somewhere over there to the west the HSE had brought in some disused London Underground trains for testing after the 7 July bombings in the capital, when forty-two people were killed by bombs on the Tube in 2005. The carriages had been subjected to test explosions in a makeshift tunnel. As a result of the testing a series of burned-out Jubilee Line units with their windows and doors blown off had stood around the site for years, only a couple of hundred yards from a public footpath through the old RAF base.

They were on one of the public footpaths now, probably the one walked by Sandra Blair's group. Becky Hurst pushed open the broken door of a concrete shed, which revealed a stack of old drums of Shell Tellus Oil.

'What *is* that?' she said.

'Hydraulic fluid. That's all.'

It was strange that the HSE had made no attempt to divert the footpaths, the way Deeplow Quarry had done. Instead, they had installed CCTV cameras and warning signs, and red flags to indicate when an explosion was imminent. They also recorded use of these footpaths, and the HSE's security teams had sometimes asked people to leave. B Division response officers were occasionally despatched to make sure that suspicious individuals had actually departed the site.

Hurst had reached a fence and worked her way along to a stile that led over the hill towards the far side of the site.

'I wonder where that track goes from here?' she said.

There was no need to consult the map this time. Cooper knew the answer perfectly well. He could picture the funeral party picking their way carefully down this hill, a coffin shifting precariously on their shoulders as the slope became steeper. He was able to imagine the weary sighs as they halted at the gate a hundred yards below him on the hillside, resting the coffin on the large, flat stone until the relief bearers took it up again.

'We know where it goes,' he said. 'It comes out at the Corpse Bridge.'

Chapter Thirty-two

VILLIERS AND IRVINE had left Jason Shaw's cottage in Bowden and were driving back towards Edendale.

'Did you hear that?' said Villiers. 'He offered us a suspect in Sally Naden, then said himself how ridiculous an idea it was.'

'Not very helpful.'

'Deliberately unhelpful.'

When they got back to West Street, Ben Cooper was out of the office. He'd disappeared, taking Becky Hurst and Gavin Murfin along with him.

'What do we do now?' said Irvine, turning to Villiers.

Villiers grimaced and nodded across the office. 'You know there's only one thing we can do, Luke,' she said. 'We have to report to DS Fry.'

Molly Redfearn had returned from Paris that morning. Diane Fry had taken over the interviews with the victim's wife and was writing up her report when Irvine and Villiers came in.

Mrs Redfearn had been just the sort of woman Fry disliked most – cold, middle class and materialistic. Exactly the kind of woman she was afraid of turning into herself, in fact.

The perfume Molly Redfearn was wearing had been almost overpowering. Fry had been glad that they weren't talking to each other in one of the interview rooms at West Street, with their archaic lack of ventilation. They would all have been stifled and found dead in their chairs an hour or two later.

But the results of her interview were disappointing. Mrs Redfearn had been out of contact with her husband throughout the whole of her trip to Paris with her girlfriends.

When she saw Irvine and Villiers approaching she willingly put her half-finished report aside to listen to what they had to say.

'So that's his story,' said Irvine when they'd finished. 'He basically put the blame on everyone else.'

'And there was no one on the bridge with Mrs Blair that night?'

'Not according to Shaw. He admits taking her there with the effigy and all that stuff, but then he left her to it.'

'And what do you think of that, Luke?' asked Fry.

'I think he's telling only half the truth again.'

Fry looked at Villiers, who agreed.

'His attempt to blame Sally Naden looks a bit weak, but you can never tell.'

'No.'

Fry was interested in Jason Shaw's job as a gamekeeper. She would have to get a check done on the firearms register.

She looked up at Irvine and Villiers.

'By the way,' she said. 'Do *you* know where DS Cooper is?'

On the far side of the Harpur Hill testing grounds Cooper realised how close he was to Buxton Raceway. There was no race meeting today, but he could see the circuit and the stand where he'd talked to Brendan Kilner. It was Kilner who pointed him in the direction of the graveyard, yet here he was coming full circle within thirty-six hours.

He'd left Becky Hurst and Gavin Murfin checking their way through the old buildings, the former RAF bunkers that had been abandoned or even demolished. They would be grumbling to each other by now. They might not appear to get on, but they'd developed an understanding. Hurst respected Murfin's experience, though she would never have said so, and Gavin wouldn't have wanted her to.

Cooper parked the Toyota by a structure of rotting timbers like the skeleton of a beached ship. From the number of old car tyres lying around, he guessed it was the remains of a long-disused silage clamp.

Across the road a small group of ponies with long manes trotted eagerly to greet him as he climbed over the stile into their field. From here he had a view down a shallow valley to the HSE laboratories, with one building shaped like a flour mill gleaming a startling white in the sun. Beyond the buildings the little tower that people called Solomon's Temple stood on the crest of a hill, overlooking the town of Buxton.

Further on a gate was fastened with a series of lengths of baler twine. It was probably a subtle deterrent for walkers, without quite making the path inaccessible.

A farmer appeared on a quad bike and entered the fields where sheep grazed on the fringes of the HSE testing grounds. When Cooper got closer the white building turned out to be a mysterious structure of scaffolding and pipes shrouded in white plastic sheeting, with a large tank standing next to it.

A few employees from the laboratories had taken the opportunity during their lunch break to stroll or jog along the roadway where a disused railway line had once run. They were still wearing their yellow high-vis jackets, as befitted employees of the Health and Safety Executive.

A few minutes ago he'd driven past a nursery in Harpur Hill village, where the children were out playing. They'd been wearing high-vis jackets identical to those the workers wore at the HSL. Health and safety got everywhere. Cooper could hear Gavin Murfin's voice in his head. *Elf 'n' safety. You can't argue with that.* It was one of Murfin's favourite sayings.

Just out of sight of the path a dead sheep had been dismembered on the hillside. He found severed leg bones, an almost intact spine and ribcage, a bloodied fleece and part of the skull. It could have been scavengers, arriving after the carcase had begun to soften and disarticulate. A fox perhaps, or a pair of crows. But you could never be sure.

Cooper passed a large concrete-lined watering hole for the cattle and sheep, formed into ledges to provide a safe footing for the animals when the water was low. And it was certainly low now. There were only a few inches lying below the final ledge. He could see glimpses of the muddy bottom, though most of the water was choked by weeds. A few chunks of limestone had fallen in, along with a rotting timber or two, and a rusted iron feeding trough.

And something else caught his eye. No more than a slight, flapping movement in the wind. It was a white plastic bag, one corner protruding above the muddy surface. If the water had been a fraction deeper, he would never have seen it.

Becky Hurst appeared at the top of the slope. Cooper signalled to her to join him and waited until she scrambled down.

'What have you found?' she said.

'I'm not sure. Probably nothing.' He looked up the slope. 'Where's Gavin?'

'Having a quick sulk.'

'And a snack?'

'Probably. I didn't wait to see. There's only so much I can take.'

Cooper found a length of wood, hooked a handle of the plastic bag and fished it out of the water. When he prised it open he discovered some sodden clothing inside. Thrown away instead of being taken to a charity shop or disposed of properly?

He teased the clothing out and spread it on the ground. A crumpled shape turned out to be a woollen hat, with ear flaps and a Scandinavian design. He'd been right about the reindeer.

Something metallic rolled out of the hat on to the ground. It was a small LED torch. A tiny thing, but it would have provided a bright light, if its batteries hadn't been submerged in water for the past four days.

'Sandra Blair's possessions,' said Cooper.

'Wow,' said Hurst. 'Why would someone take the trouble to dump them here? Why not leave them with the body?'

'They probably handled them.'

'So they were worried about fingerprints or DNA?'

'Exactly.'

'Do you reckon we'll be able get anything from them?'

Cooper slipped the items into separate evidence bags. 'Let's hope so. It's about our only break so far.'

'You really think there'll be another victim, Ben?' asked Hurst.

He straightened up and looked out over the Harpur Hill testing grounds, with the remaining route of the old coffin road heading away across Axe Edge Moor. The breeze fluttered a scrap of wool on the dismembered body of the sheep. It seemed inevitable.

As if there had to be a death before anyone could cross the Corpse Bridge.

'I'm certain of it,' he said.

CHRIS THORNTON WAS shift supervisor at Deeplow Quarry that day, when the crusher jammed. He was standing outside the office, checking the time sheets and cursing one of the dump truck drivers who'd failed to turn up for work. As far as he was concerned the first sign of trouble was the screech of metal. It shrieked across the quarry above the rumble of engines and the crash of broken stone. Then an alarm sounded for a few seconds before somebody hit the button and stopped the motor.

'What the hell was that?'

Thornton began to run up the roadway towards the quarry face, kicking up limestone dust and veering aside to avoid a truck manoeuvring to deposit its load in the bottom hopper. He could see a group of men in orange overalls and hard hats, who were slowly gathering around the crusher. Someone had climbed on to the inspection plate and was staring down into the belt mechanism. Then the worker straightened up and said something to the other men below, shaking his head as if he couldn't believe what he was seeing.

As Thornton covered the last hundred yards, the entire group turned to look at him. He read a mixture of shock and relief on their faces. He knew the reason for the relief – they'd just set eyes on the man who was going to take responsibility from their shoulders. He didn't yet understand why they were looking so shocked.

In a moment, though, Chris Thornton would find out. Within the next few hours the whole of Derbyshire would know.

Chapter Thirty-three

THE ROAD TO Deeplow Quarry ran steeply down through neighbouring villages, carrying the telltale signs of quarrying. The unnaturally white surface of the carriageway and the crash barriers on every bend were the clues.

Ben Cooper knew that limestone lorries ground their way down this hill every day. No matter how well they were sheeted or how often their wheels were washed, they left their traces on the roads in the neighbourhood and reminded everyone of the quarry's existence. The barriers were there to protect residents living directly in the path of the lorries. If the brakes failed as one of them descended the hill, it would turn into an uncontrollable twelve-ton missile capable of demolishing a house. It had happened only once in living memory. But that was once too often for the people whose properties had been damaged.

Most of the quarries in this area were run by large multinational companies now. The name on the sign at the entrance would usually be that of Tarmac, or Omya, or Lhoist. But Deeplow was one of the few that had survived the spread of the conglomerates.

It remained a locally owned operation, thanks to a source of good quality limestone which enabled it to produce pure lime, and kept it productive and profitable.

It was also thanks, perhaps, to the existence of a loyal work-force – local people who'd worked at the quarry for generations and relied on its existence for their livelihood, much as the workers on the Knowle estate did. Those quarrymen didn't want to see Deeplow swallowed up by a multinational with its headquarters in Switzerland or Mexico.

Cooper turned his Toyota into the quarry entrance. The crusher, where the stone was ground to a powder, was one of the most prominent buildings on the site.

There had been a quarry at the Deeplow site for over a hundred years. The present plant extracted and processed calcium carbonate, a carboniferous limestone more than a hundred and eighty million years old, formed from the compressed skeletons of millions of prehistoric animals and sea creatures.

There were four bigger quarries nearby – Hindlow, Hillhead, Brierlow and Dowlow, all lying close to the A515. A public footpath had crossed the site between the main road and a green lane on the west. Though it had been a public right of way for many years, the footpath had been diverted by the county council under the Highways Act.

So the old coffin road that once ran across this part of the countryside had gone, the ground ripped up and excavated, the route switched to the south.

'It's mad,' said Chris Thornton, taking them into the Portakabin he used as an office. 'I mean, why would anyone do something like this?'

'We don't know, sir.'

'Although I suppose it could have been worse. There have been a couple of bodies—'

'Yes. But nothing for you to worry about.'

'There was one at Pilsbury, which isn't very far away from here. Do you know who it was yet?'

'We haven't released the victim's identity at this stage.'

Thornton removed his hard hat and ran a hand across the top of his head, making his hair stand up as if he'd just received an electric shock.

'Well, someone obviously got on to the site and did this. It scared some of the blokes to death. They thought it was real at first. The older ones can be a bit superstitious, you know.'

'I understand.'

'Anyway, it's in here,' said Thornton. 'I suppose you'll want it.'

He opened the door of a storeroom for Cooper to look in. The object had been ripped to shreds by the machinery. One of the legs was missing and the head hung from the neck by a few threads. Rips ran right up the plump torso. It was covered in white dust and Cooper coughed as he brushed some of it from the face.

There was no mistaking it, though. He could even take a good guess at who had made it. It was almost an exact copy of the Corpse Bridge dummy. But this time the effigy of Earl Manby had been through the crusher.

'Could it have been one of your own employees who did this?' asked Cooper.

'I'd be surprised,' said Thornton. 'About a hundred people work here at Deeplow. But they're like a family. Some of their jobs have been passed down from father to son, the way it's always been.'

A siren went off – the first blast a long one, giving a two-minute warning of firing. Outside, near the quarry face, the blasting engineer had his det-line and detonator with two buttons like a simplified TV remote. The blasts followed each other within milliseconds. That vibration would be felt down in the valley.

'What do you use for your explosives, Mr Thornton?' asked Cooper.

'It's a coarse mixture of ammonium nitrate pellets and diesel fuel.'

Cooper nodded. 'Do you happen to have any missing?'

Thornton went pale and dropped his hard hat on the desk with a thud. 'We haven't reported it yet,' he said. 'How did you know?'

WHEN COOPER WENT to report to Detective Superintendent Branagh at West Street, they were joined in Branagh's office by DI Walker. The superintendent was clearly unhappy with the new development.

'We're waiting for one more,' said Branagh. 'But you can give us the outline, Cooper.'

But Cooper had no sooner begun to tell his story, than the door opened after a brief knock, and Diane Fry came in.

'Sorry I'm late, ma'am,' said Fry.

The superintendent just waved a hand. 'Take a seat,' she said. 'Carry on, Cooper.'

Fry seemed to listen impatiently. Out of the corner of his eye, Cooper was aware of her fidgeting and leaning forward as if about to interrupt. It didn't help his temper. When Cooper had finished, Fry was the first to react.

'Explosives?' she said. 'And what do you think their target might be?'

Cooper turned to her. 'Well, what do you think? An effigy of Earl Manby is found hanging from a noose, curses are packed into a witch ball with the Manbys' eagle's head emblem, an anonymous letter is received about death, and acts of vandalism are committed at the family chapel. Then we find a note arranging a meeting at the Grandfather Oak at one o'clock in the morning.'

'You mean the target could be Knowle Abbey itself?' said Branagh, calmly intervening.

'Yes, ma'am, that's exactly what I mean.'

'That would be a pretty dramatic statement.'

'I'll say.'

Yes, dramatic hardly covered it. According to what Mr Thornton had told him at the quarry, in the brief instant of an explosive detonation, the pressure could reach more than three million pounds per square inch. The detonation front travelled at twenty thousand miles per hour, with temperatures of up to five thousand degrees Celsius. The shockwave shattered rock by exceeding its compressive strength.

Cooper tried to imagine what kind of damage that would cause to the crumbling façades and sagging walls of Knowle Abbey, with its wooden floors and rooms packed full of antique furniture and dusty specimen cases. He tried, but failed. The devastation was beyond imagining.

Even worse was the possible fate of the earl and his family, not to mention the scores of staff and any visitors who happened to be enjoying the tour at the time of an attack.

'It would be impossible to do an efficient job, of course,' he said.

'Oh, that's good news?'

'In a quarry, blasting is only carried out after laser equipment is used to survey the rock face. The surveyor has a computer program to calculate the most effective blasting plan, drill positions, the firing sequence. They might not cause much damage at Knowle Abbey. Unless someone knows what he's doing.'

'We won't be able to keep this one quiet,' said Branagh. 'Too many of the workers at Deeplow Quarry know about it. It will be all around the area by now. All over the county.'

'Agreed, ma'am.'

'Well, one thing is obvious,' she said. 'We'd better make sure extra security precautions are being taken at Knowle Abbey. If some disaster happens that we had warning of, then it would be all of us being fed through the crusher.'

THAT WAS ALL very well. But how did you ensure the security of a place like Knowle Abbey? It seemed an unanswerable question as Ben Cooper and Diane Fry drove once again through the ornate gates and into the sprawling parkland towards the abbey.

There were hundreds of acres to cover, much of the landscape hidden by plantations of trees. There were so many buildings ancillary to the abbey – the restaurant, the craft centre, the gift shop, all the offices in the coach-house block. And then the abbey itself, vast and rambling, at least three storeys high, with attic rooms in the roof space and probably cellars under the servants' quarters. How many rooms would that be? Cooper hardly dared to think.

There was only one practical solution, the one he'd come away with from the meeting.

'Your friend Ms Burns isn't going to like this at all,' said Fry as they pulled on to the gravel by the estate office.

'I know,' said Cooper. Then he added: 'But she's not my friend.'

'Everyone is your friend. Or, at least, you think they are.'

Cooper shook his head at her jibe, but didn't feel resentment. Over the years he'd concluded that Fry did this as naturally as breathing. She didn't mean any personal animosity. In fact, she might regard it as a normal form of small talk.

'Let's see if we can get a look at their overall set-up anyway,' he said.

'I can't wait.'

Chapter Thirty-four

THE MORE ECCENTRIC members of the Manby family had amassed a vast collection of hidden treasures at Knowle Abbey. Dozens of rooms contained an eclectic accumulation of exotic artefacts and souvenirs of foreign expeditions, as well as antique objects. Some of them might have been fashionable or interesting at the time, supposed Cooper. There were stuffed marmosets and narwhal horns, mechanical toys and African tribal masks, not to mention a host of other mysterious, dusty objects whose purpose had long since been forgotten.

He remembered that a few years ago the Duke and Duchess of Devonshire had cleared out their attics at Chatsworth House. They raised almost six and a half million pounds from the sale of valuable antiques and curiosities like the 6th Duke's Russian sleigh and alabaster Borghese table. But no one would pay a fiver for this lot at Knowle Abbey. Even the seediest antique shop in Edendale would give it a pass. There were cases of crumbling butterflies and semi-precious stones, toy soldiers and porcelain dolls, stuffed antelope heads and sporting prints.

Cooper made a mental note to check on the earl's gun licence. He felt sure there would be one. He imagined a cabinet full of shotguns somewhere in the house, perhaps even a few ancient blunderbusses and an elephant gun. Some poor licensing officer would have had the job of checking whether they were functional firearms or purely ornamental.

'Yes, some of the Manby ancestors were avid collectors,' said Meredith Burns. 'The Victorians went in for natural history, and the eighteenth-century earls for religious texts. Of course, more than a few of them were army officers too.'

'It's amazing how much stuff they came back from Africa and India with,' said Fry. 'They must have used soldiers like pack-horses to cart all their loot.'

There was a virtual tour of the state rooms on the first floor, an idea Cooper suspected had been copied from the National Trust, which had used them in its historic properties for years. He supposed it was an attempt to deter visitors from wandering around parts of the abbey where they shouldn't go. But did it work? Well, it would take more than a glossy video and a bit of velvet rope across the doorway.

Cooper felt sure a determined and experienced snooper would have no trouble getting into any of the state rooms. There wasn't exactly a high level of security. This was just someone's home, after all. If an intruder could get into Buckingham Palace and chat to the Queen in her bedroom, there wasn't much hope for an amateur set-up like this. The earl and his family would be sitting ducks, if someone had seriously decided to make them a target.

'The private family apartments are in the west wing,' said Burns. 'Walter has an office of his own up there on the first floor, in the library. But many of the rooms in the north wing are now staff flats, offices, workshops and storerooms. Then we have these areas, which are accessible to the public. The visitor route alone is half a mile long. And it all gets vacuumed and dusted every day.'

They found themselves in the final doorway of a long corridor, gazing into apparent chaos. It was such a cluttered room. Every inch of floor space seemed to be crammed with furniture, and every available surface covered in ornaments and trinkets of no discernible use. How would you live in a room like this? He would hardly dare to move.

'You can't be serious about this threat?' said Burns.

'We do have good reason to be concerned. You should step up your security as much as possible, both in the abbey and around the park. We'll have officers here to advise on additional security measures you can take. Also a dog unit will be arriving, in case there are already explosives on the premises.'

'Our visitors aren't going to like that,' said Burns.

'Visitors? Didn't we say? We're recommending that you close the abbey to the public for the time being, until we're sure the threat has passed.'

'That's ludicrous. Have you any idea how much revenue we would lose? All our Christmas bookings would be cancelled, for a start. Walter would never agree to it.'

'Could we speak to the earl himself perhaps and explain the situation?'

'I don't think so, Sergeant,' said Burns stiffly. 'Perhaps a more senior officer…'

Cooper nodded. He didn't feel offended. Well, not as offended as Fry looked, anyway.

'I'll have a word with my superintendent,' he said.

'Yes, do that.'

Fry was staring with baffled revulsion at a huge glass cabinet full of stuffed birds. And it *was* full. There had been no half measures for this particularly fervent collector among the Manbys. Against a painted background of a seashore, he'd crammed in a heron, a couple of bitterns, a whole flock of curlews, turnstones and lapwings who crowded against each other in the foreground. A shelduck and a trio of plovers dangled from the top of the case in simulated flight. There was hardly an inch to spare between one set of feathers and the next.

And it was just one of many cases full of birds in this room. They were stacked right up to the ceiling on every wall. Some former earl must have been going for a complete collection of British bird species, thought Cooper, as he surveyed the room. Well, except for that pelican, resplendent in a case of its own, just about to swallow an equally stuffed fish.

'What is your energy supply here?' asked Cooper.

'There's a wood pellet-fuelled biomass heating system installed in a former agricultural building. It was one of Walter's first projects when he inherited the estate. The system is fully automated and provides heating to various properties on the estate.'

'Underground piping?'

'Of course. About five hundred metres of it.'

'Very vulnerable.'

'Well, oil and electric storage heaters were the wrong sort of system to be using on such a big house, so investing in a green energy system seemed to be important. It lowers fuel costs and significantly reduces the estate's carbon footprint. It even produces a financial payback through the government's incentive scheme.'

'One of his lordship's most productive ideas, then.'

'Precisely.'

They examined the main entrance with its wide steps and pillars, and a smaller side door where visitors paid their entrance fee. The locks were adequate, the alarm system modern. The earl would never have been able to get insurance for his historic mansion without those precautions.

'I've been told the burial ground will be tarmacked over and become a car park for the holiday accommodation,' said Cooper.

Burns shook her head. 'That's nonsense. We would never be allowed to do that, even if we wanted to. Most of it will remain an area of open space, with a bit of landscaping.'

'I can't emphasise enough how important it is to step up your security measures. There's a good private security company based in Buxton. You should contact them.'

'I'll note your advice.'

Outside the main entrance, Cooper heard voices above him and looked up in astonishment.

'Who are those people on the roof?' he asked.

'Oh, they're a group of historic house enthusiasts,' said Burns.

'Members of the public?'

'They paid twenty-five pounds each for a behind-the-scenes tour of the abbey today.'

The party had been led up a flight of narrow stairs from the top floor, through the attic, and out on to the roof, where they were able to gaze over the stone parapets at a mist-shrouded view of the Dove Valley. Directly below them was the crumbling Lady Chapel. They would have a good view of the missing tiles and the cracks in the walls. They would probably glimpse the corroded face of a stone angel. Or, if they were really lucky, they might witness an entire section shearing off the façade, like a calving glacier.

Cooper shook his head. Was there any point in wasting his breath urging extra security precautions when there was a crowd of complete strangers being allowed on to the roof?

THEY ARRANGED TO leave the park through the north entrance, taking a winding route through sheep pastures on the lower slopes of the hill, backed by more woodland. A member of outdoor staff was on hand to unlock the barrier and let them through.

Outside the north gate they were forced to slow to a crawl. A group of about twenty people were milling around with placards. Cooper stopped to speak to one of the two uniformed officers keeping a discreet eye on the demonstration.

'What are those people doing?' he asked.

'Oh, them? They're environmentalists. They're protesting against the quarry plan.'

'Quarry plan?'

The officer gestured to the hillside behind Knowle Abbey. The white scar of the limestone face was visible above the trees of the parkland.

'For Alderhill,' she said. 'There's a plan to bring it back into operation.'

'And that looks like the earl himself talking to them.'

'Yes, it is.'

Walter Manby was an ordinary-looking man in many ways. Yet somehow he gave off an aura of money, a peculiar glow that made him stand out from those around him. He stood casually among the protestors, chatting amiably to their dreadlocked leaders, his hands thrust deep into his pockets, yet unable to resist the occasional supercilious smile.

COOPER TAPPED HIS fingers on the steering wheel of the car as they drove back towards Edendale.

'Who did we ask to look into Eden Valley Mineral Products?' he said out loud.

'We?' said Fry.

He'd almost forgotten she was there. She was becoming his conscience, haunting him like all the guilt he'd ever felt, all the uncomfortable doubts over his own competence.

'Me, then,' he said. 'I asked somebody to look into Eden Valley Mineral Products.'

'Luke Irvine,' said Fry. 'I believe he was tasked with following that up.'

And she was right, as usual. Cooper got hold of Irvine as they were climbing the hill on the other side of the valley.

'Yes,' said Irvine. 'Did you know that Deeplow Quarry is owned by Eden Valley Mineral Products?'

'The company where George Redfearn was a director?'

'That's the one.'

'Well, it's a link,' said Cooper.

'Of a kind. But what does it mean?'

'I have no idea. Anything else we should know about the company?'

'They've been doing okay. In fact, they're planning to expand into a new site soon. They won a bidding war to get the contract. It's a big deal.'

'Where is the new site?'

'Alderhill Quarry,' said Irvine. 'Have you ever heard of it?'

Cooper turned and gazed towards Knowle Abbey, sitting down there by the river in its parkland – a perfect picture, but for the white scar on the hillside behind it.

'Alderhill Quarry?' he said. 'I'm looking at it right now.'

'Seriously?'

'And what about the protests?'

'I don't know anything about any protests,' said Irvine.

'Well, make sure you do by the time we get back to West Street,' said Cooper as he ended the call.

He sensed Fry smiling. But when he turned to look at her, she was staring out of the window. And he'd never been able to read her mind.

Luke Irvine was waiting eagerly when Ben Cooper and Diane Fry arrived in the CID room. Cooper didn't even bother to take off his jacket.

'Those protestors,' he said. 'The quarry plan. What do we know about it?'

'It seems the environmentalist crowd are protesting against the destruction of a protected area through opencast quarrying,' said Irvine. 'The site of Alderhill Quarry is on land owned by the Knowle estate and the contract has been signed by Lord Manby himself. As part of the lease agreement, the landowner will receive thirty pounds for each ton of rock extracted from the site.'

'It doesn't sound that much.'

'Well, the quarry has vast potential apparently. The reserves of limestone go right back into the hillside. In fact, it sounds as though there won't be much of the hill left by the time they've finished digging. They'll be quarrying out there for decades to come.' Irvine looked up from his notes. 'That's a hell of a lot of rock, Ben.'

'Is there an estimate?'

Irvine nodded. 'A ballpark figure. If the quarry development goes ahead at Alderhill, the Knowle estate stands to earn more than two hundred million pounds.'

Chapter Thirty-five

FIREFIGHTERS HAD CHOSEN the evening before Bonfire Night for another strike over changes to their working conditions and cuts in their pension rights. The strike had started at 6.30 p.m. and was due to last until eleven. Contingency crews had been formed from half-trained volunteers, though strikers had agreed they would obey a recall if lives were at risk.

When vandals set the Bowden bonfire alight that Monday evening, there were judged to be no lives at risk. In fact, a small crowd of people gathered from the houses to watch it burn. The blaze could be seen right across the park and staff came out of the abbey itself to see what was happening. A security guard and a couple of gamekeepers were tasked with checking the parkland near Bowden for the intruders who'd started the fire, but they could find no one.

The stack of wood had been blazing into the night sky for almost an hour before a volunteer crew eventually arrived from Buxton. And it was already too late. The Buxton crew soon extinguished the remaining embers. But by then Bowden's bonfire was dead and gone.

STERNDALE MOOR WAS an odd little collection of houses, like a chunk of an urban council estate sliced off and dumped in the countryside. It was handy for workers at the quarries, Cooper supposed – the entrance to Deeplow stood almost directly across the A515.

As he drove into it that evening Cooper found only one short street, with a branch off it to a patch of wasteland used for parking and the entrance to a social club. The club building matched the housing. It was low, grimy and pebble-dashed. To one side stood a corrugated-iron smokers' shelter, open-fronted and containing half a dozen chairs and a couple of plastic bins. It looked a grim place to spend even part of an evening during a Derbyshire winter.

He wondered where Rob Beresford was planning to spend the night. There had still been no sightings of him the last time he checked, and Beresford's parents had received no contact from him. The longer he was missing, the more worrying it would be.

Since there was nowhere to park on the street, Cooper turned the Toyota on to the waste ground. He parked next to a van attached to a trailer that was loaded with a battered stock car. Perhaps it was used for racing up the road at Axe Edge. On the back the vehicle was decorated with the slogans 'Work to live, live to race' and 'If you can read this, I need more mud'. More bafflingly, the bonnet said, 'Pennine Pikeys Runyagit'. Cooper shook his head over that. It was probably best not to ask.

The club was closed, but Cooper peered through one of the windows and caught sight of two porcelain figurines standing on the ledge inside. A cowboy and Indian. They seemed a strange pair for a social club in a Peak District village. But then Cooper had a memory, a flashback to that occasion years before. How many years was it? Fifteen? Or perhaps more? So the country and western club still met here.

This was one of those odd places the Peak District was full of. Above Sterndale Moor, on Red Hurst Hill, a fake stone circle called Wheeldon's Folly had been built by a local farmer from random stones, lumps of concrete and even an old gatepost. In this area you never knew what sort of place you were arriving in or what might lie behind its façade.

Yet Sterndale Moor had one thing in common with Bowden. There were almost no people around. It was dark and the residents all seemed to be shut behind their own doors. All he could see was a young woman with a small child waiting in the bus shelter outside the social club. There was no sign of a bus.

Brendan Kilner lived in a small, pebble-dashed semi-detached house. The tiny front garden had been removed and concreted over to create just enough space to park a couple of cars off the road, a Ford Fiesta and a Peugeot.

Kilner looked surprised to see Ben Cooper standing on his doorstep. He'd been relaxing in front of the telly, judging by the sound of the *Coronation Street* theme tune drifting from an open door. Kilner was wearing jeans and an old checked shirt, and had come to the door in his socks, with a beer can clutched in one hand.

'Something up?' he said.

'Just a couple of things I wanted to ask you,' said Cooper.

'You're working late, aren't you?'

'You know what it's like, Brendan. No rest for the wicked.'

'Oh, er…' Kilner glanced over his shoulder, as if calculating what might be on view inside the house that he wouldn't want anyone to see. But his conclusion must have been on the positive side. 'I suppose you'd better come in.'

As he entered the house Cooper thought he detected that whiff of fried onions again, but perhaps it was just a memory of their meeting at Buxton Raceway. Just a bit of bad déjà vu.

'Come through to the back,' said Kilner, with a wary glance through an open doorway.

Cooper took a peek too and saw the back of a woman's head on a sofa in front of a large TV screen. He felt certain the Kilners had a couple of sons, and perhaps a daughter. But they would all be well grown-up by now and probably extending the clan in their turn.

'Just you and the wife at home?' said Cooper. 'Sorry, I've forgotten her name.'

'Lisa.'

Kilner had lowered his voice, perhaps worried in case he attracted her attention.

'Is she okay?'

'Fine.'

There was a small room at the back of the house, adjoining the kitchen. Kilner seemed to have converted it into a workshop. There were air filters and boxes of suspension springs, a crankshaft and even a couple of tyres.

'I do a bit of work on the stocks now and then,' said Kilner.

'On the side, I suppose?'

Kilner shrugged. 'Everyone does it.'

'And does Lisa not mind you bringing all this stuff into the house?'

'As long as I clean up the oil, she doesn't yell too much.'

Cooper was trying to recall exactly what Brendan Kilner said to him at the raceway on Sunday. It was Kilner who'd said: 'They've all got an axe to grind.' But there was something else. *It's all about family. Ancient history if you ask me. But that stuff means a lot to some people, doesn't it? Me, I can never bring myself to visit the place where my mum and dad were buried.*

He looked across the hall, glad of the noise coming from the sitting room, the TV turned up a bit too loud. It was such a different home from the expensive Georgian property rented by Marcus Everett and his friends near Pilsbury. Yet there was a similarity, which Cooper had suspected. It had been put into his mind by the sight of that drooping Mexican moustache, the fake Confederate soldier. That same man had offered him a joint outside the Sterndale Moor Social Club on the night he'd been dragged to the country and western evening.

And Gavin Murfin was right to remind him about Brendan Kilner's background too. Cooper had checked the intelligence.

The items on view in Kilner's kitchen were different from those he'd seen in the rental property at Pilsbury. There were no silver trays or plastic straws for sniffing lines of cocaine. Instead, he saw small cotton balls, a pile of bottle caps and a narrow leather belt with a series of teeth marks visible on the end, as if it had been chewed by the dog.

At least the Kilners disposed of their hypodermic needles, even if they were only in the pedal bin. That wasn't the case in some houses Cooper had visited, where the floor might be covered in used needles and you had to be careful where you put your feet when you walked across a room. Some illegal drugs gave the user a sense of invulnerability. Individuals began to believe they would never be found out, that no one would ever notice their paraphernalia or suspect what they were up to when they took a spare belt into the toilet to tie off a vein.

Brendan Kilner probably felt he was safe when he took that moment at the door to reassure himself that his needles and his wraps of heroin were safely out of sight.

But perhaps it wasn't Kilner himself who was the user. It might be his wife or one of his adult children. It wouldn't make any difference. It was all about family, after all.

Kilner had stopped and was watching him resignedly. He was an old hand and he knew the score. Cooper didn't have to explain it to him, the way he had to Everett. Some people grew up confident they would never have to deal with the law. Others expected it. And they were rarely mistaken.

'So what do you want?' said Kilner. 'I dare say there's something.'

'Yes, as a matter of fact,' said Cooper. 'There is.'

DIANE FRY GOT a call-out in the middle of the night. She always hated that. Yet at the same time she experienced an immediate buzz of excitement when her phone rang. This was what she lived for, after all. All the hours of tedium and paperwork were worthwhile, just for this.

The drive through Derbyshire had been dark and wet, the transition from city streets back to muddy rural lanes almost too painful to bear. She needed her satnav just to guide her to the A610 and on to the A6 towards Matlock. After that it was like entering the twilight zone.

At Knowle Abbey she had only to follow the signs of activity. By the time she reached the outer cordon the crime-scene tents had been erected and the scene itself was lit by powerful arc lights.

With the dark outline of Knowle Abbey as a sinister backdrop, the whole effect was of a badly illuminated scene from a melodrama. It looked to Fry as though Earl Manby had decided to stage a modern, open-air version of *Hamlet* in the grounds of the abbey. A perfect setting for Ben Cooper's ghosts haunting the mock battlements.

When she'd struggled into a scene suit and joined DCI Mackenzie inside the larger tent, Fry could see the gruesome reality. The earl's body lay sprawled on the grass, a splatter of blood and shredded flesh in a wide arc round him. His head was unrecognisable from this angle. One bloodied pulp looked much like another.

'Shotgun?' she asked. Nothing else did that kind of damage to a human body at close quarters.

Mackenzie nodded. 'He was shot twice. The second barrel was the one that killed him.'

Fry covered her mouth as she examined the injuries caused by the lead shot. The smell of raw meat rose from the ground under the hot lights.

'And we're sure it's the earl himself?' she said.

'He was found by one of the staff, who called the family. There's no doubt about it. I'm afraid there's been a lot of trampling of the scene and contamination of the evidence already, before we got here.'

Gradually, Fry moved around to the other side of the tent. She could see now that the left side of the earl's face was more or less intact. Most of the damage had been done to the back and side of his head. One ear had been shattered and the jawbone gleamed through oozing blood.

At least it looked as though the earl had tried to defend himself. The palms of his hands were also shredded by pellets, as if he'd made a defensive gesture at the last moment, trying to protect his face from the blast. But it had been futile. It was a pity he hadn't taken one of his own weapons from the gunroom with him when he went out in the grounds. His attacker might have thought twice.

But why had the earl gone out into the grounds of the abbey last night at all? It seemed an odd question to be asking herself, really. Why shouldn't any individual walk around his own property in perfect safety, whenever he wanted to? It ought not to matter who they were. But Walter Manby had been under threat. He'd been warned there might be an imminent danger to his life. And he'd still felt able to wander alone in the dark through the wooded parklands of Knowle.

In a way Fry had to admire the courage or self-assurance this man must have felt. Perhaps it was a quality that came with the position he'd been born into, like that air of affluence that had turned out to be such a façade. Maybe it was being on his own property that gave him confidence. The earl and Knowle Abbey had certainly seemed inseparable.

'Do you think he came out here to meet someone he knew?' she said.

'We don't know,' said Mackenzie. 'Let's see what evidence Forensics can turn up.'

'It's a bad business.'

Mackenzie smiled grimly. 'Tell me about it. We'll need to start interviewing staff.'

'Where are we going to get the help from?'

'Why, how many are there?'

'About three hundred,' said Fry automatically.

'Seriously?'

'Guides, housekeepers, office staff, the maintenance team, shop assistants, kitchen and serving staff in the restaurant, gardeners, gamekeepers, farmers, river bailiffs, car park attendants … where do you want to start?'

Mackenzie frowned at her tone. 'With those who were on duty here when the shooting occurred. That's simple enough, Diane.'

Fry took one last look at the body before she left the tent and stripped off her scene suit.

'When word gets round about this,' she said, 'I know someone who'll say, "I told you so".'

Chapter Thirty-six

Tuesday 5 November

THAT MORNING COOPER was due to give evidence in a trial at Derby Crown Court. Luckily, he didn't have to go all the way to Derby any more and waste an entire day sitting around waiting for his few minutes in court. The new video-link technology allowed him to give his evidence from a desk right there at the divisional headquarters in Edendale.

Other officers had been busy working on the George Redfearn murder inquiry. As he arrived at West Street, Cooper had seen Diane Fry's boss DCI Alistair Mackenzie there from the Major Crime Unit. Mackenzie would no doubt be acting as senior investigating officer.

For a moment Cooper wondered if the MCU had considered the Sandra Blair case to be too unimportant to merit their full attention from the start, even before doubt was cast on its status as a murder inquiry by the post-mortem results. He would have to make the best of that. While everyone else's attention was on the murder, he had the chance to resolve the situation at Knowle Abbey.

But when he came out of the video-link room later in the morning, Cooper began to hear people talking about Knowle Abbey in urgent tones. He had no idea what was going on. He felt as though he'd been locked into suspended animation for the past hour or so and emerged to find the world had moved on without him.

'What's going on?' he asked Luke Irvine, who was the only occupant of the CID room. 'What's all this about Knowle Abbey?'

'It's the earl.'

Cooper detected the air of disaster. 'Is he dead?'

'He died last night. He was fatally wounded with a shotgun while everyone's attention was distracted by the fire at the estate village.'

'And I don't suppose it was an accident, or suicide.'

'No chance.'

COOPER SLOWLY GATHERED his team together from their various assignments. It seemed more important than ever that they concentrated on making connections that could explain the whole story, and not just a small part of it.

He'd asked for background enquiries on all the people involved in the protest group and there ought to be some results by now.

'Talk to us about the quarry plan for Alderhill first, Luke,' he said.

Irvine explained the position of Eden Valley Mineral Products and their plans for Alderhill Quarry.

'George Redfearn was Development Director at the company,' he said. 'Mr Redfearn was responsible for winning the contract to bring the quarry back into operation. His name is signed on the dotted line. Along with the earl's of course.'

'So, the protest group,' said Cooper. 'The people we're interested in include Jason Shaw, aged thirty-two, with an address in Bowden on the Knowle estate, where we're told he works as a gamekeeper.'

'Here's an interesting thing, though,' said Irvine. 'At the end of last year Jason Shaw's hours at Knowle Abbey were cut back. So he managed to find some part-time work at Deeplow Quarry. He's been there a few months now.'

'So he may have been the one who learned how to put an explosive charge together?' asked Irvine.

'With diesel fuel and ammonium nitrate, you mean?'

'Exactly.'

'He wasn't actually given any training in the use of explosives,' said Irvine. 'They were pretty clear on that. He had no authorisation or experience. But I suppose you can pick up a few things just by observing and asking questions.'

'A little knowledge can be a dangerous thing,' said Cooper. 'Especially when it comes to making explosives. Anything else?'

'Well, before he got a job at the abbey, do you know Shaw worked at the cheese factory in Hartington?'

'No, I didn't know that.'

'He was a warehouseman and forklift truck driver.'

'A real jack of all trades.'

'From some of the hints I've been given when I followed up on Shaw, gamekeeping is the job that's most up his street, though.'

'What do you mean, Luke?'

Irvine smiled. 'It seems Jason Shaw is known for producing the occasional rabbit or pheasant in return for a favour. No questions asked about where they came from. You get the picture?'

'He's a poacher.'

'And so was his father before him. They say that's where his skill came from – he learned the tricks of the trade from his dad. In fact, Shaw has a conviction on file for an offence fourteen years ago, when he was a teenager. He was caught out with his father taking a deer. So whoever gave him the job as a gamekeeper probably made a smart move.'

'The tricks of the trade,' said Cooper. 'He'll have learned how to use a shotgun at an early age too.'

'We don't have any real evidence against Jason Shaw,' pointed out Hurst. 'It's only speculation. All circumstantial.'

'What do we know of his whereabouts now?'

'He's not due at the quarry today, but he has a late shift at the abbey. Apparently, they're drafting in some of the estate staff to provide a bit of extra security at night-time.'

'Wait a minute – who interviewed Shaw? Wasn't it you, Luke?'

Irvine shifted uneasily. 'Me – and Carol Villiers. When we came back, we reported to DS Fry.'

'I see.'

'You weren't here, Ben.'

'Right.'

Cooper found he couldn't fault Irvine. Though the excuse he'd just relied on was the same one he'd used at the scene of George Redfearn's murder, when it was the other way round and Fry had been absent. It sounded like a shift in loyalties. But he was probably imagining things.

'It seems to me that Shaw developed a relationship with Sandra Blair after they met in the protest group,' said Carol Villiers. 'We know it was Jason Shaw she met up with in Longnor on the evening she died.'

'Anything else?'

'Well, he does have a link with the Nadens,' said Becky Hurst.

'Does he?'

'Yes.' Hurst consulted her notes. 'Geoff and Sally Naden were both made redundant from the cheese factory in Hartington. Mr Naden had been a cheese-maker for twenty-five years and his wife worked in the offices. When they lost their jobs he became a parking attendant at Knowle Abbey and she went to work in the kitchen making sandwiches for the café.'

'Interesting.'

Cooper imagined those jobs weren't as well paid as the Nadens had been used to, but they had probably felt they were secure working for the earl. With so many visitors, their services would always be needed. But then they must have found out that Lord Manby was planning to get rid of them – and the visitors too. He had no interest in the welfare of his staff, only in the money he could make from the estate's assets.

'We know about Rob Beresford,' said Hurst. 'He appears to be an open book. A bit hot-headed maybe, but he doesn't seem the type to be violent.'

'And Sandra Blair we know too,' added Irvine.

'There was the note in her diary about a meeting at the Grand-father Oak. What was that meeting all about?'

'I'm not sure it ever took place,' said Cooper.

It seemed to Cooper that the graveyard protest campaign had drawn attention away from the real issue. Among the protest group there must have been a more extreme faction, one or two individuals who wanted direct action. Well, more than direct action – they intended violence. They were very angry.

'I think there were two factions, who had a disagreement,' said Cooper. 'And it all fell apart that Halloween night. Somebody wasn't where they were supposed to be according to the plan. That person was out killing George Redfearn at Pilsbury Castle. Mr Redfearn's murder was a message the earl couldn't ignore.'

'But who was that?' asked Villiers.

'Whoever Sandra Blair was supposed to meet at the bridge that night.'

'We've talked to the members of the group we can identify. They all insist there were only five in the core group – the Nadens, Jason Shaw, Rob Beresford and Sandra Blair herself.'

'It's not true, though,' said Cooper.

'Why, Ben?' said Villiers.

He indicated the group photo on his screen, the one taken at Harpur Hill with the Nadens, Shaw, Beresford and Sandra Blair.

'Well, think about it,' he said. 'This photo was taken on Sandra's phone. But she's in the shot herself. So who took the picture?'

BEN COOPER WAS anxious to get an opportunity to see inside Jason Shaw's house. But at the moment he didn't have enough justification for a search warrant. As Irvine had said, it was all speculation and suspicion. It was a shame, though. A person's home told you more about them than any amount of background checks you could do. No matter how many friends, colleagues and neighbours you talked to, you wouldn't ever get a true picture of the person. Everyone created a public façade for themselves, sometimes several. You could be one person at work, a different one with the family, and another when you were down the pub with your friends. But inside the home was where the façade broke down. You could see the aspects of a person's life that they didn't want anyone to know about.

It was only inside Sandra Blair's home that he'd got a proper feeling for the sort of person she was. And, though she had some unusual interests, he didn't feel she was the fanatical type who would be willing to take violent direct action, as she'd been described by the Nadens.

And of course he'd seen inside Knowle Abbey too. That was an eye-opener. Yet he'd learned almost nothing about its present owner, while learning perhaps too much about some of his eccentric ancestors. Earl Manby remained an enigmatic figure, a sort of figurehead for the estate, like the eagle's head emblem of the Manby family, representing something more than just itself.

Cooper would have liked to be able to see behind the façade being presented at Knowle on behalf of his lordship, if only for the sake of his own curiosity. But it probably wouldn't happen now. He wondered if Detective Superintendent Branagh had ever managed to get a few words with the earl, as he'd suggested. That was a conversation he would love to have overheard. They were two people accustomed to exercising power.

In a way coffin roads represented the worst aspects of the hierarchical structures so many people had lived with. They weren't legacies from an ancient past, but were deliberately brought into being during medieval times. They were an unintended side-effect of an old canon law on the rights of parishioners. As Bill Latham had said himself, they were just one more exercise in power and privilege.

Cooper put on his jacket and set off to visit Knowle Abbey for the final time.

STAFF INTERVIEWS WERE under way at Knowle. The Major Crime Unit had taken over the estate office, ousting Meredith Burns from her desk.

Cooper thought of that message they'd found: 'Meet Grandfather, 1am'. But that must have been a different meeting, surely? It had been marked in Sandra Blair's diary for 31 October. And this killing had happened earlier than one o'clock. It had been planned for the period when the bonfire was blazing away in Bowden, a time when many of the staff from the abbey were either at home themselves or distracted from their duties.

'A shotgun,' he said when he met Fry at the outer cordon. 'That's a totally different situation altogether from the other deaths, Diane.'

'Absolutely.'

Of course, there were many legally held shotguns in the possession of ordinary individuals in an area like this. Farmers always had them. Cooper owned one himself, though he kept it in the gun cabinet at Bridge End Farm with Matt's.

But right now he was thinking of the men he'd seen at that remote farmstead on Axe Edge Moor. Bagshaw Farm, the home of Daniel Grady. Had one of those men been sent on a different kind of rat hunt?

He hadn't liked Grady and felt sure a bit of digging would turn up all kinds of dubious activities. But was Grady so closely involved with the protest group? Or did somebody simply have enough money to pay him for this kind of service?

Cooper told Fry about the plans for Alderhill Quarry and the link to George Redfearn's company. Her mouth fell open when he mentioned the sum of two hundred million pounds.

'Do you remember what Meredith Burns said that first time we visited Knowle Abbey?' said Cooper. 'When I offended her by asking for a photograph of the earl?'

'Yes, she said he wasn't a rock star. I thought that was stating the obvious myself.'

'No, not that. She said he would much rather find some other way of paying for the upkeep of the abbey, instead of letting all these visitors in. Because it was his home.'

'Oh, yes. I do remember,' said Fry.

'Well, this is it, isn't it?'

'This is what?'

'The quarry scheme is his alternative way of funding the repair and maintenance of Knowle Abbey.' Cooper waved a hand at the visitors being turned away at the gate, at the car parking area, and the buildings converted for use as a restaurant, a craft centre, a gift shop. 'The revenue from the quarry would have enabled him to put a stop to all this. No more crowds of visitors coming in to gawp at his home.'

'Well, it would be a shame, I suppose,' said Fry, 'if you're interested in that sort of thing. But there are plenty of other historic houses in Derbyshire. Chatsworth is much grander, they tell me. And Haddon Hall is supposed to be better preserved.'

'No, no, you're missing the point,' said Cooper. 'Think about it for a minute. No paying visitors means no restaurant, no craft centre, no gift shop and no plant nursery. And without those there would be no guides, no car park attendants, no catering staff or shop assistants. A lot of people would lose their jobs.'

'You're right.'

Cooper sighed. He didn't want to be right. Not all the time. Not when the truth seemed so tragic and so inevitable.

'At the moment Knowle Abbey is putting a lot of money back into local communities through the wages paid to all these staff. That would stop if the quarry goes ahead. Eden Valley Mineral Products would have no interest in employing local people.' He shook his head in despair. 'It's just like the cheese factory all over again.'

'What?' said Fry, puzzled.

'Never mind.'

'You know, that's not what I expected you to say.'

'What did you expect me to say, Diane?'

'"I told you so."'

Chapter Thirty-seven

'So it's a smokescreen, isn't it?' said Fry.

'What is?'

'This business about the Corpse Bridge. It was all designed to distract our attention, to make us think the deaths were connected with the redevelopment of the graveyard. I have to say that if I'd been the investigating officer myself in those initial stages, the idea would never have occurred to me.'

'That's because of your local ignorance,' protested Cooper. 'You'd never heard of the Corpse Bridge or a coffin road.'

'Exactly,' said Fry. 'Except that I wouldn't describe it as ignorance. I'd call it the advantage of an unbiased mind.'

Cooper thought about it for a moment. Could she be right about this? To be fair, she sometimes *was* right. That cold objectivity of hers had its place.

'But if it was a deliberate distraction,' he said slowly, 'that would mean…'

'Yes, Ben. That whoever was responsible expected to be dealing with a local person, who knew the history of the Corpse Bridge. They anticipated it would be someone like you, in fact.'

Cooper shook his head. 'Surely anyone would have made the connection eventually, once they started asking a few questions.'

'Eventually, perhaps. But we'd have picked up more useful lines of inquiry by then. And we'd have saved ourselves a lot of time and effort. And perhaps some lives.'

'So you're fixing your mind on the quarry protests.'

'And you're still fixated with the Corpse Bridge and the Bowden protest group.'

'Someone planned all this,' said Cooper. 'An individual who knows all about lying and when to tell the truth – or, at least, a partial truth. They all followed the same strategy. They gave us the truth when there was no point in trying to conceal it. Rob Beresford admitted straight away that he knew Sandra Blair. Both the Nadens and Jason Shaw came forward to admit they were in the area at the time she died. It made them look innocent and willing to cooperate. And Brendan Kilner pointed me in the direction of the burial ground at Bowden when I enquired about a connection between the names. Once I'd asked him that question, he knew I'd find out the answer some other way. So he told me. But even Kilner only gave me as little as he needed to and no more.'

'So what are you saying?'

'I think there was a policy at work here. Rules of engagement, if you like. It's a bit too neat for each of them to have thought of doing that separately. People just don't react in that way without some advance preparation. The instinct of the guilty is to tell a lie.'

'There's still a big question for you to think about, though, isn't there? Who was with Sandra Blair at the bridge that night?'

Cooper couldn't answer that question, no matter how much he would have liked to. He had to let it pass. Instead, he considered the crime scene, with its tents and arc lights and figures in white scene suits going backwards and forwards to the forensic vans.

'So the earl was attacked at the Grandfather Oak?' he said.

'His attacker was standing under the tree,' said Fry. 'The earl was shot at close range the first time. He probably saw his attacker and turned away to escape. The first blast caught him in the back of the right shoulder.'

'Yes, I see.'

Then the earl had run. He almost reached the back of the abbey, the west wing where the family apartments were located. The killer must have pursued him before firing the second and fatal shot.

Cooper walked past the crime-scene tent to look at the abbey. While he was alive the earl himself had come and gone from this side of the house, probably to avoid meeting the public. This section of parkland was fenced off and gated to prevent access. He could see a stable block and a building with a glass roof like a conservatory. An orangery? Was that what they called it?

Cooper hadn't seen the back of the abbey buildings on his previous visits. From here the place looked totally different. He was no longer seeing the over-elaborate façade that made Knowle Abbey look like a tourist postcard from the east. On the west side the buildings were random and grimy, almost ramshackle. Weeds were growing in the orangery, but no oranges. The stables were abandoned and derelict. They might have housed a few rats, but no horses.

The woodland was neglected too. Trees were diseased and damaged. Brambles and bracken had infested the woodland floor where once there might have been swathes of bluebells. There were no visible trails. A bridlepath from the stables had become choked by birch saplings and blocked by fallen branches.

Closer to hand, he could see that the wilderness was encroaching on to the gravel drive. In fact, it had probably crept closer to the abbey than it should have done by several yards. The gravel itself sprouted weeds, and heaps of rubbish had built up against the rear walls – rusting metal, broken plastic, a crumbling mess of wet plasterboard. The windows here were dirty and cobwebbed, some of them actually broken. Cooper thought back to the discussion with Meredith Burns about security measures. Did the insurance company know about this part of the abbey?

One of the opening lines from Daphne du Maurier's *Rebecca* came into his mind. *The woods crowded dark and uncontrolled to the drive.* Well, Knowle Abbey was no Manderley, but Rebecca would have noticed the same phenomenon here. All the estate work seemed to have been concentrated on the front of the abbey, the façade that visitors saw. Here the trees had been left unmanaged for years, by the look of them. It was a criminal neglect of valuable woodland. Not to mention the damage it must have done to the view from the west wing.

It seemed that all the time and effort the earl had talked about had been put into those parts of the estate that were on show to the public. He'd created a façade of elegance, with a ramshackle dereliction behind it, like a Hollywood film set. All appearance and no substance. A hollow charade.

Cooper turned to look at the house. He pictured Lord Manby at his desk in the library. The window was right there, on the first floor. The earl would have glanced up now and then from his paperwork and seen the evidence of neglect for himself. Had this untamed undergrowth seemed like the portents of inevitable ruin, creeping ever closer to his walls?

MEREDITH BURNS LOOKED a bit lost, like a woman who no longer knew what her purpose was. She'd been standing watching Cooper as he examined the abbey. She said nothing, until he turned and found her there.

'We took your advice and called in the security company,' she said.

'But too late, it seems.'

'Yes.'

'I'm sorry.'

Burns flapped her arms helplessly. 'We've found something else,' she said. 'I don't know if it's relevant or not.'

'What is it?'

'I'll show you.'

An intruder had tried to force open a Manby family tomb in the Lady Chapel. It was a marble sarcophagus with a cut-glass lid, but coated in grey mould from the damp of generations. Now a corner was broken off, as if someone had prised at it with a crowbar.

'Could this have been what brought the earl out into the grounds last night?' asked Cooper.

'That's what I wondered. If Walter heard a noise or saw someone near the chapel.'

'It's a possibility. I'll get a crime-scene examiner to check it for fingerprints.'

Burns gazed round the crumbling walls and eroded statues of the chapel. 'What do you think anyone would be looking for in here?' she said.

'Nothing,' said Cooper. 'I think they were probably intending to cause some damage.'

'Like the graffiti?'

'Yes, but a step further.'

'It's awful to think they would come here with the intention of causing damage to a tomb.'

'Or to the occupant.'

Cooper saw the shocked expression on Burns's face. But what Brendan Kilner had said still held good. It was all about family.

'Your superintendent has arrived, by the way,' said Burns as they left the chapel.

'Detective Superintendent Branagh is here?'

'Yes. She's meeting with the earl.'

'The earl? Lord Manby?'

'I mean Peter Manby,' said Burns. 'He's the new earl, of course. With the death of his father, he's just inherited the Knowle estate.'

'Of course he has.'

Cooper looked out over the parkland towards the front of the abbey. What would the arrival of a new owner mean to the master plan for the development of Knowle? Would the latest Lord Manby steer the estate in a different direction or would he be too much under the influence of the Dowager Countess? Would the quarrying plan still go ahead? And might the bulldozers still move into the old graveyard, despite everything? Time would tell. But now at least there was a chance that someone could make a difference.

Chapter Thirty-eight

FROM KNOWLE ABBEY, Cooper took a detour via the Corpse Bridge. He was able to bounce the Toyota halfway down the track, with the steering wheel lurching violently in his hands.

Off-roaders had been blamed for destroying many of the stone setts and churning up the ground into muddy ruts on either side. Although this had been designated as a byway open to all traffic for many years, the national park authority had imposed a traffic regulation order to exclude trail bikes and four-wheel drives.

But Cooper had heard off-roaders say they had as much right as anyone to enjoy the landscape. They pointed out that all kinds of recreation caused damage. If local authorities were too cash-strapped to maintain rights of way properly, that was a problem for everyone. As usual there were two sides to every story.

The police presence had gone from the scene of Sandra Blair's death. The tape had been removed but for a few scraps still fluttering from a tree, where an officer had cut it instead of trying to untie a tight, wet knot. The forensic examination had been complete, the search had reached its outer perimeter, and the scene had been released for public access.

Not that there were many members of the public around. Unlike some more accessible murder scenes, the Corpse Bridge hadn't attracted ghoulish spectators.

He walked towards the bridge and stopped at the parapet. Though it was daylight now, he was taken back to the moment he saw Sandra Blair's body lying in the water just down there under the arch, tangled in the roots of a sycamore. Those dark, wet boulders and the roaring of the water. Cries of pain and a victim's last, dying breath.

He relived that light-headed feeling, the result of a lack of sleep, and felt himself almost slipping again in the mud on the bank of the river. There had been so little blood. No more than a few drops on the stone.

Cooper didn't need to spend any more time thinking about it. He was sure that his original impression had been perfectly correct when he stood here early on that morning after Halloween. Sandra Blair wasn't alone when she died.

THAT AFTERNOON COOPER took a call from Brendan Kilner. He sounded nervous and he was practically gabbling down the phone, like a man afraid of being overheard if he didn't finish the call quickly.

'Okay, so,' said Kilner. 'First of all, promise me my name doesn't get mentioned in any way, shape or form.'

'As long as you weren't involved in a murder, Brendan,' said Cooper. 'Then all bets would be off.'

'We both know I wasn't. It was one of those people at the bridge.'

Cooper didn't need to ask what bridge. 'Which of those people exactly?'

'I don't know. Honest, I don't. It could have been any of them or all of them, as far as I'm concerned. They're all as mad as each other.'

'Can you arrange a meeting?'

'I suppose I could. But I wouldn't do it. It would be too dangerous for me.'

'I'm not expecting you to go to the meeting,' said Cooper. 'I will.'

The line was silent for a moment and Cooper thought Kilner had gone. But he must have been covering the phone with his hand, because his breathing suddenly came back on the line.

'Okay,' he said finally. 'But I don't need to arrange anything. There's a place you'll find the person you want. At least, you will if you go there tonight.'

'Excellent. Where is this place? Not the Grandfather Oak, preferably.'

'No, that was just a one-off. But there's a spot they've used before for meetings, where no one ever goes now. That's where they'll be. But they're all canny, though, so don't scare anyone off. No lights or sirens, you know what I mean?'

'Yes, Brendan,' said Cooper. 'But where is this place?'

'You might know it. The old cheese factory.'

Cooper put the phone down and sat at his desk for a few minutes, turning the situation over in his mind. It was a challenge, of course. But he had to prove that he was up to it.

He had a decision to take. There was one phone call he ought to make. Though it might put everything he hoped for at risk.

BY LATE EVENING the air was cold, with a bright moon high in the sky behind a haze of fog, casting a pale-green sheen over the landscape. The streets of Hartington were very quiet. A smell of woodsmoke hung in the air, with a faint roar of central heating systems venting steam.

Ben Cooper couldn't explain the feeling of unease this corner of the village gave him. He knew he'd been to the old cheese factory before, years ago when he was a uniformed PC. The factory had been working then, a thriving enterprise. The bays had been busy with vans and lorries. Men in blue boiler suits and yellow high-vis jackets walking around outside, the hum of machinery from inside the buildings. There was none of that now. The factory was dead.

Standing empty and abandoned, there was nothing attractive about the old stone buildings, or the newer sheds of green steel sheeting. They belonged firmly to the utilitarian side of the village, not the tourist part. Yes, the factory was only a short stroll from the duck pond and the Old Cheese Shop, but it was a step back into Hartington's past.

Cooper walked between an empty car park and a long shed with a corrugated-iron roof covered in dense clumps of brown-green mould. Where a tall chimney was attached to the building, an orange stain had spread across the wall and run down on to the ground, discolouring the base of the chimney itself as if the lifeblood of the factory had slowly been draining away since its closure.

Two tall grey tanks stood in their own pond of green water. What the tanks had held, he couldn't imagine. A network of steel pipes ran along the back wall of the factory, with weeds growing in all the crevices. There were CCTV cameras here, but he doubted they were working.

There didn't seem to be much to steal here, though perhaps people would find ways to break into the factory for other purposes. It was inevitable with any abandoned building, especially in a spot like this where you wouldn't be overlooked.

Cooper saw a small door standing open at the back of the main building. It was half-hidden under the mass of pipes and a steel platform supporting the hoods of a massive cooling system. Above it metal steps ran up the wall to a set of doors on the first floor. He watched and listened, but saw no movement and heard no noise from within the factory.

Then there was a metallic reverberation, a boom like a heavy object dropped on one of the empty tanks. But it came from behind him, not from the factory.

His heart thumping, Cooper whirled round. On top of a tank he glimpsed a figure just disappearing as someone descended a ladder. Where the person had been standing was a perfect vantage point to observe Cooper's arrival. If it hadn't been for that stray boot against the side of the tank, he might never have known anyone was there.

He cursed himself for not taking a more wary approach. But what had he been expecting when he came to Hartington, if not someone hiding out here? It was almost as if he'd deliberately given them a warning. And allowed them to escape.

But whoever it was, they hadn't gone. Somehow they'd slipped round the back of one of the smaller sheds and reached the door into the main building, which had now closed behind them.

Cooper shivered and looked up at the sky. The moon was so bright it had created a ring of colours through the prism effect of the fog, like a circular rainbow. Well, a rainbow was supposed to be a sign, a portent that something was about to happen, or a direction to a pot of gold. But a rainbow at night seemed all wrong. Was it an omen of something terrible about to happen?

DIANE FRY WAS surprised to be handed a couple of forensics reports by an officer entering the CID room at West Street.

'What are these?' she said.

'Results from some items that Detective Sergeant Cooper sent through for processing.'

'Really?'

Fry became aware of Becky Hurst bobbing up like a child who always knew the right answer in class.

'Those will be the items from Harpur Hill,' said Hurst.

'Yes, you're right.' Fry frowned at the first report. 'A hat? And an LED torch?'

Hurst came over to her desk. 'That's it. We believe they were Sandra Blair's possessions.'

'We?'

Fry smiled. She knew that when Becky Hurst said 'we' she actually meant Ben Cooper.

Hurst didn't flinch at her tone. 'They were found concealed in a plastic bag and dumped in a drinking hole for cattle. Somebody must have taken them away from the scene of Sandra Blair's death at the bridge to dispose of them. There's got to be a reason for them doing that.'

'I suppose there has,' said Fry.

She was interested now. She opened the report and gazed at its results for a moment. Hurst began to get impatient.

'Well, what does it say?'

'They got a hit from a print on the casing of the torch,' said Fry. 'And from the inside of the plastic bag the items were in too.'

'A hit? Seriously? So it was someone who's already on the database.'

'Yes.'

Fry had turned to the second report. 'And what's this? The lid of a marble tomb? These are prints recovered from the Lady Chapel at Knowle Abbey this morning. And the results match.'

'They got a hit to the same person?'

'Yes, the same.'

She put the report down and began to speak more briskly. 'We need to assemble a team for an arrest. Request an armed response unit. We need to use all precautions. He's known to possess two shotguns. And there's a dog on the premises too.'

'But who is it?' insisted Hurst.

'An individual with a conviction for poaching fourteen years ago. Jason Shaw.'

'Great.'

Hurst began to make calls, but she stopped and turned back to Fry.

'Diane, there's one thing we've forgotten,' she said.

'What's that?'

'What happened to the explosives stolen from Deeplow Quarry? Where are they now?'

THE FIRST EXPLOSION was shocking in its suddenness. It caught Cooper completely off-guard. He should have known it was coming, but the moment of expectant silence before the detonation made it all the more shocking when it happened.

The loud boom echoed across the village green and bounced off the walls of the limestone houses. It startled a flock of wood pigeons out of their evening roost in a sycamore tree on the edge of the churchyard. For a few moments the birds flapped in a panicked circle, passing overhead and silhouetting themselves against a cascade of light the explosion had hurled into the air.

Cooper looked round, embarrassed at his own reaction, ready to laugh it off if anyone had noticed. Tonight was a test. Fire, heat, explosions, the sight of blazing timbers. When he'd decided to come out on Bonfire Night, he had no idea how he would cope with these sights and sounds. But it was something he had to face. He couldn't avoid it for ever. There was no future in trying to run away from the past.

A barrage of missiles shrieked across the sky like hunting demons. Cooper was deafened by the screeching and jumped in shock at a volley of bangs on the hillside behind it.

He stopped for a minute to pull himself together. Despite the cold air, he could feel sweat breaking out on his forehead and his hands trembled. The reaction was deep down inside him, impossible to deal with on a deliberate, conscious level. He would have to fight his way through it.

Cooper stood in the yard, his face lit by the coloured flashes, surrounded by crackling and the smell of charcoal and sulphur. He felt once again that he was standing in the middle of a raging inferno, caught up in the heart of that burning building, with flames leaping around him and smoking timbers crashing to the ground, his skin scorched by the heat of the fire.

But there was nothing else for it. He would have to go inside.

Chapter Thirty-nine

THE LIGHTS OF three police cars arriving in convoy created quite a stir, even in Bowden. They certainly attracted the attention of the residents who were at home that Tuesday evening, including Caroline Mellor, who appeared at her window across the green to observe the activity.

Two of the vehicles pulled up outside the home of Jason Shaw and officers piled out. The third car swerved across the road and blocked the access to the village. Two armed officers went to the front door, while another covered the back yard. Diane Fry waited at a safe distance with Luke Irvine and Becky Hurst, while uniformed officers were stationed to keep spectators away.

Fry had checked with the Knowle estate office whether Shaw would be working, but he wasn't on the staff rota for this evening. And his blue Land Rover Discovery stood by the side of the house.

'Don't give him time to react,' she said. 'Don't forget there are firearms kept on the premises.'

When there was no response to their hammering on the front door and shouts of 'Police!', the entry team produced a small battering ram and swung it at the lock. The door burst open after two strikes and they entered the house. Jason Shaw's dog could be heard barking hysterically from the rear of the property.

After a few seconds one of the officers appeared in the doorway and signalled to Fry. The CID team moved into the house. But they were disappointed to find it empty.

'All the rooms are clear, Sergeant.'

'His Land Rover is here.'

'Even so, there's no one home.'

Fry went through the rooms herself and found the gun cabinet. It was securely locked, as it ought to be, so there was no way of telling whether both shotguns were still inside. Not without breaking it open, which would take time.

She looked round for Irvine and Hurst. 'Get out there and start talking to the neighbours and find out if they know where he is. We don't want him to get a warning, in case he decides to go to ground.'

'We'd never find him in these woods, even in daylight.'

'Exactly. We might need to request the air support unit.'

As Fry looked around the untidy sitting room, she wondered whether she'd made a mistake in trying to make the arrest after dusk. Perhaps she should have waited until morning and conducted the operation at first light. It was galling to think that Shaw had vanished into those dark woodlands. He would know the grounds of Knowle Abbey better than almost anyone. If she didn't locate him quickly, she might never see Jason Shaw again.

While she waited she examined the items strewn across the surface of a small table. Shaw had gathered a lot of magazines about country sports. *Shooting Times*, *The Field*, *Sporting Gun*. Many of them had cover illustrations of men in ear defenders aiming shotguns at unidentified targets, or dogs with dead birds in their mouths. Fry recalled a failed attempt by an animal rights organisation to get this sort of magazine banished to the top shelf in newsagents, along with the soft porn.

She pushed some of the magazines aside. Underneath she found an object she couldn't identify. It seemed to be a hoop of something like dried willow, wrapped with a thin band of leather. A web of white string filled the space inside the hoop, decorated with tiny beads, and someone had attached a couple of feathers to the bottom.

'A dreamcatcher,' said Luke Irvine, jolting Fry out of her distraction.

'Is that what it is?'

'They're Native American originally. But they're popular here now.'

Fry frowned. 'Popular with who?'

Irvine shifted uncomfortably. 'Well, you know – people interested in spiritual things. There was one on the wall at Sandra Blair's cottage. I think she probably made it herself. I bet she made this one for Mr Shaw.'

'What is it supposed to do?' asked Fry.

'It stops you having bad dreams.'

Fry turned the dreamcatcher over and laid it back on the magazines. It looked incongruous lying against a picture of a slaughtered pheasant in the jaws of a Golden Retriever.

'I wonder if that worked for Jason Shaw,' she said.

'It doesn't look as though he ever used it.'

'No.'

'I came to tell you the dog unit has arrived,' said Irvine. 'They've brought the sniffer dog for the explosives.'

'Oh, yes. Let's get them in.'

An officer entered with a Springer Spaniel, which began to sniff its way enthusiastically around the house.

Fry checked the phone for messages, peered into the cupboards, walked out into the back yard, trying to ignore the barking dog. Becky Hurst appeared, with Mrs Mellor trailing behind her, looking alarmed but flushed with excitement.

'Oh,' she said, when she saw Fry, 'isn't Detective Sergeant Cooper here?'

'No. But you remember me, don't you?'

'I suppose so,' said Mrs Mellor, though Fry suspected it wasn't her memory she was dubious about.

'You're aware that we're looking for Jason Shaw?'

'Yes. I told your girl here. When I saw Jason half an hour ago, he said he was going down to the gift shop. They wanted him to help out with something.'

INSIDE THE HARTINGTON cheese factory Cooper found that the buildings hadn't been entirely cleared of their contents. In a corridor he passed pairs of white wellies that looked as though they'd missed their last wash when the factory closed. A few ancient bits of broken equipment stood around, with a metal filing cabinet and a scatter of Stilton cheese leaflets still lying on the floor.

The modern part of the factory was quite different from the old stone buildings. He passed through large cheese storage areas with quarry-tiled floors, and one building like the lower level of a multi-storey car park, with a low ceiling, hefty pillars and shadowy alcoves.

'Jason? Where are you?' he called.

There was a muffled laugh somewhere in the darkness.

'Come on. I know you're there, Jason. We're long past the time for playing the fool.'

Something metallic banged against a wall. Cooper wondered if there was a shotgun pointing at him from a dark corner of the building. He moved sideways, away from any residual light that might be creeping through the doorway behind him or from the skylights in the roof.

The fireworks display still showered the sky with cascades of colour and created a background din of bangs and crackles. The blast of a shotgun would hardly be noticed on Bonfire Night. It would be just one more distant explosion to frighten the pigeons. No one would bother to dial the emergency number or come to see what was happening in the old cheese factory.

Then he glimpsed something light-coloured, moving across an opening. The figure was ahead of him in one of the cavernous rooms, slipping through another doorway deeper into the abandoned factory.

The person moved with a lightness and agility that surprised him. He recalled Jason Shaw's description of the woman he'd seen in the woods near the Corpse Bridge that Halloween night, the ghostly white flicker and swirl as a figure dodged through the trees. Was he seeing the same phantom that Shaw had described so convincingly? Could the same apparition be right here in the cheese factory? Even for the most impressionable mind, that didn't make any sense.

But that pale shape reminded Cooper of something else. He could see an individual sitting across the table from him in Interview Room One at West Street.

Chapter Forty

AFTER THAT IT was easy. Even Jason Shaw wouldn't have walked into the gift shop at Knowle Abbey with a shotgun.

Fry directed the police vehicles round to the back entrance, where their presence wouldn't be noticed from the shop. With officers outside each entrance, she simply walked in with Irvine and Hurst, told Shaw he was being arrested and read him his rights while Irvine put the cuffs on.

'You do not have to say anything,' she recited. 'However, it may harm your defence if you do not mention when questioned something that you later rely on in court. Anything you do say may be given in evidence.'

It felt odd saying it surrounded by tea towels and bookmarks with pictures of Knowle Abbey, and shelves of mugs saying 'Keep Calm and Carry On'.

'What's this all about?' said Shaw.

'I'm sure you know.'

'Is it Sandra?' said Shaw as he was led out to the car. 'I think I was in love with her, in a way. It's not often you meet a woman like that.'

'Save it,' said Fry.

'She had so much life in her. I had to avenge her.'

'Really?' said Irvine as they put Shaw into the back of the car. 'Weren't you responsible for her death?'

'No. It was Manby to blame for that.'

Hurst grasped Irvine's arm. 'We can't question him now or take into account anything he says.'

'I know.'

'And if you mean the quarry man Redfearn,' he said, 'I don't know anything about that.'

Fry stopped the car from driving away.

'There's one thing we have to ask him,' she said.

'But, Diane,' protested Hurst.

'If we believe there may be immediate danger to life.'

Hurst backed off then. 'You're right.'

Fry leaned into the car and stared hard at Shaw.

'Where are the explosives, Jason?' she said. 'You took some explosives from Deeplow Quarry. Diesel and ammonium nitrate pellets.'

Shaw shook his head. 'I took them. But I don't have them now.'

Fry watched the car drive away across the parkland towards the gates of Knowle Abbey. She hadn't taken much notice of the phone call she'd received from Ben Cooper. She knew that Jason Shaw would be under arrest long before Cooper was due to meet him at the cheese factory in Hartington.

Guiltily, she'd been imagining Cooper waiting at the derelict building for hours in the cold and the darkness, hoping for his coup, while she was busy doing the real work here at Bowden.

But if it was true that Shaw hadn't killed George Redfearn, who had? And who was Cooper meeting in Hartington?

THOUGH THE TALL, athletic figure was familiar to Cooper, she was no longer the young woman who'd sat nervously in Interview Room One staring at a cup of cold coffee. He couldn't imagine this woman being intimidated by her surroundings. Her hands were steady now and the rings on her fingers glinted in the glare of a rocket as she stood in the darkness of the abandoned factory.

'Poppy,' said Cooper. 'I wasn't expecting you.'

'I'm sorry.'

Cooper peered into the gloom, trying to make out her face. 'What for?'

'Everything, I suppose. It wasn't meant to be like this. It all went wrong.'

There was no light in here, except for a few patches of greenish light from the fog-shrouded moon filtering through the skylights in the roof. Poppy Mellor stood on the edge of one of the rectangles of light, making the shadows around her seem so much darker.

'Are the rest of the group here?' asked Cooper.

He looked round, but could see nothing in the darkness. It was another of the large storage areas. The low ceiling and heavy pillars seemed to press in on him and made him feel claustrophobic, though he knew the room must be extensive.

Poppy didn't answer him. It was as if she weren't really listening, but just wanted the opportunity to talk.

'The group have been like a family to me,' she said. 'Closer than my real parents or my brother. And just like a proper family, I didn't really choose them.'

Was she armed with something? Her right arm was pressed too close to her side for him to be sure. Cooper realised he would have to let her talk. He needed her to stay calm and relaxed, and then he might find out what was going on. He also needed time for his back-up to arrive.

Cooper glanced nervously around again. If back-up *was* going to arrive.

'Yes. We just came together for this one purpose. It was almost random. We talked to each other all the time on those walks. We talked like I've never been able to talk to my dad.'

'They were loyal too,' said Cooper.

'You're right. They were. None of them gave away the fact that I was there at the bridge, did they?'

'No. We accepted your story completely.'

'Thank you.'

She spoke as if it were a genuine compliment.

'So what did happen at the bridge?' asked Cooper.

'It was bad luck. The fact is, Sandra was out of control that night. I don't know what she was on exactly, but she was totally out of her head. She began to run around in the woods like a crazy woman. Then she came after me and chased me towards the bridge. She scared me. I thought she was going to do me some harm. God knows what she was thinking, but I'm sure she was hallucinating. The others had no idea what was going on, though. We were supposed to be quiet and not draw any attention to ourselves. When they heard all the commotion they didn't know what to think.'

'They imagined someone else must be there,' said Cooper.

'Yes, exactly.'

'And that would have ruined the plan.'

Cooper felt his phone buzz in his pocket. He reached for it slowly, but Poppy backed away again and he lost sight of her in the shadows.

'Sandra caught me near the bridge,' said Poppy. 'I seriously thought she was going to do something bad to me, she was so nuts. I think I must have screamed. Jason says he heard a scream anyway. I suppose that must have been me. Though Sandra was making plenty of noise too, crashing about in the trees. But then she seemed to start coughing or choking and she fell on the ground. I had no idea what to do. I thought she was still messing around.'

'And no one came to help you?'

'Yes, Jason did.' Poppy moved her head sideways so that he couldn't see her eyes. Was she looking towards someone who stood in the darkness? Or was the gesture merely theatrical?

Cooper moved too, trying to maintain eye contact. Perhaps he ought to arrest her right now. But what had she admitted to, really? Perverting the course of justice? Conspiracy? There wasn't much of a case against her. He needed to know more.

'It was lucky I wasn't relying on Rob,' said Poppy. 'He's not the bravest of people.'

'What happened to Sandra?' persisted Cooper.

Poppy sighed. 'She should never have come out with us on something like that. We didn't know she had a heart condition.'

'I don't think she knew either.'

'If she had a family history of heart disease, she ought to have gone to her GP for a review. I bet she was a prime candidate for heart disease. A bad diet, smoking, too little exercise, a family history...'

'So. At some point on this particular evening she simply dropped down dead in front of you,' said Cooper.

'Pretty much.'

'And what did you do?'

'I've got to admit, I had no idea what to do. I was about ready to panic, to be honest. But Jason said he'd done a bit of first-aid training. He tried CPR. You know, pressing on her chest, mouth-to-mouth, and all that.'

'But no one called an ambulance, did they?'

'No. Well ... no, we didn't.'

Cooper was silent for a moment. 'No matter how long Mr Shaw performed CPR, it was pretty useless without defibrillation, which is what actually restarts the heart.'

'That's what I said to Jason. I mean, we both knew that Sandra was dead. It was so obvious. There was no way she was going to be brought back to life. Right in those first few seconds, she was dead. She was already a ghost.'

Cooper shivered at her choice of phrase. The factory had made him feel uneasy as soon as he'd entered it. If your imagination ran in that direction, you might think there were phantom presences here, the spirits of the former occupants imprinted in the walls. But his senses were warning him of whispers and movements in the darkness. He couldn't tell yet whether they were real or illusory.

'We both panicked a bit, then,' said Poppy. 'Jason had touched her hat and her torch, so he took those away with him, in case of fingerprints. Then we rolled her body off the bridge. Her head hit the rocks, which was a bit nasty. But she wasn't feeling any pain by then, was she?'

She was actually appealing to him for reassurance.

'No, Poppy,' he said.

'It was funny, but it was only when I got home that I thought about her mobile phone. But it must have been in the river, I suppose. I dropped my phone in water once. It didn't work too well after that.'

Cooper took a cautious step towards her, but she noticed and backed out of the light. That was worse. Now she was almost invisible and he was the one standing directly beneath the opening, bathed in the odd light. He could see the green tinge on the skin of his hands, like the discoloration of flesh after death.

'Poor Jason was upset,' said Poppy. 'He was quite keen on Sandra. He likes them a bit weird, I think.'

Cooper could have kicked himself as he listened to her story. He'd noticed all those people coming forward and telling him part of the truth, as if they'd been told to do that. The Nadens, Jason Shaw, even Brendan Kilner. But he'd never thought to himself: And what about Poppy Mellor? She'd come forward voluntarily and appeared to be a willing witness. But she'd only told part of the truth too.

Yes, she'd been clever in some ways. Yet she was so young, so inexperienced about life. And about people too.

'And George Redfearn?' he said.

'Unfortunate. But it was just like Sandra's death.'

'No.' Cooper shook his head. 'You can see a heart attack coming. It's there in the tests. It's in the blood. But this is different. You don't see a murder coming.'

'Sometimes you can.'

'But it wasn't you who killed George Redfearn, Poppy. That's something I can't believe.'

'Can't you, really? But it's so easy, isn't it? To get someone up on a high place like that and shove them off. You don't need much strength.'

'No, that's true.'

And he had to admit it *was* true. A quick push, a momentary loss of balance. He'd imagined it himself on the sharp ridge of Parkhouse Hill just yesterday.

But Poppy was still backing away from him as he crossed the walkway.

'You are right, though,' she said.

'Right?'

'It wasn't me. I was back home by then. You can check with my dad, if you want. He'll be only too happy to talk to you.'

Cooper held his breath, listening for a sound, any sound, in the darkness. He was beginning to feel disorientated by the blackness all around him. His eyes couldn't adjust because of the light he was standing in. He felt like a character on a stage, pinned by the spotlights, and about to perform his big scene in front of an audience he couldn't see.

'You're a different person from the one I met before, Poppy,' he said.

'I was in character before.'

'I'm sorry?'

'I took a joint honours in drama studies at De Montfort,' she said. 'I wasn't great. But good enough.'

Poppy was backing away steadily and Cooper had to follow to keep her in view.

'And you coached the rest of your group, didn't you?' he said. 'They all played their parts well. Congratulations.'

'Thank you,' said Poppy again. Then she paused. 'But the final act isn't over yet, I'm afraid.'

Cooper found himself at the foot of a flight of metal steps leading up on to an overhead walkway. It might once have passed over the cheese vats, but now there was nothing but a bare concrete floor below.

He thought he saw Poppy's pale figure above and ahead of him, and he mounted the steps on to the walkway.

'Where are you?' he said.

But the voice came from behind him.

'I'm here. Very close.'

Cooper stopped moving. He became certain that there was more than one other person in the factory with him. Someone had been here all the time. They'd been keeping very quiet in the darkness. But now he could hear their breathing and a footstep coming closer. So Jason Shaw had come after all. Or had he?

Chapter Forty-one

DIANE FRY SLAMMED her foot down on the accelerator pedal as her Audi hurtled down the A515 towards the Hartington turn-off.

Ben Cooper wasn't answering his phone, which was typical. He'd probably got himself into a situation where he couldn't answer it or had no signal. Or perhaps he'd simply turned it off.

Fry cursed him under her breath. Did he really need her help, after all? Had his call been a test: request her help knowing she wouldn't come, just so he could point to a final betrayal? She couldn't let him have that satisfaction.

There was a marked car behind her, but the other had taken Jason Shaw back to the custody suite in Edendale, where Becky Hurst would process him. With Luke Irvine in the car with her, she hoped there would be enough manpower. There was no one else available at such short notice, unless she sounded the alarm. And she couldn't do that yet, without any clear idea about what was happening.

'Turn here, Diane,' said Irvine, pointing at the junction to the left.

He seemed to be as worried as she was herself. But then, Irvine knew as well as anyone that his DS was capable of doing something rash.

'Try Ben's phone again,' she said. 'And keep trying.'

ANOTHER FACE APPEARED from the darkness, lit for a second by a bursting firework, a blue-and-white flash and crackle through the broken skylights high in the roof of the old cheese factory.

'Are you on your own?' said a voice.

'What do you think?' replied Cooper.

'I think you might just have made a mistake.'

Cooper experienced another disorientating memory. The thickset, middle-aged man who'd been raking leaves in the churchyard at Hartington vigorously. He was wearing the same baseball cap, forcing those same untidy clumps of grey hair to stick out at the sides. Cooper remembered that grimly determined expression as he'd lashed out with his rake at the weeds. A deep anger in his expression, an intense physical concentration.

'Hello, Mr Naden,' he said.

Naden didn't reply. Cooper looked from him to Poppy and back again. These two made an unnerving team.

'It should have been obvious you were the leader,' said Cooper. 'I could see it on that photo taken on the testing grounds at Harpur Hill. The one on the old coffin road. The photo that Poppy took, I imagine, since she wasn't in the shot herself.'

Naden glowered at Poppy Mellor, who shrank a little further into the shadows.

'What about it?' he said.

'We would have been able to identify all the members of the group from that photo anyway,' said Cooper. 'I suppose you guessed that. And you were right at the front, Mr Naden. As if you were conducting a guided walk. The others were looking to you. Nothing could disguise that.'

'I told Sandra to delete that photo from her phone,' said Naden grimly.

'And she may have done. But she emailed it to herself first. She must have wanted a memento, I suppose. We found it on her laptop.'

'Idiot woman. She was mad, you know.'

'She *is* dead.'

'Well, I didn't kill her.'

'No. But I know who you *did* kill, Mr Naden.'

Naden had moved closer without him noticing. He didn't know which way to face now, which direction the threat might come from. The training manuals said you should make sure to have an escape route if you were likely to face a threat. But Cooper was aware only of the drop to the concrete beneath him, the low rail that wouldn't stop anyone going over.

'That night, when you were supposed to be at the bridge with the others,' he said. 'It didn't all go wrong by accident, did it? You had a different plan from everyone else.'

He could sense Poppy stiffen and draw in a sharp breath.

'You said it was the wrong day,' said Cooper, 'but your wife thought it was the right day. You knew who was actually wrong, didn't you?'

With a smug smile, Naden leaned closer to stare into Cooper's face. 'She kept insisting it was the right day,' he said. 'She didn't believe me, but kept on and on about it, even after we got home. That gave me the excuse to go out again later that evening, to check what was happening.'

'But you went to meet George Redfearn instead.'

Naden nodded. 'Well, he never suspected me. I looked too harmless, I suppose. But I've thought about it often enough over the years. Just not in relation to Redfearn.'

'So how did you do it?'

'I told him I knew his wife. I said I had some information to give him about her.'

'Mrs Redfearn was in Paris at the time,' said Cooper.

'Exactly. One of her regular trips. She's ten years younger than him, you know. He was bound to have a sneaking suspicion about what she was up to.'

'But how did you know personal details about the Redfearns like that?'

Naden pursed his lips. 'It's general gossip.'

Cooper could tell Naden was lying.

'Oh, I get it now,' he said. 'You employed Daniel Grady from Eden Valley Enquiries. He purported to be a property enquiry agent asking questions on behalf of a prospective house purchaser. His job is to pick up all the bits of gossip about the neighbours. I bet he's very good at it, too. Even when money doesn't change hands. He must be a godsend to potential blackmailers.'

Naden shrugged. 'It doesn't really matter, does it? I had the information I needed. And it worked. Redfearn came to meet me at Pilsbury Castle. It's a very quiet spot, you know. No witnesses.'

'Except there were,' said Cooper.

'Were there? That's a shame.'

'Some tourists staying at Pilsbury saw your car.'

Naden shrugged. 'It hardly matters. As long as you realise Sally had nothing to do with it. I wouldn't have involved her in something like that.'

'How did you know she would keep insisting it was the right day?'

Now Naden laughed. 'I take it you're not married, Detective Sergeant?'

Cooper swallowed. 'No, I'm not.'

'It was obvious. Well, take it from me, when you've been married for a few years, some things become all too predictable. You don't need to be able to read minds to work out what your partner will say. Sally has become very easy to predict.'

His tone of voice seemed to contradict the sense of his words. Cooper detected something deeper that Naden wasn't saying, some aspect of his relationship that wasn't on the surface.

'But why do something so drastic?' he said. 'Why take the risk? It doesn't make sense.'

'Doesn't it?' Naden looked at the ground, as if contemplating the distance of the fall. 'Sally is very sick, you know. She's in a lot of pain most of the time.'

'No, I didn't know that.'

'We've been together for so many years. It's funny how nothing else seems to matter when you know someone's going to die very soon. You consider all the things you've ever wanted to do, that you ought to do but have never dared to because of the risk to your liberty and reputation. And you start to think, Well, why not?'

Cooper nodded. That was something he could definitely understand. For months after Liz had been killed in the fire, he'd driven around the steepest roads in the Peak District late at night thinking, Well, why not?

'I think that's why Sally thinks about murder a lot too,' said Naden. 'She once told me that the best way to kill someone and get away with it is to lure them on to a high place and push them off. As long as there are no eyewitnesses, it's impossible to prove forensically whether they were pushed or just fell.'

'I'm not sure that's true,' said Cooper. 'It depends on a lot of factors. For one thing, you'd need a good pretext to get someone into that position.'

Naden's footsteps clanged on the metal walkway. The sound reverberated around the empty shed. And bounced off the hard concrete floor below.

'Oh, it's not that difficult,' he said.

DIANE FRY AND Luke Irvine entered the factory through the same door Cooper had used. Outside in Hartington, the last few fireworks were spluttering to a halt after a spectacular finale.

Fry kicked against a pair of wellington boots standing by a doorway and crunched through a pile of dusty leaflets on the floor.

'What a mess,' said Irvine in a hushed tone.

'Let's hope we find nothing worse,' said Fry.

They moved steadily through the rooms and were joined by two uniformed officers. The beams of their torches illuminated the darkest corners, alighting on old filing cabinets and mysterious heaps of abandoned equipment.

'Ben?' Fry called.

She moved ahead, passing through a doorway, then another, following some instinct she couldn't explain. She knew Cooper was here, because his car was parked nearby. But she didn't know who else was.

BEN COOPER HARDLY knew what happened next. He and Geoff Naden were staring into each other's eyes. He was aware of Naden's left hand reaching out to grasp his shoulder, and Naden's right hand coming up with a length of steel pipe he must have picked up from the floor.

Cooper instinctively grabbed his wrist. He wasn't as heavy as Naden. He could feel the difference as soon as they made physical contact. He didn't want either of them to go over that rail. But he was also conscious of Poppy Mellor immediately behind him. Cooper needed to turn round to see what she was doing, but he was reluctant to take his eyes off the other man. He felt for his extendable baton, concealed in a pocket of his coat.

'Be sensible, Mr Naden,' he said. 'This won't help anyone. It will only make things worse for you.'

'It doesn't matter to me any more,' said Naden grimly.

And then there was a chaos of people shouting and lights swinging across the ceiling, picking up the figures on the walkway, then passing on and reflecting off the skylights, flashing like the starbursts in the sky over Hartington. Cooper heard his own name called, boots clanging on the metal steps.

In an explosion of light he saw Naden raising the length of pipe. Then an impact from behind threw him off balance and he dropped his baton as he threw out a hand to clutch at the rail and save himself from falling.

He dropped to his knees with the breath knocked out of him, expecting a blow to fall at any second. He heard Naden cry out – one loud, angry yell that turned into a scream of fear. Then a sickening impact thudded through the empty shed.

Cooper raised his head. He saw Diane Fry standing at the top of the steps, white-faced and ghostly behind the light of her torch. And Geoff Naden had gone.

Chapter Forty-two

Wednesday 6 November

BEN COOPER'S TOYOTA was booked in for a service on Wednesday morning. There was some problem with the suspension, which was making the steering feel unpredictable. He must have been neglecting it recently. That made him feel guilty, as if it were a person close to him that he'd been mistreating. Cooper knew you had to work at relationships. He supposed it was as true with cars as it was with people.

So today he'd walked to the office in West Street. It wasn't far from the flat, and the brisk November air helped to clear his head and wake him up.

IT WAS FUNNY how the offices at E Division headquarters seemed busier today than during the whole of the inquiry that had followed Sandra Blair's death and the subsequent killings. Officers and civilian staff who Cooper had never seen before had turned up and were working on the case, now that it was all over.

Of course, there had been a lot of people involved in the incident at the old cheese factory. That meant statement after statement to be taken, including Cooper's own. Yet his account might be the least useful to the prosecution, in some ways. He didn't see the moment of Geoff Naden's death. It happened in the darkness as far as he was concerned, another life snuffed out in the shadows.

So it was lucky that Diane Fry, Luke Irvine and the other officers present were able to give coherent and consistent witness statements, confirming that Poppy Mellor gave Naden that fatal push, just as he was about to strike with the steel pipe. There had been no plan for that. In Poppy's case, things had gone badly wrong now.

It was still unclear what the group had intended to do with the explosives stolen from the quarry by Jason Shaw. The dog unit had located them in the factory, hidden in a disused office. But the experts said they were in no condition to be used. So perhaps Knowle Abbey had been safe, though not Earl Manby himself.

Cooper thought back to that first morning at the Corpse Bridge and the way he'd been caught up in the legends around it, the stories of the coffin roads and their associated ghosts and spirits. It had seemed to him then that the Devil had manifested at the bridge. But now he wasn't sure who the Devil was in this case.

Gavin Murfin had some news of his own to break that morning. He took Cooper aside for a quiet word. His manner was surreptitious, almost furtive, as if he feared some of the civilians around today were spies of the management and might overhear.

'I'm telling you first, Ben,' he said. 'I thought you should know.'

'What is it, Gavin?'

'I'm calling it a day, Ben. This is the end.'

'So you're finally going?' said Cooper. 'You've resigned?'

'It's by mutual agreement, like.'

'You're starting to sound like a politician, Gavin. So you're going to spend more time with the family.'

'Not exactly. I've been offered another job.'

'Really? What about the grandchildren? Weren't you looking forward to spending more time with them?'

'We tried it this week,' said Murfin glumly. 'Have you seen the amount of baby stuff you have to carry around with you these days? It's like taking Pink Floyd on tour.'

'I'm sorry that you felt like this.'

'It's all the fault of that woman,' said Murfin.

'Gavin, you know what happens when a police officer uses that term. You get dragged in front of a parliamentary committee to apologise for being disrespectful.'

Murfin laughed. 'I might,' he said. 'Except I wasn't referring to the Home Secretary.'

'I suppose this means you won't be a police officer much longer. It's hard to grasp, Gavin. You've been in the job such a long time.'

'It feels like about three centuries. I ought to be handing in my top hat and cutlass.'

'So – a new job offer? What are you going to do?'

Murfin looked round as if about to confide a secret. 'You've heard of Eden Valley Enquiries?' he said.

From somewhere in the past, Cooper heard an echo of his own voice asking that same question. *Have you heard of Eden Valley Enquiries?* And a scornful answer coming back to him: *A firm of second-rate enquiry agents? Divorces and process-serving, that sort of thing.*

But Cooper didn't repeat the answer that Diane Fry had once given him. He sensed it would be the wrong thing to say just at this moment, with the expression on Gavin's face suggesting he was screwing himself up to some kind of embarrassing confession.

'Of course,' Cooper said instead. 'They have an office in one of those small business centres on Meadow Road, don't they?'

'That's right.'

'Discreet confidential enquiries. No questions asked.'

Murfin looked even more uncomfortable. 'Mmm,' he mumbled.

Eden Valley Enquiries. Daniel Grady was only his latest contact with that outfit. Cooper recalled that one of their operatives had actually been given the task of following Diane Fry one night, as a result of her connection with a murder case. The man tailed her into Sheffield by car, then followed her on foot as far as some railway arches, only for his assignment to end in a painful confrontation when Fry realised she was being followed. Cooper himself had been obliged to tell Diane who her stalker was, after following up the name 'Eve'. Not a friend of the victim's, as they'd thought – but an acronym. Eden Valley Enquiries.

'Looking for a new job, are you?' Fry had said when he mentioned the name. 'Thinking of joining the private detective business?' And Cooper had made some facetious remark in response.

Now, as he looked at Gavin Murfin, Cooper hardly needed to ask the same question. But he asked it anyway. He knew it was expected of him.

'Thinking of joining the private detective business, Gavin?'

'Well, actually…'

'No, seriously? I can hardly believe it.'

'It's good money,' said Murfin defensively. The words came out automatically, as if he'd been rehearsing his justifications all week. Perhaps for longer than that. 'They say I've got valuable experience. I'll be a big asset to the firm. And, you know … it'll keep me occupied.'

'But it might not keep you out of trouble,' said Cooper.

'You know me, Ben. I'm Mr Squeaky Clean. It's because I always avoid trouble.'

'Yeah, right.'

Cooper was thinking of Diane Fry's violent reaction to EVE's role in that murder inquiry. They'd gathered information that had helped to locate a victim. And even after the news broke that she'd been killed, they didn't come forward.

'Discreet and confidential,' said Cooper. 'No questions asked.'

'That's the motto,' said Murfin.

'I wish you luck in your new career, then, Gavin.'

'Thanks.'

But Fry's voice still echoed in Cooper's head. *I'd string them up and break every bone in their bodies.*

Maybe the doom-mongers were going to be proved right. Gavin Murfin wasn't the first copper to go into the private sector. Perhaps one day they would all be privatised, willingly or not.

JASON SHAW HAD been interviewed repeatedly that day. His defiant attitude was either part of the overall plan or it might be due to a realisation that his case was hopeless, whatever his duty solicitor had said to him in their consultation.

For a start Shaw hadn't taken the trouble to clean the shotgun he used before putting it back in its cabinet at Bowden. His instinct to put the weapon safely out of sight had outweighed the more logical calculation that a forensic examination would show that the gun had recently been fired and would be able to match the shot removed from the earl's body and traces of wadding found at the crime scene to the cartridges in Shaw's possession.

Worse, he'd even left cartridge cases at the scene with his prints on them. That was the disadvantage of doing your shooting in the woods at night. Once you'd dropped your cartridge cases, it took much too long to find them again, especially if you were anxious to get clear of the area.

There was even a shoe mark in the grass, preserved by the soft ground and the morning dew, with a spatter of the earl's blood lying in the impression. The forensic evidence was piling up and Fry felt confident there was more to come yet. The case against Shaw was going to be watertight.

'Well,' he said, when he was pressed on his motivation, 'it was purely a family matter.'

'What do you mean?' asked Fry.

Shaw glared at his questioners across the interview-room table.

'You know the way it is. Generation after generation, the Manbys spent hundreds of years exploiting the people of this area. One death makes up for a thousand sins.'

IN THE CID room at E Division headquarters they'd spent the day on paperwork. There were mountains of it. Reports to write, statements to take, interviews to conclude with Poppy Mellor and Jason Shaw, and with Rob Beresford and Sally Naden too. Reviews of the evidence, discussions with the Crown Prosecution Service. It could all go on for a while yet.

At the end of the day Ben Cooper had been called to Detective Superintendent Branagh's office. She looked tired. But then, they were all tired.

'You know we're losing DC Murfin?' she said.

'Yes, ma'am, he's told me.'

'It was expected, of course.'

She didn't sound as though she was too disappointed either. Within a short space of time Gavin's existence would be wiped from the memory of E Division. But Cooper had a feeling he hadn't heard the last of Murfin yet.

'But it may not be your problem,' said Branagh.

'I'm sorry?'

'There's always some good news,' she said.

At the end of the day, still feeling dazed, Cooper pulled on his jacket and felt in his pocket for his car keys.

'Damn,' he said.

'What's the matter?'

'I forgot my car was in for a service.'

He checked his watch. It was much too late to collect it from the garage now. They would have closed over an hour ago.

'Oh, well, it can wait until tomorrow,' said Cooper. 'I can walk home. It's not far.'

'Have you seen the weather?'

When it was dark and the lights were on in the CID room, he could see nothing outside. Even without the blinds drawn, the windows only threw back their own exhausted reflections. The weather could be doing anything and he would have no idea until he left the building.

'Is it raining?' he said.

'Chucking it down, mate. And blowing a gale with it. It's shocking out there.'

'I'll give you a lift,' said Fry. 'I pass that way.'

The offer came out of the blue. Gavin Murfin's mouth fell open like a cudding sheep. Cooper was shocked and he hesitated before replying, searching his mind for an ulterior motive. He couldn't think of one and realised he was hesitating too long for politeness. So he had no option but to accept her offer.

'Thanks, Diane, that would be great,' he said.

'No problem.'

She picked up her car keys and they left the office together to drive through the streets of Edendale.

Chapter Forty-three

IT WAS SO difficult to know what to talk about in the car with Diane Fry. She had so little in the way of small talk. But Cooper knew he had to make conversation, because he was getting a lift, was on the receiving end of a favour. So he asked her about the outcome of her interviews with Jason Shaw.

'For some reason Shaw became more extreme in his intentions after Sandra Blair's death,' said Fry, when she'd outlined the results.

'Well, don't you think he was in love with her?' said Cooper.

Fry looked at him. 'That's what he said. I didn't believe it.'

'Why not?'

'Well, he's not that sort of person.'

'Are you kidding? Anybody is capable of love, no matter what else they do in their lives. Yes, even people who commit murder can be in love. You understand that, don't you, Diane?'

She didn't answer directly, but gripped the steering wheel a bit tighter. 'That still doesn't explain his reaction,' she said.

'It was jealousy, I think,' said Cooper.

'Who of?'

'Poppy Mellor perhaps. Oh, not in that way. But Sandra and Poppy were enjoying themselves too much. It was as simple as that. Jason didn't see it as fun. With Sandra gone, he only had two options – to give up or take it to the extreme. And he wasn't a man who would just give up.'

Fry looked as though she were struggling to understand the emotional complexities of ordinary human beings. She concentrated on the traffic as they headed out of the town centre and over the bridge towards Welbeck Street.

'I dare say you're right,' she said in the end.

'So in a way, you see,' continued Cooper, 'the earl paid the price for Sandra Blair's death, not for his development plans at Bowden, or even for the quarry scheme. He became the target for one individual's thwarted passion, an unfocused rage.'

He watched Fry trying to digest the interpretation. He knew it wouldn't fit with any of her logical constructs. In fact, in Diane Fry's world, motive could be pretty much dispensed with, once you'd collected enough evidence to prove your case. Guilt was important in the criminal justice system, not reasons. The system represented by Fry didn't want to know why people did things. It was much too hard to understand, impossible to write down on a report form. It was too human.

Cooper wished he could tell her that one day, when he thought she would understand.

They turned into Welbeck Street and Fry drew up outside his flat.

'That was a big help,' he said. 'Thanks a lot, Diane.'

Fry waited while he got out of the Audi. Cooper turned and stood on the pavement, expecting her to accelerate away. He was planning to give her a little parting wave as she disappeared from his life round the corner of the street. But she didn't do that. And his instinct for politeness kicked in again.

'Do you want to come in for a bit?' he said.

'Sure.'

He could hardly believe that he'd asked her in. Even more alarming was the fact that she'd accepted. Cooper couldn't get to grips with what was happening to him today. The world had taken a strange turn.

Inside the flat the cat padded forward to greet Cooper, then paused suspiciously before sitting down and staring at Fry.

'I suppose you'll have another funeral to go to soon,' said Fry. 'Your landlady.'

'Mrs Shelley, yes. It's next Monday.'

'What's going to happen to this house?' asked Fry.

'I think the nephew will sell them. He doesn't want to be bothered dealing with pesky tenants. He'll do them up and get a good price for them when he puts them on the market.'

'But as a sitting tenant you have legal rights.'

'I know, but…'

'It won't be the same?'

Cooper had thought it would sound odd to her if he'd said that himself. But she'd hit on what he was thinking exactly. He'd almost forgotten Fry's ability to read his mind so well. It had never seemed like a positive asset before. But now her insight made it easier to explain his feelings. For once he felt she might actually understand what he meant.

'No, it won't be the same at all. In fact, it doesn't feel the same now. Number six is empty already. They took Mrs Shelley's dog away. I imagine he's gone in a sanctuary or more likely he's been taken to the vet's to be put down. Well, he was quite old, I suppose.'

Cooper found Gavin Murfin drifting into his mind, remembered the impression he'd been given in Superintendent Branagh's office that Murfin was regarded as an old dog past his day, a useless mutt who lay around sleeping and eating and was no good to anyone. At least there was a sanctuary for an aged copper.

He was still acting on instinct, following the accepted practices of hospitality, despite the unlikely presence of Diane Fry in his flat.

'Would you like a drink?' he said.

'That would be good. What have you got?'

'Oh. Well, there are some beers in the fridge. And I've got a bottle of cheap Australian white somewhere. That's all, I'm afraid. I don't entertain very often.'

'It's lucky I brought this, then,' said Fry.

She opened her bag. Where Cooper had thought she was carrying reports back to Nottingham, the bag was heavy because it contained a bottle.

'Champagne? Are you kidding?' he said.

Fry held the bottle up and peered at the label. 'Isn't it a good one? I have no idea really.'

'I'm sure it's fine.'

'Good.'

Cooper opened the bottle, poured them each a drink and put the bottle down on the coffee table. Fry had settled on his sofa and he sat down opposite her in the old armchair, with the cat rubbing anxiously against his legs.

'Cheers,' he said.

He watched Fry take a long gulp and cradle her glass, and found himself copying her. It *was* good champagne too, so far as he was any judge. There hadn't been many occasions in his life to celebrate recently.

'So what did you make of your little protest group in the end?' asked Fry. 'Poppy Mellor and her crew of armchair anarchists.'

'They were a strange bunch,' admitted Cooper. 'But I think Poppy Mellor was right in something she said to me. They were like a family. They didn't choose each other, but they were thrown together, almost against their will or their better instincts.'

'Is that the way it happened?'

'Of course,' said Cooper. 'Think of all the things that happen in people's lives. Coincidence, fate, circumstances beyond their control. It's all just the nature of events. They bring individuals close together and they pull them apart again.'

'That's very true. Very true.'

Fry got up and poured him a second glass. He seemed to have finished the first one very quickly. He always drank too fast when he was nervous.

He watched Diane Fry drifting around the room with her glass. It reminded him of the first time he'd ever set eyes on her, as she walked into the CID room at West Street. He'd just returned from leave and she was the new girl on a transfer from the West Midlands.

But then she stopped and reached out to straighten a picture on the wall. Cooper's heart lurched. She'd effortlessly replaced that first memory with another one. The day he moved into this flat in Welbeck Street, Fry had turned up unexpectedly, the way she had last Friday. She'd even brought him a gift to welcome him into his new home. A small, decorative clock. It was standing on the mantelpiece now.

The rarity of that occasion made it all the more memorable for him. He'd witnessed a strange transformation that day, suddenly seeing a side of Fry that was usually hidden, the vulnerability behind the cynical façade. It was the Diane he'd been looking for, ever since she walked into West Street that first time, all those years ago.

'So – you've been offered an inspector's job?' she said. 'I hope I'm right. It's the reason I brought the champagne, after all.'

'Yes,' said Cooper, with a guilty surge of triumph. 'I'm sorry, and all that.'

She raised an eyebrow and put down her glass. 'Sorry? Why?'

'Well, I can't imagine it's what you wanted. You've been watching me so closely for the past few days, hoping I'd slip up. And then, in the end, I did what I never wanted to do. I had to ask you for help. It must have been satisfying for you.'

'Is that what you think?' said Fry. 'Don't you realise that I was asked to make an assessment? It was my input that helped you to get the job.'

'Seriously?'

'I'm always serious.'

Fry laughed then, as if she'd made a joke. That was twice Cooper had witnessed it. Something was definitely happening.

'Well, I don't know what to say. Except thank you, Diane.'

'That's okay.'

She took another drink and looked thoughtful. Cooper waited on tenterhooks for the next direction the conversation might be about to take.

'I visited my sister in Birmingham the other night,' she said. 'You remember my sister, I'm sure.'

'Angie?'

'I only have the one.'

'Is she well?' said Cooper.

'Amazingly well. Ridiculously well. You'd hardly recognise her. I certainly didn't.'

'That's ... good, I suppose.'

'Yes. She's deliriously happy in a new relationship. And now she's pregnant.'

'Pregnant? Really?'

'That's what I said. My big sis is having a baby.'

'Good for her.'

'Absolutely,' said Fry. 'Good for her. I hope she's very happy.' She tilted her head on one side and gave him a quizzical look. 'But here we are, you and me, talking about murder. I suppose it's whatever turns you on.'

Cooper was beginning to feel exactly the way he had with Poppy Mellor in the old cheese factory, trying to talk calmly to a woman whose behaviour had become unpredictable, who might do something completely unexpected at any moment.

'We don't have to talk about murder, if you don't want to,' he said.

'No, we don't. We could talk about something else. Any ideas, Ben?'

'Er...'

'No? That's not like you.'

Fry seemed to be slightly tipsy. He'd never seen her this relaxed before. She was even saying things that didn't make any sense.

'But it's strange, isn't it?' she said. 'Strange that a corpse could turn out to be a bridge.'

'You're mad.'

But Cooper smiled. Wasn't that exactly what had happened? A new sort of connection had formed between them with that first body lying in the shallow water of the River Dove. He hadn't understood what it was until now. But it was true – a corpse might provide a bridge in a way. And more than that. Three corpses could be enough to carry you across a void, transporting you from one place to another. They could take you away from a world you didn't want to be in to a different universe altogether. A place where … well, where anything could happen.

But something was wrong here. Fry wasn't going to be around after today. She had a whole new career of her own to look forward to.

'So that's your parting gift,' he said. 'When you finally leave Edendale, you want to make sure that you leave me feeling in your debt.'

Fry dropped her gaze to the floor. 'Something like that, I suppose. Yes, something like that.'

Cooper was feeling very strange. Perhaps it was the alcohol. The first real drink he'd had for months. Well, the first time he'd felt relaxed enough to enjoy it. It was odd that he'd spent days working out how he could get away from Fry and now he discovered he didn't want her to leave.

'Are you really going, Diane?' he said.

'I'm already gone.'

'You can't be quite gone,' said Cooper, putting down his glass.

'Why not?'

'Because I've still got your TV in the boot of my car.'

'So you have.'

'You'll need it for the new apartment in Nottingham. You've moved everything else. That old place at Grosvenor Avenue must be empty now.'

'Pretty much. But we can't move it tonight,' said Fry. 'You've been drinking.'

'So have you.'

'True.'

Fry gazed at him. And it felt as if everything that had ever passed between them over the years dissolved in that moment, in that one look. Cooper's doubts about Fry fell away. For the first time he found himself looking past the brittle façade and seeing the real person underneath, vulnerable and lonely. Fry was like a 3D picture, baffling at first. But if you stared at it for long enough, your eyes slipped through the surface to a different focus and found something surprising that took your breath away.

'So, Diane...'

'So let's leave the TV where it is,' she said. 'We're not going anywhere tonight.'

COOPER WAS AWAKE early next morning. Quietly, he opened the back door into the garden behind Welbeck Street.

A strong wind had been blowing from the north all night. He walked out of his flat into a world of bare branches and swathes of dead leaves covering the ground. So that was it, he thought. Autumn was truly over. Nothing could stop the winter now.

For a while he sat on a garden chair and watched the sun rise. Fry had been right that a death could provide a bridge to the future. It meant a new start in so many ways. But nothing was quite so simple, was it? It was all very well trying to look ahead, to think about what might still be to come. But it was all daydreams, a lot of wishful thinking. Whatever you did, there was no escaping your fate. No one had any idea what the future would bring.

Cooper gazed up at the hills around Edendale, the ever-changing landscape of the Peak District, the countryside he'd grown up in. The colours of those hills altered season by season, month by month. They might look bare and bleak now, but new life was just below the surface, waiting to burst through again, if it was only given half a chance.

Yes, winter always ended. And, if you could look far enough into the future, spring was just around the corner.

Read on for an excerpt from

Lost River

A Cooper & Fry Mystery

Available now from Witness Impulse

Chapter One

Monday

ON THE BANKS of the river, Ben Cooper was running. His breath came ragged and hot in his throat. The sweat ran into his eyes. All around him, water rushed over stones, pale rocks gleamed under the surface, wet slabs of limestone caught the glare of sunlight trapped in a narrow valley. As he splashed at the edge of the water, he saw shimmers of steam rising from the wet grass, bursts of foam on the edge of his vision. And he saw long streams of blood, swirling in the current like eels.

A hundred yards away, someone had started to scream. The noise echoed off the limestone cliffs, and shrieked among the caves and pinnacles of the dale. He wanted to put his hands over his ears to block out the noise, to stop the pain of the screaming.

But he knew it would never stop, would never be out of his head again.

Behind him, other people were running. He could hear them stumbling and gasping, crashing into trees, cursing each other.

The outlines of the Twelve Apostles swayed against the sky above him, jagged stone spires bursting from the hillside like teeth.

Cooper stopped to swipe the sweat from his eyes, wondering whether he was seeing anything properly. The sun reflecting off the water created impenetrable shadows and glittering fringes of light, caught strands of grass waving below the surface like hair. A fish popped up to the air, another jumped and splashed across the river. Water foamed around an obstruction, a shape lying deep on the gravel bed.

Cooper shook his head. Who was screaming? Why didn't someone tell them to stop? There were enough people here by the river. Scores of people. Dozens of families had been drawn into Dovedale by the hot May bank holiday weather. Sensing the sudden burst of excitement, they milled aimlessly on the banks like panicked sheep. In the distance, he could see them lining the stepping stones in a dumb row.

Nearby, a man stood on the bank, his hands raised, water dripping from his fingers. Cooper had the mad impression that he was some kind of priest, performing a blessing. High on an arch of rock another figure hunched, silhouetted against the sky, his face invisible. A predator on its perch, scanning the valley for prey.

In the water, Cooper saw another rock. More rocks everywhere, lying half in and half out of the river, worn as smooth as skin. Pale, wet skin, everywhere in the water. What chance did he have of distinguishing anything? No chance. No chance, until it was too late.

He looked up again. Was it really someone screaming? Or was it just a bird, startled from its roost in the birches on the limestone edge? A whole flock of birds screeching to each other, over and over, a cacophony of despair. It felt as though the rocks themselves were screaming.

He breathed deeply, tried to focus, forced himself to be calm. Now wasn't the time to lose his head. He was a police officer, and everyone was looking to him to do something. He lowered his eyes, and kept running. Still there was too much light glaring off the water, too many shadows, too much random movement. The roots of an ash tree covered in algae crouched at the edge of the water. A broken branch lay like a severed limb.

There were shouts up ahead now, and the sound of an engine. Voices calling questions, and shouting instructions. Finally, someone was trying to take charge of the chaos. He stumbled into the water, splashed spray in a wide, glittering arc. The coldness of the water was a painful shock, a blast of ice on his hot skin. He missed his footing on a wet stone, slipped, found himself crouching low over the water, staring at a broken reflection of his own face.

No. Not his own face. It was smaller, motionless – a white face, hair floating, the blood washed clear by cold, crystal streams, a green summer dress tangled on the body like weeds. A green shroud of weeds barely stirring in the water.

He plunged his hands into the river and grasped the limp arms. With a heave, he drew the body up out of the water, into the air, and held the cold form in arms, hardly daring to look at the white face. The limbs flopped, her head lolled back on her neck. Water cascaded from the folds of her dress and oozed from the sides of her mouth.

Finally, Cooper raised his voice.

'Here,' he called.

And then the screaming stopped. The limestone gorge fell silent. And there was only the roar of rushing water – the endless sound of the River Dove, never stopping, continually washing clean. A torrent of water, purifying death.

Cooper turned towards the bank. And that was when he saw them. They were standing close together, but apart from the crowd, as if the onlookers had instinctively drawn away. Two adults, and a boy of about thirteen. He stared at them in despair, his mouth moving but no words coming out.

Their isolation, the tense attitude of their bodies, the desolation of their expressions – they all told him the same story. This was the dead girl's family.

Chapter Two

Well, the tourist authority would love it. They'd be sending out the ice-cream vans and unfolding the awnings at the tea rooms. For once, summer had come early in the Peak District.

The thought was no consolation to Detective Sergeant Diane Fry, as she sat in her car on a hot street in Edendale. The windows were open, but there wasn't enough breeze here to ruffle her hair, let alone to cool the clammy interior of a black Audi. She cursed herself for having parked with the front seats in full sun, so the heat had been focused on the fake leather like a laser aimed through the windscreen. She couldn't even use her air conditioning without risking the battery. Now the heat was rising all around her in a mist, steaming up the mirrors. Another half hour of this, and she might spontan-eously combust. That was, if she didn't die of boredom first.

She thumbed the button on her handset.

'Anything happening?'

'Not yet. It's all quiet.'

'Okay, thanks.'

Fry sighed, glanced in her rear-view mirror, and shifted uncomfortably in her seat. The Audi was a new car, since she'd finally got rid of the battered old Peugeot. But she hadn't been able to tear herself away from black. These days, everyone seemed to go for silver grey or metallic blue, but personally she tended to agree with Henry Ford – anything, so long as it was black.

Of course, it wasn't the best choice when the summer decided to start early, with a heat wave at the end of May. Black seemed to absorb every last drop of heat.

What she needed was movement. Her foot on the accelerator, a breeze whipping past the windows. The air con going full blast. She wouldn't really care where she was heading, if only she was moving. Out of this housing estate, out of the town of Edendale, and into the Derbyshire countryside for the sake of a cool breeze on the hills. She never thought she would hear herself say it.

A voice crackled.

'Still nothing. Shall we call it a day?'

'Not yet.'

'I'm dying here, Diane.'

'I'll make sure you get a good funeral, Gavin.'

In the CID car, DC Gavin Murfin and young DC Becky Hurst would really be getting on each other's nerves by now. Murfin would be dropping crumbs on the floor and sweating, and Hurst would be talking too much and spraying the interior with air freshener. One of them would probably kill the other, if she made them sit in the sun any longer. Fry pictured the contest. If she had to place a bet, her money would be on Hurst. She was younger, faster, and meaner.

Fry looked up the street again at a suggestion of movement. An old man walking an ancient dog. Neither of them was moving at more than half a mile an hour. The dog was black, like her car. Its head drooped as it slowly put one foot in front of the other on the pavement, heading towards the corner shop at the end of the street.

They weren't what she was watching for. Her target was a fair-haired man in his late twenties, wearing a baseball cap. Intelligence said that he was living in one of these houses halfway along the street, a typical Devonshire Estate council-owned semi. But she was starting to think he might have moved home.

'I'd better start making a note of what music I want,' said Murfin.

'What?'

'At my funeral. I don't want any of this happy-clappy, celebrating-his-life sort of stuff. I want everyone to cry when I go.'

'Gavin, can we keep the chatter to a minimum, please?'

She heard him sigh. 'Okay, boss.'

In the last few months, Fry had found herself thinking about moving home, too. She wasn't sure whether it was the new car, or all the other things that she had to think about, particularly the major decisions she had to make. Decisions that she'd been putting off for weeks.

Whatever the reason, her flat at number 12 Grosvenor Avenue had begun to feel narrow and confining, as if she was living in a cell. The detached Victorian villa, once so solid and prosperous, had started to flake at the edges, the window frames warping with damp, tiles slipping off the roof during the night and frightening her half to death with their noise.

'Is this him, Diane?'

Fry watched a white baseball cap emerge from behind an overgrown privet hedge on to the pavement.

'No, it's female.'

'Oh, yeah. You're right. Female, and suffering from a recent fashion disaster.'

Despite herself, Fry smiled. 'You being the expert, of course, Gavin.'

She could hear another voice in the background. Hurst, giving Murfin some earache.

'Becky says I'm being sexist,' said Murfin. 'So I'm going to have to go and kill myself.'

'Fair enough.'

Fry looked at the row of council houses, wondering about the kind of people who lived here, rent paid out of their Social Security benefits. Some of them hardly seemed to care about the conditions they brought their children up in.

When she'd first moved into her flat, there had been a private landlord – absent, but at least a real person who could be spoken to occasionally. Last winter, the property had been sold to a development company with an office somewhere in Manchester and an automated switchboard that put you on hold whenever you phoned with complaints.

It was a shame. When she looked around the other houses in Grosvenor Avenue, she saw what could be done by a responsible owner. But the present landlords didn't worry about their steady turnover of tenants, who were mostly migrant workers with jobs in the bigger Edendale hotels, and a few students on courses at High Peak College. The former tended to disappear in the winter when the tourist season was over, and the latter were gone in the summer. Fry had been the longest surviving tenant for two or three years now. No doubt the owners wondered why she was still there. She was starting to wonder that herself. It was probably time to say goodbye to the mock porticos, and the flat on the first floor, with its washed-out carpets and indelible background smells.

But where would she go if she left Grosvenor Avenue? Well, that was yet another decision – one she wasn't equipped to make right now. She had far more important things to think about. Subjects that would dominate her thoughts, if she let them. Decisions that would change her life for ever.

Fry swore under her breath and turned up the fan to coax a bit more action out of the air con. When she first joined the police, back in Birmingham, she hadn't anticipated how much of her time would be spent sitting in cars. And always uncomfortably, too – wearing a uniform that didn't fit because it was designed for a man, strapped into a stab-proof vest that pinched her skin in awkward places because . . . well, because it was designed for a man.

And then, when she moved to CID, she'd been too excited to take in what everyone told her – that she'd spend just as much time in car. And when she wasn't in a car, she would be sitting at a desk, filling in forms, compiling case files, answering endless queries from the Crown Prosecution Service. Like so many other police officers, she lived for the moment when she got a chance to get out of the office. Well, maybe she had the answer to that. Perhaps she had a road trip coming up.

Recently, she'd been working hard to get back in physical condition, to regain all those skills that she'd learned under her old *Shotokan* master in Dudley. If you didn't train regularly, you lost those skills. But now her body was tuned and fit again. Her natural leanness was no longer taken as a sign of poor health. As for her mind . . . well, maybe there was still some work to do.

Then her phone rang. Though she'd been getting desperate for something to happen, Fry was actually irritated. She checked the caller ID and saw it was Ben Cooper. It had better be important.

'Ben?'

'She's dead, Diane.'

'Who is?'

The connection was very bad. His voice was intermittent, crackly and fragmented like a message from outer space. Detective Constable Cooper calling from Planet Derbyshire.

'The little girl. The paramedics tried to revive her, but she was dead.'

'Ben, I have no idea what you're talking about.'

'I tried, Diane. But she was already –'

'You're breaking up badly. Where are you?'

'Dovedale. It's –'

But then he was gone completely, his signal lost in some valley in the depths of the Peak District. Dovedale? She had an idea that it was way down in the south of the division, somewhere near Ashbourne.

Fry frowned. Just before Cooper was cut off, she thought she'd heard a siren somewhere in the background. She dialled his mobile number, got the unobtainable tone. She tried again, with the same result. No surprise there. So she used her radio to call the Control Room.

'An incident in Dovedale. Have you got anything coming in?'

She listened as the call handler found the incident log and read her the details. There was no mention of DC Cooper, just a series of 999 calls recorded from the public at irregular intervals, probably as people got signals on their mobiles. Units were attending the scene, along with paramedics and ambulance. One casualty reported. She supposed it would all become clear in due course.

'Thank you.'

When she thumbed the button again, she got Gavin Murfin's voice yelling for her.

'Diane, where are you? He's on the move, on the move. Your direction. Repeat, your direction. Have you got a visual?'

'What?'

Fry looked up and saw movement on the pavement a few yards ahead of her position. But it was only the old man coming back towards her, flat cap pulled over his eyes, dog lead in one hand, plastic carrier bag in the other. The dog dug its heels in and stopped to water a lamp post.

'Nothing. Nothing in sight here.'

'He's long gone,' said Murfin. 'He was legging it. Didn't you see him?'

'No.'

While his dog performed its business, the old man stood and stared at her defiantly like some ancient accusing angel.

'Bloody Hell, Gavin,' said Fry. 'We've lost him.'

FOR THE PAST half hour, Cooper had been listening to the yelp and wail. The modern tones of emergency response vehicles, howling up the dale one after another. The noises merged inside his head with an echo of the screaming. The noise still bounced off the sides of his skull in the same way it had rico-cheted among the caves and pinnacles of Dovedale.

He still didn't know who had screamed. Perhaps it was the mother. Or it might just have been some random bystander, reacting with horror to a glimpse of a body in the water. A small, white face. Long streams of blood, swirling in the current like eels . . .

'Their name is Nield.'

The tall uniformed sergeant was called Wragg. Cooper remembered him vaguely, and thought he'd probably turned up at a couple of major incidents in E Division when he was still a PC. He was fairly recently promoted, and was based at Ashbourne section now. He was wearing a yellow high-vis jacket over his uniform, and had removed his cap to reveal close-cropped fair hair. He looked harassed, but it might just be the heat.

'Local?' asked Cooper.

'Yes, by some miracle. Among all these crowds, you'd think it'd be city people who suffered an incident like this. You know, the sort who've never actually seen a river before. Folk who don't think you can drown in water unless there's a sign telling you so.'

'You've seen too many tourists.'

'You got that right,' said Wragg. 'I never want to catch duty on a bank holiday again, I can tell you. Do you know how long it took me to get my car through those jams? You won't be able to move down here later.'

'That will be somebody else's headache.'

'I wish.'

Cooper was leaning against Wragg's car. He had a clear view up the gorge towards the weirs, and beyond them, the pool where he'd pulled the body out of the water.

'How old is she?' he said.

'Eight.'

'She's only eight years old?'

'Yes.'

'She was here with her parents. How the hell did it happen?'

'They say their dog went into the water to fetch a stick. A golden retriever, it is. It seems the girl ran in after the dog. Only the dog came out.'

Cooper shook his head in despair. 'Where are the parents now?'

'Gone with her to hospital.'

'They surely don't think she'll be revived. Do they?'

Wragg shaded his eyes with a hand as he watched some members of the public being shepherded away from the scene.

'You don't give up in these circumstances,' he said. 'That's the very last thing you do.'

Events had moved pretty quickly once the girl's body had been recovered from the water. Cooper had carried her to the bank and laid her on the grass. Then a woman had come forward from the crowd of bystanders, saying she was a nurse. Cooper had handed over resuscitation efforts to her, and she kept it going until the fast-response paramedic arrived, closely followed by the ambulance and Sergeant Wragg and his colleagues from the Ashbourne section station.

'We'll need a statement from you, of course,' said Wragg.

'But it will do later. We're trying to catch as many witnesses as we can among the public before they disappear.'

'Of course.'

'But there doesn't seem any doubt it was an accidental drowning.'

'There was blood, though,' said Cooper. 'Blood in the water. She had an injury on her head.'

'She probably fell and hit her head on a stone. That would explain why she drowned in such a shallow depth.'

'"Probably"?'

'There's hardly going to be any trace evidence,' said Wragg irritably. 'The stone is somewhere out there being washed by thousands of gallons of water every second. We'll see what eye-witness statements say, but I think you'll find that's it.'

'Yes, all right.'

There had been no blood on the girl when he'd picked her up. But Cooper remembered seeing the wound now, an abrasion and broken skin on her forehead. The toughest thing he'd ever done was putting that body down, handing the little girl over to someone else. It felt like abandoning her to her fate. For some ridiculous reason, his instinct had been telling him he was the only person who could save her.

It was strange what your mind could do in a crisis. Sometimes, the rational part of your brain cut out altogether and you acted entirely on instinct, with no conscious thought involved. But occasionally your mind presented you with odd flashes of information that didn't even seem to be relevant at the time.

Right now, Cooper was remembering images from the last hour or so. Paler rocks under the surface, streams of blood swirling in the current like eels. Jagged limestone spires at crazy angles. A dead, white face with floating hair. And a man with his hands raised, water dripping from his fingers.

'Anyway, the Nield family . . .' said Wragg, consulting his notebook. 'Father is a supermarket manager in Ashbourne. Mum is a teacher. There's a boy, about thirteen years old, name of Alex. They're all in a state of shock, as you can imagine.'

'And the girl?' said Cooper.

'What?'

'The girl. You haven't mentioned her name. She must have a name.'

Wragg looked taken aback.

'Of course. Her name is Emily – Emily Nield. She's eight years old.'

'Thank you,' said Cooper. 'That's what I wanted to know.'

He was aware of the noise of tourist cars rattling over the cattle grids out of Dovedale. Streams of scree had spilled from Thorpe Cloud like ash from a small volcano, slithering slowly towards the valley bottom. Two spaniels splashed in the water, scattering the mallards.

Many visitors were still clustered on the smooth, green slopes of the lower dale, where the limestone grassland had been grazed short by rabbits and sheep. Some were making their way down to the car park from the slopes of the dale, where they'd been exploring the woods or the limestone pinnacles and caves.

Suddenly, Cooper pushed himself away from the car.

'Just a minute.'

'Where are you going?' asked Wragg.

But Cooper didn't bother answering. He ran over to the car park and began to dodge between the groups of people, searching for a face. Some of them stared at him as if he was mad. But he was sure he'd seen someone he recognized. It was just a glimpse, a face half turned away in shadow, but the angle of a cheek and the tilt of a head were distinctive. It was a face he remembered for a reason, one that should mean something important.

He stopped two women getting into their Land Rover Discovery.

'Excuse me, did you happen to see . . . ?'

But he didn't know what he wanted to ask them, and they hurriedly slammed their doors, fearing that he was some lunatic.

Cooper stopped, shaking his head. Maybe he *was* mad. But that face had been important, if only he could pin down its meaning.

Frustrated, he walked slowly back to the police vehicles. The River Dove was returning to its normal state after the excitement. Small brown birds with white bibs hopped from stones and plunged into the water after food. Dippers, they were called. It was said that crayfish and freshwater shrimps lived in this river. The water gave life to so many creatures. But it could take life away, too.

'DC Cooper, are you okay?' asked Wragg.

'Yes. Why wouldn't I be?'

'You're shivering.'

'Oh, I'm just cold.'

Wragg stared at him with a baffled expression. He wiped the sweat from his own face with a handkerchief and squinted up at the glaring sun.

'Oh, yeah. Chilly day, isn't it?'

Cooper didn't reply. He couldn't tell Wragg what he really felt. It sounded too ridiculous. But right now, he felt chilled to the bone.

About the Author

STEPHEN BOOTH was born in the Lancashire mill town of Burnley and has remained rooted to the Pennines during his career as a newspaper journalist. He is well known as a breeder of Toggenburg goats and includes among his other interests folkore, the Internet, and walking in the hills of the Peak District, in which his crime novels are set. He lives with his wife, Lesley, in a former Georgian dower house in Nottinghamshire.

www.stephen-booth.com

Discover great authors, exclusive offers, and more at hc.com.